RETURN
TO THE
CONTINENT

The Second Book of *The Continent* Trilogy

by

Douglas T. Bradshaw

DORRANCE
PUBLISHING CO
EST. 1920
PITTSBURGH, PENNSYLVANIA 15238

Dorrance Publishing Co
585 Alpha Drive
Pittsburgh, PA 15238
Visit our website at *www.dorrancebookstore.com*

ISBN: 978-1-6480-4394-9
eISBN: 978-1-6480-4569-1

RETURN
TO THE
CONTINENT

The Second Book of *The Continent* Trilogy

CHAPTER 1

SQUARING OFF WITH THE CIRCLE

The Continent, a land of wonder and magick, after the progressive rule of the last regimes, now finds itself falling into tyranny and despair. As a newcomer, one might ask, what happened to this land? How did things get to be this way? What force has caused this reversal of fate? Questions which are certainly worth asking and all can be answered with a single word, for this one word caused the lion's share of what is now transpiring on the Continent. One force caused it, a force that was known once by this land and is now known again, magick.

Now, this deterioration did not happen all at once. As with most things on the Continent, it happened slowly. One could say that the times that are present now are a direct result of the last Queen of the North, Queen Clarissa. Late in her long and prosperous reign, she issued a royal decree that stated that everyone had the basic right to an education, and that it should be free to all who wanted it. This radical change met with much resistance among the noble classes, as they wanted to keep a monopoly on education to keep the lower classes in line, but Clarissa was queen, she knew that this state of affairs would not last, and before long, the people would rebel and plunge the North, and perhaps the entire Continent, into war. She spent about half of the North's treasury on building a total of 25 schoolhouses, along with enough teachers and guards to ensure that lessons would not be interrupted by dissenting nobles. It took less than one cycle for all this to occur, and before long, the peal of the school bell could be heard not only in the North, but across the Continent as the Western and Southern Kingdoms followed her lead.

3

So, it came to pass that the lower and burgeoning middle classes started to get an education. Fathers and mothers sending their little ones off to school; adults learning to read and write for the first time in their lives. Even the elderly, whose bodies were no longer suited to work, got into the act learning alongside everyone else, combining their wisdom amidst the more traditional facets of education, so that the oral traditions and stories of the Continent would be remembered by a new generation. Over the next 10 cycles, the nobles calmed down, seeing the positive aspects of a more educated workforce, but not everyone was convinced. Changes started brewing, particularly with the nobles who owned the mines, and the booming factories noticed that their workforces had declined because no one who was educated wanted to do that sort of work.

To combat their declining workforces, they increased wages and included some benefits to entice more workers, and as a result of that, more people wanted to educate themselves to get the increased wages being offered. Other industries suffered as well, particularly the more agrarian pursuits of times past, but a more educated population led to new ideas and new technologies being developed meaning less manual labor and better productivity. As fields started producing more, landowners got more money and started to improve wages and working conditions to attract more workers onto their fields.

All these benefits took a long time to come and evolve, and even after 50 cycles, there were still holdouts, but it was mostly seen in those industries that were in decline at the time. As the populace got more educated, even at a basic level, they started to ask questions about their lot in life. They wanted more of everything, including more say in government. Though monarchy was still the government of choice over the Continent at this time, many could see that monarchy's suns were numbered. At the time, no one knew what could replace the current system of government, and many people were afraid that if the king or queen were deposed or replaced in some way, anarchy would result and that wouldn't benefit anyone, so while people were afraid of what might come as a result of a new system of government, they knew the current arrangement was on its way out.

Given an increase in educational opportunities, those in the lower and middle classes took advantage of one other area of education that was previously forbidden to them. Starting in the North, the three major academies of magick at the time started opening their doors to all that could afford to attend. Previous to this momentous paradigm shift, only the sons and daughters of nobles and the elite classes could apply to attend a magickal academy. However, with an increase in applications, prospective students found that getting into an academy of magick, the "Ivy League" of the time, was a combination of intestinal fortitude, intelligence, and of course, gold. Lots of gold. The magickal academies of the sun had around a 3 percent acceptance rate and only the best of the best could get in. If your son or daughter failed to get in, nothing, not even a healthy bribe would work to sway an opinion. In the world of magick, no meant "NO." Additionally, the academies of magick had abysmal graduation rates as the 10-cycle course of study was so rigorous and difficult that over 80 percent of students who started dropped out for a myriad of reasons, but most drop-outs were because the academics were so challenging.

As magick was a part of mainstream society, thanks to Thaddeus, those who did graduate and survive the challenge of the academy, thereby earning the title of Wizard, had a problem. After graduation and the question of "Now what?" came to their minds, they found that there wasn't really much for them to do besides set up herb shops or infirmaries where the sick would go to be healed by magick or with the natural remedies of the sun. Over time, Wizards got bored with this limited career path and started to branch out on their own, exploring the Continent's mysteries and trying to find fame and fortune. Their reasoning was that if Thaddeus did it, why couldn't they?

As a reaction to the magickal climate of the time, a new group formed, centered particularly in the West and North, calling themselves the Circle of Wizards. In their minds, they were all equal; each had survived the rigors of the Academy, and in the guild mindset of the time, they realized that in numbers, they would have more of a say in making things better for their small group. After another 20 cycles, in 1027, the Wizards had sufficient membership in the Circle to be considered for an official guild charter. A guild charter was official recognition of their group by the kingdom. It also legitimized their group in the eyes of other guilds, in addition to providing them license to operate their group according to their charter. Much to their surprise, this normal part of Continent life was denied them as they were resoundingly rejected by the three main kingdoms in existence at the time.

Being Wizards, however, they were undaunted and set to work. After 13,482 individual revisions and clarifications to the charter document (which is still the longest guild charter document in Continent history, as it contains

5

493 handwritten pages) and 41 separate applications, the Circle of Wizards finally achieved their goal in Cycle 1030 and obtained a charter from the most unlikely of places, the Kingdom of the West, where magick was once banned. Their group remained one of the smallest guilds in the West, though what they lacked in numbers they more than made up for in intellect, and for some members, this opened up a new purpose for them, as advisors to nobles of all sorts, even royalty. Doing some digging into history, the Wizards thought that it would be apropos that Sapphira should be remembered as the first magickal advisor, and a sub-guild was formed in her honor called the Sapphiran Knights serving as the official advisory arm of the main Circle of Wizards guild.

All this hobnobbing with high society meant that the Circle of Wizards guild gained the one thing it needed to survive: influence with those who made the laws and rules. All monarchies of the time had advisory councils set up, and as more Wizards became members of those advisory councils, they started to advise those in power to make laws that were favorable to the Circle of Wizards. These laws made it easier for Wizards to find work and to garner more gold and glory for the guild. The Circle of Wizards guild grew in size (albeit slowly) and most importantly in power and influence as the leaders that they were advising often relied on the Wizards for sage advice and thought nothing of letting their "house Wizard" make decisions and allowed the Wizards to execute those decisions into actions.

As the Guild started to grow more and more, murmurings of dissent started to form both inside and outside of the Guild. Those on the outside were growing afraid of the rapid rise of the Guild's power and influence, and those on the inside started wondering why they themselves were not in power, as in their minds, they were smarter than those who held the power in the first place.

Over time, Wizards eventually gained a majority on most advisory councils and through magickal means actually transformed the reigning King of the West, Noran IV, into their puppet. The reason they were able to do this is because the young Noran was only 10 when his father, Noran III had died, and the Wizards seized upon this opportunity to ensure that the new king would serve them. They realized before anyone else that the vacuum left by the departing regime could be filled by a king who listened and puppeted every word that the Wizards told him to, instead of having to constantly struggle with the king or the advisory council to get things done for the Circle of Wizards guild. While the King was technically in charge, he was little more than a figurehead because it was the Wizards that were the driving force in leadership.

CHAPTER 2

THE ELVEN EXODUS

What had started in the West eventually spread to the North and to the South, but not among the elves, as they had a long-standing practice to never allow anyone practicing magick to become a member of the Consulate, the ruling body of the Elves, because of the fifth Magickal law, set down by Kimshila herself, which stated:

> *No elf who practices or has practiced any theory of magick, whether natural or not, shall at any point in his life serve on the Consulate, or participate in any advising of said body at any time.*

As a result, the Consulate has remained firmly out of the hands of magick since its inception, as if the founders of the first Elven societies knew that what was happening to the humans now could happen to them. Also, it should be noted that, the Consulate was dedicated to the affairs of the elves as it had been since the first Consulate was convened over 5,000 cycles ago, and as such, they were also usually loath to involve themselves in the affairs of humans. So, when the Consulate decided to send a warning to the human kingdoms about the rise of the Circle of Wizards, it was considered very "un-Elven" by just about everyone, and the Consulate faced a lot of backlash because of it. Even worse, for the Consulate, is that they received no reply from the human kingdoms about their warnings. Elves do not take very kindly to being totally ignored, especially when, to their eyes, they went to extraordinary lengths to warn the humans about the Circle of Wizards and their growing power.

After an appropriate amount of debate amongst themselves which took the better part of three seasons, the elves felt that no one was paying attention and felt that they did not want to bear witness to what, in their collective minds, was an entirely avoidable situation. The elves decided to uproot their entire civilization and move further to the South, to their ancestral homes along the Southern Coast. This massive exodus of elves was unprecedented in modern times and was certainly cause for alarm, especially in the South, where Elven troops were utilized in defense of the Southern Kingdom.

The elves felt that though it was sad to leave what had been their home for a thousand cycles, they decided to revert to the "old ways." This ancient set of laws, some of which were abandoned when the elves decided to co-exist with humans, formed the backbone of their society for thousands of cycles before humans came to the Continent. A common Elven saying is, "Colis tam nertil, samre tau sauta," which translates to, "What was then, it is now," reflecting a desire to be one with the past and live as their ancestors did. By doing this, some elves feel that they honor their ancestors, but that view is not universal amongst the elves, particularly with younger elves. Most knew that the old ways consisted of shunning humans, and though it bordered on xenophobia, even half-elves were not welcome into the enclaves that the elves rebuilt in their ancestral homeland. In effect, they decided to leave the society of humans, and either the humans would repent and recover, or descend into total anarchy…

Either way, the elves were having no part of it.

The Southern King, Vistor II, asked why they were moving and they replied, "We have seen this before and have no desire to see it again, repent and stop this before it consumes all you have worked for."

Though the progress of the Circle of Wizards guild was slowed somewhat in the South due to the Elven exodus and the King's efforts, he bowed to the will of his advisory council, and it eventually came to pass that all three kingdoms had a Circle of Wizards guild, with a Sapphiran Knights sub-guild, which is where the guilds' real power came from.

While Thaddeus was never a fan of the elves, he knew of their knowledge and wisdom. The fact that no one was paying attention to them, portended poorly for humankind despite his teachings that the elves should be heeded, especially if they take the time to tell you something. He felt bad for the people, for it is always the commoner that suffers when leadership is too blind to realize when a mistake is being made. This indifference by the new leadership on the Continent indicated to him that the worst was yet to come, but even he was unaware of the scope of the evil that was about to befall the Continent and everyone in it.

Thaddeus looked upon all this with a certain measure of pride as he saw the Wizards as his "creations," but also with disgust. He knew that Wizard leadership could be a blessing and a curse at the same time. On the one hand, Wizards were unusually intelligent and highly focused, able to solve complex issues that would stump lesser people, but on the other hand, Wizards were usually too self-centered to be effective leaders, and while there were some exceptions, they were too few to have their voices heard. He also was greatly concerned with the "puppet" governments that were coming into fashion across the Continent, and he, with a certain knowing air, decided that it was time to prepare for the worst.

It took two cycles for the entire population of 750,000 elves to move 1,670 leagues to the Southern Coast. All that they had built further north was gone, as if they were going to "sit this one out," but unbeknownst to them, the evil that would infect the Continent and all the humans on it would affect them as well, but one of their number was to become humanity's saving grace, and the reason that human life will continue on the Continent.

Thaddeus was also concerned with the decline of belief in the Gods, as that started to be supplanted with a belief in the power of magick. People started to put their faith in things they could see, and magick certainly had visible effects, especially when that magick helped to save someone from an illness that could kill them, or an injury that would have left them crippled. To the average person, especially ones who were educated, science and technology were winning the battle over organized religion which was something that Thaddeus was witnessing firsthand. The Moon Goddess was starting to weaken after hundreds of cycles of belief in her; with fewer worshippers, her abilities started to wane. Thaddeus tried to "prop" her up, but in spite of his best efforts, while she did not succumb to the same "death" that most other deities faced during this time, her powers were greatly diminished.

Many temples fell silent, and the faithful who would still worship in them were too few in number to resurrect the now forgotten deities of old. To a god or goddess, the worship of humans gave them life and abilities to help their charges, but over time, many deities had forgotten that and used their powers in more self-serving ways, and now that something more concrete was available to believe in, many humans flocked to the "new" belief in magick and its effects. With an increase in education, it was no longer enough for people to just have faith in something and hope that their god or goddess would make something happen for them...Now it was gold and magick that caused that something to happen, not a deity.

Unlike their human counterparts, the Elves never stopped believing in the Moon Goddess, and as such, though her powers are greatly diminished, she was still able to watch over her Elven charges with Thaddeus' help. A few human deities managed to hold on, in particular the Snow Queen, whose charges never had magick and continued to live life as they always had. Over a couple of cycles, those minor deities who were popular in a few regions quickly succumbed to the lack of worshippers as belief in magick spread far and wide across the Continent.

Though Thaddeus ascended to the Moon Goddess' side, he was not reliant upon worship as she was for his energy. He relied upon his magickal skill to ensure that he remained alert and by her side at all times, until he could think of what to do to counter this threat. As more and more deities succumbed, it was Thaddeus who ended up as the only male "resident" of the above, watching in horror as long held beliefs and institutions were slowly declining, save one, the institution of magick.

The elder Thaddeus recalled what life was like when he was alive on the Continent, particularly with Sapphira, who he loved with all his heart and who loved him...He recalled the first magickal academy he opened and his first students who he wanted to teach the ancient and honorable craft of magick. In some ways, in retrospect, that is the only decision that he regrets now more than ever, for the First King was correct, as he said that there would be some that would disobey the Natural Law, and that has come to pass on the Continent, which has turned dark and foreboding, the kingdoms that once were, were but shadows of their former selves, struggling to survive, as a dark shadow had taken over the Continent, and though the elder Thaddeus was saddened to see all this, deep inside, he knew it was of his making.

CHAPTER 3

~⊰⊱~

THE DESCENT INTO MADNESS

More time passed, and the Wizards' Guild, being one of the most powerful guilds across the Continent, continued their rule through puppet kings. However, the current system of rule, which worked for everyone, even though no one except the Wizards' Guild knew what was really going on, was all about to come crashing down.

Noran IV, though now a man of 30 cycles and a king for 20 of those cycles was now quite mad and was rarely seen in public as his mind, thanks to 20 cycles of control by Wizards, was so feeble that it just shut down one sun. Realizing that Noran was no longer capable of even feeding himself, the Guildmaster, a man named Boral, decided that the only option was for him to rule in Noran's stead, as the King had no wife and no heirs, yet another consequence of the Wizards' control of him. The backlash that Boral faced was unlike anything the Continent had ever seen. The three million-plus residents of the Kingdom of the West did not approve, and over the next season, though guards tried to beat back the waves of protestors, they were overwhelmed. The Wizards did what they thought was necessary to maintain their control and unleashed spells on the populace that they had never seen before, and many thousands of people died.

These clashes with their own people were called massacres by the populace, but it was called "Law Enforcement" by the Wizards, who created a law that stated:

> *Any person at any time, caught protesting or otherwise creating a*
> *disturbance, in the presence of a member in good standing of the*
> *Circle of Wizards guild, shall be ordered to stop immediately. Fai-*

lure to do so, will result in sterner measures, up to and including use of baleful magick against such persons.

Many people took this new rule to mean that non-lethal magick would be used to stop any protests, as the Circle of Wizards were not known to be killers, but it so happened that the scene of the first of these disturbances, the Wizards present were trained to use elemental magicks, which they did, to devastating effect. The death toll was in the thousands that sun, as the 10 Wizards present unleashed a flurry of spells designed not only to disburse a crowd, but also to kill. This sparked more protests all over the Continent, and many subversive plots were hatched to "take the Wizards out." Some of these attempts on the lives of Wizards caused others to hire retinues of security guards to protect themselves. Other Wizards who weren't able to do so found themselves on the wrong end of a sword, even if they hadn't done anything wrong. Every Wizard who died served as a stern warning to the others to continue to beef up their security, increasing their paranoia that everyone was "out to get them."

Becoming a guard of a Wizard was a very lucrative profession during this time, and highly skilled warriors could command sums of gold that would make even the greediest blush, but those sums were paid and then some, as Wizards thought it wise to part with gold in exchange for continuing to live. As time passed, these highly educated people started to turn on each other, and soon it was Wizard against Wizard, as their paranoia worsened and they started to lash out at each other. Massive bonuses were given to warriors who killed a rival Wizard. In desperation, one Wizard even made a deal with the Assassin's Guild, but even the combined might and stealth of that powerful guild was insufficient to save his life, as in the end he succumbed to disease inflicted by another magician using biological agents against his enemies.

The streets ran red with blood, killings were commonplace and humanity started to slip into anarchy, exactly what many did not want, but that was reality during this terrible time as the Wizards fought each other for supremacy and control. The Wizards divided the cities and towns amongst themselves and fought each other for territory and resources; people became pawns, and the land was but a game board to them. Many people protested this state of being, and many people died, killed by spells or swords, but regardless, dissenting voices became fewer as the Wizards tightened their grip on the Continent.

For the survivors of that terrible time in the West, it didn't get any better. Fearing their beloved King was dead, many started to leave their homes, seeking a new life in more stable kingdoms. Emigration at this time was the highest it had ever been, and makeshift villages in more and more remote places became the norm. However, Noran's untimely lapse into madness was only a harbinger of things to come, as the other two royals in the North and South suffered the same fate as Noran IV did. Though no one knew exactly why, some suspected it was the Wizards, but it could not be proven. Despite more protests and more emigration, Wizards started to take control of the established kingdoms of the time. Many more protests were staged, and many more thousands of people died across the Continent.

Those Wizards who managed to stay in power tried to stop all this killing and mass exoduses by clamping down even tighter on the people, establishing curfews and limiting travel, which failed spectacularly. Some Wizards didn't agree with this, and though the Wizards' were educated, they did not have the capacity to rule very well because every Wizard had an opinion on how things should be done, and over time, that led to petty squabbling and divisiveness amongst the Wizard Guilds. Fortunately, the Wizards' Guild charter came to their rescue, as on Page 394 of the charter it stated that:

> *In the case of a dispute with another Guild Wizard that cannot be resolved between the members, a tribunal of an odd number of Wizards, but no less than 13, neutral to the disagreement, shall be convened. The tribunal will hear the arguments on both sides and render a decision. A simple majority vote will make a decision which is binding on both parties in dispute.*

So it came to pass that Wizard Tribunals were set up to settle these disputes, but the good intentions of the original founders of the Wizards' Guild charter, many of whom were still alive, did not take into account the greed of men, as they formed this Guild out of brotherhood with their fellow Wizards, they certainly never imagined that within a few short cycles that they would be the leaders of the Continent. Bribes of money and promises of power were routinely given to anyone who was a Tribunal Wizard to find in favor of one of the parties and whereas there were no rules or laws that forbade it, it turned out that the person with the most gold won the disputes and the person who lost frequently found themselves on the wrong end of a spell shortly after a decision was rendered.

Things went on like that for a while, and while the Wizards were fighting back and forth, the people under their rule dwindled, as they started to find other places to live that were not under the Wizards' control. Many people did not trust them, and rightfully so, as it was commonly noted that Wizards were arrogant and very self-centered, thinking all others were beneath them due to their station. In the North, people went to the Far North to live with the Barbarians there, who, under the direction of the Snow Queen, continued to be completely free of magick as they had always been. The population in the Far North swelled as more and more settled in their lands and the Barbarian tribes welcomed them, remembering that the humans welcomed Sapphira and many others into their lands during the Barbarian Wars. New towns were established among the snow-capped peaks of the North, some even settled in the very inhospitable Deep North.

In the Deep North, some new settlers happened upon a cave. Deep within the cave, they found evidence of someone who had lived there…and died there. Carvings on the walls indicated that the man's name was Bjor'ma and that he lived here for many cycles before finally succumbing to the harsh conditions. What the settlers did not know was that Bjor'ma's spirit lived, and while gone from this place, what they found here would become very important to historians of times future as they pieced together what happened during this time.

In the West and South, people started moving to the mountainous regions in their respective kingdoms, and some even sought refuge with the Narsum in the East. Given that the Narsum had a human live among them in times past and become a legend among them, they did not shun the outsiders, and while they were not welcomed with open arms, they were not driven out either. The humans and Narsum formed an uneasy peace, which would become stronger in the cycles to come as the Narsum discovered that the humans were capable warriors, combining education and strength together, which is something that the Narsum could never do.

In the space of three short cycles, the pettiness and corruption of these highly educated people reduced the Continent to a shadow of its former self. For the decimated population of the Continent, now living in makeshift hamlets and villages either in the mountains or amongst other races of beings, it was a very tough time, having to scratch out a living from the land which many could not do. They started to harbor a definite hatred towards the Wizards who forced them from their homes and caused all this nonsense. Even within the Circle itself, what were once considered petty squabbles, even a few skirmishes between lower level Wizards, had turned into a full-blown war as the paranoia of the Wizards worsened. Rival Wizards were now fighting each other, as treachery, lies, and deceit became the currency of the realm as the Wizards continually fought with each other over land and resources eventually touching off the so-called War of the Wizards.

This war lasted a total of five and 30 suns, when it was Wizard versus Wizard, until the forty-third sun of Simcha in cycle 1073, which was a sun that started with the Circle being somewhat complete, in that there were still enough Wizards on the Continent to actually make the shape of a circle, but that would not last. And as the second sun set on that fateful sun, only two would remain. Of the two, only one, Boral, the Wizard-King of the West, had the upper hand and, in the fashion of the time, exploited his advantage to eliminate his last rival from existence.

His victory complete, Boral declared himself a living God, and in that moment, he could not have known that his pronouncement would set in motion a series of events that would forever change the Continent once again.

Chapter 4

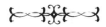

Boral

Boral, a human from the West where magick was once outlawed, was now the sole Wizard surviving from the Circle of Wizards, but the question has been asked, who was he and how did this one man manage to overthrow a once respected guild to establish himself as a living God?

In answering such a question, we need to go back to his beginning. He hailed from the village of Farhill, in the foothills of the Western Mountain Range. His parentage was common, though his father wanted his son to do something worthwhile with his life instead of being a blacksmith as he was. Boral was very precocious even as a very young child, and his parents noted his intelligence and his ability to focus on something and continue at it until he completed whatever it was that he was trying to do. Unfortunately, while he had a sharp mind even in his youth, he was a very sickly child and was frequently ill.

He was a regular at the infirmary, though he was able to avail himself of the cures of the sun. He hated being ill all the time and fought it for all he was worth. He would always wait until he couldn't function before he would avail himself of a remedy because he often thought that the cure for his various ailments were worse than being sick. If there was one thing that he always said about the cures of the time, it was: "They stink, and I hate them," becuase they usually tasted bad or burned as they were applied to him. Boral's parents weren't sure what to do with their son, as opportunities for children like Boral were very limited. As luck would have it, when the Magickal Academy grand opening was announced in the West, Boral's father decided that he should learn the craft of magick, as he viewed it as something worthy of his intelligence in the hopes that he might learn magick and gain the ability to heal himself. So, at the tender age of 10, his father sent him to the Academy in the hopes that he would be accepted.

Boral's father had saved over many cycles to acquire the entrance fee of 1,000 gold ducats (a considerable sum at the time), as he was accepted as the seventeenth student in the Academy's first class of 25. He actually met and talked with Thaddeus during his entrance examination and personal interview. He studied under him as a young man, and despite his sickly nature, decided to focus on the destructive magicks that Thaddeus specialized in instead of the curative magicks that would actually help him due to his distaste for them as he often said, "I wouldn't want to inflict those cures on anyone." While he excelled at the Academy, something turned within him during his time there, something caused him to reject the Natural Law and substitute it with the evil that now infests his mind.

As for what happened to him, theories abound, but there are only two people that know the truth. Unfortunately for the Continent, the elder Thaddeus, who some say is the cause, is one of them, but history recorded that he did nothing to stop it before it snowballed into the situation that existed now. Thaddeus knew that Boral was an exceptionally driven young man in everything he did, as he told Thaddeus that his father instilled in him the need to win at everything. In his younger suns, if he didn't win at something, his father told him he wasn't good enough and routinely put the boy down because he didn't win. His drive to be the best at everything stemmed from this upbringing though Thaddeus didn't necessarily see this trait as a problem. He personally selected the first 25 students at the Western Magickal Academy and appreciated Boral's drive to be the best, as he thought it would serve him well as magick is a difficult art, and only the best and brightest are able to attain the highest levels.

Boral's drive and desire to be the best led him to be at the top of his class as he focused on little else except the craft of magick. He sacrificed much of his youth to the betterment of his magickal ability, and it paid off, as he was an accomplished magician even during his long and rigorous training. While his fellow students were enjoying life and having fun given the copious amounts of free time that magician students were typically given, Boral could always be found at the library, studying and learning.

This whole situation might have never occurred, but fate was about to intervene and a perfect storm was just starting to brew in his young life. As Boral entered his ninth cycle of study, his father died, never knowing just how good his only son was. As he was going through school, with each triumph and each new spell that he learned, he would secretly tell himself that he would show his father just how good he was at the craft of magick as he was the top student in his class until that time. He was so angry that he couldn't show his father how good he was, he couldn't get the praise that he wanted from the one man he wanted it from…It was as if his life had lost meaning, and for a time, he brooded about what to do with his life now that the whole reason he was here had died.

As luck would have it, it was the season of Samhein, and Thaddeus was in the West tending to his normal teaching duties, when a student came to him and told him about Boral. Thaddeus sensed the boy's magickal ability and tried to speak to him about this problem but said something that one would expect a teacher of magick to say in that he repeated the Natural Law. He said, "One learns magick to help people, and to better everyone around you, not to impress others."

Unfortunately, while Boral did hear that and understood the Natural Law, he totally disregarded it. At this stage in his magickal career, all he could focus on was being the best. During his final two cycles at the Academy, he needed someone to show off to and chose Thaddeus. He spent a lot of time in Thaddeus' classes, learned the destructive magicks that Thaddeus knew, and Thaddeus would praise him lavishly for completing an assignment or learning a difficult new spell. He studied Thaddeus, learned all he could about him. Upon gaining this new focus, he once again excelled in his final two cycles at the Academy and graduated with the highest honors the school could bestow at that time.

Shortly after he graduated from the Academy, Thaddeus died, and once again, his life was without focus. Out of respect for his teacher, Boral attended the showing of Thaddeus' body and heard Sapphira speak about his life and times and immediately purchased a copy of Thaddeus' memoirs to read for himself how he got to be as great as he was. He was so focused on learning to be great that his social skills were left undeveloped, and no members of the fair sex would come near him. No one loved him, and he only loved the pursuit of knowledge.

21

Though he read Thaddeus' memoir from start to finish, he failed to take into account the one lesson that Thaddeus had hoped he would learn: to find love and the acceptance of another is life's greatest challenge. Sadly, he only focused on the magick and how to be the best because it seemed to him that the two greatest men in his life, his father and Thaddeus had died, and he had no way of showing either of them how powerful he was at the time. His foci were gone, and he needed something else to focus his mind on, and it wouldn't take long for that something to find him.

At this time, he was a strapping lad of 20, though his mind was exceptionally sharp, honed by cycles of magickal teachings, his body was still plagued by a weak constitution. He continued to get sick often and did not avail himself to the curative parts of the magickal curriculum at the Academy because he came to enjoy having power at his command, and like Thaddeus, he enjoyed the flashiness of destructive spells. Also, he sometimes went suns without food or drink in researching a new spell or a new bit of knowledge; he wouldn't sleep for suns on end because he wanted to keep going to finish what he started and gain the knowledge faster than anyone else ever could.

During one particularly long night, he was on the brink of a discovery, he thought to himself, "Only a few more tolls…" but he was very tired, and his mind was dulled because of it. He felt a dark presence in the room with him that night but paid it no mind, instead focusing on his research. He did not realize that a spirit of one who had every reason to hate Thaddeus was in the room with him…and it was through this hatred that he managed to become what he is now. Through means dark and nefarious, he made a "deal" with those who dwell below. In exchange for eternal life in spirit form, he would deliver the Continent and all of its people to his masters. He also wanted to finally gain revenge on Thaddeus and to set the story right in his mind, as it was supposed to be from the original author's pen. This spirit was none other than that of Bjor'ma, the half Elven Wizard who Thaddeus exiled a very long time ago. He lived a lonely and dangerous life out on the steppes of the Deep North, but in death, he vowed to have his vengeance. Bjor'ma knew that Thaddeus was dead, and with magick alive and well on the Continent, combined with his skills in mind control, he was determined to make Boral the vessel of his final conquest of the Continent that was taken from him by Thaddeus.

Thaddeus had ascended at this point in time, so he couldn't have done anything to stop this initial meeting, but history has judged, however falsely, that he could have done something…but did nothing. In his new form, Bjor'ma fed on magickal energy, and he could find no better source of it than Boral. He knew that Boral didn't have the protection that Thaddeus did, not to mention he shunned every other living being, so the spirit would not have to worry about being detected because of the evil that it emanated. The spirit rejoiced that he found such a person to feed on and that Boral would be an easy mark upon which to feast, and that is how he achieved his meteoric rise within the Guild and how this whole mess started.

Being fed upon by an evil spirit is painless, as the spirit veils what it is doing by melding with a persons' shadow during the sun, and masks its presence further by causing the person to shun everyone and everything. The spirit knew that Boral already did this, and that magick was everything for him. It was a match made in heaven, if the gentle reader will pardon the pun. For cycles on end, Boral got stronger, and the spirit did as well.

Of course, having an evil spirit feeding off of you, and having no one else in your life to counter the effects, slowly changes a person, though the spirit itself did nothing to change Boral; the nature of the spirit being as close as it was to Boral, sun in and sun out, slowly changed his mind to evil thoughts… angry thoughts…thoughts that would forever change the Continent and would set in motion the devastation that is now a reality across the Continent.

It should be noted that Boral was a good and honorable man in his youth, and while exceptionally driven to be the best at his craft, he wasn't evil and to this sun would not realize that the changes within him were because of the spirit of Bjor'ma, not to mention Bjor'ma still had the ability to control a person's mind.

CHAPTER 5

A NEW HOPE

As Thaddeus' mind recalled the unfortunate events of the past and given the sheer amount of magick that was present on the Continent, the lines between the Continent and our world blurred even further. The elder Thaddeus put his considerable magickal might to work to open a portal large enough for him to slip through, crossing to another place. A place where a young man named Thaddeus was sleeping in his darkened room.

The young Thaddeus, his head filled with the adventures of his namesake, written in an ancient tome that his father read to him every night. His mind was aflutter with all the adventures in it, the heroes, the monsters, and the excitement of never knowing what's around the next corner. He often saw himself as Thaddeus, fighting and casting spells just as his namesake in the book did. As each page turned and the adventure continued, he often asked in his mind, *Will Thaddeus and his companions survive or succumb to the trials he faces?*

For our young man, tonight was a special night, a night where he and all he knew would be thrust into a world that he had read about, and had fantasized about for a long time (at least to him). As that unseen spark lit up in the sky, one could see a tall man standing over his bed, with a long, white beard and a dragon on his shoulder. The elder Thaddeus saw a young man, one who had his story in his mind and heart, and mayhaps within him was the power to save a place that he had come to know and love.

Thaddeus said to Sairys, "Well, here he is...Never thought I'd meet anyone like 'im. See how he glows with life and with belief?"

Sairys nodded.

The elder Thaddeus always believed in allowing people the freedom to do what they thought was right, but desperate times, at least in his mind, called for desperate measures. He cast a sleeping spell on the young boy, left a note on the boys' bed, and took him through the portal to a new world. For a brief moment, the boy glowed brightly as his thirst for life and adventure was abundantly apparent, and it is here that our story begins in earnest as the Moon Goddess finally awakened due to the life energy and belief in her that has just entered her realm.

The Moon Goddess opened her eyes after what seemed like an eternity to her; though she was still "alive" by deity standards, she required a lot of rest to maintain the meager powers that she retains. Thaddeus had laid her on her bed, so it would appear to the untrained eye that she was resting, but he knew that deities did not need to rest, but he wanted her to appear that way because he had to find a way to save her and hopefully the whole of the Continent from the magickal mess of which he had a hand in creating. As she awoke, he looked into her bright green eyes and felt her zest for life washing over him, and while he was no longer a mortal, he still felt a boost in his mood and demeanor whenever she entered the room, which was a welcome respite from the gloom and doom that the Continent had been in over the last few cycles.

Her first words were, "Thank you, Thaddeus" as she touched his cheek and smiled. As she looked behind Thaddeus, she said, "And who do we have here, a bringer of light and belief in me?"

Thaddeus said, "Aye, this here be my namesake Thaddeus, from another world. Somehow, his father got a hold of my memoirs and has been readin' them to this boy. Perhaps it is a coincidence that his name is Thaddeus, too. I thought mayhaps that he could help us with his belief in you to start with, so that we can think o' somethin' ta do about this mess."

The Moon Goddess examined the new arrival carefully as if to understand who he was and what he could do against the threat of magick that now plagues the Continent.

She asked, "Is he here of his own free will?"

Thaddeus said, "No, I took him from his bedchamber and brought him 'ere. I didn't ask the boy if he wanted to be here, but..."

The Moon Goddess cut Thaddeus off and said, "You know my rules. I understand why you did it, but the rule is absolute. We will have to awaken the boy and explain to him what has happened…and what dangers he is in for should he acquiesce to helping us."

The elder Thaddeus nodded and released the sleeping spell on the boy. He started to stir and woke up slowly.

As the young Thaddeus opened his eyes, he knew that he wasn't in his room, and the first person he saw was the elder Thaddeus as he said, "Am I dreaming, Thaddeus?"

The elder Thaddeus smiled and said, "No, my son, you are not. I have searched the multiverse looking for a special someone, one who knows of my story, who is of good heart and intention, and I have found that some-one. It's ye…I brought ye here without yer knowledge and consent, but we are in need of yer help. Will ye stay and listen to what we would have ye do?" He continued, "Then ye can make yer decision of what ye intend ta do. Know that if ye decide not to help, I'll take ya back ta yer home…But if ye do decide ta help, there's plenty of adventure fer ye and perhaps ye might learn a bit of magick."

The boy looked with wonder as he saw Sairys, and the Moon Goddess herself. As he looked around, he was in a large room, clean with subdued light-ing with a mostly green hue to just about everything.

He asked, "Where am I?"

The Moon Goddess looked at him and smiled, "You are in my home and domain."

The younger Thaddeus was transfixed by the Moon Goddess and her charismatic beauty. He had a great deal of difficulty looking away, and though he was young, he still appreciated the female form, especially one as attractive as this. He had never seen a real deity before, and the women and girls he had seen to date all paled in comparison to the one who stood before him.

The young man turned to Thaddeus while still casting furtive glances at the Moon Goddess and said, "Wow! You're exactly like the picture in the book my pa reads to me…I can't believe I'm actually here! But you said you needed help before?"

Thaddeus said, "Aye…We did. Let me tell ya what has happened. Or may-haps I should show ya." Thaddeus moved his hands about and a window formed on the Continent below. Thaddeus said, "This is the Continent, though I wish ye could have seen it a few cycles back…It did not appear as blighted as it does now. This is why we brought ye here, we want ye to help us bring the Continent back to it's former glory, so that all peoples might live in peace as it was before."

The boy looked with horror as he noted the burned-out cities, the cries of despair, and the utter devastation of the land and said, "What happened here?"

Thaddeus said, "Magick happened here," as a tear formed in his eye. He said, "Now ye see what happens when those who study magick fail to heed the Law."

The young Thaddeus said, "I remember the Law. One uses magick to help others and better those around you."

The elder Thaddeus looked at him a bit surprised, in that this boy from another world knew the Law off the top of his head and said, "That is correct. And ye should know that ye are about the right age to start trainin'. It is a long and arduous process, but mayhaps we could speed it up under the circumstances."

The young Thaddeus glowed brightly and said, "Does that mean you are going to teach me magick? But how? It takes so long to learn. My pa would miss me if I was gone that long."

The elder Thaddeus stoked up his pipe and said, "I will teach ye, if ye are willing to help us. And about yer pa: not to worry, time in this world is different as it moves much more quickly than it does in yer world. If we do this right, he won't even know yer gone. Besides, I left him a note, in case it takes longer than I thought."

The young Thaddeus looked around, still taking everything in, stealing a few glances at the very attractive Moon Goddess standing a few arms away, while thinking about his life to this point. He was a typical boy, nine cycles old, brown eyes and brown hair, about four arms tall, fairly skinny, but possessed a strong mind and excelled in his studies. He was in good health, weighing about six stone or so.

He wasn't really interested in sports or more athletic pursuits, as some other boys were at his age. To him, he was always looking for something else which he could never put his finger on until his father started reading Thaddeus' memoirs, which sparked something in his mind. He realized that his life was typical in every respect, though short by any standard, was completely devoid of true adventure, except the adventures that his father read to him. He longed for something more, which is why he loved Thaddeus' adventures so much because it's what he wanted to do, to live a little outside of his modern comfort zone, perhaps learning a skill or two along the way.

The elder Thaddeus sat in his chair, eyeing the boy, smoking his pipe, seemingly allowing him to make up his mind, without his interference, as to what he wanted to do. He seemed content to read the boy's thoughts and decide if he was magickal material just by observing his thought process.

The Moon Goddess decided on a different tactic, as she was dressed in a long, green, form-fitting silk dress that accentuated her curves to a great degree. She decided to lay on her side on a chaise, reading a book, displaying her feminine form for the boy's benefit in an attempt to "help" him make up his mind. Every so often, the boy's eyes could be seen eyeing her curves while he was deciding whether or not to help, which Thaddeus could "pick up," and those thoughts amused him.

After a long while of silence and contemplation, the boy spoke up and said, "I've thought about it, and I want to help. When can we get started?"

At that moment, the sound of those words echoed throughout the Continent, it was nothing more than a sweet-smelling breeze to most, but to a select few who could understand what was happening, the magnitude of that moment was a welcome turn of events. It signaled for the first time in a long time that something was about to happen that was to stand up to the evil that had plagued the Continent.

Of the few that could hear, Bjor'ma was the first to react, as he caused Boral to explode in a hysterical rage, though no one was in the room with him. With this action, Bjor'ma knew that a clock had been set in motion, and the infernal deed that he was compelled to do, now had the added complexity of a time limit. He knew that if he failed in his task, his soul would be forever damned to the depths of the Land of the Dead, and he would never again know the joys of life.

CHAPTER 6

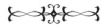

PLANS FORM FROM BELOW AND ABOVE

After calming down a bit, Bjor'ma collected his thoughts and allowed Boral to continue to work, though truth be told, Boral couldn't seem to focus as well as normal because Bjor'ma had drained a lot of energy from him during that fit of rage, including of his life energy. Bjor'ma had figured out that, because Boral was a young man and he wasn't as powerful as Thaddeus, he could drain magickal energy and life energy from him. This constant drain was a reality for Boral, who accepted it, but allowed Bjor'ma's spirit to strengthen and permitted him to further tighten his grip upon Boral.

Over time, Bjor'ma developed a liking for life energy and took it whenever he could without Boral noticing. As a result, Boral was frequently tired, in addition to being ill more often than usual, and at the age of 30, actually had some white hair on his head, but no one ever spoke ill of him; but then again, there wasn't anyone around him because he had killed all his rivals. He also had no other companions due to his extreme paranoia and the fact that the evil emanating from him was now very strong. No one would voluntarily work with him because of the evil he exuded, even for the vast, copious quantities of gold which he was able to offer. It should be noted that Boral's mind was completely under the control of Bjor'ma who perfected his technique by controlling animals in the Deep North to do his bidding and still retained that ability in death as part of the "deal" he made with the infernal powers.

Boral decided to lay down to rest as it was his custom to take an afternoon nap. While he was sleeping, this was Bjor'ma's time to enjoy other pursuits, like attracting a new plague to the Continent, the undead. Bjor'ma's "employers" allowed him the ability to bring these creatures to bear against any opposition to their plans for the Continent and its people. These horrors, who had no minds of their own, ambled around aimlessly in what was once a thriving kingdom, waiting for their chance to do their masters' will. Of course, there were those undead horrors, who were stronger and had minds of their own, mostly the spirits of Wizards that Boral had killed, that were now under the command of Bjor'ma because of his ability to control their minds. Their hatred for Boral was evident, but they could not act upon it because of Bjor'ma's control over them.

His plan was to lead these undead creatures, and send them all over the Continent to destroy the last pockets of humanity, and once they were disposed of, gather up their souls and deliver them to his employers for eternal torment and anguish. Then, he thought, with Boral's magickal might, to wreak havoc on the elves and destroy them, damning them to an eternity of wandering the wastes of the Continent. With no humans or elves on the Continent, all the deities tied to this place would die, and then he would take over as the Overlord of the Continent. He relished what he thought would be an appropriate final act before taking his rightful place as Overlord. He would shed the worthless mortal coil that he was forced to inhabit and watch Boral die a painful and slow death, while he drank in the last sweet vestiges of life from his dying body. He liked his plan, as did his employers. And with his army numbering in the hundreds of thousands, he should have no troubles at all…

Or so he thought.

It should be noted that with so many under his control, that Bjor'ma's control over this undead horde wasn't perfect. Every now and again, one creature would break free and act out, but almost always there were others around the now free creature who squelched any rebellious intent that creature may have had. What Bjor'ma didn't know was that there was one who broke free who had a mind of her own and who was smart enough to not act out right away. Seeing what happened to those that did act out, she decided to bide her time and wait until the opportune moment to take action. She played along with her deception and did as she was instructed to do.

This spirit was a spirit of a Wizard, an Elven Wizard at that, who was given a new lease on consciousness, though not life as she knew it. Her name was Kamatrista, but she preferred to be called Kama. In life, she was an uncommonly good Wizard, taught in the finest traditions of elfish magicks, and one of the top students in the Southern Academy for Magick Craft, having graduated from that worthy institution seven and 10 cycles ago. She was killed when a Wizard stormed into her shop and killed her with a bolt of fire for no apparent reason other than to eliminate another potential rival. Kama always upheld the Natural Law and believed that healing others was a noble craft, in the finest traditions of her people. She also drew inspiration from Clarissa and had read her memoirs to understand what her craft could be with enough practice. Hers was one of many stories of the Elven Exodus, but she knew that the bulk of the elves had escaped to their ancestral homeland, but instead of going with them, she stayed behind to continue to help others, humans included, because of the Natural Law.

While Bjor'ma's army was gathering strength, he needed to decide on the first place to attack and decided on the Narsum to the East. He thought that they would be easy pickings and too few in number to put up any serious resistance to his army of undead. He sent spirits out to do some reconnaissance and understand just how powerful the Narsum were and their approximate numbers. He made the mistake of sending Kama out one night, who did as she was told and began the long trek to the East. While flying east, she attracted the attention of someone else. The Moon Goddess happened to feel her presence in the air as she was heading east because the Moon Goddess had attuned herself to the only charges she had left, the elves. The Moon Goddess thought it was odd to see an Elven spirit this far North and, to her delight, one who believed in her. Little did Bjor'ma know that, in this small routine act, the Continent's history was about to change.

Kama got halfway across the Continent and then she saw something that surprised her. A bright light, right in front of her, as bright as the First Sun coming up in Somar, at which point she stopped, and while far out of the reach of Bjor'ma's sight, she heard, "My child. There are some who are pleased to see you. I pray you know who I am…"

Kama said, "You are the Moon Goddess, I'm sure of it! What do you wish of me?"

She heard, "Aye, you are correct. Mayhaps this is the start of something miraculous, for it will take a miracle to undo what has been done, a miracle that you may be a part of, if you wish to be that is."

Kama was taken aback; she had so many questions in her mind like, *Why did the Moon Goddess abandon the elves? Why didn't she do anything to stop the slaughter of thousands of people?* and *Is there a plan to thwart the plans of Boral?* While in these thoughts, Kama found herself in another place, in a warm quiet room with green, subdued lighting all around, with a lone person sitting on a chair directly in front of her. She could feel the power emanating from the Moon Goddess, and it felt wonderful, like the sun warming your entire being, a far cry from the darkness from which she had come.

The Moon Goddess said, "Welcome to my home and domain. Only those who believe in me can come to this place, and only those who are unwaveringly faithful to me will ever see this room. I warmly commend your belief in me despite what has been going on. I've been somewhat incapacitated lately, but I feel much better now, thanks to some happenings of which you have now become a part, provided you do so of your own free will."

Kama was astonished, for only in Elven legends did anyone ever actually see the Moon Goddess in her domain. She read that of the elite group that actually saw the Moon Goddess, even fewer were blessed by her, and she knew that the only woman to ever get this most sacred blessing was Mystara, a warrior of legend from times long since past.

Kama stuttered out a reply while dropping to her knees, "W…What…do…ye…wish of me? Whatever it is, I will do it."

The Moon Goddess smiled and said, "Rise, Kama of the Elves. Your faith in me has renewed my strength and strengthened my resolve to do something about the blight that has taken hold of the Continent. I need you to continue what you are doing: play along with Bjor'ma, report to me whatever you hear or see." She continued, "However, as in times past, this is a mortal problem, and hence requires a mortal solution. To that end, while you are no longer mortal, this must fall to someone who is."

Kama said, "But who? Boral is the last Wizard on the Continent with an army of foul creatures and evil beings behind him, what mortal can stop him?"

Hearing voices in another room while exploring what was to be his new home for a little while, the young Thaddeus strode confidently into the room and said, "What's going on?"

He was followed by the elder Thaddeus, who said, "Ah, I see another has chosen to join our cause…Excellent!"

Kama looked at the young boy with an old man behind him and said, "You're Thaddeus, aren't you? I read all about you at the Academy, and I obeyed the Natural Law that you set down. I am honored to help in any way

I can...I never got to see you in person. This is such an honor! I am truly blessed this sun to see my Goddess and a legend, here in this place."

There was no emotion in her voice, only the hauntingly low tones that escaped from her spirit, which put a bit of a damper on the moment, but it was a moment that was not lost on the younger Thaddeus, who said in a very excited voice, "Wow, we haven't even gotten started yet, and I've already met a spirit! What an adventure this will be!"

At that point, something changed in the young boy. He started growing, not in stature, but in knowledge, as if the gates of his mind opened up and started allowing solutions to the issue to come to him. It was as if his mind threw off the shackles of ignorance, and though youthful exuberance was still a part of him, all in the room could sense that there was a greater wisdom now present in his mind.

At that moment, the elder Thaddeus said, "Well, my boy, I think ye are ready now. Let's begin yer training!"

While the elder Thaddeus could feel the effects of this change, only the Moon Goddess knew what really happened in that moment. She smiled and thought to herself, "Alotraxas...is that you? Why have you come after all this time?" She got no reply but her curiosity was piqued as she said to Kama, "Are you ready to spy on Boral and Bjor'ma?"

Kama said, "Yes, my Goddess. Anything..."

The Moon Goddess said, "Very well. Then go and do what ye must. I wish you well!"

CHAPTER 7

THE LONG DARK NIGHT

Time passed on the Continent. Kama did as the Moon Goddess had wanted and passed along vital information to the Narsum and her for a full season until the darkest night came, a night unlike any other, when Boral cast a spell of truly infernal design and blotted out the light from the three moons, rendering the Continent completely dark for the first time in recorded history.

Under cover of darkness, his undead hordes numbering in the hundreds of thousands fell upon the villages of Narsum and their new human allies, but when they got there, there was a surprise waiting for them. As Boral crested the last hill, right on the border of the lands of the Narsum and he looked upon the largest of the Narsum villages, he saw that it was totally devoid of life…

There wasn't anyone there to fight. Everywhere he looked, it was the same thing, nothing but empty towns and villages. He ordered his army to attack the villages anyway, thinking that they were hiding, but after several tolls of searching, no trace of anyone was to be found in any village.

Oh, how he raged at that sight, both the spirit within and the man! They screamed and yelled and raged long into the night as the undead hordes blanketed what once were thriving villages and towns, where life took hold and flourished even under these harsh conditions.

He yelled loud into the night, "We have been tricked, deceived! I will have my vengeance!" He realized a few moments later as he looked around that there was no one left to deceive him, all around him had been eliminated and only the undead remained, then he thought that perhaps a spirit had deceived him, but how? He knew that he had complete control over them, unless he sent too many spirits out, and perhaps they were spotted by the village shamans who he knew could work a primitive magick. Damning himself for his failure (as there was no one else to blame), he vowed to find the Narsum and destroy them.

Kama had done her work well, warning the villages and the disparate tribes of Narsum to flee further into the mountains, where the undead could not go and where they would be safe from Bjor'ma and Boral. She told the village shamans what was coming and when, along with the most likely routes they would take to get here. Hearing this news and seeing the undead horde for themselves, the Narsum and their human allies went deep into the mountains where the undead could not follow in force, though spirits could do so easily.

The spirits that Bjor'ma sent after Kama had betrayed him mistook the movements of the Narsum for raiding parties as the Narsum were travelling very light, however, over many thousands of cycles, they have learned how to survive anywhere so they didn't bring food or water with them, relying on their knowledge of the mountains to survive. As the spirits reported back, Boral and Bjor'ma reveled at the news that they were helping in their ultimate destruction by fighting among themselves. What these spirits didn't realize was that the village population was getting smaller and smaller…and since they had no knowledge of Narsum ways, they could only report back that everything was normal and that the Narsum were unaware of what was coming.

Kama knew that Boral and Bjor'ma were reliant on the might of their undead horde and used spirits as reconnaissance only so she knew that though Boral might find out where the Narsum were, he would not be able to get to them with the might he needed to annihilate them and that the Narsum were formidable warriors on top of that.

Boral and Bjor'ma were also working with false data, in that Kama had told them that the Narsum had only numbered 40,000 along with another 30,000 humans among them. Other spirits reported the same thing as it was difficult to see all the Narsum and humans at the same time because they were so spread out. Boral did not realize that the Narsum and their new human allies numbered closer to 175,000, replete with cavalry using steppe horses. These grayish colored horses typically stand at nine arms high, weigh an impressive 105 stone on average, and sport long gray hair to protect them from the cold. They were bred by the Narsum over hundreds of cycles specifically for mountain travel and combined the strength and speed of a large horse, the cloven hooves and iron nerve of a mountain goat, and the sight of a mountain eagle into one large and very dangerous adversary especially with a Narsum rider trained in the use of dual broadswords and the most fearsome weapon of all, the Narsum bow.

The long dark night continued on as the mindless undead horde picked through what little there was, looking for something living, but they found nothing. Nothing but the sounds of their own shambling feet as Boral raged on, sending spirits into the mountains to find the Narsum.

As the mass of spirits closed in upon the highest mountain range on the Continent, the Dragonscape Mountains, they faced one other danger, one which gave this mountain range its name…Yes, here there be dragons! Dragonkind are a rarely seen, reclusive bunch and rarely take notice of anything that occurs outside of their homes; in fact, some of the favorite hiding places of the Narsum are in old dragon caves, their former owners long since dead, but large enough for an entire village to fit comfortably within its cavernous interior.

Dragons are, and always have been, very sensitive to spirits and always take notice of them, a fact lost on Boral and Bjor'ma, as neither of them knew anything about this part of the Continent, or about the denizens therein because this area was so poorly studied. So, when the army of spirits descended on the Dragonscape Mountains, they inadvertently awoke several older dragons, all of whom flew out of their homes searching for the invading spirits.

Having no knowledge about the danger they were in, the spirits followed their leader's commands to the letter and started searching caves, and that's where the trouble began. The spirits should have known the night was going to go badly for them when several spirits entered the first cave and found a female dragon with her clutch of eggs. She was incensed by this intrusion and went on the attack, blasting the spirits with baleful magick which had no effect, until she played her trump card: a magickal mind attack. Waves of thought energy shot forth from her mind and dispelled some of the spirits that were in close proximity to her while others left the area post-haste. This scenario of spirits getting blasted by waves of thought energy was replayed throughout the mountain range that night, leaving the spirit's numbers decimated. Of the 4,372 spirits that went into the mountains that night, fewer than 800 returned.

Even worse, six of the oldest dragons followed the spirits back to the empty villages of the Narsum to familiarize themselves with the situation.

While the dragons knew where the Narsum were, they did not know why, assuming it was another human army trying to drive them out. The dragons were surprised when they noted the dark moons and the hordes of undead now meandering about, decided that they did not want these creatures befouling their mountain range, so they decided to go on the offensive and deal as much destruction as they could to these mockeries of life before they could despoil the rugged beauty of the mountains.

Their attacks were well-coordinated, well planned, and very destructive; that is until they met Boral standing on the top of a hill listening to what was happening in the mountains through his spirit informers. Boral saw them coming and launched a barrage of magick that caused them to scatter as he screamed, "Now, dragons…I rule this place! Bow down to me while you still can, and witness the glory of the coming transformation!"

The dragons were unimpressed and launched a mind attack on him that separated Bjor'ma from Boral's body. Bjor'ma had heard about what happened in the mountains and flew off to avoid the fate that befell so many spirits that night. After Bjor'ma left him, Boral felt weak at first and didn't know what to do as he looked around and saw six dragons coming at him, but he was able to fend them off using his most powerful magickal spells. While the dragons inflicted terrible damage to his army, reducing it by 90 percent, and Boral felt the claws of a dragon rip into his body in several spots, he felt good knowing that he inflicted damage on them as well, and now he knew where the Narsum went; it was just a question of finding them.

As the night wore on, Boral was bleeding profusely, and his weak constitution caught up with him as he decided to sit down and care for his wounds, though he was a bit confused as to what had happened. It was as if his drive had left him and for all intents and purposes, it did. Bjor'ma was several leagues away, recovering his strength and trying to understand what he could do now with his diminished forces. He was unsure that his "employers" would allow him more of the undead to replenish his numbers. So, he asked them.

The stench of evil permeated the air where they gathered, with Bjor'ma in spirit form waiting in an open field as they appeared one by one. The first appearance of the Entities of Evil as they were called on the Continent, this so-called brotherhood consisted of three members, the Lord of the Dead, commander of the legions of the undead, the Lord of Blight, able to kill just about anything with a touch, and the worst of the three and Bjor'ma's "boss," the Dread Lord, Overlord of Evil whose capabilities are unspeakably terrible, hence his name. The fact that they are able to appear here bodes poorly for the Continent for they cannot appear if there is a champion of good willing to fight anywhere on the land. The place they landed was known as the Dread Hallows and would forever bear their mark, in that nothing would ever grow and anyone passing over this spot would grow sick and die in a matter of tolls.

Bjor'ma bowed low and said, "I have meekly asked you here…"

The Dread Lord interrupted him, "I know why you have called us! YOU HAVE FAILED! Can you do nothing right…?"

Bjor'ma was now quite afraid of his boss as he said, "My Lord…"

The Dread Lord interrupted him again saying, "You want more troops, better troops, faster troops? You have to earn them. Win a victory with what you have, consecrate the fallen to the Lord of the Dead and we shall see. But know this: fail again, and we will have another 'agent' take care of this miserable world and as for you…Well, you know your fate. Now GO!"

Bjor'ma flew off quietly as the Entities of Evil left this world. On his way back to Boral, he wondered how he was thwarted so easily, as if the Narsum knew he was coming…But how? Then it came to him: he did not have perfect control over the minds of all the spirits. Perhaps one of them went rogue on him, but how? He thought that even if one of them did get loose, that all Wizards were just like he was in life…But what if one of them wasn't? What if one of them was an innocent victim who happened to be a Wizard? He thought long and hard as to who it could be, but he didn't know, and he was resigned to the fact that he might never know, but he thought that perhaps whoever it was met their end tonight, though that could never undo the decimation that occurred. As he approached where he thought Boral was, he stopped in his tracks as he saw Boral laying on the ground, his wounds wrapped up in cloth, barely breathing. Bjor'ma rushed over and entered Boral's body, but Bjor'ma discovered that Boral didn't have any magickal energy in his mind, having expended it in fighting the dragons, or any life energy that he could spare, having bled much of that out on the ground.

After about a toll of convalescing on the ground, somehow defying the pain that he was experiencing, Boral was able to get up and started to walk away (albeit slowly) from Narsum lands. While he may have declared himself a living God, he didn't feel very Godlike tonight as he needed two of the undead to assist him in moving, and following them was a much smaller horde of undead and several hundred spirits. On the way back to what remained their home base, the Circle of Wizards Guild Hall in the West, both Bjor'ma and Boral were thinking about all the planning, the gathering, the reconnaissance, all for naught, as they were outsmarted by a single Elven spirit. They thought that they needed to learn a lot more about warfare, and fast.

Two suns later, Boral barely made it back to the Guild Hall and began rummaging through an emergency pack that he designed, just in case he was attacked by a rival Wizard, and he found what he was looking for, healing poultices, which he applied generously to himself. As the poultice did its work, he started to feel a little better, but was totally exhausted and as close as he had ever come to death. While Boral was a brilliant Wizard, he never learned healing magicks, as he found that he couldn't win contests with those, but now he was cursing himself having used the last of his poultices, and he didn't know how to make more.

As he laid on his bed that night, he remembered the clarity of thought that he experienced while laying on the hill, and he wondered why that was; it was as if he was thinking on his own, and as he recalled, he wasn't very good at it, but he chalked it up to almost dying out there and paid no more mind to it as he closed his eyes. Just then, the spell that Boral had cast expired, and once again, the three moons shone brightly as if to say that there was hope for the Continent. And there was.

CHAPTER 8

A LIFE RETURNED AND A LIFE TAKEN

While all this destruction was happening, Kama was still doing what the Moon Goddess asked her to, helping the Narsum whilst avoiding dragons. This was not an easy task because she knew of their terrible mind attack power and what it could do to a spirit, thanks to the elfish magicks she learned. Fortunately for her, dragons are highly intelligent and can be reasoned with, which she did brilliantly, helping them destroy much of the undead horde that had been brought to bear on the Narsum. After the long dark night was over, the Moon Goddess did something extraordinary, though it took every ounce of strength she had. She blessed Kama.

This blessing is perhaps the greatest gift that the Moon Goddess can give, as it does two things. First, it cements one's name in the annals of Elven legend, but more importantly, it allows the recipient to regain a corporeal form and allows them to "be themselves," just as they were when they were alive. Though the Moon Goddess could not give her life, this was as close as anyone who was dead could get to their former life.

Kama knew that she had joined an elite group of elves after her blessing. She knew that she had joined the Continent's most famous female elf, Mystara, as one of the few who had received this exceedingly rare gift. Being an uncommonly kind and caring elf, under the circumstances that the Continent found itself in, she wanted to pay it forward and do whatever she could to ensure that the Moon Goddess' faith in her was not misplaced, so she joined Thaddeus and trained the young man in the magick she knew best, elfish magick. This Elven teaching placed him in much esteemed company, as one of only a handful of humans to learn the ways of the elves from a real elf, the last of which was Clarissa.

The young Thaddeus was a quick study, which augured well for him as he was now learning elfish magicks, thanks to Kama, as well as the flashier (and destructive) magick that Thaddeus wrought. He took a liking to elfish magicks; though they didn't have the same visual appeal, they were faster to cast and allowed one to heal others. It seemed to the young Thaddeus that the Natural Law and elfish magick went hand in hand, and while he knew that destructive magick certainly had its place in the world, he thought that elfish magick was more in line with the spirit of the Law as he interpreted it.

Over that time, unlike his elder namesake, the young Thaddeus developed a liking for the elves, though he had only this one example to judge them by. Truth be told, he couldn't have picked a better example to follow in what elves are truly like, not to mention that Kama was what could be considered beautiful by Elven standards, which the younger Thaddeus appreciated. Though now corporeal, she could appear how she wished and chose to appear as she did in life. Kama had a pleasant round face, lavender eyes, and short pixie-style hair. She dressed simply in plain Elven style dresses, taking a page from Clarissa's playbook in that regard. Unlike Clarissa though, Kama would add a colorful accessory of some kind in a contrasting color, as she had a very playful personality and liked to have that contrast displayed in what she wore.

She and the young Thaddeus were about the same height and body type, so neither was intimidated by the other, and with Kama's playful personality and Thaddeus' youthful exuberance, they could often be found talking as part of their lessons together as Kama would tell the young Thaddeus about the elves, and he would regale her with tales of our world and the wonders within. The elder Thaddeus noted that he seemed to enjoy being taught magick by her, and while he always excelled at his lessons no matter who was teaching him, he seemed to be taking more of a liking to elfish magick.

While elfish magicks were strong, the elder Thaddeus knew that this would require a change in strategy when he was to face Boral, for he would need to engage in more of a defensive strategy and try to wear Boral down rather than to go on the offensive. As his training continued, the young Thaddeus truly excelled at the healing magicks that Kama taught him and started speaking a few words in Elven under her tutelage.

The elder Thaddeus understood why this was, thanks to him teaching so many students while he was alive. He could pick out with stunning accuracy who would excel at his type of magick or elfish magick. He knew that it all had to do with the students' life experiences to this point. Unlike him, his younger namesake had no bad experiences in his young life that would steer him towards the awesome destructive powers that the elder Thaddeus taught him. While the boy loved the flashiness of the effects, and the sheer power that he was able to command, it appeared that he was more inclined by his very nature to help rather than to harm.

Thaddeus, on the other hand, had tragedy befall him when he was a young man, when he lost Sapphira in a bandit raid, and as such, he delved into the most destructive magicks that he could at the time. He also was craftier than his contemporaries in that he added new effects to his magicks because he was a showman at heart and loved to show off his spell effects. While he did have his revenge on the bandits that cost him his love at the time, it did nothing to bring her back to him. He knew that it was the desire to bring her back which served as the impetus behind many of his more illustrious adventures.

Meanwhile, on the Continent, a gravely injured Boral rested for many suns trying to regain his strength. His condition was exacerbated by the spirit of Bjor'ma taking his energy away and the lack of food and fresh water in the area, not to mention his poor health was starting to take its toll. This was definitely not part of Bjor'ma's plan as he expected Boral to live another 30 or so cycles, which would be enough time for him to execute his plan, but it certainly didn't look like he was going to last another season. Bjor'ma was worried for his vessel because he knew another like him didn't exist, as all the other Wizards of his ability were gone, leaving only the elves, whose magick made them notoriously difficult to inhabit, save a select few individuals who might be open to Bjor'ma, but they were mere shadows of Boral and the power that he possessed.

He needed a victory in battle, just as the Dread Lord had said, but the Dread Lord did not say *how large* of a victory it needed to be. If he sent his undead horde after a hamlet of 100 to 200 people, and defeated them, wouldn't that be a victory? He needed to find a poorly defended populace in a remote area, so he sent his spirits out looking for just such a place.

It took a season to find a populace that wasn't near anything else and that didn't have a lot of people, that Bjor'ma thought could be easily decimated by his horde, which was growing smaller each sun as the undead started to "rot" because of exposure to the elements. They would just collapse and crumble to dust. Bjor'ma knew that it was late in the season of Samhein and soon colder weather would take over, slowing his army to a crawl, as they were almost unable to move in the deep snow that typically fell around this time especially in the mountainous areas where he found this population to be.

He had to do all this planning alone and with little energy because his vessel was doing so poorly, but he could wait no longer, as he inhabited Boral and caused him to rise and lead his undead horde towards this populace of humans that his spirits had found. Boral was in rough shape, only looking marginally more alive than many of the undead. Bjor'ma had a litter made and caused 10 of the undead to carry Boral around because he couldn't walk for more than a toll before needing to rest.

Finally, he reached the hamlet, seeing the 100 or so inhabitants preparing for the colder weather which was on its way. Without warning, he unleashed his army of undead upon the small hamlet, and within two tolls, the population was completely destroyed. Bjor'ma performed a ritual and cast a spell of his own, which consecrated those that died to the Dread Lord in the hopes that he would receive more troops as many of his troops had fallen, some due to the heroic actions of the populace, but many others to rot. A few moments later, many of the humans that fell in battle rose again as undead themselves. Bjor'ma wasn't really happy about this, but getting an additional 100 troops was better than nothing, though he lost about 200 in the engagement.

He knew that he had to act fast and decided to continue on the march to win more engagements before the snow came to bolster his troops. Over the next 15 suns, he found and defeated four other smaller hamlets, which had a negligible effect on his total troop strength, but at least he seemed to be replacing that which he lost in each engagement. With each engagement he won, Bjor'ma returned to Boral and witnessed a battle he was losing. Boral was dying, and there was nothing he could do about it.

By the oddest of coincidences, the last place Boral would see would be his home village, Farhill, in the foothills of the mountains. The place where he started this epic journey 20 cycles ago, which was a thriving place back then, home to over 2,000 souls. As he lay on the ground, racked with pain, his face contorted in constant agony, he uttered his last words, "Father, I have failed, I just wasn't good enough."

All the cycles of Bjor'ma taking energy from him had finally taken its toll as his body had no more to give and on the last sun of Samhein, Boral died of his injuries and the harsh conditions in the mountains.

Bjor'ma was angered at this and consecrated his death to the Dread Lord in the hopes that he could be resurrected. In a sense, he was; the only difference was that now there was no life in his glowing red eyes, only a burning hatred of life and a desire to see it extinguished as quickly as possible.

Bjor'ma heard, "He is one of us now, follow him to victory."

Bjor'ma was happy he got his vessel back, and while he would no longer have any life energy, there was plenty of magickal energy to feed off of and no worries about Boral and his poor health.

The new Boral decided to head back to the Guild Hall and plan his next moves for when Simcha arrived, one season from now to wreak havoc and devastation upon humanity and then the elves. Bjor'ma found that he was quite comfortable with his new vessel and thanked the Dread Lord for hearing his request.

Boral's body was left where he said goodbye to this world, unburied, when a beam of moonlight fell from the sky as the first moon, Trirance, came over the horizon, and a new Wizard appeared in place of the Wizard that had just perished. As the young Thaddeus set foot on the Continent for the first time, he thought to himself, *Wow! I'm really here...The Continent at last!*

This action had two effects, the first of which was that many unseen entities saw him for the first time, some cheered at his arrival but others wanted him dead. The second effect was that he was able to see Boral clearly for the first time and look into his now lifeless eyes. He saw no malice or evil there and decided to help him. Thanks to his training in healing magicks, he put a small amount of his own life energy into Boral as he opened his eyes and said, "I'm alive...I...I can't believe it..." As he looked up, he saw the young Thaddeus and said, "Who are you? My name is Boral."

The young Thaddeus said, "I am Thaddeus, a Wizard. We don't have much time. I can help give you back what was taken from you...Would you like to live again?"

Boral looked around, seeing his home village in ruins, its buildings destroyed, its people slaughtered, and he remembered all the evil that he had done and what befell the Continent because of him as he said, "No, I've done enough harm for one lifetime I think. I can't forgive myself for what I've done, and perhaps it's better this way. Thaddeus, you are the last human Wizard on the Continent now, take a lesson from me and always follow the Natural Law. I…I want you…to have what is in my robe…'s yours now…goodbye…"

As the last of Thaddeus' life energy left him and Boral's eyes closed for the last time on that cool Samhein night, Thaddeus shed a tear, as this was the first time he had ever seen the moment of death. Thaddeus felt around Boral's body and found a strange scepter in his pocket; it was small, made of a peculiar silvery metal, devoid of decoration, but Thaddeus could feel power radiating from it as he held it. It didn't appear at first to do anything, so he put it in his pocket. Afterwards, he used earth magick to dig a hole, and ceremoniously put the body of Boral in it, said a prayer to the Moon Goddess, and filled it in.

He cast another spell and willed himself back to the domain of the Moon Goddess, a changed person. He had seen death, and before this was over, he would bear witness to much more.

CHAPTER 9

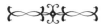

BITTER COLD AND SWEET DISCOVERIES

The coldest season of the cycle, Sarodan, came with a vengeance. It was particularly vicious this cycle, more snow and much colder than usual, as if unseen forces were trying to purify the Continent before the new Boral and Bjor'ma defiled it for what could be the last time. They planned a three-season blitz of the mountainous regions of the West to root out the last humans there, then onwards to take on the Barbarians of the North, followed by a return to the Dragonscape Mountains of the East and finally ending with the Elves in the South. They estimated that by the time they were ready to take on the elves, their army would have well over two million soldiers, which would overwhelm any defense that the elves could mount.

Their plan was simple; fight battles and win, consecrating all deaths to the Dread Lord, and then those who opposed them would be forced to fight with them as they pressed inexorably on. They decided to start small, as their forces would be almost non-existent by the time Simcha came. The primary reason for this was that the undead raised have a shelf-life of one season before their bodies collapsed and crumbled to dust. At first, they would be reliant on magick from the new Boral, who fashioned a new name for himself. He was now Thanatos, which is the Elven word for death, since that was his only purpose here, to cause as much of it as possible. Bjor'ma knew that Boral's magick was strong, but it seems to have gotten an upgrade when Thanatos was created. Bjor'ma witnessed the awesome power of his magick, as he would frequently unleash his spells on the mindless undead that surrounded the Guild Hall.

There was one other effect in the upgrade from Boral to Thanatos, Bjor'ma found that his formidable mind control power did not work, and it seemed that Thanatos was being controlled by his superiors or he was immune to Bjor'ma's abilities. This left Bjor'ma without a job as it seemed that he was reduced to just "being along for the ride" with no real purpose or function, other than to watch. While he did not mind the break, he quickly realized that he was being phased out of this operation, and he knew what that meant, that he could be disposed of at any time. Thanatos sensed Bjor'ma's thoughts and attempted to set his mind at ease by saying in a low deep voice, "Your job is to control the hordes of undead that the Dread Lord will give to us. Rest now, regain your strength. At this time in the next cycle, the Dread Lord will claim this place as his own, and you will rule over all…"

Ever the cynic, Bjor'ma didn't believe him, and a plan started to form in his mind. What if he betrayed the Entities and thwarted these attacks at the opportune time? He might be lauded as a hero. He put that thought away for now and rested, but he was increasingly wary of Thanatos and what he was doing.

Sarodan took its toll on the Continent, particularly in the West, as many humans perished as a result of being in the mountains. The extreme cold and lack of food did not help their situation and in many cases, entire villages ceased to exist. Some were more prepared than others, but because they were forced to move, many could not carry all the supplies that they would need and even worse, many did not know what it took to live in the mountains. Those living with the Northern tribes and with the Narsum had it relatively easy as they were experts in winter survival, and were generous with their help and sharing their knowledge with the millions of souls that moved there.

The humans dwelling in the North were also easily converted to worship the Snow Queen, bolstering her abilities, making her one of the strongest deities during this time in the Continent's history. While a good deity, concerned with watching over her charges, she loved the snow and the cold. It was during Sarodan that she made the most appearances on the Continent to revel in the weather. Most people believe that a purification ritual is taking place given the events of late, that the Snow Queen is doing something about this mess. It should be noted that those people, the true faithful of the Snow Queen were right, in that she is the cause of this brutal Sarodan.

Those who took up residence in the Deep North, lived in the mountain caves during Sarodan, as the temperatures outside were fatal to humans and

Barbarians alike. Further excavation of these caves led to a discovery about Bjor'ma, though no one really knew what it meant, except one man named Harold. He attended the Northern School of Magick and dropped out after his fourth cycle owing to the extreme difficulty of the curriculum there, but he was there long enough to know what he was looking at.

It was a book of spells, penned by Bjor'ma himself in an attempt to preserve what he knew, but it was also a journal, detailing his life and times spent here in exile. In the tome, Harold noted a few spells that Bjor'ma knew, but more importantly, it spelled out why he made a deal with the Dread Lord, in that he was so angry and bitter about Thaddeus, and the original storyline that was irrevocably changed because of his arrival. He ranted for pages about what was taken from him, the opportunity to be a Lord himself. For this one man though, who was the leader of his village, the tome detailed how that contract with the Dread Lord could be broken if need be because Bjor'ma thought that once this deal was made, he could not break it, and it could very well fall to someone else to stop the evil that the Continent was now rife with.

As Harold read further, he discovered that the only way the deal could be broken with the Dread Lord is if Bjor'ma performed a good act, no matter how small it was; that would be enough to break the contract and cause Bjor'ma to cease being a spirit and spend an eternity in anguish and torment. Of course, Bjor'ma was careful to hide this fact in his writings because he wrote it in magickal script, a language that only a fellow Wizard could read, but it was there nonetheless. Harold didn't know who Bjor'ma was, but documented his discovery and made detailed drawings of the pictures that Bjor'ma had drawn on the cave walls. In a small crevice, just large enough for a small man to crawl in and rest, Harold found animal skins on the floor and writing on the walls. He wrote down what he saw:

My name is Bjor'ma, and I have lived in this cave for 37 cycles, having been exiled here by Thaddeus Brimstone because of my powers to control the minds of men. While I could have attained greatness, that honor was stripped from me by this newcomer. I know that my life is coming to an end soon, and while I will never be anything other than a footnote in history, I wanted it known to anyone who reads this that I can never forgive him for what he did to me.

I do not know why I have the powers I do, or why I felt compelled to use them for so long, but I suppose I want what every man wants, to make his mark on the world and leave it a better place than when he found it. I know that the Continent will forget about me and perhaps that is best for everyone…that I should die, lonely and forgotten, is perhaps the greatest service I can perform for the Continent and its people…

To whoever reads this, I bequeath to you my worldly possessions: my sword, my coat, and most importantly, my journal, may it shine a light on me and my struggles to live in this alien place…

Bjor'ma

Harold was taken aback by what he read because he did know who Thaddeus was. In his mind, the fact that Bjor'ma claimed to be able to control the minds of men, and that he may have been tempted to use that ability, is probably why he was exiled here, because he knew that Thaddeus was an honorable and just man, or at least that is what he was taught. More importantly, Harold was now in possession of knowledge that no one else had, how to break the Dread Lord's contract and perhaps stop the madness that Harold and his entire village came here to escape.

Meanwhile, in the Circle of Wizards Guild Hall in the West, Thanatos was endlessly planning and plotting and while Bjor'ma's spirit was able to provide detail and reconnaissance, most of the plan belonged to Thanatos. Bjor'ma noted that he seemed to be less like Boral and more attuned to those who dwell below. He never rested, never ate or drank anything and seemed to have an endless amount of magickal energy that he would need to "expend" by casting devastating magicks about once every seven suns. Bjor'ma noted that it was one of his weaknesses. It was as if, he was instilled in some way with an excess of magickal energy, probably for him to feed on, but Thanatos produced much more than he could ever need, but maybe that was part of the plan. Bjor'ma thought that if he started consuming that energy, growing stronger and more powerful that perhaps he might be able to thwart Thanatos at some critical point, because he didn't like playing "second fiddle" to anyone, much less someone who, to his mind, was sent here to supplant him. So, he started feeding, and feeding, and feeding. He spent entire suns feeding voraciously and grew stronger as a result in a very short period of time. He still wasn't able to control Thanatos, but he was able to determine a second weakness, that he needed to be on the ground constantly or he would lose contact with his masters. Bjor'ma discovered this quite by accident as a result of his continued feeding, oddly enough while Thanatos was walking outside. Though he couldn't be sure what would happen if both feet were off the ground, he surmised that the energy supply would be cut off, rendering Thanatos unable to act. Bjor'ma noted that as he lifted a foot off the ground, there was less energy for him to feed on, but in that split second when both of his feet were on the ground, there was a brief surge, followed by another lull.

Bjor'ma continued to feed heavily and perform reconnaissance as needed as Sarodan continued its assault on the Continent and its people. He also noted that Thanatos did not need to "expend" any more energy every seven suns due to his incessant feeding, so Bjor'ma was proved correct in his theory that the excess energy was for him and that he should take as much as he could ever want. Thanatos did not seem to notice or care that Bjor'ma was discovering things about him, and continued to plot and plan his assault. It was as if Thanatos and his masters were unimpressed that Bjor'ma was a Wizard and a very intelligent man when he was alive, which motivated Bjor'ma to find out all he could and at the opportune moment when no one expected it, to use that information to his advantage just as Boral did in eliminating all his former rivals.

Meanwhile in the Moon Goddess' domain, upon his return from his first trip to the Continent, the younger Thaddeus said to the elder Thaddeus, Sairys, Kama and the Moon Goddess, "I saw Boral, I…I saw him die. He did not want to be saved, but he gave me this. It doesn't seem to do anything but he seemed adamant that I have it…Does anyone know what this is?"

The elder Thaddeus looked with some disbelief and said, "So that's how 'e was able to do it!"

Everyone looked towards Thaddeus as Kama said, "Do what?"

Thaddeus replied, "That there be the Eyes of the King. It is able to find any Wizard alive and tell ye where they are. If Boral had this, he would know where to find any other Wizards alive, and in 'is case, kill 'em."

The young Thaddeus held the Eyes of the King and said, "But I don't see anyone else…"

Thaddeus cut him off and said, "That's because ye are the last Wizard on the Continent, and I'm technically dead, and that device never could find me anyway. Elves are tough to see with that…though half-elves weren't a problem."

As he said that, he thought of Bjor'ma and wondered what became of him. Little did he know that he would find out soon enough. He also thought of

Sapphira and the Heart of the Queen. He missed her dearly and wondered what became of the Heart, knowing that no male could wield it.

Thaddeus said, "So…Ye have it now. I suppose that's as good a place as any fer it ta be. At least it's in good hands." He continued, "Would ye mind if I held it for a moment or two?" The younger Thaddeus handed it over, and the elder Thaddeus was stunned at what he saw saying, "Well, isn't that interesting. Sairys, would you care to join us?" The dragon flew in quickly as everyone else just stood around wondering what it was that Thaddeus saw when he said, "Seems one of yer kind is at work here, an ancient one at that. A name…Alotraxas…is coming to mind…"

CHAPTER 10

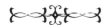

ALOTRAXAS THE ANCIENT

While the young Thaddeus didn't realize it, his newfound learning ability was due to a dragon spirit, assisting him in learning as much magick as he could, for the inevitable showdown with Thanatos, Bjor'ma, and the Entities of Evil. Alotraxas knew the gravity of the situation and saw this opportunity to allow the race of men to live on. He also noted that all other human Wizards were dead, except for this boy, and once he left, there would be no others.

The question has been raised, why did Alotraxas choose to appear now? Why did he choose to inhabit this boy from another world? What the gentle reader should understand was that there was a time in the ancient past when dragons flew about in far greater numbers than they do now; they were imbued by the Ancient Gods, also known as the Creators, to watch over the races of men and to protect them from evil, so that they might grow and flourish on the Continent.

Alotraxas was their last king, before he and all his kind were brutally killed by a single event so powerful that it wiped out life on the Continent well over 50,000 cycles ago. Though there are no records from that time, ancient legends said that it was the Entities of Evil who grew jealous of the dragons and the success of their charges that caused them to take the extraordinary step of wiping out the dragons, humans and elves along with all life on the Continent, though no one alive now really knows what happened.

Unlike his predecessors, before becoming king, Alotraxas swore an oath that he would always protect his charges, in life and death, provided they continued to be worthy of that protection. Alotraxas was particularly fond of humans, as he noted that they could be anything and do anything that they set their minds to. He saw the young Thaddeus, burning brightly with life and good, wanting to help the Continent recover from this horrible tragedy, deemed him worthy of the protection that he swore to provide, and so took up residence within his mind, opening it up to the infinite possibilities of what magick can do.

Alotraxas noted the innocence of the young Thaddeus, along with his unquenchable desire for adventure and his bright, keen mind. He noted that he was from a different place, seeing things that did not exist on the Continent, technologies that would not be invented for a thousand cycles hence, yet this boy knew of them.

What no one else could see, except Sairys that is, is that there are certain telltale signs of dragon spirit possession, many of which are so small that they are not noticed by most, but one of the more outward signs is the ability to speak dragon tongue, an ancient language that ties all dragons together as one.

Sairys said, "Good evening, my king," in dragon tongue and heard back:

"Good evening, Sairys. I was wondering when I would have a chance to speak to you."

Everyone present heard the words coming out of the boy's mouth; it certainly wasn't a language he knew before, but he spoke in the ancient tongue of dragons, there was no doubt about that.

The Moon Goddess approached the young Thaddeus and said, "So I was right. Why now, Alotraxas?"

In a low and deep voice that sounded out of place coming from a nine-cycle-old boy, Alotraxas said, "Long ago, I swore an oath to protect humankind when I became king, and as I have never been released from that oath, it is something that I am still sworn to do. I have appeared now because I saw this boy, who wanted to save not only the Continent, but all humankind from utter annihilation. Part of my oath was that I needed to continue to deem humankind worthy of my help. This boy is a shining example of what humankind can be, which is why I chose him to act as my champion because though he is not from this place, he wants to save it despite having no personal stake in whether this place lives or dies. His selflessness was what drew me to him, his spirit caused me to take notice of him, and it was his courage that made him truly worthy of the gifts that I have bestowed upon him. It was I who opened his mind to the wonders of magick, and I instilled in him the desire and the will to defend all of humanity from the devastation that has been perpetrated upon my charges. With your help, he will succeed in his task, and he will restore humanity to its former glory…This I vow!"

The boy's mouth closed and for an instant, seemed confused, but then he said in his normal voice, "I spoke in a different voice, didn't I? This is getting better by the day!"

Everyone had a brief laugh as Alotraxas said, "We don't have much time, the season of Sarodan is coming to a close, though some friends will make it last longer than it should."

The elder Thaddeus took out his snowflake, which was a gift from the Snow Queen herself, and said unto it, "Anything ye can do would be appreciated. We all need this boy to be as prepared as possible."

Alotraxas' soliloquy made it apparent that he knew what was at stake here, and if he believed that this boy was strong enough to stand up to the evil that currently was infesting the Continent, then that was good enough for most… except for the elder Thaddeus.

As everyone went off to do their own things, Thaddeus pulled the boy aside and said, "Now ye listen ta me, that was a good speech ye gave, but I fer one believe in having a backup plan, based on my experience in savin' the world, as it were. I might be a clumsy old fool, but I lived a long time cuz I always had a backup plan, and I survived in the face of certain death on many occasions becuz I was prepared for anything…What say ye?"

The boy answered in his normal voice, though Thaddeus could tell that it wasn't him who was actually answering, "Thaddeus, that's where you come in. While I will give him the ability to learn all he can from you and Kama, when it's his time to face the evil, he will stand alone. This is a mortal problem and needs a mortal solution, but I've always been one to stack the deck in my favor. We can all use a bit o' help, every now and again…Mayhaps let him borrow a few items that he can use to put the odds in his favor, yes?"

Thaddeus said, "Aye, this be true…let me see what I can scrounge up that might help."

Thaddeus walked away after that, seemingly satisfied about the boy's chances and thought of a few things that the lad could use to help himself. After Thaddeus disappeared, Sairys came flying in and landed on the boy's shoulder and said, "My king, seems strange calling you that because you look like a human boy, but these are strange times. Might I ask a question?"

Alotraxas said, "Yes. What do you wish to know?"

Sairys said, "As you know, like Thaddeus, I hail from a different place, and I have been his familiar for a very long time, but now that we have passed on, I've been thinking…Do you think that one of my kind might be able to help him?"

Alotraxas said, "Perhaps…Having a familiar of dragonkind would be very helpful to a young Wizard like him, as I'm sure you know. Weren't you and Thaddeus joined when he was the boy's age?"

Sairys said, "Yes! I remember like it was only one sun ago…Oh, what adventures we had! But now is the time for his adventure, it would be nice if he didn't have to do it alone. Remember that dragons are mortal!"

Alotraxas said, "Aye, we are…Let me see if I can find a suitable candidate, as you know it is a lifetime commitment, and what if he chooses to go home afterwards? What then? More study is certainly warranted on this, because as you know so well, where one may fail, two will succeed!"

Sairys stayed for a bit on the boy, and the young Thaddeus didn't seem to mind, petting Sairys every so often during the difficult and intense study sessions that were a part of every waking toll.

Given what the boy knew now, Alotraxas knew it would take at least another cycle for him to become proficient enough to have any success against the forces that were aligned against him, though he was learning fast, he needed to learn 10 cycles of knowledge in a single cycle, which under normal circumstances was not possible. He hoped that the elongated Sarodan and the fighting spirit of the humans would give the boy enough time to become what he needed to be. As Kama started another lesson, Alotraxas hoped and waited.

CHAPTER 11

SOMETHING EVIL THIS WAY COMES

The long, cold season of Sarodan was much slower to recede than normal, causing delays in Thanatos' plans and causing more suffering and hardship for those who were living in the unforgiving mountains of the West. The jagged peaks were home to thousands of humans and half-elves who had come here in search of a new life, but the mountains were a tough place to lay down roots, but as has been noted by many sages of times past, humans were able to find a way to survive and, in some cases, flourish in the most harsh and unforgiving places. While it wasn't the home that they wished for, many found that living among the peaks of the Western Mountains was a blessing. While farming was impossible amidst the granite that made up the vast majority of the mountains, these peaks were home to thousands of species of animals, so food was plentiful, and given that one of the largest lakes on the Continent was there, cool, clear water was also in good supply.

Humans had done something remarkable in that in this time of need, all of the humanity that made its way there decided to come together in one common cause, to survive; in the hopes that they might live to see peace once again reign on the Continent. To that end, trade was very important; people traded all kinds of things, like wood for stone, animal hides for finished clothing, meat for various wild vegetables that grew in the vast alpine forests, and so on. Builders in particular, were in great demand, as were stonemasons. Healers and priests were of paramount importance in villages because of various injuries and to stave off the effects of the cold. People of all sorts would travel from village to village, to ply their trades, travelling over long distances in the bitterest conditions imaginable, and while travelling was dangerous particularly in this most inhospitable terrain, people did it because of a genuine desire to help their fellow man and to garner more trade goods.

Another effect of being in the mountains was that gold was not the currency of choice, and humans reverted to an age-old system of exchange, barter. When the first humans arrived on the Continent, there were no gold coins, so a system had to be set up where the values of trade goods were set. For example, a large animal skin was worth a man-stone. A man-stone was a stone that weighed as much as a man, cut into the shape of a building block. Food items were typically traded on a weight basis. One stone of meat equaled one stone of vegetables, and so on. This worked out particularly well during this time because people just set up somewhere without necessarily knowing what was in the area and traded for what they needed.

Trade relationships grew stronger between the small hamlets and villages, and while some perished during this time, others flourished as Sarodan was slowly leaving the land. Many thought that Sarodan was leaving very slowly and wanted to hold the land in its frigid grip for as long as it could, not knowing the danger that awaited them once Simcha came.

Finally, the season changed, and Simcha came. As the temperature slowly went up, and the snow that had come started to melt, the humans that made their home in the mountains of the West celebrated their triumph over the cold, having survived the harshest Sarodan in recent memory. The first thing that many villages did was to bury those that had perished in the cold, and mass funerals were planned to honor those that had died, noting their sacrifice during this difficult time.

Despite the hardships of living in the mountains, most adapted well to the harsh conditions. Younger folks had an easier time of it than older folks did, but the strength of the human spirit was demonstrated time and again, and life in the makeshift villages became one of helping your neighbor. Acts of altruistic behavior were commonplace, helping to foster a spirit of generosity towards your fellow man. It was noted in the journals of those who survived during this time that the bonds they formed with their fellow man were among the strongest that they had formed throughout their lives. Little did they realize that the strength of those bonds would be tested to their limits in the coming suns.

On the third sun of Simcha, Thanatos launched his initial attack on yet another unnamed village, some 50 leagues from his home base at the Guild

Hall. The magicks he unleashed were devastating to the small populace, and all but four were killed within a few moments of his arrival. The makeshift buildings erected by the people here were quickly levelled, and any militia that was formed didn't have time to muster and was killed by successive waves of fire unleashed by Thanatos. The four that survived were a young family who happened to be out picking berries for the village. They were laden with full baskets of berries, and the children were talking about the fruit tarts they would make when they came upon the scene of destruction that lay before them. They were dumbstruck at the totality of the carnage, in that not one building remained standing. They also saw no dead bodies, just burnt and charred buildings. The children started crying, and the parents just stood there, awestruck at what they saw.

The fires that were still burning extinguished themselves having run out of fuel within a few moments, leaving a thick pall of smoke in the air as the young family witnessed firsthand the wrath of Thanatos, without even knowing who he was. It was as if they had never been here, so complete was the destruction he wrought to this peaceful village. This was the only warning that others would receive, as this scene repeated itself five times this sun.

As night came and Trirance rose over the horizon, over 1,000 souls had died, and most were now unwilling members of the undead army of Thanatos and Bjor'ma. Bjor'ma's control over them was stronger than before, owing to his increased power due to the magickal energy that he was feeding on almost constantly. Bjor'ma came to a realization—an epiphany if you will—in that he realized that he was being placated with magickal energy in an attempt to get him addicted to the incredible amounts of energy that he was consuming each sun, but, he wondered, *What happens when this is over and Thanatos' victory is complete…?* Who would provide the energy that he will need and at what cost? Could that be used as a bargaining chip against him? Would he be able to resist the demands of his masters, if they were controlling the energy that he needed to survive? He thought he might be in too far and didn't see a way he could be ever be free again. He supposed that perhaps this was his fate as he made a slave of King Noran all those cycles ago, perhaps now he was getting his comeuppance. He knew the risks and understood the bargain he made, but he wasn't sure he was ready to betray the deal he made. At least not yet. He thought that at least in exile, he was free to do whatever he wanted, but now, he was a slave to those that controlled Thanatos and the energy he provided.

While in those thoughts, a dark and sinister voice came into his mind, "We know your thoughts. Continue down this path at your peril, you know what happens to those that betray us…"

In his mind, he saw the foul, smoking pits of the Land of the Dead. Though he surmised that this was a special place reserved for beings that had betrayed the Entities of Evil, in that all he heard were screams and the sounds of torture; he saw himself standing shackled to a black post made of stone in a large fire-walled room. He could feel the presence of others around him, all being tortured. He could feel the heat given off by the flames; he could smell the burning of flesh all around him. He could see what looked like people being tortured in insidious devices…He himself was watching as he saw a be-ings' skin slowly being removed by a gruesome looking blade wreathed in flames, only to have it grow back again and the process repeated as the victim looked at him pleading for release from this torment. He heard the sounds of a large creature approaching…

The creature's footsteps grew louder in his mind as he could feel the glee in the creature in carrying out the grisly task of whipping him endlessly and inflicting as much pain as he possibly could. The footsteps stopped, and he could feel the eyes of the creature on him, his bare back facing the creature as he heard the sound of a whip, also wreathed in flames, coming within a hand of his right ear. As he heard the creature grunt and the whip going back, he prepared for the blow, but it never came, as he felt the cool breeze of a Simcha evening…

He snapped back to reality and saw the glowing red eyes of Thanatos upon him, and he heard in a deep and menacing voice, "Do not falter now, for that which you saw awaits you should you fail…"

A feeling of helplessness overcame him; now he knew he had no way out, and it was only a matter of time before he would really be in that room for all eternity. He had to think…But how? They could hear his thoughts, but could they read magickal script? Mayhaps he could write down his thoughts in magickal script, as only those trained in Wizardscraft could read it. Through writing, he could put his thoughts on parchment and not carry them in his mind where they were not safe, but where to find parchment and ink, and how to carry it, as he was a spirit now? Then he had an idea, one that came to him rather suddenly, he would write it on the stones as he went from town to town. He knew that magickal script was invisible except to those who are Wizards, so perhaps that was as good a means as any, so he started to write, releasing those thoughts from his mind at the same time.

Bjor'ma covered the blackened stones of their latest conquest with script, detailing his thoughts, and in some cases giving away Thanatos' plans, but he didn't care; he didn't know why he was writing all this other than to release these thoughts from his mind, which apparently was no longer a safe place to harbor thoughts of dissent. He counted on the fact that there were no other Wizards capable of reading what he had written because Boral had done such a good job in eliminating them. It took him a few tolls to get all his thoughts on the stones, but once he completed his writings, he felt content that he had an outlet to release these thoughts and that he could exercise it at any time with impunity. If questioned about what he was doing, he could claim that he was inspecting the ruins for traces of potential hideouts hidden underground.

The suns and nights of Simcha came and went, and many more thousands of humans died, and at least 60 villages were wiped off the mountains as the complete destruction of the humans in the West as nearing completion. Sometimes a handful would escape, but they were usually tracked down by spirits, killed and resurrected as an undead creature, ready to do Bjor'ma's will. Bjor'ma continued to write profusely in magickal script and to his delight, what he wrote seemed to go unheeded and unnoticed by Thanatos, which proved that he was not Boral reborn, but another creature entirely. Even though the Bjor'ma's army had spirits, all of whom were former Wizards, given their depleted numbers and Bjor'ma's increased ability to control them, they never bothered to read what Bjor'ma had wrote, and if they did, they never reported it to anyone. It seemed to Bjor'ma that had discovered a way to purge his mind of these thoughts and keep everyone ignorant of what he really thought along with his plan for what he planned to do about it. What he didn't plan on was the ranks of the undead swelling to the degree that they had, because each being he had control of meant less ability to hide these thoughts before he could write them and meant less control over the horde that was quickly amassing. He kept on feeding off of Thanatos more and more to compensate for the increased control he needed over the horde, and whatever Thanatos was, he had the ability to generate as much energy as Bjor'ma wanted.

As Simcha came to a close, the destruction of humanity in the West was complete, a few thousand scattered survivors notwithstanding, and the horde numbered in the hundreds of thousands. Bjor'ma was able to control them, but he was feeding almost constantly from Thanatos to maintain control of the horde as its ranks swelled. He knew that the horde was headed to the North and that would be a challenge, because he knew of the strength and skill of the Barbarians in the North, but with a force this large, even the Barbarians would be hard pressed to achieve victory. As Thanatos, Bjor'ma, and the massive horde left the mountains of the West, they didn't leave much behind with the exception of the writings of Bjor'ma, and his fervent hope that someone, somewhere would read them and put a stop to this, even if it meant his eternal torment in the Land of the Dead.

Bjor'ma felt very guilty because these were his people; he was a Westerner too, though he was born in Taras'la, where almost all half-elves come from, he emigrated to the West to practice his art. They adopted him as one of them, and King Noran trusted him implicitly, and how did he repay their generosity and kindness? He murdered them and then raised them again to serve him in this massive horde of undead. His mind was a battleground: one the one side, his desire to not be tormented for eternity, but on the other side, his guilt for killing a group of people who were kind to him, even without his powers. How could he escape from this conundrum? Each passing sun it got worse and as the death toll rose, so too did his guilt...

Why did he make this deal? Who could save his eternal soul? Who would want to now that he was thoroughly consecrated to evil?

There was no one to talk to, and no one to assuage his guilt. He was alone with his thoughts all the time as Thanatos was focused on death and nothing else. The undead had no minds of their own, and he feared releasing a spirit because of what they could say about what he wrote along the stones that bore silent witness to the villages that he decimated.

CHAPTER 12

THE TREK TO THE NORTH

Thanatos knew that the trek to the North would take about a half of a season, given the very slow pace of the undead horde over uneven ground, and it would get even slower as they approached the foothills and come to a near standstill once they got into the heart of the mountains. While he would not be slowed, his force would be. He noted that since Bjor'ma was feeding on him almost constantly, he didn't have an excess of energy to fling spells at the Barbarians, and he was reliant on Bjor'ma's ability to control the minds of the horde to keep them moving in one direction. Thanatos had a modicum of spells at his command, mostly to distract and harass, though a few could cause some damage to oncoming troops, but what he did not know was the tenacity of the Northern Barbarian tribes and how strong their warriors were.

Thanatos also did not know that he had been spotted by an advance "guard," so to speak, in the form of a trained hawk, who plucked some hair out of one of the undead now shuffling their way north. These hairs were all the warning the Barbarian tribes needed to fortify their forward defenses against the onslaught that was coming. They didn't know the number of troops yet, but they would see them soon enough. The horde kept to the lowlands at first, wanting to move as quickly as possible, but they were not out of range of the Barbarian artillery, in the form of catapults, trebuchets, ballistae, and a new weapon among them, the ground cannon, which could lob a flaming projectile over half a league.

On the twentieth sun of the horde's march north, they met with the might of the Western Advance Corps. This group of soldiers, over 5,000 strong manned the border with the West and was on high alert, seeing the fires that had been started in the Western mountains. They were heavily fortified in the mountains and had 20 catapults, 15 trebuchets, 60 ballistae, and 40 ground cannons along with trained and experienced soldiers, all of whom were formidable warriors.

The shelling began at about 10 tolls as a heavy barrage of projectiles of all sorts rained down upon the mindless horde, tearing into their ranks as they pressed inexorably forward. Thanatos knew that they couldn't get to the soldiers high in the mountains, so he commanded Bjor'ma to move the horde further south in an effort to save as many troops as he could, and it was here that Bjor'ma could do a little to thwart his masters as he was slow in issuing the order and allowed thousands more undead to be neutralized. He didn't want Thanatos to start unleashing spells, so he stepped up his feeding stating that he needed this energy to effect Thanatos' commands. The horde moved slowly to the south as the spirits still in Bjor'ma's army went to deal with the troops up in the mountains. Little did he know that many would not return because of the one type of magick that Thaddeus thought was unpredictable and unreliable: shamanic magick.

As the 800 or so spirits bore down on the fortress, they saw something they were not expecting. It seemed that this fortress had everything, including some form of defense against them. They saw five individuals, dressed in furs and strange masks dancing about in the courtyard, chanting. As they focused on these five Barbarians, what the spirits saw amazed them, as the shamans' pleas were answered by draconic spirits. Five dragon spirits came swooping down from the fortress and using their mind attacks, proceeded to decimate the mass of spirits once again. The fighting, which lasted for over four tolls was terrible, but in the end, the draconic spirits got the upper hand, and only 15 spirits returned from the battle, which upset Thanatos, as he said to Bjor'ma, "Did you know about this magick?"

Bjor'ma said, "No, my Lord Thanatos. I was exiled to the Deep North and had no knowledge of this part of the mountains or this shamanic magick. Should we send our troops up there to deal with them?"

Thanatos said, "No, they would be annulled rather quickly, we press on."

The shelling on Thanatos' troops stopped as Trirance came up over the mountains, but he had sustained heavy losses. Over half of his troops, over 150,000 were lost, many more were damaged, and he could not so much as strike a single blow in return. In addition to that, most of the spirits were lost as well. He could hear the cheers of the Barbarians as they sounded their victory horns.

Thanatos gathered more energy from the ground but was unable to get much as Bjor'ma was feeding constantly now and was a much bigger drain on his energy levels, stating that he could repair some of the troops and get some of the troops back to a fighting state when in fact, he could not. he was just feeding to feed and get bigger and more powerful. Thanatos finally cut off Bjor'ma's energy supply and said, "This is needed to teach the Barbarians the power of my masters."

Thanatos flew off, and Bjor'ma followed along, seeing what he would do. He heard Thanatos say to the encamped Barbarians, "Now, listen well, for Thanatos, the Messenger of Death now speaks to you. Though you may have won a victory this sun, all victories will be paid for...in DEATH!!"

A volley of tiny fireballs appeared in his hands, and as he set them free, they all got a lot bigger, and as they hit the fortress, they exploded with a might heretofore unknown and shattered the forward walls of the fortress. Some 500 troops fell from the walls as the rest fought back with bows and ballistae, but Thanatos was impervious to normal weaponry, or so it seemed, as the arrows seemed to go right through him without damaging him at all.

As the shamans started their familiar chants, Thanatos said, "I claim the magick here as mine and all who practice it are mine!"

What Thanatos did not realize was that shamans cannot do magick. It is done for them, which is why shamanic magick is so unpredictable because the entities with which you entreat may choose to twist your request to suit themselves. Thanatos cast his own spell in an attempt to dispel whatever it was that the shamans were doing, but it had no effect on the shamans who continued to entreat their entities until finally the shamans got what they wanted, and a shimmering field of force went up all around the fortress, which Thanatos could feel would stop any further magick from getting through as he said, "You've won this battle, but you won't win the war!"

Thanatos flew down with Bjor'ma in tow. He started to feed on Thanatos once again, but found no energy there until Thanatos touched the ground, and then the energy flow started once again in earnest, proving another of Bjor'ma's theories correct in that Thanatos needed to be in contact with the ground to get energy, and if he could be lifted off it and kept off of the ground, he might cease to exist. Bjor'ma knew that this fact could mean that he could be rid of Thanatos forever, but to what end? He would just be replaced as the legions of the dead are without end. Then he had a thought, with Thanatos gone, he could stop the attacks all together and refuse to lead their troops, but that might only buy a couple of suns, as all that would be needed is an exceptionally powerful undead creature to lead the troops that he had and it wouldn't take long to find one willing to lead, but at what cost? The only thing that would be lost is time, but perhaps that is all that would be needed, but it would need to be a long time. He flew off and wrote this in magickal script on one of the boulders used to crush several of his troops.

The horde pressed relentlessly forward into the night with Thanatos and Bjor'ma leading them along with the 15 spirits that were left. Bjor'ma thought that the sky above them was once black with the combined might of over 4,000 spirits, but now they were so few in number, and that is all that remained of the Wizards that were once so much a part of the Continent…but not anymore. He lamented that there were no more human Wizards on the Continent and technically he was right, but there was one that he would come to know quite well, but not yet.

The next sun, fresh from the victory they had won, the Western Advance Corps sent a runner to General Morshand, the aging Western general, once a part of the great army of the West, now a general of 250,000 troops strung along the 500-league border of the Far North. Having been getting reports all night about troops on the move, he sent a reconnaissance force of 25 to spy on the troops and understand what and who they were. He sent his First Expeditionary to investigate. These expertly trained women were small and fast, experienced with bows and swords, not to mention, veteran falconers. They were also adept at camouflage, keeping themselves hidden at all costs.

What they saw amazed them, as none of them had ever seen this many undead creatures in one place. They scrawled notes about numbers, and the condition of the troops as they saw them, attached them to their falcons and send them aloft to await instructions while staying out of sight of the approaching horde.

Upon receiving the messages, the General decided to attack the horde now heading north to try to stop their advance, so he and his soldiers could garner glory for themselves as that was the Barbarian way. What he didn't know as he had never faced an undead horde before was the fetid smell of the rotting undead assaulted even the hardiest troops and that made fighting them that much more unpleasant. General Morshand decided to take his First Division, 100,000 disciplined and hardy soldiers, to face the horde dead on, from a position of advantage, of course. He designed the attack plan to fit his army's strengths, in that Barbarians are experts at defensive fighting and are best when formed as a wall, particularly when situated above their attackers. However, to mix it up and potentially confuse the opposing army, he decided to take his Third Aerial Division as well. This division, exclusively consisting of women, were experts in missile weapons of all sorts. They numbered well over 10,000 and would provide another line of offense depending how the battle went.

The two armies approaching each other were as different as two armies could be, one alive, the other not; one organized and disciplined, the other mindless and sloppy; one having weapons, the other having only their rotting, scabrous fists to defend themselves. The only advantage Thanatos' army had was it was numerically superior, but not by as much as he would like. Thanatos knew that he would need help in defeating the Barbarian troops, and he called upon the Dread Lord.

Once again, the army of undead stopped in its tracks at Bjor'ma's command. The foul scent in the air got stronger as evil once again permeated the area, and once again the Continent would bear another scar as a result of this war. The Dread Lord returned...

The overpowering stench of foulness saturated the air as he materialized in front of Thanatos and Bjor'ma. He surveyed the situation and looked upon the horde of undead assembled behind them. One could sense that he was proud of his creation, Thanatos, but increasingly disappointed in Bjor'ma. The Dread Lord knew that Bjor'ma wasn't "fully onboard" anymore and would probably need to be eliminated—but not yet. The Dread Lord thought that perhaps he could redeem himself. He thought that perhaps the use of future promises would be appropriate to win the seemingly fleeting loyalty of Bjor'ma as he looked down at Bjor'ma and said, "Bjor'ma, I have noted that your mind is faltering in its total devotion to me. Let me reassure you that when you have taken the last life from this place, and consecrated them to me, you will be Overlord of the Continent. Your powers will be formidable. For now, stand with Thanatos, and see to it that his victories are complete for in doing so, you serve me..."

He turned to Thanatos and said in a dark and forboding voice, "You are not outnumbered, but you are outgunned. You will lose this engagement unless you can bring magick to the battle, which you cannot as you have a leech attached to you. Mayhaps we need to remove said leech and see how it fares for a few tolls without the constant supply of energy it is currently consuming. Bjor'ma…Cease your feeding and allow Thanatos to bring magick to the upcoming engagement. You will be rewarded for your sacrifice."

Bjor'ma said, "Yes, my Lord. I have stopped feeding, but what is my reward?"

The Dread Lord looked angrier than usual and said, "Your reward is… THAT YOU CONTINUE IN SERVICE TO ME!" The ground shook as he said those words, and Bjor'ma was genuinely scared now, as he had never seen the Dread Lord this angry.

Bjor'ma squeaked out, "Yes, my Lord, as you command…" He appeared beside Thanatos, and one could see Thanatos begin to glow brighter as more and more energy coursed through his being.

The Dread Lord said, "Now go, and grow your army." as he disappeared, giving Bjor'ma one last look of disdain.

Being rebuked by the Dread Lord did little for Bjor'ma's desire to serve his master nor did he believe that he would be the Overlord of the Continent as he was promised. He thought that it was time to seek a "Plan B," and try to figure out another way for a positive outcome for him. Little did he know that the little bit of ground shaking that the Dread Lord caused, caught the attention of others who were in a position to thwart the undead army as it began to climb the mountains in search of the Barbarian army which was heading towards them.

The Snow Queen felt the ground shake and wondered what was happening as she appeared high in the mountains amidst the drifts of snow and saw two armies approaching each other. She picked out Thanatos immediately as he had so much magickal energy flowing through him that it was difficult to hide. She wondered what would befall her troops if he was allowed to let that magick loose upon her people and so, she caused the temperature to drop as the sky turned to an iron gray, and then it began to snow…

The young Thaddeus was now through the equivalent of his seventh cycle of study and had a repertoire of spells that was impressive, though he had more spells dealing with protection and healing than true destructive forces at his command. He also felt the Continent shake, and his instructors thought that it was time for his first major encounter with his enemy. The young Thaddeus was excited and took some items designed to help him, the first being a Wizard's Staff. This seven-arm staff belonged to the elder Thaddeus and had innumerable uses but could protect the young Thaddeus from evil spirits. Thaddeus also lent the young Thaddeus a unique item, known only to him and not from this world, a void stone. This large, black, and very smooth stone about the size of a cantaloupe, had but one use, to void all magick cast at the wielder, hence its name. It should be noted that the void stone also allows the user to utilize that energy to cast spells.

Thaddeus said, "This'll protect ye from spells pointed at ye, but use the energy quickly, so it can continue to absorb it fer ye."

The young Thaddeus was visibly excited and looked every bit a Wizard, with his Wizard's robe and hat on, both a basic green as he was primarily a healer and protector, instead of the engine of destruction that his namesake was. Armed with his knowledge, his staff, and the void stone, he willed himself to the Continent. He landed behind the Barbarian army and caught the attention of the Snow Queen, who watched from afar as to what the boy could do. She sensed strong magick from him but knew nothing else.

The two armies were now within bow range, and the Barbarians took full advantage of this fact and started to pelt the undead horde with arrows…flaming arrows. This did not cause the reaction that they had hoped as the undead paid no heed to the fact that they were now walking fire sticks. Soon, much of the army was alight, and while it was snowing, that did nothing to quell the flames, or to slow down their inexorable march forward.

Thanatos said, "Playing with fire, eh? Two can play at that game!" as he cast a spell of epic proportions and flung a 100-arm wide ball of fire back towards the Barbarians, but it took a sudden turn behind them and went straight into the young Thaddeus' void stone, as he used it to immediately cast a powerful spell of protection on the front half of the Barbarian force.

Both Thanatos and Bjor'ma looked up and saw flying behind the Barbarian force was another human, dressed in green as he sent his spirits to investigate.

The young Thaddeus said, "Cross this sphere at your peril, spirits, for I am well-protected from the likes of you."

A white sphere encapsulated the young Thaddeus as a spirit touched the sphere and promptly ceased to exist, which surprised not only the other 14 spirits, but also Thanatos and Bjor'ma.

CHAPTER 13

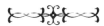

MAKING FRIENDS WHILE FIGHTING

The two armies met on the battlefield, sword and sinew against rotting flesh and bone. Magick against countermagick. The Barbarian line held strong as the waves of the undead came, but time and again, the undead were stopped by the solid wall that the Barbarians formed. On top of that, they were slowed somewhat by the snow and ice, and they were coming uphill, thus allowing the Barbarians a massive combat advantage. The Barbarians were also used to fighting as defenders and employed several strategies to keep the slow but steady attackers at bay throughout the sun.

The Barbarians never advanced beyond the forward fortification line that they had set up, which provided them a great vantage point to swing their blades down upon the hapless attackers. Though Thanatos was casting spell after spell, none of his spells seemed to be having much of an effect on the Barbarian troops, on top of the fact that this battle was taking place under white-out conditions, which again played into the hands of the Barbarians as they were used to the cold, snowy conditions in the mountains. After several tolls of battle, Thanatos realized that he would not advance this way as the Barbarian line was just too strong, on top of the fact that they seemed to be protected from his spells by the small green Wizard in the back of their force. He ordered Bjor'ma to pull his remaining troops back. All told, the casualties to the undead were 30,000 along with 14 spirits, leaving 120,000 undead and one spirit remaining—all others were stacked as cordwood in front of the Barbarian line. On the Barbarian side, only 500 were lost, but of that number, 400 or so were injured and were expected to recover. General Morshand called it a rout, and a huge cheer went up when the Barbarians saw the undead retreating under the withering fire of flaming arrows.

The young Thaddeus went to work after the battle as the wounded started to come in, and he helped an innumerable number of soldiers to recover from their wounds, which he expertly healed. He felt more alive than he ever had before as he healed the Barbarians from wounds large and small. Even the Barbarians were amazed at the speed at which he worked and the competence he displayed in practicing his craft. The elder Thaddeus, Kama, and the Moon Goddess looked on, smiling, as they saw their protégé protecting the Barbarians and then healing those who were injured, and they all agreed that he could certainly hold his own in a tough combat situation. During this time on the Continent, Alotraxas called to his kind to see if there was anyone who was willing to serve the young Thaddeus as his familiar. After some debate amongst dragonkind, and considering the victory he had won against evil, he found a candidate to serve as Thaddeus' familiar who would arrive in two suns to begin the joining process.

His name was Agham-Ix, and he was a stone dragon, so named for the grayish color of his rock-hard scales. Though young and small by dragon standards, it was decided that he would be a perfect accompaniment to the young Thaddeus and his mostly defensive magickal powers. Though small, stone dragons had an impressive array of defensive abilities, most of which could be transferred to the dragon's familiar, all of which would benefit the young Thaddeus as he continued his adventures on the Continent. Of all the things that could be transferred, it was the protection the dragon provided that would be the most valuable. The stone dragon gives his familiar's skin the same toughness as the dragon has, which is quite formidable. They are also exceptionally intelligent, could learn to cast spells of their own, and like all dragons, they can fly, albeit very slowly. Lastly, they only reached a length of about 20 arms when fully grown, though Agham-Ix was exceptionally small, being only two arms long at this stage in his life.

While this debate amongst dragonkind was in full swing and his army in full retreat, Thanatos had an idea…Since a frontal attack during the sun did not work, he would attack at night and from the air. He would raise as much of his army as he could, put them over the Barbarian fortress and then drop them upon the unsuspecting Barbarians, in the hopes that by using the element of surprise that the Barbarians would be less effective and his forces could score some kills. He realized that using his spells in a direct damage assault was useless, but using them in this way, it would be much more difficult to thwart. So he waited until nightfall and put his plan into action.

That night, though it exhausted him magickally, Thanatos was able to raise 25,000 of his troops and send them flying off to the Barbarian fortress. He didn't want to use all his forces in case the tactic was unsuccessful, but he had to try something. Unfortunately for the Barbarians, the undead were spotted too late, and the horde was able to get into the fortress and wreak havoc among the Barbarians. The undead were able to run quietly from room to room and kill; they displayed some intelligence in doing this as they were assisted by Thanatos in this endeavor, as Bjor'ma found himself sitting on the sidelines watching, which angered him again.

The Barbarians recovered quickly enough and started fighting back, but not before thousands of Barbarians died, all of whom returned to fight as undead as they were chased out of the fortress by the combined might of the Barbarians and by the young Thaddeus, who chose to spend his first night on the Continent as a guest of General Morshand himself. Though Thaddeus was able to inspire the Barbarians to fight beyond what they normally could, they lost quite a few soldiers that night.

Thanatos called the encounter a success and bolstered his numbers by 5,000, while Bjor'ma just sat and brooded over what to do. Half of him wanted to thwart Thanatos right now because he was angry, but the other half told him to wait and that the opportune moment was coming. He knew that Thanatos was becoming more powerful and soon he may not be able to be stopped, but how would he know when the opportune moment would come? Would there be a sign? Just then, he heard a voice…very quietly…it had an Elven lilt to it, and it sounded pleasant, like the songs of the elves that he heard when he was a boy.

He perked up and looked around, only to see the ugliness of the undead horde all around him, just milling about mindlessly. As he listened, it was definitely Elven. As he tried to recall the last time he spoke any Elven, which was at the age of seven and 10, when he left his home in Taras'la to seek his fortune. He remembered the melodious tones of his mother speaking to him when he was a boy, he could picture her so clearly in his mind, speaking to him, singing to him. After he left Taras'la, he never saw her again and wondered what had become of her. While in those thoughts, he had another realization, that the constant anger and bitterness over what Thaddeus had done to him was gone from his mind, as if the thoughts of his mother made them go away. It was like a great weight had been lifted from him and he could think clearly for the first time, in a long time. He didn't know why he didn't feel angry or bitter anymore towards Thaddeus, he thought that perhaps his anger and bitterness over his current situation far outweighed what Thaddeus had done to him.

That was it, he thought to himself. Maybe the one man who caused all this in his mind could help him to undo it, and perhaps he didn't have to spend the rest of eternity in torment. But Bjor'ma had a problem. How could he communicate with Thaddeus, especially as he was being watched by Thanatos and the Dread Lord? He resolved to find a way to do it, but little did he know that a way to communicate with Thaddeus was about to present itself.

As the night wore on, Thanatos launched three more aerial assaults on the Barbarians, but he did not focus on the fortress, instead he focused on the villages. He found that he had the magickal strength to cast these mighty spells now that he didn't have Bjor'ma constantly feeding from him. Thousands more died that night as the now flying undead horde descended upon the hapless villagers. The undead had a unique way of killing a victim; all it takes is a touch from their scabrous rotting flesh, and the victim is dead within a few moments ready to be raised again. No cure has been found as of yet, but the Barbarians were unaware that there was a cure and it was among them, in the nine-cycle-old boy who came to assist them. He carried the power to eradicate the rot and return a human to life.

If the cure is not effected on the victim, he/she dies and once dead, the Lord of the Dead senses them and causes them to rise again as undead, though once risen this way, they cannot be raised again.

Meanwhile, Bjor'ma now unable to feed, has an idea. He saw the floating green wizard thwart much of what Thanatos could do. Perhaps he would be willing to save Bjor'ma from his fate. After the night's attacks, he decided to fly off to the Barbarian fortress and see if he could talk to the wizard. As he entered, it didn't take him long to find the young Thaddeus, sharing a victory meal with the Barbarians. Bjor'ma saw that he was only a boy but could sense the incredibly strong magick radiating from him.

Through all the noise that over 400 Barbarians made while eating, drinking and boasting about the victory they had won, the young Thaddeus sensed something, something evil. As he turned his body to look behind him, he pulled out another one of the elder Thaddeus' handy gadgets, which was a monocle that detected spirits of all kinds and, when he put it up to his eye, saw Bjor'ma. He flew into action, surprising the Barbarians he was sitting with, grabbing up his Wizard's Staff and saying, "Cross the sphere at your peril, spirit, for I am well-protected from the likes of you, and I stand here to protect those around me…BE GONE!"

All noted a white sphere enshroud the young Thaddeus as the top of his outlandishly large staff glowed white.

The Barbarians were surprised, as the spirit of Bjor'ma appeared amongst them as swords were removed and even the two shamans in the room looked up to see what the young boy was going to do. The Barbarians backed off, except for General Morshand and the young Thaddeus, waiting to see what the spirit was going to do.

Bjor'ma did not react or respond, for he expected them to react like this to him, given what he was as he said, "Greetings. I am Bjor'ma, and I wish you no harm. I only wish to pass on a message to Thaddeus Brimstone. Will you hear it?"

The young Thaddeus said, "Speak it, spirit…and be quick about it!"

The General gave Thaddeus a bit more room, and Thaddeus stepped forward a bit as Bjor'ma said, "Tell Thaddeus that I wish to speak to him, that I understand what he did to me, and that I need his help. He will know where to find me."

The spirit of Bjor'ma backed off and left the Feast Hall where 400 Barbarians were seated, and for a moment, all was quiet, as if they didn't know what had happened and were waiting for their General to tell them what to do.

The young Thaddeus was the first to react after Bjor'ma left and said, "It's okay. He's gone, which means that I should probably go as well. I'm sorry for bringing this trouble to you as he probably sensed me here."

As he turned to leave, the General put his massive hand on the boy's shoulder and said, "Boy, you have nothing to be sorry for. You protected my soldiers in battle, and many of the men and women here owe you their lives. You are always welcome here among these people." He handed the young Thaddeus a pouch and said, "Take this. It's a token of our gratitude to you for what you did this sun."

Thaddeus opened the pouch and took out a simple leather cord. On it was a large, yellowed tooth held in place by two beads.

The General said, "A token of these people. This tooth was taken from a cave bear a long time ago. It is an ancient relic to these people. It instills strength in he who wears it. Legend says that if they welcome someone to their tribe with this, that he will do great things for these people as you have done. I give it to you, this sun, as these people gave it to me when I arrived here seeking refuge from the madness that has overcome the Continent."

Thaddeus went to put the cord over his neck, but the General stopped him saying, "Young man, since I am technically not one of these people, they must put this on you to welcome you among them…" In a powerful voice, he said to the assembled people here in the Feast Hall, "Who will welcome this boy to stand among you, given what he did for all of us?"

Some murmurings could be heard as a female voice rang out from the back of the Hall.

"I will welcome him."

Everyone noticed that it got a lot colder in this room, and one could hear 400 Barbarians going down on one knee in honor of the Snow Queen making a rare appearance.

She was dressed in her usual white, slightly revealing gown, with a white crown on her head and a staff of solid ice in her hand. He noticed that her features were slender and her skin was the palest white as she gracefully walked forward. The only accents were her blood red lips and her long, dark hair.

As she got closer to Thaddeus, looking at him with her ice blue eyes, she said, "I welcome you to stand among my people. You are now one of us…and take this." Thaddeus could feel the cool breeze that wafted over him as she spoke to him. She put the simple cord over Thaddeus' head and then added another necklace, this one looked like a very large snowflake on a white cord and said, "You are now a friend of my people. Know that few are rewarded in this way." She disappeared as a flurry of snow replaced what was the Snow Queen as Thaddeus marveled at the gifts he had been given.

The Feast Hall, usually a place with plenty of noise, was eerily quiet and conversations were slow to pick up as if everyone in attendance knew the gravity of what had just happened. No one in the room could re-member when the Snow Queen herself welcomed anyone; it was usually a job relegated to a leader of some kind or a shaman, but to have the Snow Queen herself perform that task was almost unheard of and usually indi-cated that the new member was of great significance to the tribe. While no one questioned what he did this sun, they could not believe that such a young boy would be that significant.

While everyone was in those thoughts, Thaddeus said, "I will see all of you again. Thank you and may the Snow Queen bless you!"

He willed himself back to the domain of the Moon Goddess bearing his new gifts.

CHAPTER 14

TWO BATTLES

Despite winning many engagements against the undead, the ranks of the Barbarians and human counterparts continued to thin as time wore on. Thanatos made a strategic decision having learned that he could not defeat the Barbarian army in a frontal assault, so he decided to go after villages and towns with a small portion of his total force to bolster his troop strength and avoid a direct confrontation with a superior foe. The issue that the Barbarians were trying to overcome was very slow communications because time and again, by the time the armed forces got to a village that was under attack, the village was completely dead and the populace converted to undead soldiers. While the Barbarians were used to fighting a defensive war, they were not used to being attacked in five places at the same time.

Thanatos used Bjor'ma's skill in mind control to control each regiment of soldiers individually and return to a set location along with new recruits. The undead did not possess any particular skills, except for their tenacity, in that unless they were completely neutralized, they would press on and try to fight. With no minds to guide them, they were dependent on Bjor'ma for commands. He only issued one command to them: press on and kill. So they did. And what they lacked in skill, they made up for in numbers.

Soon, Thanatos' strategy was paying off and he was able to augment his forces to a great degree, replacing those which he lost when he first arrived here. Within five suns, many villages, particularly human ones were gone and only those who lived further north were left. Thanatos again commanded an army of over half a million, and he chose not to squander them needlessly in trying to attack those who had gone further north, particularly to the Deep North. He thought that he would lose too many troops in trying to kill every last human, but something within him stirred. He knew that it was his only purpose for being here, but he was intelligent if nothing else and not a blood crazed madman, so he performed an act of extreme altruism (for him) and decided to leave those in the Deep North alone, figuring that he would lose far more troops than he stood to gain, not only due to the weather, but due to the ferocity of the Barbarian defenses that he had already experienced.

Thanatos was very confident in his army now, though Bjor'ma was having a tough time controlling them as there were so many now and it seemed that Thanatos was rationing the energy he was able to take. It was just enough to do what he needed to, but no more. Thoughts of dissent were rare in his mind now as he could think nothing else except to control the horde and feed. Suddenly, he heard, "Bjor'ma…" as he was flying alongside Thanatos, leading the army to yet another part of the mountains to continue their assault on the Far North.

He noted several in the horde who were close to him; one of them was staring at him directly. She looked familiar to him somehow; though her face color was a dull gray, he saw a ring on her earlobe. It was very distinctive, and he recognized it—it was a gift from him. He recognized her, and a wave of memories started to flood his mind as the horde stopped dead in its tracks as he lost control of them, so powerful were these memories. The undead creature approached him, disguising it as mindless movement and said in a strange monotone voice barely above a whisper, "My son, I'm here for you…let me help you."

Thanatos looked at him with a disapproving stare, approached him, and said, "Why has the army stopped?"

Thanatos noted that Bjor'ma was holding the sides of his head and fell over, collapsed from the strain of the memories flooding his mind and the constant pressure of controlling a vast army of undead. What Thanatos didn't realize was by rationing his energy to Bjor'ma, these memories were able to disrupt his ability to control the horde, and now their army was stopped dead. While Bjor'ma had thoughts like this before; when he was feeding constantly, he had enough energy to prevent these memories from doing this, but no more.

With a half million troops stretching out for a half league on open ground, Thanatos knew he was in trouble. An attack now by the Barbarians would be devastating regardless of his magick. He knew that he couldn't control this many troops and cast spells; he had little choice but to try to inject a bit more energy into Bjor'ma.

Though a spirit, Bjor'ma wasn't moving as he saw Thaddeus in his mind, they were sitting in a tent just as they did during his first and last meeting with Thaddeus. He remembered the command tent, he remembered everything in it, the sights, the sounds, the smells, the thoughts on Noran's mind, especially those of Bethany.

They were seated across from each other as Thaddeus was smoking his pipe, the scent of fruit lay heavy in the air, and Thaddeus said, "I hear ye wanted an audience with me. Ye have my ear...speak!"

Bjor'ma said, "That woman...that's my mother...I know it...I killed her... I gave her that ring in her ear..."

Thaddeus said, "Aye, it is. She fled here along with many from Taras'la when the elves left. So what did ye want?"

Bjor'ma said, "I felt so much anger towards you. I could have been a Lord..."

Thaddeus interrupted him, "And ye would have died shortly after becomin' one, and now look at ye."

The scene started to fade as Thanatos was putting some of his considerable energy into getting him up off the ground.

Thaddeus fought back with energy of his own to keep Bjor'ma here as he said, "I picked this time to speak with ye, as what we say here will not be known by anyone but us while ye be in this state. What did ye need from me?"

Bjor'ma felt an icy hand upon his head pulling him away from this familiar scene as he said, "Help me, please."

Bjor'ma returned to his reality with Thanatos standing over him, his hand on Bjor'ma's head saying, "We need to move. You can feed..."

While Thanatos and Bjor'ma were not watching, the young Thaddeus appeared about 500 arms to the north of the undead horde. He was dressed in his green robe and hat, along with his white staff as he yelled out amidst the cold winds of the Far North, "Ye will take no more into your horde, and those ye have taken will be laid to rest!"

Thanatos looked up and saw the young Thaddeus and said, "I am Thanatos, Messenger of Death, I would know your name before I annihilate you."

In what was to be a defining moment in his young career as a Wizard, the young Thaddeus defiantly planted his staff into the ground and said, "I am Thaddeus, and I am your nemesis! Behold!"

As he said that, the tip of his staff glowed white and a great light appeared from it, repulsing the undead horde; though Thanatos was not repulsed, he did not like what the staff was doing as he said, "Thaddeus, eh? Well, Thaddeus, I have many at my command, and you are alone. Do you think you can stop them all?"

Thaddeus said, "They retreat at my presence, they cannot come forward, and I have friends, too…Comrades, to arms!"

Much to Thanatos' surprise, 1,000 Barbarians emerged from their hiding places along the rocks and trees and formed a shield wall with the young Thaddeus floating above them saying, "We are outnumbered, but these people are under my protection, and none but yours will fall today. Leave the North now and never return and perhaps I may have mercy on you!"

Thanatos stepped forward, though it was difficult for him due to the effects of Thaddeus' staff and said, "Never, we will fight!" as he cut off Bjor'ma's energy supply and cast a bolt of lightning right at Thaddeus, which went right into his void stone. With that energy, Thaddeus followed up with a spell of protection for the vast majority of the troops under the command of General Morshand himself.

The undead were driven on by Bjor'ma, but as they got to within 10 arms of the Barbarian shield wall, they crumbled to dust. Seeing this, Thanatos cast spell after spell at the Barbarians assembled, but his spells were ineffective as the energy from Thanatos' spells was used to bolster the protection that the young Thaddeus had cast over the Barbarians. Growing increasingly exasperated by the ineffectiveness of his troops and his spells, Thanatos tried his new tactic and raised 1,000 of his horde up to a height of 20 arms and dropped them over the shield that the young Thaddeus had erected. As they hit the shield, they were instantly transformed into dust, though one could see that the young Thaddeus was straining to keep the shield active as it was being heavily bombarded by the forces arrayed against them. Bjor'ma knew what that shield was that Thaddeus had erected over the Barbarians, and that his undead could never cross it…

But perhaps he could.

As he floated over to it, he could feel the energy coming from it, and he knew that if he was not evil, he could cross that barrier easily. He lamented that after all this time, voraciously feeding on evil energy, he could not be redeemed and seemed resigned to his fate as he went forward, only to be pulled back at the last minute by Thanatos who said, "We must pull back. They will pay for what they have done, but we will find no victory here!"

Bjor'ma snapped back to reality, feeling copious amounts of energy coming from Thanatos, he tried to feed, and Thanatos allowed his somewhat faithful servant to replenish his energy as the undead horde started to pull back under Bjor'ma's command. The Barbarians pulled out their bows and started to pepper the horde with their signature flaming arrows.

Thaddeus yelled out, "And stay out!"

To accentuate his victory, he cast a purple-hued fireball at the retreating horde. It exploded in the middle of the horde, causing many thousands to be burned to a crisp as the horde inexorably marched on, now partially on fire. After some frantic searching, Bjor'ma found his undead mother amidst the horde and tried to protect her, but he realized that in the short span of that battle, her mind was gone now, having been eaten up by the rotting disease that caused one to become undead, the last of it being used to say goodbye to her only son.

Bjor'ma was saddened now more than ever. His own mother was one of this horde, sentenced to die again at his whim as she mindlessly fought his enemies. He was so close to perishing himself, as he knew that he would not survive the encounter with the shield put up by the young Thaddeus. If he wasn't close to faltering before, he was on the brink of it now as he remembered what he needed to do to break the contract he signed...*Do something good*. That phrase repeated itself in his mind over and over again as the undead horde continued east.

The Barbarians cheered as they saw the undead retreating with many of them on fire as they saw the dust that the undead had turned into—and not one of them was harmed, so complete was the protection that the young Thaddeus had given them. After some hearty goodbyes and victory cheers, they started back on the two-toll journey to their fortress high in the mountains as Thaddeus willed himself back to the domain of the Moon Goddess.

As he arrived, the place was abuzz with plans for the Joining.

CHAPTER 15

THE JOINING

As the boy arrived fresh from his second victory over Thanatos, he was visibly excited and relieved as he knew that the battle could have gone very differently than it did. As he went to find Kama to tell her all about it, the elder Thaddeus got his attention and said to his young protégé, "Sit ye down. This is an important sun fer ye, and a sun of decision."

The young Thaddeus looked puzzled as he said, "What's going on? What do I need to decide?" His youthful exuberance got the better of him as he followed his questions up with another question as his voice got louder, "Did you see my victory? That was WAY cool! All those things just turned to dust, and then the purple ball of fire! If my friends could have seen that…"

The elder Thaddeus, while happy his protégé was victorious, continued in a more serious and sedate tone and said, "As ye know, ye have a dragon spirit in yer head, which is one of the reasons yer magick is so strong. Sairys here thought that the fight against the forces of Evil would be too much fer one and so suggested to Alotraxas that ye get a familiar. Normally, ye find one yerself, but under the circumstances, Alotraxas asked for one on yer behalf. He found a dragon fer ye. His name is Agham-Ix, and 'e is a stone dragon."

The young Thaddeus said excitedly as his face lit up, "I…I get my own dragon? This is SO cool! Wait till my friends—"

The elder Thaddeus interrupted him, "Now, don't get ahead of yerself. There are some things that must be discussed before the Joining."

The younger Thaddeus asked, "What is this Joining, and what needs to be decided?"

The elder Thaddeus conjured a chair, stoked up his pipe and said, "Have a seat, so we can talk like civilized gentlemen…" A chair appeared beside the young Thaddeus, and he quickly took a seat as Thaddeus continued, "Well, first ye have to decide if'n ye want a familiar. Let me explain, a familiar can be of great benefit to a wizard, in that some of the dragon's abilities can be transferred to ye, and vice versa. You'll also gain some additional knowledge based on what yer familiar knows and vice versa. The downside to all this is that ye be responsible for yer familiar's life and vice versa because as Sairys knows, once ye die, yer familiar does as well and vice versa. If'n yer familiar dies, so to do ye."

Thaddeus continued, "Once ye go through the Joining, it cannot be undone. It's a contract fer life, and I don't know what will happen to ye or yer familiar if'n ye decide to go back from whence ye came. So it comes down to a choice: If'n ye take a familiar this sun, ye may not be able ta go home to yer pa, but if not, ye be weaker against what yer up against, and if ye think ye seen the worst of what Evil has to offer ta stop ye, ye would be sadly mistaken…

"So as ye can see it's a big choice. I only wish ye had more time to decide…Unfortunately, ye don't. If it's to happen, the Joining must take place this sun because it takes two suns for it to become fully effective during which time ye be asleep, but once ye awake, ye and yer dragon will be quite a pair, just as Sairys and I are. What say ye?"

The young Thaddeus sat back in his chair as he just took in a lot of information at once, but he was used to it, as that is the way that Thaddeus taught him. Though only nine cycles old, he understood that his life would never be the same after this adventure, and could he go back to his ordinary life after living this adventure of a lifetime? The young Thaddeus thought that all the things that he had done and the things that he would be able to do would be more than he could have dreamed, and much more than he would be able to do in our world, where eventually he would have to do a job each sun, instead of living here, where each sun was an adventure.

The elder Thaddeus just sat back in his chair and puffed on his pipe while reading the boys' thoughts. Alotraxas, too, remained silent as he, like the elder Thaddeus, knew that it had to be his decision and only his decision. Both the dragon spirit and the elder Thaddeus knew the gravity of the choice that they had set upon this young boy. The fate of their world might well rest upon what he decided; the difference between success and failure in this herculean task they have set before him may be decided this sun. The young Thaddeus thought of school and his friends, along with his pa, his home, but then he thought about something that Boral told him as he lay on the ground dying on that cool Samhein night; that he was the last human Wizard alive on the Continent.

He reflected on that statement, that he was the last of a long line of people to have studied magick and quite possibly he could be the last human to ever cast a spell in this place. He thought of all he learned in his world and in this one, how what he learned from school prepared him for what he learned here and made him the person he is. He thought that it would be an honor to help rebuild the Continent to its former glory, but then he thought about his world. Would they wonder about what had happened to him? He thought that perhaps he would be forgotten by most in a short time, except his by father, who would always remember him and have his memory in his mind always. But what about everyone else? He thought about what he could do here in the future, and what he had already done here to help the Continent, he thought about what he could do in his world and then he came to a realization, did it matter where he achieved greatness? Did it matter the reality that it occurred in?

In his mind, he saw something that he learned through Alotraxas, the vast multiverse, the seemingly endless places where he could be right now making this decision. He thought that no matter where he was, that he should strive to bring good to that place. In doing so, he reasoned that his life, like the lives of so many before him might be remembered by future people because of the good he brought and the lives he helped save.

This line of thinking caused the elder Thaddeus to raise his eyebrow, and though it was the line of thinking he was hoping for, he remained silent until the young Thaddeus said, "Can I see and talk to my pa whenever I want, if I stay here?"

The elder Thaddeus said, "Aye, we can arrange that. Won't be easy, but we can find a way."

The young Thaddeus felt so alive especially after two victories against Evil and receiving the bear tooth from the Barbarian clans, not to mention the blessing of the Snow Queen herself. Nothing like that had ever happened to him before when he was back home. He thought that he could really make a difference here, and back home, he could as well, but he was already making a difference here, and it would be another 10 or 15 cycles before he could realize his potential back home.

The young Thaddeus thought for a long time, seemingly weighing every consequence in his mind, until he said, "I've decided. I want to stay here and live my life here. Thaddeus, you came here and found a life worth living, why can't I? Besides, back home, all I have is my pa ta come home to…but here, I could be the one that makes the Continent safe again, and with a dragon by my side, following the Natural Law, of course, my life will mean something, not only to me, but to everyone on the Continent."

The elder Thaddeus said, "So, ye've chosen to stay here. While I'm happy to hear that, ye have to be happy about it as well."

The young Thaddeus replied, "I am happy about it. It's like my whole life has been leading up to this; from the first time I heard about you and your adventures, I knew that's what I wanted as well. Can I meet Agham-Ix now?"

The elder Thaddeus said, "Well, if ye're sure, aye, ye can."

As he said that, a grayish-colored stone dragon came walking into the room. Thaddeus looked with delight seeing a real (albeit small) dragon at his feet, though he looked more like a dark gray lizard than a dragon, but the young Thaddeus was enthralled nonetheless with this creature. Agham-Ix sensed the magick from the boy and smiled, knowing that he would be able to cast some of that himself one sun. It took some time as the dragon flew up to Thaddeus' height and looked him in the eye. Agham-Ix saw the good in him, which made him smile, and felt a connection to this young boy right away. He also saw that unlike Sairys, he could not rest on the boy's shoulders, as Stone Dragons are very heavy and somewhat slow due to their incredibly hard and thick skin and bones. Though Agham-Ix was small for a Stone Dragon, he weighed in at 40 stone but as usual, the elder Thaddeus had a solution for this rather weighty problem. He handed the boy a brooch and said, "It's best when ye and yer familiar are touching each other. To do that, you'll need this. Make sure ye have it on, and when yer dragon rests on ye, he will be light enough where ye can support him easily. If'n yer not wearing it, he can crush you especially as he gets older."

Thaddeus said to all assembled, which included the Moon Goddess and Kama, remembering what was said during his Joining to Sairys, "This sun is the sun of Joining, an auspicious and rare event in of itself. Every wizard who chooses to have a familiar goes through this…when ye and yer familiar are joined as one for as long as ye both shall live."

The elder Thaddeus said, "Thaddeus, are ye ready to take on this dragon as a familiar, knowing that this is a bond for life? If that bond is broken, ye

and yer familiar die. Yer thoughts and his thoughts will be as one, ye will function as two halves of a whole for as long as ye both shall live. If ye assent to
this, put your hand on the dragon's back and say, 'Aye.'"

The young Thaddeus put his hand on the dragon's back, noting how
stone-like the scales were, realizing that the dragon that was about to be his
familiar was aptly named. He liked the thought of having another creature
around that could be his guide and companion as he started a new life on the
Continent. He smiled at the elder Thaddeus and said, "Aye!"

The elder Thaddeus said, "Agham-Ix, are ye ready to take on this human
as a familiar, knowing that this is a bond for life? If that bond is broken, ye
and yer familiar die. Yer thoughts and his thoughts will be as one, ye will function as two halves of a whole for as long as ye both shall live. If ye assent to
this, put your claw on the human's back and say, 'Aye.'"

Agham-Ix nodded and made a sound. Alotraxas said through the boy, "He
has assented."

The elder Thaddeus raised his arms above his head, cast a spell from a wand he
had in his pocket, and said, "Then I now pronounce that you are a joined pair. From
this sun forward, you will live as one, be as one, and grow as one. Now, ye must
sleep, and ye must be connected for two suns, after which you will be fully joined."

As those words were spoken, Agham-Ix flew up and landed on Thaddeus.
His weight was magickally reduced from 40 stone to a mere one stone, while
Thaddeus' strength increased somewhat, and he took on a slightly grayish tone
to his skin and features. Unbeknownst to him, his skin was as hard as stone and
would be difficult to cut so long as he was in contact with his familiar. Alotraxas
rejoiced and was happy that he would have someone to talk to, as the knowledge
of dragon tongue would be passed on to the young Thaddeus; not to mention he
could fill Thaddeus' mind with knowledge and dragon lore from the ancient past.

To the young Thaddeus, it was like a superhighway of knowledge had just
opened up in his mind as the vast storehouse of what Agham-Ix knew and what
he knew was being exchanged. Alotraxas also helped in this transition by providing Thaddeus with the knowledge of dragon tongue, so it would be easier
for them to communicate, and for Thaddeus to understand the vast storehouse
of knowledge that he would have available to him.

The young Thaddeus and his new familiar went to sleep…a deep sleep. A
sleep unlike either of them had ever had before. They were joining, becoming
one as they dreamt of the times to come.

CHAPTER 16

TWO PROBLEMS

As the young Thaddeus slept, the elder Thaddeus had two problems brewing at the same time. First was the situation with Bjor'ma and his plea for help, and then with finding a way for his protégé to be able to talk to his father. Since the more immediate issue was Bjor'ma and the fate of the Continent, he decided to tackle that issue first, as it could yield some results that could swing the balance more in favor of good. He thought about how long had passed in the place where the young Thaddeus was taken from, as he opened up a small window on the boy's world, just big enough for his eye, and he was pleased that it was still dark. He surmised that only half a night had passed by based on the movement of the single moon, and figured that he had some time yet to continue to work with the boy to get his magickal ability up to snuff before the inevitable final confrontation with Evil.

He wondered what would happen to the boy as he progressed through what remained of his training and how fighting this much evil would affect him. Thaddeus had taught many students before the young Thaddeus, but they were different for many reasons. The first is that the young Thaddeus is from our world, a place where magick does not exist, at least not the kind that he cast anyway, and second, this was the first student he taught in so short a time. Thaddeus knew that it took time for the mind to be able to fully utilize what he was teaching and would allow students the time to "swallow" what they had been taught. He adopted much of the elvish way of teaching, in that he would only hold class for three tolls each sun with the rest of the time for the students to learn on their own and practice that which he taught. He hoped that he would be okay, but if nothing else, at least he had someone to talk to now that he had a familiar, and he noticed that the boy seemed to be really taking a liking to Kama, and she really enjoyed spending time with him. She had even taken to teaching him Elven, and even she was surprised at how fast he was learning it. Even though the young Thaddeus knew that Kama was a spirit and was not technically alive, she looked like a young elf and acted like one as well, and the two were always talking and learning together. The elder Thaddeus noted that her teaching style was one of reflection and constantly asking questions, which was typical for an elf, while his was much more direct, but interspersed with his wit and boyish charm. He thought that his young protégé was getting the best of both worlds and hoped that he could synthesize what he was learning from both of them into a cohesive magickal style. He knew that everyone developed their own way of doing magick, and the boy seemed very focused on protection and healing magicks, with some very colorful destructive magicks thrown in for good measure.

While he was musing in these thoughts, his mind switched to Bjor'ma and what might be done for him given his current situation. He decided to do some research on the problem while he had some spare time. He wanted to find out the nature of the "deal" he made and who he made it with. He was surprised at the magickal might they had, as they were able to pull Bjor'ma out of his protected sanctuary with relative ease which is something that he wasn't used to. Thaddeus believed that he was not dealing with ordinary terrestrial creatures, he was dealing with deities. This revelation didn't frighten him as he has had many dealings with deities throughout his long magickal career and he was currently "living" with one, but he didn't know who they were and what powers they had, at least not yet.

He pored over texts and tomes for tolls on end, referencing and cross-referencing anything he could find about what power could do that, which he surmised was certainly infernal in nature. He remembered a tome that he had, but had never read; he came across it whilst reading in an Elven library. It was in a stone room, guarded night and sun by a cohort of elves preventing anyone from entering the room and becoming corrupted by a tome that the elves said came from the Lower Planes of Gehron. The planes of Gehron were where evil gods supposedly lived and plotted against those who lived in the Light. The tome had no name but was very recognizable due to its black charred cover and the red ink with which it was written, supposedly the blood of an elf. Due to his lofty station at the time, he was allowed to take the tome "for research and teaching purposes," figuring that it might come in handy one sun. To protect himself and his library, he buried the tome under a stack of stones. It was buried there because of its infernal origins and it's ability to immolate itself to protect the evil secrets it held (which he found out about the hard way).

After casting a spell of protection on himself, whilst sitting in his chair surrounded by a pentagram, he started reading. The book described the planes of Gehron and in so doing he came across a name, the Entities of Evil. He learned that there were three of them, and each one had certain powers. As he read, he came across an interesting passage:

...And so they fought until all the Ancients had perished; save one, Chagdrom, the most evil of the Ancients, as his last act, in his dying breath, set a pestilence on the land making all in his gaze wither and die...

After the land was rendered sterile and lifeless, he perished with the rest of his Kin never to be reborn again...

From his rotting, putrescent husk came his progeny...three beings, while mere shadows of the evil that bred them, still served as a reminder of the terrible power that the Ancients had...

The first and the oldest was the Lord of Blight, with his terrible power of decay and rot, bringer of pestilence and sower of poison and bitterness...

Next, armed with his sword, came the Lord of the Dead, commander of the legions of dead to forever fight the armies of the Light...

Finally came The Dread Lord, Overlord of Evil...his powers centered on the power of the mind...his sole desire to corrupt and twist thoughts to his will...his magickal ability was unique amongst these entities, as he was able to cast magicks that no mortal could...

Thaddeus read that passage many times and thought that perhaps that was who Bjor'ma had entreated with in becoming what he was and how all this happened in the first place, and once again, he blamed himself and his short-sightedness in not knowing the Continent and its legends. Instead of tolls of self-recrimination, Thaddeus decided to read on and learn all he could until he came across another passage, written in magickal script, seemingly between the lines of the blood-red script of the book. It read:

...The Entities of Evil cannot appear on the Continent if there is a Champion of the Light anywhere on it, provided he has been so named by the Ancients of the Light. If one of them joins with their respective protected race, the Entities can only work through intermediaries and cannot bring their full powers to bear upon said Champion...Hail to the Light!

Thaddeus couldn't believe his eyes! It was like an ancient Wizard was speaking to him from beyond the grave; maybe someone who was there, maybe another Champion of the Light, a Wizard who wrote in this most evil tome how to weaken the Entities of Evil and, in so doing, give his young protégé a fighting chance. He stoked up his pipe and continued to read, picking up little things here and there, bits and pieces of how to stack the deck in his favor until he came upon the passage he was looking for, which read:

Mortals entering into a blood contract with the Entities of Evil do so under the pains of eternal torment and anguish should the contract be broken. If an act, which can be considered to be even slightly beneficial to any enemy is performed willingly by said mortal, the blood contract is broken. Once broken, the mortal is then immediately taken to the Pits of Hatred, there to spend an eternity in pain and anguish.

Those who manage to complete their contracts with any of the Entities of Evil, will gain the rewards promised to them under their contract, subject to the terms and conditions therein.

Again, written in magickal script in between these paragraphs was written:

They CAN be intercepted by an Ancient of the Light or a Guardian, but only if the deed breaking the contract was sufficiently worthy to warrant complete absolution of their crimes against the Light...

Thaddeus sat back in his chair, took a drag from his pipe, and released a large puff of fruit smelling smoke. He was elated that he had found a way to save Bjor'ma from his fate, but the deed breaking his contract would have to be really big, as Thaddeus knew that he was behind the scourge of undead that was roaming the Continent, not to mention hundreds of thousands of murdered people, one of whom was his mother, and the bigger problem was, where to find an Ancient of the Light and convince him/her that Bjor'ma was worth saving? He also wanted to know more about who wrote the magickal script, having noted it interspersed throughout this evil tome giving commentary mostly on the events of the time and how his version differed from the events written in the book.

After reading, Thaddeus decided to read a more enlightened tome, found in this realm, one that might shed some light on who this Wizard was and where could he find an Ancient of the Light; unbeknownst to him, he wouldn't have to wait long to find one piece of what he was looking for...

He found the tome he was looking for, entitled *Ancients of the Light*, and opened up the large, metallic covered tome here in the Moon Goddess' library, which was quite extensive and had much knowledge contained within it, some of which he had already read. What he discovered was that there were thousands of Ancients of the Light going back into times immemorial even by deity standards. A sigh of despair escaped his lips as he started reading, taking notes as he went through the many thousands of names and their heroic deeds that caused them to be recorded in this tome.

After a marathon session of reading, on the sixth to the last page of this rather long tome, he found a familiar name: Alotraxas, the Last King of the Dragons. He was an Ancient of the Light! He noted that all of his story was also recorded here, but the one odd thing recorded in this tome was that he was the only Ancient of the Light in this entire tome to swear an oath to defend humans in life AND death, provided he deemed them worthy of that protection, until released from his oath, which no other Ancient had done, as he was the sixth to the last Ancient to have lived.

As Thaddeus read Alotraxas' story, which was one of the shorter stories he read in this massive tome, he came across another name which was unfamiliar to him, a human named Toril, apparently a Wizard of some renown, being listed as the only Champion of the Light that Alotraxas had personally named. Thaddeus found this odd because most of the Ancients of the Light named hundreds of Champions of the Light during their incredibly long lifetimes, and each one of them was detailed in this tome, along with their more notable deeds and family histories. Toril apparently served Alotraxas for many cycles, fighting the forces of Evil for his entire life. He also read that it was Toril who created the two relics that he held for a brief time while he was alive on the Continent, The Eyes of the King and the Heart of the Queen, which are the only two relics which survive from that time that have ever been found. He also wondered how the First King came into possession of the Eyes of the King in the first place. Perhaps he had some connection to Toril, but the tome was mute on this point, having been written long before the First King was thought of. Thaddeus wondered if that's how he knew of magick, and why he banned it; perhaps this sort of thing had happened to him and his people, and he beseeched the Gods for help.

Thaddeus was dumbfounded and increasingly upset with himself. All these connections that he was totally unaware of now making themselves known to him—if only he had put more safeguards in place to prevent this…He thought that maybe he should have stuck to only teaching healing magicks, but it wasn't who he was. Besides being a showman at heart, he learned these magicks to wreak vengeance on those who took his love away all those cycles ago.

Besides exacting revenge upon your enemies, he knew that his magick was useful, when applied in the right circumstances. He spent a lot of time teaching others about his magicks and how useful they could be, along with copious examples of the right ways to utilize magick in conjunction with the Natural Law. While he was teaching others, he hoped that since he eventually learned to control himself and his magicks that others would be able to follow, but they didn't and now his magick has destroyed the world which he loved. While thinking of the past, he remembered something that he once told Clarissa: that magick will consume you, in life and in death, it never stops consuming; and now it had consumed the world he loved. But while he was thinking about all the things that magick took from him, he remembered all the things that magick gave him as well, including having the opportunity to save this world and to set things right again as he closed the tome.

He left the library with heavy thoughts and went back to his favorite chair and reflected on what he learned…and how much a part of this world he had become.

CHAPTER 17

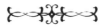

THE AWAKENING

Two suns passed by as most do, but for the elder Thaddeus, that time was spent in study and contemplation about his life and times on the Continent. When he came here and decided to stay, he thought he was helping this world, but as he looked at the mounting evidence against him, he realized that by bringing magick here, he did more harm than good to this place. He hoped that history could forgive him for what he did, and he hoped that he would be judged by what he did to fix this world. Even the Moon Goddess could sense something amiss and came to him whilst he was brooding as she said, "Am I to be alone this sun?"

Thaddeus looked up and sighed. He said, "I'm sorry fer abandonin' ya. Been havin' some tough thoughts of late, realizin' what I did ta these good people by bringin' magick ta them. It's my fault entirely. I killed them...all of them...millions of voices silenced becuz of me and what I brought ta this world. They weren't ready. If only I had seen this coming, but divination was never my strong suit...which begs a question. Why did ya allow me here?"

The Moon Goddess looked at him, smiled, and said, "You're here because you're a good man, you always were, and you inspired a lot of people while you lived. Teaching people about your life and times, along with magick and the Natural Law was a good thing ,and perhaps this boy will be the father of a new magick here, one that is controlled and can be learned by anyone with the wherewithal to understand it. My dear Thaddeus, everyone makes mistakes, even me. But it's what we learn from them and how we set things right again that determines how history will judge us. Admittedly, these are some very dark times for the Continent, but I think you are doing right by the Continent, and think about how you are changing the boy's life."

She continued, "I implore you to stay the course because you are giving a lot of people hope through your actions, so that while many will die, many more will live and remember us long into the future." She sat down next to him, hugged him, gave him a peck on the cheek, and said, "Come with me. There is something you need to see that should cheer you up!"

Thaddeus got up with a bit of a spring in his step, which was a consequence of having a Goddess next to him. As he followed her into the garden, there he saw something that put a smile on his face: his protégé and his new familiar flying about; albeit very slowly, and the pair looked a little unsteady, but they appeared to be having the time of their lives. Thaddeus thought about all the times he had seen this same scene play out over his life, and it always made him smile. A young Wizard and his new familiar, together, learning and exploring their world as one…It reminded him of when he and Sairys were joined all those cycles ago and the fun they had during their first few suns together. Sairys sensed that Thaddeus' mood had changed and came flying in to see what was going on. He saw what was happening, took up residence on Thaddeus' shoulder as he said into Thaddeus' mind, "Remember when that was us?"

Thaddeus replied, "Aye, that I do…seems like it was only a sun ago, old friend."

The Moon Goddess said, "They awoke a few tolls ago, and they seem so happy together. I thought that you could use a sight like this as proof of the good that you are doing, not only for the boy, but for the entire Continent."

Thaddeus said with a smile, "Sairys, what say you…should we show them how it's done?"

Sairys transformed into the grand creature he really was and took off, with Thaddeus on his shoulders as the two of them took to the air. The young Thaddeus and Agham-Ix had no hope of catching up to them, but they enjoyed the acrobatics that their elders were engaging in as they tried to steady themselves. Thaddeus thought that what he was witnessing could be him in a few cycles, riding a much larger dragon. He could only imagine the bond that his elder had with Sairys and how devoted they were to each other. He could hear Agham-Ix echoing his thoughts, wondering what was in store for them as they progressed through their lives together. The young Thaddeus realized for the first time that the entire exchange of thoughts between them took place in dragon tongue, not in his native language. He liked communicating by thought as it was very quick, and no one around him could know what they were talking about. He realized that this was a huge advantage to him, having the power of two minds instead of one to make decisions and decide courses of action though at the moment there were three minds taking up residence in the young Thaddeus' head.

After a short time of doing acrobatics and flying about, the elder Thaddeus and Sairys landed and said, "Always loved doing that!"

...as the Moon Goddess said to him, "You're smiling again. It's good to see it..."

Thaddeus realized that he was smiling and that despite his mistakes; he thought that in the end everything would turn out right, but that there was still lots of work to be done.

The elder Thaddeus and Sairys looked at the new pair and said, "Well, how do ye both feel? Sleepin' fer two suns like ye were?"

The young Thaddeus said, "We feel great. I know so much that I didn't know before, so much about this land's history and legends, but we are ready to get back to work and finish our training in magick. What say you?"

The elder Thaddeus looked at them, so eager, so ready to take on the world and said, "Aye, we start on the morrow. Take the sun and enjoy it. Every Wizard needs time to enjoy himself, as there will be trying times ahead, and it's always nice to look back at the good times ye've had and look forward to the times ye'll have ahead."

The young Thaddeus and Agham-Ix nodded to Thaddeus' wisdom and headed back to the garden, so Agham-Ix could practice flying with a rider, which was something that he had never done before. Though the young Thaddeus was a small fraction of his weight, and Agham-Ix could support him easily; flying with something as un-aerodynamic as a human on your back required some practice, not to mention that stone dragons were poor flyers in the first place. They were slow to gain altitude and were prone to plummeting down instead of gliding due to the stone dragon's weight. It didn't get any better as they got older because as they got bigger, their weight increased exponentially. Stone dragons could weigh as much as 800 stone, yet only be 20 arms long. Their primary ability was not their speed or their limited ability to fly; it was their dense skin and bones, and their resistance to just about anything, including

101

a high resistance to magick, which their familiar would also gain. They were also exceptionally long lived, another trait that they could pass along to their familiar, and it should be noted that stone dragons could live 750 cycles or more. Unfortunately, no one knew the effects that having a human familiar would have on stone dragons as no one had ever had one as a familiar, but Agham-Ix was chosen due to his moderate temperament, resistance to elemental effects, and his stability in both mind and body, as these were seen as critical to ensure the young Thaddeus' survival against the forces that were aligned against him.

While Thaddeus and Agham-Ix were joining and getting lessons in aerodynamics, other things were brewing on the Continent. For the last three suns, Thanatos, Bjor'ma, and their undead horde continued to head east, realizing that the total conquest of the Barbarians and the humans with them would result in catastrophic failure due to the skill and tenacity of the Barbarian warriors, not to mention the winter weather that would mysteriously begin whenever they would engage with the Barbarians, which slowed Thanatos' army greatly. He cursed the powers that saved the Barbarians from his army, but vowed to exact revenge upon the next group to feel his wrath, the Narsum and their human allies. Thanatos estimated that they would need a million more troops to face the elves in two season's time, as they would lose some to rot and others to battles; the problem for their next targets was that the Narsum and the humans did not number that many, but neither Thanatos nor Bjor'ma knew their true strength.

Bjor'ma kept the undead creature that was his mother close to him at all times, so he would not lose her in the massive horde that trailed him. Though she didn't know who she was anymore, he did, and it pained him greatly to think about what he had done to the woman who gave him life along with the rest of the city of Taras'la. A city unique on the Continent due to the high number of half-elves that lived there, it was a city that exemplified living together in peace and harmony with those of a different race. How he wished he was there now, just sitting outside, enjoying a glass of chilled Elverquist with a fresh stem of grapes, listening to the elves talk of philosophy and the wonder of everything.

Thanatos was too busy leading his army to worry about Bjor'ma's issues; it was as if, he no longer cared about his only leftenant and believed at some point that he would have to be eliminated, but Thanatos did not know about

Bjor'ma's contract with the Dread Lord. Truth be told, since his contract stated that every humanoid life on the Continent had to be delivered, Bjor'ma's existence as a spirit was already forfeit and had no real reason to continue, as he could not succeed given the troops that he had combined with their new leader. Bjor'ma knew this though, and had already awoken to the fact that he was going to endure an eternity of suffering and torment because of his failure, but from his point of view, given the sadness of the last few suns, especially finding his mother, he figured it was what he deserved. He was biding his time in the hope that perhaps he could do something to thwart Thanatos and the Dread Lord at the right time to spoil their plans and maybe save the Continent from the evil that he helped bring to it.

Thanatos was confident that not only could he find and defeat the Narsum, but that he could add their strength to his forces. He believed that since the Narsum were not human, the effects of becoming undead might be different for them, and it might benefit him in some way. Onward they marched, sun and night, without rest, as no one in the army required it.

Travelling with a half million troops presented certain difficulties, which Thanatos was finding out about. First, a great deal of control was needed, and while Bjor'ma was good, the 500,000 number was about as much as he could manage given his current allowance of energy. Thanatos realized that he would have to allow his less-than-faithful leftenant to feed voraciously as he did before if he wanted to get his two million troops marching in the same direction at his command.

The other issue was that given the sheer size of his disorganized force, his force would be easily seen and heard from a distance or from the air. He couldn't hide his forces, as they were too many in number, nor could he only march at night, as he would lose too many of his army to rot. His only option was to press on, hope for the best, and try to increase his troop strength as much as he could.

Looking out to the horizon to the east, he could see the mountains to the North falling away, and the most rugged terrain on the Continent ahead of him, the vast desert known as the Crying Fields. Some of the worst conditions imaginable existed here; scorching temperatures when the suns were out, massive sandstorms and bitter cold at night, not to mention a complete lack of water. The Crying Fields were an ancient burial ground from times past, where people would go to bury their dead in one place on the Continent. This ancient custom fell out of favor when the human populations started to spread out more and more, and getting to the Crying Fields would take a season or more for more remote villages. However, for many hundreds of cycles, this was where all of the Continent's dead were buried.

Thanatos thought that an opportunity might present itself here and he could bolster his troop strength by huge amounts and make conquering the Narsum that much easier. As he entered the Crying Fields though, he was in for a surprise.

CHAPTER 18

FATE IN THE FIELDS

His first steps in the Crying Fields were easy, as the scrublands of the Central Plains gave way to the desert beyond, and he didn't feel anything, but Bjor'ma was afraid, as he knew about the ancient legends and said, "My Lord Thanatos, we need to stay out of here. We will not be welcomed."

Thanatos glared back at Bjor'ma with glowing red eyes and said in a deep voice devoid of inflection or emotion, "We press on. I know what is here, and I know how to deal with them."

Bjor'ma kept his mother close to him as they ventured forth onto the most sacred yet unforgiving ground on the Continent, where hundreds of thousands of souls were interred in the ancient past. Bjor'ma was the only one feeling uneasy as he floated over the sand because he knew what was here, but didn't know how Thanatos was going to "deal" with them. Small stone markers were everywhere, but nothing accosted them, as now the entire horde was walking over sand. Onward they trudged, through the sand dunes and over the sun-scorched hills of this massive desert.

Several tolls into their march, the horde came to a stop when Bjor'ma saw a huge sandstorm coming right at them. It almost looked like a giant hand pushing the sand towards them in an effort to erase the blasphemy that Thanatos had brought to the desert. The wall of sand was over 200 arms high, and it went on for as far as either Thanatos or Bjor'ma could see.

Thanatos said, "We press on. Get them moving."

The horde lurched forward and continued on as the sandstorm struck the throng of undead. It was a surreal experience for Bjor'ma, having never been through a sandstorm in life, but he was amazed at the destructive power of it. He couldn't believe that small grains of sand could do all this. The storm raged for tolls on end; it was as if all the sand in the Crying Fields was being flung at them in an effort to stop them.

After the storm passed, though they themselves were unaffected, they looked behind them, and their entire horde was gone, having been buried under seven arms of sand. The vast horde was silenced, and the only thing that could be heard was the wind, almost laughing at them. Bjor'ma tried to move them but was unable to, as the undead did not have the strength to free themselves, nor did they have the intelligence to dig themselves out. Thanatos used one of his old tricks that he used successfully in attacking the Barbarians; he started raising them up out of the sand and dropping them rather unceremoniously. Many that he raised were missing limbs or other body parts, and some had crumbled to dust under the weight of the sand piled on them.

For two tolls, he raised as many as he could, but something happened that he had never experienced before; he ran out of energy. He noted that the energy that he expended wasn't being replenished, even though he was standing on the ground…What could this mean? It was as if his supply of energy had been cut off, and Thanatos knew that without his constant supply of magickal energy Bjor'ma could not move his horde, and they would be stuck here, at the mercy of the elements, among other things.

While Thanatos was raising parts of the horde, Bjor'ma saw something that the sages of times future would mark as a turning point in his struggle; he saw his mother's body, but her face was obliterated by the sandstorm, and she was missing an arm, but she shambled around like all the rest, so he knew she was still able to move, and she couldn't feel anything, so at least she was spared that pain. Bjor'ma knew that he would never see her face again for as long as he lived; it was like he was losing his mother, piece by piece, and he wasn't sure how much more of this he could bear. His sadness was almost overwhelming, and without energy from Thanatos, it was as if he had no purpose. He felt his life was wasted even before he was exiled. He questioned why he didn't use his powers for good, to help people who took the wrong path. He mused that could have been a spiritual healer of some kind and put a suggestion into someone's mind to get them to do what they needed to, so they could better their lives…

But he didn't do that. He was greedy and used his gifts to control someone for his own purposes. He cursed himself and wondered when it would all be over. He would almost welcome eternal pain and torment at this point, because at least he wouldn't feel like this: despondent and dejected.

Thanatos, ever the leader, said, "We must retreat from this place, can you move those which I have raised? We will come back for the others later…"

Bjor'ma tried to move them, and to his surprise they responded to his command, but as he looked around, he understood why. The sandstorm had buried all of the troops, and Thanatos was only able to raise 25,000 of them; there were still 475,000 more buried beneath the sand. So he moved them to the west, keeping an eye on his now faceless mother, her earring barely dangling off her ear, most of which was removed by the storm, but he noted that the sand really shined up the gold and made her a lot easier to pick out amongst the thousands of shambling bodies. Over the next few tolls, Bjor'ma moved his much smaller force to the scrublands and waited. He felt low on energy and low in general, as if he just wanted to get it over with and pass on to wherever it was that he was meant to go. He had no more energy to direct the horde, and so just floated there waiting and wondering when Thanatos would return with some much-needed energy.

As he waited, he noted the undead colliding with one another as some of them could not see, which he normally would have found highly amusing, but he didn't care, so dejected was he right now. As his energy reserves kept getting smaller, he saw Thanatos coming out of the Crying Fields, though he wasn't quite himself. He appeared with 4,000 more troops behind him, but he didn't have his usual more militaristic bearing; his shoulders were slumped, his gait was shambling, and he was just barely keeping pace with the faceless undead that were with him. As he approached the scrublands, Bjor'ma saw energy begin to flow into him, he regained his posture somewhat but collapsed as he reached Bjor'ma.

Thanatos said, "We won't be able to cross this place. We will have to find another way; there are forces in there that are very dangerous to us."

Bjor'ma said, "Yes, my Lord. What would you have us do? What about the troops we lost in there? Can we recover them?"

Thanatos looked at Bjor'ma, his cold, red eyes staring at his leftenant as he said, "We could, but it will take too much time. You will find another way… but first, feed…"

Bjor'ma was stunned by this rare altruistic moment and decided to take full advantage as he glutted himself on energy for tolls on end. While Thanatos and Bjor'ma were recuperating and their comparatively small horde mindlessly wandering about, they did not know that something was coming—something dangerous.

During the time that Thanatos and Bjor'ma regained their energy, trying to figure out the path forward, something happened that surprised the pair of them, as they had never seen anything like this before. What was left of their undead force just ceased to exist, having turned to dust at his call, their spirits finally able to rest; but soon enough they heard it.

The wailing. This was how the Crying Fields were named, supposedly by the cries of the millions of the living who came here to bury the dead over thousands of cycles and consecrate them to the Ancient Gods. It got much louder as Thanatos and Bjor'ma came face to face with something from out of a legend—a Guardian. Taking the appearance of a large glowing human dressed in plate armor, with wings of the purest white and standing at 20 arms high, they were truly sights to behold. They were tasked with sheperding the spirits of the dead inside the fields and keeping evil out. The Guardian saw many spirits trying to get in and two evil creatures that needed to be kept out. Thanatos and Bjor'ma saw what used to be their horde of undead, now turned to spirits which were unable to cross the border of the Crying Fields. They saw the Guardian opening up what appeared to be a pair of giant golden doors, and the many thousands of undead spirits entered the Crying Fields, their last home. Bjor'ma saw his mother cross the border into the Crying Fields, so noted by a bright glint of light from her golden earring, and he shed a tear at seeing her go but was happy at the same time, in that her suffering at his hands was over now, and she could finally rest. Thanatos and Bjor'ma had bigger problems though, as neither of them had any idea what this Guardian could do; but whatever it was, both were sure they wouldn't like it.

The Guardian turned to face them and willed a large, glowing sword into existence. The Guardian took the sword into what appeared to be hands, planted it into the ground and said on the wind, "You shall not enter this hallowed ground again, I forbid it! You shall never again desecrate this most holy place! Be gone from here, or suffer the consequences!"

Thanatos stepped forward boldly and, not realizing that he was totally out of his league, said with conviction, "I will never back down from you. My strength returns. Now taste my fury!"

Thanatos unleashed a torrent of spells, faster than any human ever could at the Guardian, but after what would have been a deadly amount of magick for several thousand people, the Guardian stood tall, apparently unaffected as he said, "Your feeble magicks cannot affect me. The Ancients are here and stand with me."

Bjor'ma did some quick thinking and thought to himself that this might be the opportune moment to act. He knew that the Entities of Evil could not follow him into the Crying Fields, but how to get past the Guardian, he wondered?

Bjor'ma said to Thanatos, "He's weakening. Keep at it!" Thanatos continued his magickal barrage on the Guardian while Bjor'ma got on his knees in the sand and said in his mind, "Guardian…I ask that you take me into the Fields, for it will strike a blow at him, and he will not be able to command the undead as I can. I will repent for my sins…I wish to be with my mother again…"

Time slowed down for Bjor'ma. He was watching Thanatos casting spells at the Guardian in slow motion, as he saw a vision of his mother approaching him and said, "Mother…please tell him that I'm a good man. I'm sorry for what I've done, and I will repent for my sins, but I can't do this anymore… especially after what I've done to you…"

His mother said, "Rise, my son. Drive the evil from this place, and mayhaps he will allow it…good luck!"

Time did not speed up again for him as he approached Thanatos, who did not respond to him at first; he saw the energy tendril coming from Thanatos and knew that energy could go both ways through it. He latched onto it and drove his energy into Thanatos.

Thanatos did not know what to do at first as he said into Bjor'ma's mind, "What are you doing? Too much energy…STOP!"

Thanatos had no way of stopping the energy that Bjor'ma was sending into him, something Bjor'ma had figured out a while back, but did not think about it, until now that is. Bjor'ma thought that with this inflow of energy that Thanatos would be unable to contain it, and it would eventually overwhelm him, thereby casuing Thanatos to explode, or worse. Bjor'ma was so distraught about everything that he had done, he knew that this was the right thing to do, and at the right time. He kept at it as long as he could, Thanatos was screaming in his mind to stop, but he didn't as Thanatos was quickly becoming overwhelmed with energy.

While all this was happening, he saw a vision of the Dread Lord in his mind as he said, "A good deed. Our contract is broken…and YOU ARE MINE!"

He saw a hand coming for him, a large withered hand with black claws…

He seemed resigned to his fate, an eternity of torment and anguish, a just punishment given his life of doing evil. The black, charred hand got closer, and he could smell the foulness of it. He could feel the heat as he was being pulled towards it.

He closed his eyes and just let go; he didn't care at this point what happened to him. It would all be over soon enough, and he would be tormented endlessly, but at least his mind would be occupied with pain instead of his being endlessly miserable about what he did to his mother. His last thoughts were of her. Oh, how he loved her; she was so kind to everyone, including him. She encouraged him when the whole world had him down, she lifted him up and made him see the good in himself…and she was about to do it again.

When he opened his eyes again, he expected to be in the Dread Lord's domain, but he awoke in the scrublands to the west of the Crying Fields. Thanatos was gone; he couldn't believe it. He was no longer a spirit! He heard his heart beating; he looked down and saw his feet. He was standing up and not floating…

Then he saw it, a large individual with overbearingly white glowing wings. He noted a large balance in front of him, though it was exactly in balance at the moment. He looked at this surreal scene and saw his mother behind the large individual. She looked just as she did when he left home, it was how he remembered her as she stood smiling to him. Bjor'ma saw no one else bearing witness for him, just her. No friends, no other family was there to vouch for him, as the large individual said, "Bjor'ma, I am Tyrus the Judge, the Ancients have intervened, so that we may judge you…your mother implored us to hear your tale before the contract you made with the Dread Lord is carried out. If you are a good man, you will be allowed into the Crying Fields, if not…the consequences of your contract with the Dread Lord will be carried out. Let the hearing begin!"

A large hammer, wielded by unseen hands smashed against a stone as he was carried back to his birthplace. He saw his mother and father there, in their home at Taras'la. He saw his life—all of it whizzing by, and as it did, he saw little bits of the story going into one of the two pans on the large balance. Some were going into the good side, and some were not, but all were accounted for. It wasn't until he signed the contract with the Dread Lord that things really started to go downhill. Here was all the evil he had done, every soul he condemned to die twice stood in mute witness to his misdeeds, all the murder he had committed, and though there were some bright spots, most of what he had done was going into the wrong pan. When his life story was finished, it appeared that he was too. The "bad" pan was only a finger from the ground, but it wasn't there yet, as the Tyrus said, "Bjor'ma, you have been weighted in the balance and found wanting, but you can be redeemed as neither pan has touched the ground, if there is one here who can speak to any good that you have done in your life, then you may be allowed to rest here in the Crying Fields."

His mother stood up and screamed, "My son is a good man, please don't let that evil take him!" …as another person suddenly materialized and surprisingly came to his defense.

The person who came was none other than Thaddeus Brimstone, who said, "I second that, and the testimony of two is valid in 'is defense."

Tyrus said, "Aye, it is…we now adjourn to deliberate his fate."

Bjor'ma said, "You…? You came to my defense? Why? Surely I have done nothing but harm…"

Thaddeus raised his hand and interrupted him and said, "Bjor'ma, ye've done nothing to me, other than to cause me a few sleepless nights. I had hoped ye would have died quietly, but it seems that ye wanted revenge on me, and where did that get ya? Now do ye see the value of the Law?"

Bjor'ma looked genuinely contrite as he said, "Aye, that I do. I caused a lot of pain and death, and I've no reason to expect anyone to take pity on me. I deserve my fate, whatever it is, but I wanted to thank you, Thaddeus, for coming to my defense. As you can see, I didn't rack up too many friends while I lived."

Tyrus returned a short time later, his white wings fully extended with a scroll in his hands, and said, "It has been decided…Bjor'ma, stand forward and hear your fate…"

Bjor'ma stood up and tried to be brave but broke down and cried as he said, "Aye…I am ready. Have mercy on me…"

Tyrus opened up a scroll and said, "We have heard many such tales before and have judged many an evildoer to their grisly fate, and though your mother did not sway us, this man did. He came forward to speak for you when he did not have to and confirmed that you were a good man in life. However, as a spirit, the severity of your crimes is well known to us, and those you slaughtered weigh heavily on us…therefore, we sentence you to a thousand cycles of torment at the hands of the Dread Lord per your contract, but afterwards, your immortal soul will be allowed to rest here in peace, along with your mother. Sentence to be carried out in 10 suns hence. Go, be with your mother. May she always comfort and guide you."

Thaddeus could see Bjor'ma hugging his mother as they turned towards the Crying Fields as he said, "So shines a good deed when the world needs it most..."

Tyrus said to Thaddeus, "Good luck, sojourner. Know that we are watching, for one of yours and one of ours are intertwined at the moment, though we have given pause to the powers arrayed against the Light, it will not take long for them to recover. Use this time wisely!"

Thaddeus bowed low, and as Tyrus disappeared, he saw Bjor'ma and his mother, together, entering the Crying Fields, and he smiled at that thought, knowing that his time to do evil in this world was over. He wondered why he suddenly gave up on doing evil deeds, but chalked it up to one fact: Bjor'ma was lonely in life and didn't want to be lonely in death, especially now that he was being reunited with his mother. Though he cringed at the torment and torture he would have to endure, he smiled at the endless peace that he would come to know in the Crying Fields.

CHAPTER 19

A NEW CHAMPION

With Thanatos temporarily incapacitated and without Bjor'ma, the Entities of Evil were back to square one with their plan to make the Continent theirs. Thaddeus and the Moon Goddess celebrated this victory but realized that evil will always return, and Thaddeus started to make plans for the young Thaddeus to make his stand using the knowledge from the Tome he had read and said, "My boy, yer almost done with yer trainin', but Alotraxas and I know of one more thing ya be needin' afore ye take up residence on the Continent."

The young Thaddeus along with Agham-Ix said, "What more do I need?"

Alotraxas said, through the boy, "Aye, but we need to be on the Continent to do what must be done."

The young Thaddeus said, "Agham-Ix tells me of a ritual that must be performed on the Continent…Something about a Champion of the Light…? Is…am…I…I'm going to be a Champion of the Light?! WOW! This just keeps getting better…I know tons of magick, I've got a dragon of my own, I've defeated evil, and now I'm going to be a Champion of the Light?!! This is SO cool!"

His excitement and youthful exuberance certainly got the better of him as Thaddeus said, "Aye, ye are ta be, but ye lose somethin' in the process. Once ye become a Champion, ye will fight evil until ye die, and there is always evil ta fight. O' course, you'll be able ta do other things, too, like take a wife when the time is right, mayhaps have a few kids o' yer own…but fightin' evil will be yer new job, so ta speak. So ya lose yer ability ta become anythin' else. What say ye?"

The young Thaddeus said, "So I get to fight evil all the time? What's wrong with that? More adventure for Agham-Ix and I..."

The elder Thaddeus interrupted him, "Oh, what I wouldn't give for some of that spirit and drive. Hold onto that, it will serve ya well. Let's get down ta the Continent while the gettin' is good."

In a moment, the elder Thaddeus, the younger Thaddeus, and Agham-Ix were in the city of Samsrun, though it looked nothing like Thaddeus remembered it when he first arrived here. The castle was a ruin, the stench of rotting bodies, burnt out houses, and charred trees were all that remained of this place which was once a thriving city. Thaddeus quickly made his way to his old home; it was the only building that was totally untouched by the destruction and devastation around it, as Thaddeus had reinforced the building with magick, so that it could withstand just about anything before he died and left specific instructions on how to reinforce the spell. He took a key from his pocket, and a keyhole appeared in the door, as it opened.

The elder Thaddeus said, "We're here becuz it's the safest place ta do this, where we won't be disturbed, as the ritual is complex and it takes some time. I read about it, but I know that Alotraxas knows more than I do about this."

The spirit of Alotraxas exited the boy's mind and appeared before them in the courtyard. He appeared as a grand golden dragon standing majestically on his hind legs, 75 arms tall, dwarfing everyone else in the courtyard as he said in a commanding deep voice, shaking the ground as he said it, as if to awaken the Continent to what was about to happen, "Thaddeus. Step forward..."

The young Thaddeus stepped forward still a bit confused but he stood tall as Alotraxas said in that same voice, "Long ago, before the age of humans and elves came to pass on the Continent, the First Ancient of the Light, Trantoris, named his first Champion, Malkaran. Trantoris thought it wise to have a mortal personification of him on the Continent to give the peoples of the world an example to live by. In his travels across this land, Malkaran rooted out evil, and tirelessly worked, so that all people might benefit from his crusade against the evil forces that were ever-present during his time. It is from that first example that we, as Ancients of the Light, have chosen our own Champions, so that the mortals in this world can know that there are those who are willing to continue preserving the values of Trantoris, the first Ancient of the Light. Malkaran served for a hundred cycles and he lived Trantoris' values of Rectitude, Courage, Benevolence, Respect, Honesty, Wisdom, and Loyalty. As time passed, Trantoris named other Champions, it was the teachings of Malkaran that trained them all in holding those values in their minds and hearts and to continue to personify what it was to be a Champion.

In the finest traditions of the first Ancient of the Light, Trantoris, given your heroism, bravery and courage in the face of evil, I hereby name you, Thaddeus, a Champion of the Light. You now join the many thousands of mortals to be named as such who have but one duty throughout their lives: to root out evil wherever the winds take you, to vanquish it on its own terms, and to see that the Light never falters, that it will always burn brightly in the minds and the hearts of all mortals. Do you accept this honor and privilege that few have earned?"

The young Thaddeus, with Agham-Ix on his shoulder, said, "Aye, I accept!"

As he said that, one could see Alotraxas glowing brightly as he said, "Then in my duty as an Ancient of the Light, I now join with you. Behold, the new Champion of the Light!"

Alotraxas flew right into Thaddeus, glowing brightly as the young Thaddeus began to change; his green robe and hat were replaced by a sparkling white robe with gold trim, a white cloak and hat, a staff appeared in his hand and finally a white metallic circlet appeared on his head.

Alotraxas said, "May the Light always guide your path, Champion!"

Agham-Ix took the whole thing in stride, and though he was excited for Thaddeus, he did not appear to change at all, when a white crown appeared on his head as Alotraxas said, "My dear Agham-Ix, while I cannot change you because of your ability to resist even the strongest magicks, I can grant you this: a crown of the Light. Wear it proudly, my friend!"

A rush of knowledge entered Thaddeus' mind as the full knowledge of Alotraxas and his only other Champion, Toril, entered his mind. A rush of spells and legendary knowledge was written into his mind, combining the old magick of the Ancients with the new magick he had spent the better part of a cycle learning. Places entered his mind; the actual thoughts of Toril, his notes and discoveries were passed down to the young Thaddeus. The young Thaddeus also noted a new ring had been put on his right ring finger; it was made of gold (or so he thought), and it glowed brightly. Alotraxas said to him, "This is the Ring of Light, it serves two purposes: first, it defies the dark wherever it lies, and it identifies you as a Champion of the Light. Every past champion has had a ring like this. This one is uniquely yours and will remain on your finger always. From this sun forward, you are a Champion of the Light!"

The elder Thaddeus said to the young Thaddeus, "Now that ye're here, and ye've been named a Champion of the Light, know that the Entities of Evil can't come here, as long as ye're on the Continent. Should serve ta weaken 'em somewhat. They can't bring their full powers to bear on ye, and they can only work through intermediaries, so that's a good thing. But they know ye be here now…" He continued, "This here used ta be my house, built it myself, well, with some magickal help. But ye can use it as yer home base. No safer place on the Continent." Thaddeus had a thought as he said, "I wonder…"

The young Thaddeus said, "What do you wonder?"

The elder Thaddeus said, "Come with me," and took him to a door in his home, just off the main hall as he pointed to a grouping of colored stones on the floor, and he said, "Step on that red stone three times and then, the blue stone twice, finally, the green stone once."

The young Thaddeus did as he was instructed, and the door opened.

Thaddeus saw his extradimensional home, still intact and more importantly fully charged and ready as he said, "This here is my home away from home. Can take ye anywhere ye want ta go on the Continent; it's a cinch fer impressin' the ladies, too…hehe…probably need ta attune it fer ye first, and then ye can go anywhere ya want in style, and quickly too! My boy, this home and everythin' in it be yers now. Use it well, and I hope ye are as happy here as I was. And fear not, I've got a special connection to this home, so I can come ta ya, whenever ya need me. Goodbye fer now. See ya soon!"

Thaddeus disappeared, as did Alotraxas' spirit, leaving Thaddeus and Agham-Ix alone in the home as Kama's spirit appeared as she said, "Thought you could use some company, and I was a little bored without you up there. Ain't much for an elf ta do, and besides, you're not quite done with your training yet. Thaddeus said that this house is designed to allow for spirits to roam in it without harm, so how does it feel? Being a Champion of the Light and all?"

The young Thaddeus said, "It's so cool, and I got this ring! It lights up and everything! And check out Agham-Ix…He's got a cool crown on!"

Kama listened to him and knew how excited he was but had a heavy thought on her mind, and she wasn't sure that this was the right time to ask it, even though they were alone on the Continent at the moment. She looked nervous and apparently couldn't hide it that well as Thaddeus said, "What's the matter, Kama?"

She figured that she should ask her question; it was only fair to him and to her. She thought it would be better for her if she knew the answer now instead of later.

She said, "I feel so silly asking this, but I have to know..."

Thaddeus, who was still visibly excited, said, "Ask away!"

Kama said, "Do you like me?"

Thaddeus said, "Yeah...O' course I like you. You're the best!"

Kama continued, "Do ya think you could ever...love me?"

For the first time, Kama had stumped Thaddeus; his young mind, while loaded with all sorts of magickal knowledge, had no clue when it came to matters of the heart. Back home, he had a girl that he liked—Sandra was her name—and he thought that she liked him, and they kissed once, on a dare, on the cheek, but he never thought about love before...with a woman (Kama looked young, but in reality was 75, which for an elf was considered young). That's when Agham-Ix came to his rescue and said into his mind, "Tell her that you could love her in time and give her a hug and a kiss...that's all she really wants! Go for it, tiger!"

The young Thaddeus said, "Kama, I'm only nine...I've never thought about girls that way before. But I think in time, I could love you..."

Kama seemed very excited at his answer, smiled, and said, "That's okay... We've got time!" She hugged him and gave him a kiss...on the lips. He was unprepared for that, but enjoyed it nonetheless.

He thought to himself, *Wow...I've got magick, a dragon, a new house, and now a woman who could love him, even though he knew she was just a spirit...* He was positively giddy with excitement at all the possibilities as he sat down with Agham-Ix to relax. They fell asleep together, as it had been a long and exciting sun. Being a Champion of the Light was starting out to be an okay experience, but this was only the beginning of his adventure as he dreamt of the glories of times past, thanks to his connection to Toril.

While in his dreams, he saw himself fighting evil with spells just as he imagined himself doing when he was back home. He saw terrible monsters all slain at his feet, the blood of his enemies clinging to his face and hands, when he heard a conversation in progress apparently about him.

The voice said, "Look at what he dreams about...killing evil monsters, but there's more to it than just that...Will he be merciful? Will he uphold the teachings and traditions of Malkaran...? After all, there hasn't been a Champion of the Light in over 5,000 cycles...Who will teach him our ways?"

An unseen male voice rang out, "I will teach him. He is a Champion now and must know what it means."

He woke up suddenly, he noted Agham-Ix at his side as always. Over the last few suns, he had gotten used to the immovable object that Agham-Ix was (at least to him) but noted that he was always warm, which was wonderful because the house was unheated at the moment, and the young Thaddeus felt a chill in the air. It was dark in the home, and Thaddeus used his new ring to illuminate his path as he heard two male voices talking in the next room. He prepared a spell to immobilize them as he snuck up to the room, as he crept closer to the doorway, he saw a lone figure partially shrouded in darkness as he leapt forth and cast his spell, his ring illuminating the entire room.

The figure bowed to him saying, "Ah, the prodigal son is awake...good evening, Thaddeus...I am Toril, at your service. I have been asked by Alotraxas to instruct you in the ways of being a Champion and what is expected of you while you are a Champion of the Light."

Thaddeus asked in a suspicious tone as Agham-Ix entered the room and landed on Thaddeus' shoulder, "I heard two voices, maybe three...to whom were you speaking?"

Toril replied, "Ah, one of the things I wanted to speak to you about...you see, we, as Champions of the Light are part of a family, so to speak...we all have a connection to each other, in life and in death. The power that made us what we are, and made you a Champion, also connects you to all of us. As the last and only other Champion that Alotraxas named, it falls to me to instruct you in our ways. You might call them traditions, passed down from one Champion to another."

Toril continued, "Alotraxas knows your dreams and knows that you thirst to root out and destroy evil wherever it is. But being a Champion is so much more than that. It's a way of living and a way of doing that might seem...well, foreign to you. While defeating evil is certainly part of the job; a Champion always seeks to be an example for others to follow. He is selfless to a fault, making sure that others are taken care of before himself. After all, humans from times immemorial have looked to us as leaders, to guide them when all other lights had gone out. It is our duty to ensure that the people know that they have a leader who is pure and true, one who places their welfare ahead of his own. We do not desire fame or fortune, but rather the knowledge that through our actions that people are allowed to live lives free of evil, free from tyranny and free from oppression."

118

Toril continued, "Alotraxas has asked me to be your guide, so that you might learn from me what it is to be a Champion of the Light. Remember that you are the first Champion of the Light named in over 5,000 cycles. People need to know that you are truly a good leader and a good man. There will be those who would try to subvert you, but know that my knowledge and those who came before me are always with you, and we will make you no promises save one: that we will never steer you wrong and will always guide you to be a true Champion of the Light. Know that so long as you follow the path of the Champion, you will be fulfilling a promise made by the Ancients to all humanity a long time ago."

Thaddeus said, "So, I just have to be a good person…? That's not so hard. Been doing it all my life!"

Toril said, "Yes, you must be a good person, but you must also be a good leader; in short, you must be good at anything and everything you might be asked to do because as leaders, we are expected to make the right decision all the time. Fortunately for you, you have something that no one else on the Continent has: over 50,000 cycles of experience to guide you and protect you from every situation you could come across."

Thaddeus asked, "But I'm only nine, who is going to follow me? I'm only a kid, yes; I'm a kid with magick and a dragon, but I'm still a kid."

Toril said, "Ah, youth. What you don't understand is that there are those who have led entire civilizations over the cycles who were as young as you; as they have done it, so too will you. I see great things for you in the future, and I am honored that Alotraxas has allowed me to play some small part in your success. Know that it will not always be easy, and the right path will sometimes be difficult to know, but the rewards will be beyond measure. While you finish up your magickal training, I will begin training you in the ways of the Champion, so that when it is your time, you'll be ready!"

Thaddeus asked, "My time? Time for what?"

Toril replied with a certain knowing air, "When it is your time to show the Continent that the Ancients have not abandoned them, when it is your time to lead these people to rebuild the Continent, when it is your time to vanquish the Evil that has its sights set on this land…Know that you will be ready! Rest now. It's been a long sun. I'll see you soon."

Toril disappeared after that as Kama came into the room again, she looked happy as she said, "Ready for a little practice in casting your healing spells?"

Thaddeus said, "Aye, I thought you'd never ask!"

The two of them went into the still intact laboratory to practice healing magicks, and they spent the rest of the sun together. Thaddeus noted that Kama was trying to stay as close to him as possible, but he didn't mind as she was still her normal, playful self.

And he got to be a kid, for a little while longer.

Chapter 20

Evil Returns

While a new Champion was being crowned on the Continent, the Dread Lord was furious, and as 10 suns passed by, Bjor'ma appeared before him as he said very calmly, "You faltered in service to me...you deliberately thwarted Thanatos in a last desperate act...and for what? A few suns with your twice-dead mother? Typical mortal..."

The Dread Lord looked away from Bjor'ma and said while his hand fingered his perpetually flaming trident, "When you committed that brazen, but fruitless act, I will admit, I wanted to throw you into the Pit and let the tormentors have their way with you, but it is amazing the effect of a few suns on one's thoughts, isn't it? I now see that all is not lost. You're here now, for the next thousand cycles...what shall I do with you? Torment and torture, perhaps? Endless pain and suffering, perchance? Or perhaps the most pernicious punishment of all...making you wait...not knowing when the pain is coming, only knowing that it is...Or perhaps, a chance at redemption and living in comfort until you leave here..."

Bjor'ma said, "My Lord, I broke my contract and expect to be punished for doing it, it is nothing less than I deserve..."

The Dread Lord said, "Yes, you do deserve to be punished...but how? Has to be something creative, something new and different, and something befitting your station as the lowest of the low...ah, I know...serving me as... this!"

In an instant, Bjor'ma was transmuted into something else, a three-arm tall, pinkish hued blob with eyes.

These creatures occupied the lowest rung on the demonic ladder and were called Gorpin. They could move slowly, see and think, but more importantly, they were practically indestructible, but could feel everything that happened to them. Demon Lords typically used them to blow off steam when something aggravated them, which was often. But it should be noted that most Gorpin were red, but Bjor'ma was pink, as if the Dread Lord wanted to punish him even further by making him distinguishable amidst the millions of Gorpin.

The Dread Lord said, "Now, Bjor'ma, you are a Gorpin, to even look at you in this state brings me some satisfaction…you will remain like this until Thanatos decides what to do with you. But until then, stay there!"

As he said that, the Dread Lord's fiery trident penetrated him causing him more pain than he had ever experienced in his life. Now unable to move, and feeling the searing heat coming from the trident, he wanted to scream, but Gorpin have no mouths and can only suffer in silence as he could see smoke rising up from his new form. He could only imagine what it smelled like. He thought of his mother as he dealt with the pain.

Bjor'ma stayed there for what seemed like an eternity, but he had no way of knowing how much time had passed. The heat from the trident died down after a while, but every so often a being would come along and stab him with a blade or kick him. He felt everything that happened to him, and he thought that this was better than being endlessly whipped, or having your skin removed, so he put up with it as he kept his mother in his mind. Knowing that he would see her again helped him deal with what was happening to him, but he wasn't sure how long the thought of her would help him, after all, he knew he wasn't here all that long as of right now, but he hoped that Thanatos would allow him to continue to help him on the mission he was created for, and he could be in a form that was more useful than this.

Thanatos finally recovered from his ordeal after a few more suns and his energy tendril was removed, as it was no longer needed. The Dread Lord called his faithful servant to him and said, "Thanatos…you know what to do, and you have the magick to do so, now that Bjor'ma is no longer feeding from you, you should be able to bring magick to the battle and win. Know that I do not expect you to do this alone. What do you choose to do with this?"

As he said that, the Dread Lord kicked a pink hued blob at Thanatos, who was confused at first as he said, "My Lord, what is this thing? Why is its fate in my hands?"

The Dread Lord said, "This is Bjor'ma, the traitor to our cause, serving his time with us...Can you use a faithful servant? Perhaps someone to assist you in your conquest of the Continent? I assure you, he will not betray you again...But his fate rests with you. Either take him with you and use him well, or leave him here. It's your choice. Before you make your decision, know this: a Champion of the Light has been named on the Continent. He will try to stop you. Allow him to thwart you for now, as I need to understand him and what he can do. What say you? What is his fate?"

Thanatos thought for a moment and said, "I could use him. He had his uses. But since we will have no army to build, what can he do? But first I think, a little revenge is in order..." Thanatos cast a lightning bolt right at Bjor'ma, and it had no effect, but Bjor'ma thought he would pass out from the pain of being electrocuted...then he was set on fire, then frozen solid, finally bashed with a massive hammer causing huge cracks to appear in him. Bjor'ma had never felt anything like this, but had no outlet to vent his pain; maybe that was part of the torment, he thought. It was like he was going to fall to pieces, but he didn't. Not yet.

The Dread Lord had no reaction to this treatment other than a smile and said, "What do you wish him to do? He can be changed into whatever you need. Speak it, and it will be."

Thanatos thought about it and said, "A changeling. A creature whose form I can change based on the situation."

The Dread Lord thought for a moment and said, "So be it...I grant you the power to change his form. Know that I will also grant you the power to speak of any abilities you want him to have; essentially, he is a blank canvas, waiting for an artist. Feeling creative?"

A long, full and hearty belly laugh escaped from the Dread Lord as he stabbed Bjor'ma with his flaming trident once again as he said, "Come, Thanatos, there is much to discuss that he does not need to hear. My trident will keep him out of trouble whilst we plan..."

The two beings left the Great Hall leaving Bjor'ma skewered by a giant, flaming iron trident, again.

The Dread Lord and Thanatos went into a smaller room as a map of the Continent appeared on the large black table in this room as the Dread Lord said, "You will start your invasion here," pointing at the Far North and Deep North. He continued, "The Barbarians cannot counter your magick and are very susceptible to it as you discovered, and though they have shamans, their magickal ability pales in comparison to yours, but don't be foolish with your resources: remember you have time on your side, as there is no time limit to accomplish this mighty task. If the new Champion appears, retreat and then press on with your attacks somewhere else. When he appears, run away. He will start to think that he is invincible and can defeat you easily, and THAT is how he can be beaten, by using his confidence against him. Once he is eliminated, the whole of the Continent is yours for the taking."

The Dread Lord continued, "Then the Narsum. Blast them with everything you've got, including their dragon allies, as the Narsum cannot counter your magick, but know that they can summon things through their shamans, so be careful. Also, remember that dragons are mortal and CAN die, use that to your advantage as you hunt them. This will take some time, as the accursed mountain people are spread out and will be hiding in and around the mountains. If the Champion still lives, give him more of a fight each time you meet him in combat, but still run away. By then, I will have an idea of his capabilities, and I will guide you as to how best to defeat him."

As he pointed to the South, he said, "Finally, the elves…by far the toughest fight you will face, but you will be ready, having taken out most of the life on the Continent at this time. Should the Champion still live, he will likely be with them. You'll need to have your wits about you for that battle, but it might be wise to go in with a skirmishing mentality. Wear them down over time, whittle away at their abilities slowly, and when you feel the time is right, go in with all the magick you can deliver and wipe them out in one masterful stroke. Once your task is complete, and all life of the Continent is gone, you will receive your reward for your hard work."

The Dread Lord said, "I trust in you, Thanatos, that you will deliver where Bjor'ma and Boral failed. You have the knowledge of warfare as part of you, and I have confidence that you will be able to make correct decisions on the field of battle. Battlefields change quickly. See to it that you are ahead of the curve and that you are prepared for anything. Remember that you can always run away and try again later. No one will think you a coward for executing a strategic withdrawal from a fight, so long as you return to that fight and win!"

Thanatos said, "It will be as you say; I will win, and the Continent will be yours, my Lord!"

The Dread Lord said, "As it should be. Now, prepare yourself and your servant, and begin the onslaught as you are ready."

Thanatos bowed low and said, "Yes, my Lord!"

Thanatos left the room and began to contemplate what he wanted Bjor'ma, now his faithful servant, to do along with what powers he should have to complement his magick; then it came to him. He decided to turn Bjor'ma into his personal shield against any and all attacks he might face on the field of battle with his newfound Gorpin abilities. As a Gorpin, Thanatos knew that Bjor'ma was impervious to just about anything and would protect him in case something attacked him. All that was needed was a change in form and color, as Thanatos was concerned that his current pink color did not project the right image for him as a bringer of death.

The Dread Lord was also a bit concerned with the recent naming of a Champion of the Light. He knew that this boded poorly for him, and he feared that Thanatos would not be able to win, but he had no choice now as he nor his brothers could set foot on the Continent, he had to trust that Thanatos possessed the intelligence and ability to win the Continent for him. He thought that he was sending Thanatos to his doom as he knew that Champions of the Light were tough, so strengthened by their affiliation with the Ancients. What he did not know was that his latest foe was a child, and that child was able to stop Thanatos dead in his tracks on two occasions.

After what seemed to be an eternity with a now perpetually flaming iron trident skewering him causing him unbearable pain, Bjor'ma saw Thanatos walking towards him, and he thought to himself, "This can't be good…" as he readied himself for more intense pain, though he was unsure how Thanatos would manage it.

To his surprise, Thanatos removed the trident from Bjor'ma's pink hued body and said, "You will serve me as my shield, taking the brunt of any and all attacks that might be directed at me while on the field of battle. I now transmute you into the shape of a large round shield, and I am changing your color to black. You will gain no abilities other than your current ability to take just about anything thrown at you. This is how you will serve me. Once the Continent is devoid of life and my task complete, I will give you back to the Dread Lord, for whatever further punishment he chooses to subject you to."

It was as Thanatos said; Bjor'ma assumed the shape of a large round shield, and he was now black in color. He was relieved that he wasn't being skewered anymore, and he hoped it would be a few suns before he had to endure more pain. He could still see as his eyes were on the front of the shield as he latched onto Thanatos' arm. Bjor'ma thought that at best, he might be in one battle a sun where they would face any resistance and most of the time, he would just travel with Thanatos as part of his armor, so he thought for as long as this conquest would take, his life wouldn't be so bad.

After a few more suns getting ready and preparing himself with dark rituals, Thanatos was as prepared as he could be for the battles ahead, though there was one huge question mark in his mind based on his previous dealings with the small, green wizard who he fought on two occasions and lost. He wondered if that wizard was the new Champion, and if so, how could he win against that foe that he knew was superior to him. Though he knew that no one could injure him, thanks to his new shield, he was concerned because he couldn't seem to affect the wizard, and with the protection that the green wizard provided, how was he expected to win a battle now that he wasn't trying to gain an army? Thanatos knew that in battle it was impossible to know everything, and he knew that he would have to use his cunning and his magick against any foe that presented itself.

CHAPTER 21

GOOD 1, EVIL 0

Thanatos decided to attack a remote village in the Deep North as these people had not been affected by his first attempt at conquest and thought that they would be an easy target for his high-powered magicks. He appeared suddenly on one frosty Samhein morning on the outskirts of a Deep North village of about 500 people. He walked for a bit to survey where he was; he was on a high bluff, overlooking this idyllic village as he started the onslaught anew, casting devastating magicks against the population of this place. Several leagues away, as luck would have it, Thaddeus was holding the Eyes of the King and "spotted" him, and as he zeroed in on the location, he teleported himself there. Upon arriving, he noted the black figure of Thanatos in front of him about 50 arms away casting a spell, when he said, "Thanatos, you will not harm these people. They are under my protection!"

Thanatos turned to face the voice that spoke and saw Thaddeus, but not dressed in green. He was now in white, carrying a white staff with a glowing white tip. It was as he feared, that the one person who was able to thwart him twice was a Champion of the Light, and he appeared to have a creature with him, sitting on his shoulder, a large lizard of some kind. Thanatos noted that he looked as a human child and not a full-grown adult. He could only surmise how he got elevated like this as he said, "My masters claim this place. Prepare to be annihilated!"

Thanatos had chosen to ignore what the Dread Lord told him. He wanted to see this boy dead, as his anger at being thwarted twice had gotten the better of him.

He cast a magickal flaming arrow at Thaddeus, and it bounced off his very hard skin as Thaddeus said, "You'll have to do better than that!"

Agham-Ix cast a spell that Thaddeus had never seen, and what Thanatos saw amazed him. The very stones in the village started moving towards him, larger ones moved slowly, while smaller ones were being flung at his head. Despite having a shield, he was struck by some smaller stones a few times as the larger stones moved inexorably to crush him.

Thaddeus, who was surprised at this turn of events, said with a laugh, "Ha! It appears that this village can defend itself. Leave now and live or be crushed under stone…your choice!"

As smaller stones hit Thanatos' shield, he noted a large boulder within three arms of him moving slowly towards him. He cast a lightning bolt spell, and while he succeeded in breaking it apart, that strategy backfired as the now smaller stones peppered him with their sharp edges, cutting him in many places while several more large boulders and smaller stones continued their assault on him. Thanatos was getting angrier by the moment as the stones continued to pelt him; some hit his shield, but others did not as he was being attacked on all sides by flying rocks.

Thaddeus could see rivulets of a bluish fluid on Thanatos' body, as he cast an area effect spell, called Chill the Bones. It reduced the temperature in a small area by the equivalent of 100C, making it deadly for most life, but Thaddeus knew that it would not affect the stones moving towards Thanatos. As the temperature dropped, cracks could be seen developing in Thanatos' shield, especially where the stones had struck it. The extreme cold rendered him almost still, but thanks to his status of being a demon, he could still move, albeit slowly.

Thaddeus then encapsulated the area with a shield that would allow things from outside the shield in, but would not let whatever was inside the shield out so that it would concentrate the cold, making it tougher for Thanatos to fight the effects as he slowed further. A large airborne stone just missed his head, but struck his shield as it shattered into several pieces due to the cold, which is a feeling that Bjor'ma had never experienced before and never wanted to again.

Seeing his shield in pieces on the ground, Thanatos saw Agham-Ix raising a claw in the air as a four-arm boulder came screaming at him, striking him in the legs and knocking him down. As the extreme cold continued, Thanatos was slow to rise and found that he could barely move. He knew that this battle was lost and that he could not continue and that he should heed the Dread Lord's advice and leave here before it was too late and Thaddeus finished him off.

He tried to cast a spell to escape and found that he could not, as his hands were frozen in position. He tried to move but could not as the temperature dipped further. Now frozen in place, Thanatos saw a massive boulder, the size of 100 man-stones approach him. It inched closer to him, and Thaddeus could see that it was preparing to crush the now frozen Thanatos. It rose up and rolled on Thanatos, crushing his legs and finally rolling to finish the job, completely flattening him.

As he heard the boulder crushing Thanatos, seeing an explosion of bluish fluid hit the shield, Thaddeus pumped his fist and said, "Yes! Take that, evildoer!"

Thaddeus canceled the spells he had cast and thanked the Snow Queen, along with Agham-Ix and the Earth for giving him the powers to defeat evil. He also said an Elven blessing to the earth in thanks for all the help he received. Upon inspecting the area along with Agham-Ix commanding the stone to move, he did not see Thanatos, but saw a strange sight: pieces of his shattered shield were moving! He pointed his staff at the pieces as they started to come together but did nothing to them, waiting to see what was going to happen. The weirdest part of all was when he noted that they were a light pink on the inside, except for the outer shell which was black. Thaddeus marveled at what he was looking at, but eventually the creature congealed itself together and resembled a pink-hued blob with bits of a hard, black shell sticking out from various places. Thaddeus noted that whatever it was had eyes and was looking at him. He thought that Thanatos had slunk back from the dark places he came from but left this creature behind.

At this point, the villagers started to come out to see what had happened and noted a young boy dressed in white, along with a Stone Dragon and a pink hued blob next to him. They noted that there was only minor damage to the village and that no one was seriously hurt. As they approached Thaddeus, they recognized the cave bear tooth necklace he had on, along with his large snowflake amulet. They recognized both as symbols of someone very important to the tribe but did not know who he was. A villager approached him, wearing the accoutrements of a warrior, and said, "Hail, stranger."

Thaddeus said, "Hail to you. I am Thaddeus, a Champion of the Light and friend of those in the North. This village came under attack, and I have thwarted the evil that tried to destroy all you have built and all of you."

The villager smiled and said, "So you have…what is that thing by your feet?"

Thaddeus looked at the pink blob as it looked back at him and said, "I don't know what it is, but the evil creature had this creature with him. Whatever it is, it looks harmless, but fear not, for I have it under a close watch."

The villager said, "We thank you for your timely intervention, honored one."

Thaddeus beamed and said, "It was my pleasure. Is there anyone injured among you?"

The shaman said, "A few minor injuries, well within our ability to heal. You've done enough for us, honored one…may the Snow Queen bless you for what you have done this sun! Thank you, and fare thee well!"

Thaddeus looked intently at the blob as he said to Agham-Ix in his mind, "Do you know what this is?" pointing at the creature. Agham-Ix had no idea either, but suggested that they take it back to their home for further study. Thaddeus said, "It might be evil. And I wouldn't want it in our home, but leaving it out here doesn't seem right either. Mayhaps we take it back and leave it in the courtyard? It's magickally protected, so it can't harm us in case it is more than what it seems. Let's take the pieces of black shell out of it though. That doesn't look comfortable."

Thaddeus started pulling the pieces of hard black shell out of the pink blob. It had the consistency of marshmallow, but wasn't sticky as he gently pulled the pieces out. Thaddeus noted that it didn't bleed nor did it move away from him as he pulled the black shards out. Bjor'ma was shaken up by the events of what just happened but experienced something that he had not had in a long time, a gentle touch by caring hands that were trying to help him and make him feel comfortable. After removing the black shell bits he could see, Thaddeus went to pick up the blob and found that it was light, but bulky, as he willed himself to the courtyard at his home and deposited the creature there, in hopes of finding out what it was and why it was here.

Bjor'ma saw he was in a courtyard. It was very large and flat, surrounded by structures on all sides, as he noted Thaddeus constructing a makeshift tent for him. Bjor'ma felt happy that he wasn't going to be tortured, kicked, stabbed, skewered, or burnt—at least for a little while—and would be able to rest here in relative comfort.

130

Meanwhile, Thanatos reappeared in the Great Hall of the Dead with the Dread Lord looking right at him angrily as he said calmly, "What is wrong with you? I sent you to do a job, and you come back looking like this a few tolls later? Did I not tell you to run away at the first sign of resistance, magickal or otherwise? Your only saving grace is that you are demonic in nature, and while stones can crush you, they cannot kill you…BUT A CHAMPION OF THE LIGHT CAN! You need to listen when I speak to you because the next time…well, there won't be a next time. You can just lay there and rot as I will not waste further time with you. Is that understood? And where is Bjor'ma?"

Thanatos said, "I admit my mistake, and I was wrong. The boy who thwarted me twice has done it once again, and he has the power of earth on his side. Bjor'ma was frozen and shattered by the boy's attacks. I don't know what became of him after I was defeated."

The Dread Lord said, "Bjor'ma is the least of our worries right now. Take some time and recover yourself, and I hope this serves as a lesson to you. Remember you are alone, act accordingly, and do not let anger get the better of you again!"

Thanatos said, "Yes, my Lord," as he slinked away with the Dread Lord shaking his head in disgust.

Thanatos went back to his chamber to regenerate himself, which he knew would take several suns to accomplish, and in the meanwhile wondered how he was found so quickly, and dealt with so easily. He wondered how Thaddeus could have just shrugged off one of his more powerful spells. He also wondered how a boy like that could have gotten so powerful. He thought long and hard about what to do next as he laid in the regeneration chamber.

CHAPTER 22

A BREAKTHROUGH

Back on the Continent, Thaddeus and Agham-Ix studied their new arrival, which seemed to move about slowly, and while it did give off a slightly evil aura, it didn't do anything to them while they studied it for three tolls. In that time, Thaddeus sketched the creature and wrote detailed notes about it, along with his description of it coming together after being shattered. He noted that it didn't eat or drink, nor did it make any noise to speak of. It had no means of communication but appeared to have some intelligence as it seemed to move on its own. Then he had a thought, what if he could use the creatures' eyes to his advantage, perhaps enabling some form of rudimentary communication? All he would need, he reasoned, was a common language between him and the creature. He decided to try, and as he started towards the creature, it moved towards him. As he said in Manton, which was the tongue of most of the humans on the Continent, "Can you understand me? Blink your eyes once if you understand what I'm saying to you…"

The creature blinked its eyes once.

Thaddeus seemed overjoyed and said, "Agham-Ix, did you see that? This creature understood me. It can communicate! I need to put this in my notes— this is SO huge! I can't believe it! I might be the first person to ever talk to a blob!" Thaddeus said, "Okay…you understand Manton, yes?"

The creature blinked its eyes once.

Thaddeus had an idea from his time in our world. He remembered the magnetic letters that his father used to teach him words and phrases, so he decided to use an idea like that to talk to the creature. He drew all 28 letters of the Manton alphabet on the ground and then said, "Okay…this is the Manton alphabet, and how you and I are going to talk. I will ask a question, and then I will point to each letter. When I get to the first letter in your answer, blink your eyes once, and we can repeat it for the next letter and so on. Do you understand?"

The creature blinked its eyes once.

Thaddeus first asked, "Do you have a name?"

Thaddeus moved his staff slowly over each letter, and the creature blinked its eyes once when his staff hit the letter B. Then J, then O, then R, then M, then A. His answer complete, Thaddeus ran through the alphabet again, but the creature's eyes didn't blink as he spelled the word and was dumbfounded as he said, "You're Bjor'ma…? I heard a LOT about you from Thaddeus. How did you get like this?"

Even Agham-Ix was surprised at this revelation and Thaddeus' brilliant adaptation of a simple thing in his world that is proving valuable here as he was speaking to a creature that no human had ever spoken with, let alone seen before.

The creature spelled out, "DREADLORD" in answer to Thaddeus' second question.

Thaddeus said, "Well, you're safe now from him as he cannot come to this place as long as I'm on the Continent."

The creature blinked its eyes once and looked down at the letters that Thaddeus drew. Thaddeus took this to mean that he had something to say and started to move his staff over the letters and the creature spelled out, "THANKYOU."

Thaddeus said, "You're welcome, Bjor'ma…" He looked over at Agham-Ix and said, "Let's get some lunch…I'm starving!"

As they walked out of the courtyard. Bjor'ma was happy because he knew that each sun he spent here meant one less sun he would spend down below being tortured.

Throughout the rest of the sun, Thaddeus, Agham-Ix, and Kama all studied the creature, which was just moving about on its own slowly, on this warm sun. It did not make any sudden moves and seemed to like being under the tent that Thaddeus had created, instead of being out in the two suns.

Kama said, "That's Bjor'ma…that's the Wizard that the elder Thaddeus always talked about…? How did he get like that?"

Thaddeus replied, "He said the Dread Lord somehow made him into that. I don't know how though…but he seems happy here. He even thanked me for bringing him here. I hope he doesn't turn into anything weird tonight, but I'll keep a close eye on him, and I'll be ready."

Kama replied, "Tell me about the battle you fought this sun."

Thaddeus described to her what he saw and what he did along with what Agham-Ix did to contribute to crushing Thanatos. Though she didn't care for the gory parts of the battle (though Thaddeus really liked those parts), she liked hearing how excited Thaddeus was at using magick, especially elemental magicks. She noticed that he took a particular liking to cold, as he liked that it stopped things from moving rather quickly, which made it easier to strike them with elements of the Earth, like stones and such. Kama chalked up his new found abilities with cold spells to being in the Snow Queen's domain and being favored by her, and she attributed that since Agham-Ix was a Stone Dragon, it was probable that his kind had an affinity for earth spells, especially those dealing with stone. Kama was right in her reasoning why his cold and earth spells were so strong, and she would later see that this combination of effects would be one of his favorites to use in battles and would become one of his signature effects in time. Though not as flashy as what his elder name-sake would have done, they were startlingly effective.

She liked that he asked the tribesman if they needed any healing and surmised that his asking that question was because of her influence on his magickal training. She sat enraptured by his story for a toll, all the while smiling at him, thinking of all the adventures that he would have and how wonderful it would be if he came home to her, thrilling her with tales of his adventures. She wondered if he was true to his word and that he could love her at some point. Though she was a spirit, she had a corporeal form, but she wondered if that was good enough. She thought it would be, and they sat, talked and studied together for the remainder of the afternoon.

As the second sun set in the sky that sun, the first moon rose, and Thaddeus checked in on the pink blob that he left to slither around in the courtyard. He noted that it was still a pink blob and that it was stationary under the tent that Thaddeus had made for him, its eyes closed, seemingly at peace. Bjor'ma was thankful for the fact that he was able to rest his mind for the first time in several suns, instead of being in constant pain, or constantly worrying about being kicked or stabbed. He knew that Thaddeus wouldn't do any of that to

135

him and would likely just let him stay in this courtyard, hopefully for a long time. He had heard Thaddeus talking about his victory over Thanatos, and Bjor'ma celebrated in his mind as he dreamed about being with his mother again. He hoped that the Dread Lord would forget about him, as he knew he was just a small issue compared to the Dread Lord's other problems in conquering the Continent.

Thaddeus kept a close watch on his new pink friend. He did not move for tolls on end, when Agham-Ix said into his mind, "Are you going to sleep, Thaddeus?"

Thaddeus replied, "Yes, the creature isn't moving, and he's not turning into some horrific demonic monster. Maybe tomorrow I can do a little more research on him in the library here to figure out if I can help him. Truth be told, he's kinda boring to watch at the moment. I'll be right there."

Thaddeus went into the room he picked as his own, tucked deep within the home for maximum protection from anything. This particular room was sunken into the earth and had the capability of being totally walled off from the remainder of the home, a feature that Thaddeus himself designed to protect him and his wife in case of trouble. Agham-Ix was already asleep on the special bed that the elder Thaddeus designed for him. It was made entirely of stone, perfectly smooth and flat and at seven arms long and three arms wide with a magickal radiant heat source, it was as close to perfect for a stone dragon as he could get. This was coupled with a regular mattress for Thaddeus, so the two of them could sleep in close proximity to each other.

The next morning came, Thaddeus and Agham-Ix awoke and checked in on Bjor'ma, and he was still a pink blob moving around the courtyard, as it was overcast this sun and it was expected to rain later. He decided to spend this sun finding out more about what Bjor'ma had become. He decided that he would have the Eyes of the King close at hand from now on, as it was only by sheer happenstance that he happened to have his hand on the scepter during the time of the attack the sun afore. He held it and sensed nothing anywhere on the Continent, so he started his research.

He pored over ancient texts in the home's library which was filled with all manner of magickal knowledge thanks to the elder Thaddeus who made it a point to collect these tomes whenever the opportunity presented itself. After a few tolls of research, he found out that the name of the creature in his courtyard was a Gorpin, they were firmly on the lowest strata that demonic creatures exist on. These creatures, of which there were millions, were primarily used by higher demons for sport, or to take their frustrations out on, or even to eat. He found out that they were intelligent, and could feel everything that was done to them, and were, by and large, indestructible, as Thaddeus had seen him frozen, shattered and then amazingly reformed himself. He found out that they could not speak, they never ate or drank, and their whole purpose was to entertain higher level demons.

He didn't know how or why Bjor'ma ended up like this, and he wasn't sure there was anything that he could do for Bjor'ma as he did not have any magickal knowledge about transfiguration, but then again, neither did the elder Thaddeus or Kama. It was something that was not taught to him, but he thought that there must be someone who knows about this esoteric field of study; after all, if a demon could do it, why not him? He contacted the elder Thaddeus, and asked him the question.

The elder Thaddeus said, "Transfiguration, eh? Not too many spells dealin' with that. I know a few, but never taught them to anyone as there didn't seem ta be a need fer it. Ta be honest, all the knowledge I have on the subject came from Sairys. He's an expert at it; after all, ye've seen him in his natural state. I'll write the spell fer ye, and if'n ye can help him, then I say do it."

The young Thaddeus seemed happy with the answer he received and thought that in a few suns, he would be able to transfigure him into a more natural state, preferably in a form that could communicate.

He decided to grab up the Eyes of the King again and sensed nothing from it, so he prepared some breakfast for himself and Agham-Ix. After eating, he and Agham-Ix decided it would be a good sun to explore his new home as he really hadn't done that. He was curious what other rooms there were in this place. He found that the home was really big, designed for a lot of people to live here, as the home had 12 bedrooms and an equal number of bathrooms, along with a massive kitchen, great hall and several other rooms with fireplaces, most of which were magically activated. On top of all that, there were the research facilities and a library. It appeared that Thaddeus even had a private wing with a grand study and a fully stocked larder of magickal ingredients along with a collection of pipes of all shapes and sizes.

Outside in the courtyard, Bjor'ma was exploring the finer points of getting wet, as it was raining outside. Thaddeus noted that he didn't seem to mind the water as he continued to move around in the courtyard. Unbeknownst to Thaddeus, Bjor'ma was reveling in the knowledge that he had nothing to fear in this place, and for the first time in this state, he felt truly at peace.

CHAPTER 23

A NEW PLAN

Several suns passed by, and the young Thaddeus walked out into the court-yard to see Bjor'ma. He was still a pink blob, moving around the courtyard slowly.

He said to Bjor'ma, "I've got a spell here that should be able to transfigure you into a more natural state, preferably one that can communicate and will have you walking around, so here goes!" He spoke the spell and flung a silvery powder at Bjor'ma...

The pink blob remained unchanged. He couldn't believe it; it was the first time a spell he cast had no effect, but then he remembered something he read about Gorpin. They were indestructible and impervious to just about anything, including magick, it seemed.

He sighed and said, "Well, I tried. We will have to see what else we can try because I want to help you. Also, why don't you come into the house with us? I think you've proven that you're not dangerous to anyone. At least you'll be warmer in there."

Bjor'ma was overcome with gratitude, but had no way of effectively com-municating that to Thaddeus. He couldn't believe that someone was actually being kind to him, which he wasn't used to at all.

Bjor'ma slithered into the home and started looking around. He had seen opulence like this when he served King Noran, but not since then as Thaddeus said, "Bjor'ma, I welcome you to my home. I hope you'll be com-fortable here. You must be so bored though. I know I would be. Let me take you into the library and get you set up with a book, so at least you can have something to occupy your mind. I'll set up a white glove spell to turn the pages for you."

Bjor'ma felt himself being carried to the library and set down onto a carpeted floor, which was heated. Thaddeus set up a historical tome for Bjor'ma to read on the floor, and he cast a white glove spell, which would respond to Bjor'ma's eyes.

Thaddeus said, "All you have to do is to look up at the white gloves, and they will turn the page for you. Happy reading!"

Bjor'ma hadn't read a book in ages. It felt good knowing that he could expand his mind once again. Bjor'ma noted that Thaddeus picked a book entitled, *A Compleat History of the Elves*. He dived right in and started reading.

Around this time, in another place, Thanatos' regeneration chamber opened up and he awoke, fully reformed. He had thought long and hard about what to do to carry out the Dread Lord's orders. He knew that having a huge army of troops wasn't going to help him, as it seemed that the Continent would fight him along with Thaddeus, and that casting magicks alone wouldn't do it as he would be found too quickly, but he still wasn't sure how he was found out.

So, he decided to use something that he thought would be more effective, as it didn't require expending large amounts of energy on the Continent itself. Realizing that he was attacking mortals, he thought that he should use something that was slower to work, but offered the ability for him to be stealthier about conquering all life on the Continent. He thought about using insects, plagues, and disease to do his work for him, and for that, he needed the Lord of Blight.

The Lord of Blight had his own distinct section of the place where Thanatos was created and where the Entities of Evil lived. Plants and animals abound, but all were either dead and rotting, or just rotting, shriveled, and misshapen. Even the Gorpin here did not look quite right, as if parts of them were actually rotting. The stench was enough to make even the hardiest demon run for cover, but Thanatos marched in bravely and was stopped in his tracks by the smell and gases rising up from rotting plants and animals. The stench that assaulted his nose was powerful, and he had a hard time breathing, as he was almost overcome on several occasions by the gaseous emanations of what he was stepping on. The grotesqueness of this place was awe-inspiring to Thanatos who realized that as repulsed as he was at all this, he could only imagine if what he was witnessing here took over the Continent. The humans and elves would be dead in no time, and he would return victorious.

The Lord of Blight himself appeared as a rotting bipedal humanoid creature, tall and gaunt, with glowing green eyes. His skeletal face and rotting putrescence made him a foe to be reckoned with as he said in a gravelly whisper, "Welcome, Thanatos...I've been expecting you. What can I, the Lord of Blight, do for the Dread Lord's favored one?"

Thanatos said after recovering from the stench emanating from the Lord of Blight, "I came here looking for a new strategy to use against the beings on the Continent to fulfill the mission the Dread Lord has tasked me with. Massive amounts of troops have not worked, nor has the use of powerful magicks. I was hoping that you might have an alternative idea."

The Lord of Blight said, "Ah...yes. You wish to be more effective against the mortals on the Continent...mayhaps that is something that we can arrange. You wish to be a bringer of rot, pestilence, and disease? Mmmmm...I like the sound of that, along with the wails of sadness as the mortals on the surface wither and die. Know this though, your demonic nature will not protect you from the powers that I can give you. If you accept them, you will eventually rot and die. What say you?"

Thanatos asked, "How long would it take for these powers to affect me?"

The Lord of Blight replied, "For most, a few moments. For you, a season, maybe two at most. You will be slow and travel will be difficult for you, but you will be able to go anywhere on the Continent, leaving behind a trail of death for all living things. Anything you touch will be blighted. I will give you the power to extend your reach with these..." Thanatos saw two vine-like appendages come out of the Lord of Blight's shoulders; they were long and fast, perfect for extending his reach.

Thanatos asked, "What about resistance to magick? Can you give me that?"

The Lord of Blight said, "No, my rot only affects living things. You will gain no resistance to magick by taking on these powers."

Thanatos thought and said, "Would these powers still be effective at half-strength? I think that a cycle would be enough to accomplish what the Dread Lord has asked me to do..."

The Lord of Blight said, "Aye, they would, but you would be less effective as an agent of death, but even at half-strength they would be somewhat effective and you could bring your other powers to bear as well. Are you prepared to receive these powers at half-strength?"

Thanatos said, "Aye. I am prepared."

Just as he finished saying it, a hole opened up under his feet and Thanatos fell into a pit of black vileness whose ingredients are too grotesque to mention. He plopped into the mixture and remained submerged in the stinking semi-fluid for several moments before being pulled out by the Lord of Blight as he said, "There, you have been consecrated in the black foulness of the Pit of Desecration...once the mixture dries on you, the process will be complete, and you will be ready."

Thanatos looked and smelled revolting; he couldn't even stand it himself as he was covered with a black goop that seemed to stick to him, that permeated his very skin, which contained substances that he did not want to know about. He could feel the rot in him already, changing him, making him better (or so he thought)...Soon he would be on the surface, wreaking terrible destruction upon every living thing.

A few suns passed, and the mixture on Thanatos finally seemed dry. He didn't feel quite himself as he willed himself to the surface of the Continent near a Narsum village. He decided to try to attack the Narsum first as he thought that they would be easier targets, just as Boral and Bjor'ma did. It was bright and sunny, and he could hear the sounds of Narsum young playing near him. He crested a hill and felt the grass with his hands, and it promptly died. He noted that where he had stepped, the ground plants had died, leaving behind bare soil. He squatted down, put his hands on the ground, and the plants in an ever-widening area were dying quickly, he also set forth a plague of ground insects which were common to the area, but what was a pest to the Narsum before, was now a real problem as Thanatos multiplied them by 10,000 and set them loose on this simple village.

The children playing saw what was coming and ran away as the rot continued and more plants were dying. The dead plants stopped at the village border, but the insects trucked right into the village, causing mayhem within the village as the villagers saw the black form of Thanatos coming towards them. The villagers packed up quickly and left just as fast, but some older people, who were unable to move quickly were swallowed up by the insect plague, leaving behind a bare skeleton within a few moments. The voracious insects started eating the crops that were growing as the villagers responded with their usual defense, fire. They burned their own crops and the insects along with them because they knew they could not save their crops after this many insects had infested them. As the Narsum warriors came after Thanatos, who wisely left before the warriors could figure out where he went but not before releasing a disease in the air, the Narsum breathed it in. It had no effect at first, but unless cured, within a sun, they would be dead, racked with constant pain with huge growths appearing on their bodies as the disease finished its gruesome work. The growths served to spread the disease further, because shortly after the creature died, the growths would break open, releasing tainted blood on the ground and spores into the air, starting the cycle anew. Thanatos cast no spells the entire time, simply allowing his abilities to do their work.

Thanatos was pleased with his work; he killed 12 and infected 40 with disease, and he hoped the disease would spread to all Narsum. Unfortunately for Thanatos, like Boral and Bjor'ma before him, he knew nothing of Narsum ways, and he did not know just how advanced their healers were. The warriors knew there was something wrong with them very quickly and went to the village healer, who, thanks to thousands of cycles of lore and knowledge, was able to cure the disease in them before it progressed too far. The village healer, who was attuned to most happenings on the Continent, knew that this plague was not natural and warned other healers about it, thanks to their trained hawks. As word spread about this new plague amongst the Narsum, Thanatos decided to try his luck in another village. He noted lots of birds flying about and payed it no mind, as this was a common sight here in the foothills, but little did he know that flying over his head was a superhighway of information exchange between villages, which could prove to be his downfall.

After a few tolls of travel, Thanatos was met by a patrol of Narsum warriors riding massive Steppe Horses. There were 15 of them, armed to the teeth with dual broadswords, and the rightfully feared Narsum Bow. The Steppe Horses got a little nervous as Thanatos was thoroughly evil, and it was here that Thanatos decided to let loose another insect plague. He put his arms out and thousands of insects started flying towards the Narsum. They went everywhere, stinging the warriors and their horses alike. Fortunately for the warriors, steppe horses are extremely intelligent and knew to get out of there in a hurry, but Thanatos finished them off with a fast-moving ball of

fire, incinerating the warriors and their horses. He knew that such an osten-
tatious display of magick would attract attention and made it a point to make
haste away from the scene. A few moments later, Thaddeus appeared at the
exact spot that Thanatos was standing only a few moments ago, alerted by the
Eyes of the King. He looked around and saw the scene of death, but as he examined the bodies, he noted that not all the Narsum were dead, one was still
alive, as he got to work, curing his wounds and healing his injuries.

He sat the warrior up and said in Manton, "Can you understand me?" The
warrior nodded his head as he continued, "My name is Thaddeus, and I felt
what happened here. Can you tell me who did this to you and your comrades?"

The Narsum said, "He was a small man, in black. Insects came out of his
arms, and they started biting us even through our armor, then he threw a large
ball of fire at us which killed most of my fellows. My horse, is he dead?"

Thaddeus looked around and saw 10 large gray horses apparently dead,
but 5 were standing up, but their hides were badly burned as he said, "I see
five standing, 10 on their sides. I could check them for you, but first we have
to get you up."

The warrior got to his feet and literally towered over Thaddeus, he was a
full three and a half arms taller than Thaddeus was, as he collected himself,
noting the good job that Thaddeus did in healing him.

The warrior said, "I am Nopar'Thuum. I led this patrol. We have to bury
them and their horses."

Thaddeus said, "Not so fast, my Narsum friend. Let me see what I can do
to help them."

Thaddeus started examining the fallen Narsum and was actually able to
save seven more of them, along with all but two horses. After several tolls, the
wounded Narsum and their horses started along the road back to their village,
led by Nopar'Thuum with Thaddeus right behind him.

Thaddeus felt a little out of place among these giants (at least to him),
mostly dressed in hide armor, with swords bigger than he was and a bow that
he had a hard time lifting. The horses smelled Thaddeus and immediately took
to him, which surprised the Narsum, as that almost never happened, especially
with humans. As the second sun set in the sky, the patrol made it back, and
Thaddeus saw a Narsum village for the first time. He noted the stone structures, the organization of the village, and immediately smelled cooking meat.
Nopar'Thuum said with a smile, "You eat with us tonight, warrior."

There were hundreds of huge women and lots of young children about his size. The village leader came out and noted they were somewhat short in number, as Nopar'Thuum described what happened and pointed at Thaddeus several times apparently speaking their own tongue which Thaddeus had never heard before.

CHAPTER 24

A NARSUM SECRET REVEALED

The village leader, a hulking mass of muscle, standing at eight arms tall, and weighing over 25 stone, had a huge double headed axe on his back made his way over to Thaddeus. The leader expected Thaddeus would be scared of him, but stood boldly in his presence as he said in Manton, "You save my warriors and horses. I thank you. You eat with men tonight!"

Thaddeus said, looking as high up as he could, "Thank you."

Thaddeus noted that there were two separate outdoor eating areas, and he noted a group of male Narsum congregating around one of them, he noted the female Narsum and Narsum children congregating around another separate area. He noted that the Narsum seemed to be very misogynistic; as he sat with the men, it was the women who came over and served the men, warriors first, waiting for their prodigious appetites to be satisfied before they could eat what was left for them and the children. The men had access to the best food and ale, and male warriors had access to the best of everything, including the prettiest females.

Thaddeus noted that Narsum society was centered on the male warrior; everything was given to him, but he had to be willing to fight and die for the village. Whenever he went outside the village, there was a chance that he might not return, so he exchanged his life for having the best the Narsum could offer which most thought was a good thing. Thaddeus noted that most male Narsum were young men, though not as young as he was. They mostly talked in their own tongue and looked at Thaddeus very curiously, wondering why this comparative pipsqueak of a boy was eating at a table with the men.

Thaddeus also noted that Nopar'Thuum and another large warrior sat on either side of him. He hoped that it was to protect him from other warriors who found him to be unworthy to sit with the men, especially warriors. Thaddeus didn't eat much, as he found the Narsum had no table manners at all. They smelled of dirt and sweat, and after a cycle of eating with elves, nobility (which the elder Thaddeus was) and a Goddess, Thaddeus had a hard time swallowing the food they put in front of him. Their diet was almost exclusively fatty meat and ale. There was also bread, but much of it looked moldy and was practically ignored by most. He picked over the large leg of something that he was served but couldn't drink the ale, as it smelled horrible to him, but the Narsum apparently liked it as it was being consumed in mass quantities.

While Thaddeus was exploring the finer points of sharing a meal with the Narsum, he happened to look in between two of the larger Narsum warriors across from him and noted that one of the Narsum women was looking right at him. She was huge compared to him, though a lighter shade of green than most Narsum women, standing at six and a half arms tall. He noted that she was trying to be attractive to him and was failing miserably, as Thaddeus had taken a liking to elves, especially Kama who he missed desperately at the moment.

After a toll or so, most of the men were full and took to emptying a keg of ale that had been opened this sun. Nopar'Thuum approached Thaddeus and said, "Warriors eat and drink together, then go back to wife at night. It only time that a man can be a man, among his fellow men. You have wife?"

Thaddeus looked at Nopar'Thuum and said, "No, I'm too young for that. I'm only nine cycles old."

Nopar'Thuum said, "So? Even young man need wife. You are Narsum warrior now. You need wife to take care of you."

Thaddeus said, "Well, I guess it wouldn't hurt to look."

Nopar'Thuum said, "Good. You look. Lots of women need good man. Thought I saw one looking at you…you find. Good luck, warrior."

Thaddeus set off in the moonlit glow, high in the mountains to find the Narsum woman who was looking at him. As was his custom, he always held onto the Eyes of the King, just in case, and that new custom was serving him well, when he noted a touch of magick, just to the south of his present location, and as he teleported to it, he came face to face with what looked like a shaman, who was not surprised by his sudden appearance.

148

The shaman said, "Welcome, Thaddeus."

Thaddeus said, "You...you know my name? How can that be? I've never seen you before."

Thaddeus sensed a great deal of evil coming from this shaman and willed his Wizard's Staff in his hand. His Staff confirmed the evil as he said, "You know my name, then you know who I am and what I can do. Especially against evil."

The shaman changed before his very eyes, into the demonic Thanatos as he said, "Now you die!"

Thanatos launched his attack starting with an insect plague, but Thaddeus was ready for him as a wall went up in front of him and several streaks of bright light came screaming from his staff. The streaks burned into Thanatos' goop-encrusted flesh, releasing a horrific odor. The odor repulsed Thaddeus, but Thanatos pressed the attack and touched Thaddeus, but his touch, which normally would have rotted Thaddeus' body completely in a matter of moments, had no effect as Thaddeus said, "The Ancients protect their own, especially on these mountains. Your rotting touch cannot affect me...now feel their power!" Thaddeus put two hands on his staff and said, "Behold the power of the Ancients!"

From his staff, came a very large and angry dragon spirit who went on the attack immediately against Thanatos as he silently called for Agham-Ix to join him.

Agham-Ix teleported onto Thaddeus' shoulder as Thaddeus said, "Wanted you to see this..." as he cast a very powerful cleansing spell, courtesy of him becoming a Champion of the Light, the fabled Ancient's Rite of Purification. This spell removed all evil from an area, regardless of its source or how long it had been there. A brilliant white light permeated the cave, and after it was over, the dragon Spirit and Thanatos were gone, leaving behind nothing but a powerful aura of good. Thaddeus walked out on the ledge just outside the cave and saw a large whip-like thing coming at him. It latched on to him and started to pull him towards the edge as Agham-Ix leapt down and landed on the appendage, crushing it under his weight. He heard a splat as the remainder of the whip went off the ledge, and they saw Thanatos flying away from them, his vile stench slowly dissipating as the cool mountain breezes made themselves known.

Thaddeus said, "Are you alright, Agham-Ix?"

Agham-Ix smiled at him and said, "Aye...but what a stench!"

Thaddeus said, "Aye...now then, I was going to chat with another of the Narsum. Hopefully she smells better than the men!"

Agham-Ix said, "She?"

Thaddeus retorted, "Yes...she! I noted her looking at me during dinner, even Nopar'Thumm saw it. He thought I should try to talk to her."

He teleported back to the village, and many of the men had already retired, leaving behind the unmarried women and men, along with a few of the older children. The idea was for the men and women to mingle, now that everyone else was gone. Of course, they were constantly under the watchful eyes of guards, who ensured that all was quiet, so that the warriors could rest. Thaddeus appeared in the middle of the village and noted a group of folks sitting around a large bonfire. He could see that many were paired off, but there were a few who were not. Thaddeus caused his staff to glow a bright white, so he could see (and show off) and sure enough, one of the Narsum came running at him. He could tell it was a female Narsum from her shape coming towards him in the moonlight, but could see nothing else.

As she appeared in the glow of his staff, she wasn't bad looking (for a Narsum), though Thaddeus, who had taken a liking to elves and Goddesses, was far from impressed. She towered over him, as did most around here, but said to him in Manton, "I am Li'Faran, I have something I want to show you..."

Fortunately, Thaddeus was nine and didn't take that as others might and said, "Okay...lead on! Let's see whatever it is."

She was wearing a plain brown dress that went down to her knees; it was heavily stained and didn't smell very nice. She had black hair that was dull and matted, and her lower "fang-teeth" extended well up her face. She walked ahead of him slowly, deliberately showing her female form off to him, but Thaddeus again was not impressed. She took him to a hut and said, "It's in here."

His staff glowed brightly, and with Agham-Ix on his shoulder, both went into the hut, unsure of her actual intentions. It was a pretty basic hut, and it looked lived in, with simple stone furniture...nothing extravagant and well beneath what Thaddeus was used to, even when he lived in our world. She went into another room and returned with a large wooden chest.

She put it on the floor, bent over to open it, showing him her ample posterior in the process and said, "This chest belonged to Patrick the Younger..." As she said that, Thaddeus thought it was odd that his father's name was Patrick, though he was unsure where the "Younger" part came into play. She opened the chest, and she took out a parcel wrapped in animal skin with twine around it. On the parcel written in large letters, and the strangest thing of all, in English, he read, "For my son, Thaddeus."

She said, "My mother said that there are none who can read this here, and if you can, then this is meant for you."

He read out loud, "For my son, Thaddeus."

Li'Faran looked amazed as her mother had told her what was written there, but she never mentioned it to anyone else.

Li'Faran said, "So…it is you! I get to meet my brother at long last!"

She embraced him tightly, but fortunately, Agham-Ix was on his shoulder and prevented her from inflicting any bodily damage to him, and she smelled awful as he said in Manton, "Wait…you're my sister? How is that possible? You're not human…"

An old woman came slowly in the room and said in English, "Neither am I. But she is your sister. My name is Anacra, and I guess you could say that I'm your mother. Well, sort of…"

Thaddeus was taken aback, a woman speaking English to him…a Narsum sister…what was going on here? Was this some sort of sick joke? He took out a pinch of white powder and said "aletheia," meaning truth in the Elven tongue, as he cast the powder at the two Narsum. As the white powder settled on Anacra and Li'Faran, he knew that they were telling the truth.

Anacra said, "Patrick said you'd do that. Make sure we're tellin' the truth…and are we?"

Thaddeus said, "Yes, you are…but how is this possible? You mean that my father was here? How did he get here, and what was he doing here?"

Anacra said, "We don't have the answers you seek, but Patrick said the answers you seek are in that parcel but asked me to be sure that before we gave it to you, that you could read what was written on it, as it was written in English, a language from your world. Patrick taught me some of it, too."

Thaddeus sat back in the stone chair he was sitting in; he had a whole other family in this world that he did not know existed. It was truly a momentous sun, and as he was thinking about it, something clicked into place: his father reading Thaddeus' memoirs to him; his father said that it was an ancient tome passed down from generations back. How could he have that tome, unless he met Thaddeus before, here in this world, and somehow found his way back? What other secrets did his father have? Could they help him now?

He noted that there was a marked difference between Anacra and her daughter. Anacra looked "prettier" than her daughter did; it appeared that she had used cosmetics, albeit crude ones, and that her dress was actually clean and her long black hair was shiny.

Thaddeus said, "You've been waiting all this time for me? I can't believe that I have a family here. A mother and a half-sister. This is awesome! You guys have to come with me back to Samsrun. I have a home there that you are welcome to stay in."

Anacra said in English, "Thank you for the offer, but as I said to your father when he made me the same offer, our home is here, our lives are here, and we would not be accepted in a city full of humans, or a world full of them. I won't have you being an outcast in your society because you choose to have us live with you. We know what we are, and while your father and I had a full life together and a beautiful daughter, he got restless and longed for his life again back in his world, so I let him go, though it was hard for me. But there is an old Narsum saying, *Live each sun as your last, so when it comes, you will have no regret.* But he has visited us from time to time and made sure that we are taken care of. Now that you know of us, I pray that you'll do the same."

Thaddeus hugged his new mother, and said, "You bet I will. I'm planning on sticking around for a while; after all, I'm a Champion of the Light now."

Anacra said with a tear in her eye, "You are? We have heard of Champions of the Light in our ancient past, and to think that my son is one of them... what a glorious sun this is!"

Li'Faran leaned over and kissed Thaddeus as did Anacra, as Anacra said, "You are welcome to stay with us tonight, you can share Li'Faran's room."

Thaddeus was a little concerned with this arrangement, but knew that he had Agham-Ix to prevent her from injuring him in case she rolled on him. He was also concerned because he could only imagine the vermin that infested her bed, but he was gracious and said, "I would be honored. Li'Faran, lead the way!"

She led the way to her room, he noted the straw on the floor was black and moldy and was crawling with vermin of all sorts, on top of the cacophony of odors that permeated every inch of her room as Li'Faran layed on the straw and said in Manton, "Come, brother...sleep with me..."

Thaddeus was totally grossed out…a filthy room, a disgusting bed, and a smelly sister on top of it. In times past, he would have balked at sleeping there, but now he had access to magick, so he did what any self-respecting Wizard would do in this situation and cast a purification spell on her room and was relieved when the multitudes of vermin left, the straw was renewed, and the putrescent odors left the room and his sister.

He smiled and said in his mind, "Agham-Ix, good night. It's been a long sun."

Agham-Ix said, "Pray the night is not long as well. Narsum are legendary for their stamina in certain things!"

Thaddeus looked horrified and asked Agham-Ix, "What do you mean?"

Agham-Ix smiled and said in Thaddeus' mind, "Pray you don't find out…"

He timidly layed on the straw with his new sister, she took him in her arms, kissed him goodnight, and said, "Sleep now…"

It felt weird for Thaddeus to sleep with anyone, as he had slept in his own room since he was two; it felt even weirder that this someone was a woman and was capable of crushing him, but he liked the fact that she wanted to care for him, and she was warm to boot. While Thaddeus was in her embrace, he realized there were no blankets anywhere, and he might freeze as it was still Samhein, and he was up in the mountains, so he took advantage of the resources he had. He had Agham-Ix on one side keeping his back warm and preventing him from being crushed, and Li'Faran on the other, both of them keeping him warm. Thaddeus settled into her and fell asleep.

CHAPTER 25

✂━━❦━━✂

ALL IN THE FAMILY

Thaddeus woke up the next morning with Agham-Ix at his back, noting that Li'Faran was gone but could smell cooking meat. He woke Agham-Ix up and the pair made their way to the kitchen. Anacra and Li'Faran were in the kitchen cooking, and Thaddeus noted what looked like plates on the table and utensils. After the spectacle he witnessed last night with the men, he was unsure what was happening as Anacra turned around, spotted him and said in Manton, "Ah…Thaddeus. Good morning to you. I trust you slept well. Take a seat at the table; breakfast is just about ready."

Thaddeus said, "Aye, I slept very well, thank you!"

Anacra said, "Li'Faran enjoyed your company last night. She mentioned something about you cleaning her room."

Thaddeus blushed and said, "Aye, I figured it was the least I could do to repay her kindness…"

Thaddeus noted something that his father would make for him especially on weekends—scrambled eggs, cooked meat, and potatoes; and he noted thick slabs of bread covered with what looked like butter as Thaddeus said, "This looks fantastic!"

As the ladies sat down, they put napkins on their laps and used the utensils that were on the table. Thaddeus responded in kind, and he found the food Anacra and Li'Faran made to be some of the best he'd had since his arrival here. He could taste how fresh and delicious everything was and was very impressed at the manners the two ladies displayed. They ate quietly, drinking water from large wooden goblets. Thaddeus was impressed to say the least at

155

how this meal was served and the manner in which it was served, which served in stark contrast to the travesty he viewed last night with the men.

After he finished, Anacra said, "My boy, you need to be opening that parcel this sun. I hope it answers some questions for you."

Thaddeus said, "Would you like some help with the dishes?"

Anacra said, "No, your father made that very easy for us. This home has a few magickal touches that most know nothing about. Get on with it; we are curious what's in that package."

Thaddeus cut the twine and unwrapped the parcel. It appeared to be a large wooden box with a handprint on the top; there was English writing at the top of the box which read, "Put your hand in mine, and I will show you."

Thaddeus put his hand into the handprint, and the box's lock clicked open. He carefully opened the lid and inside was a note and a large book. Also, included was a wand.

Thaddeus' heart was pumping hard, his mind racing with all kinds of thoughts as he took the note out of the envelope and read:

My dearest Thaddeus,

If you are reading this, then you've found your way to a special place… one that will always be in my heart. The two ladies there are Anacra, my wife of 25 cycles, and our daughter, Li'Faran. Finer ladies you could not hope to find amidst the Narsum. They have kept this for you for a very long time in their world, and I thank them both for making sure that you receive this.

I'm sure you have questions, but before I try to answer them, know that I loved your mother very much, and while she is no longer with us, I think of her often. I must tell you, first and foremost, that unlike a lot of other men in our world, I am a Wizard. I dabbled in magick all my life, but even in my wildest dreams, I never hoped to unlock a secret this big…a portal to other worlds. By some skill, luck and happenstance, I opened that portal and went through to the other side, finding these remarkable people called Narsum. What they lack in manners and cleanliness, they make up for in strength and honor. I found their knowledge is so deep and vast, written in ancient librams in a tongue barely decipherable today, but there are those that can read these ancient books alive today…that tradition kept alive by shamans. Seek them out to learn more of these ancient and honorable people, for their knowledge goes back to the very beginnings of their world.

For you to be there, you've either found the same portal I did, or you were taken there by a man named Thaddeus Brimstone, as he is the only other man who had the magickal strength to open the portal to this world. His magick is strong, and you could learn much from him. He is also a kind man; you would do well to befriend him if he still lives.

Since you were a little boy, I've been reading Thaddeus' memoirs to you to instill in you the desire for adventure, and if the Gods allow, learn a bit of magick yourself because I wanted you to carry on the family tradition of magick. Know that our family is different, and we come from a long line of Wizards, though they are always men. The women we marry are often unaware of our skills, though we are drawn to those who practice the craft, as your mother did. With two parents who are Wizards, we knew that you would be as well, though you have not shown any signs of the craft, but you are only five now as I write this, but if you are reading this, then a Wizard you are, and if your mother is right (and she always was), your magickal powers will be formidable.

There is something else that you should know about this world; time is different here. I spent 25 cycles with Anacra, but when I got restless and went back to our world, barely three months had passed and I resumed my life as if nothing had happened, but I still remember her fondly and all our adventures together.

Lastly, I named you Thaddeus...why? If it weren't for him and his kindness, I would not be alive. Ask him to tell you the tale one day. I wish you the best of luck here, and I hope that whatever it is that fate has in store for you, I hope that you'll be happy and healthy, no matter what world you're in!

Love,

Patrick

P.S. The book is my journal detailing my life and times here amidst the Narsum, and the wand is something I found whilst exploring the mountains, but I don't know what it does...good luck, and may the Gods watch over you!

Thaddeus refolded the letter. Everything made more sense now. It was as if he was somehow destined to be here, just as his father was before him. His father knew the kind of boy he would be and how he was always different, always looking for something else; now he knew what it was, he was looking for magick, and it found him. He thought that the note from Thaddeus would be plenty of explanation for his father as to where he went, and he thought that perhaps he could meet his father here.

Thaddeus said, "Wow…it's all so clear now."

Anacra sat down on the stone chair with Thaddeus and said, "Patrick said you'd say that once you read his letter. He told us that you were in another world, but that you would find your way here somehow. Of course, we believed him, and here you are.

"Thaddeus, I loved your father with all my heart, and though he was much smaller than me, which as you can tell, especially here, is a handicap. We had to work very hard at overcoming that handicap, for not only is it against the natural order of things among us; he was also challenged no less than 60 times for my hand. He won every challenge, and my heart for as long as I will live, and while our relationship had its ups and downs, I would say that I couldn't have found a better man for a husband. He was kind and gentle, unlike many of the paramours that I could have married. It was as if he called to me silently, and without knowing what kind of life I would have with him, I decided to take a chance on loving your father, and I think he took a chance on loving me, as I am as unlike your mother as it is possible to be. Yes, he showed me a picture of her once. She was a very beautiful woman, and you have her eyes. Your father often said that it was my spirit and intelligence that he fell in love with, but he said that it was my yellow eyes that attracted him to me in the first place.

"Your father was a passionate man and taught me to read and write, and he opened my mind up to the knowledge of his world and this one, and for that, I will be forever grateful to him. While I could never learn magick myself, Li'Faran might be able to. She is a smart girl, much smarter than the men around here.

"As I look back over the last 25 cycles, I have a lot to be thankful for, as we were still together, and he honored me with Li'Faran. You should know something about the Narsum, we take 'until death do us part' very seriously, and he is still my betrothed, and he always will be. I guess what I'm trying to say is that, while my husband is in another place, his only son is here with us, and I'm so happy you're here."

Anacra got up, with a tear in her eye after that, and said, "I've talked enough, my boy. What else have ye found out?"

He looked at and opened the tome and noted that the tome was filled from cover to cover in his father's writing. Oddly enough, he wrote it in English.

158

Thaddeus supposed that this was to prevent others from reading it from this world. However, he noted that interspersed throughout the book, his father had included some passages in magickal script. Thaddeus closed the book and picked up the wand, and he could feel it's magick in his hands. He took out a stone from his pocket and read the magickal runes on the thick blackwood. They said, "The Ancients have blessed you, and so do I."

Thaddeus repeated the phrase out loud, and the wands tip glowed white for a moment, and he felt a release of magick, and when he looked around, he could see it—a protective aura had been cast around the home, though he was unsure what the aura did, he knew that it had to be something good. What his father didn't know was that this wand, which belonged to the last Champion of the Light, could only be used by one in that most elite group of people and cast a powerful spell of protection on a very large area. Thaddeus had unwittingly protected this entire village with a spell that would always be there and would always protect them from the shadow.

He said, "Anacra and Li'Faran, thank you for your hospitality. I am honored to be part of your family, just as you are a part of mine. Know that I will always cherish this time spent with you, and I will return, but I have to return to my home here and read my father's journal, as it may contain some things that could help me in my fight against evil."

Anacra said, "My son, fare thee well in your travels, and come back to us as you are able. We will be waiting for you."

Li'Faran went up to Thaddeus and gave him a hug and said, "Goodbye, little brother. I'll see ya around." Li'Faran petted Agham-Ix, and he didn't seem to mind as Thaddeus willed himself back to his home in Samsrun.

As he returned, Thaddeus saw Bjor'ma about halfway through the book he had opened and Kama in the study as she said, "Are you alright? I was worried about you. Where did you go?"

Thaddeus said, "That Thanatos guy showed up in the mountains, and he injured some Narsum, so I helped them, and they invited me to eat with them. I won't be doing that again, at least not with the men…Yikes!"

He continued, "Then I was invited to a Narsum home and found something I never thought possible. I have a family here; my father was actually here, and I have a half-sister! He wrote me this note, and left me this book and this wand…check this out!" He read the inscription, "The Ancients have blessed you, and so do I."

As he said that, the wand's tip glowed white followed by a release of magick as he said, "It's some kind of protection spell, from the Ancients! Isn't that cool!"

Kama took it all in, and smiled as she said, "You need to bathe."

Thaddeus said, "Yeah, I do, but you should see what Thanatos can do now. Insects and disease come from him now. I think he's trying a different tactic, but I think I can beat him. He keeps running away though…"

Kama said, "Remember the Law always, and don't get cocky. Remember you're not done with your training yet; I have a feeling that you haven't seen the worst that he can do, but the magicks I've taught you should help those affected by his foulness, and speaking of foulness…Whew! Let's get you in the tub!"

Thaddeus said, "Yeah, I think it's time for a bath for us!"

He and Agham-Ix retired to the master bathroom and drew themselves a bath. They entered the large copper tub, but Thaddeus found that Agham-Ix wasn't able to float due to his weight, but thanks to the buoyancy of water, Thaddeus was able to hold him up and get him nice and clean. Thaddeus also found out that Agham-Ix liked to have his belly rubbed and made sure to do that as he was scrubbing his friend. What Thaddeus didn't know was that he wasn't alone in the tub with Agham-Ix. Kama was watching the entire time; truth be told she liked looking at his body as it was relatively thin, but not muscular like hers. She liked watching him being a kid, but at the same time, she wanted to see the adult version of him and how he would love her.

Kama fantasized about him gently taking her in his arms, kissing her as he caressed every inch of her, his mind so knowing what she wanted, what she needed, igniting her passion as she held him close to her, so they could feel as one. She imagined how he would make love to her and satisfy her carnal wants. She knew that having these feelings for him was only natural though a bit premature considering his age, as she was his only female tutor, but she did not remember having these feelings when she was a spirit…perhaps this was a consequence of the blessing she received from the Moon Goddess, that her feelings, emotions and physical needs would come back to her. She thought back and had a realization; she had never been intimate with a man before, and while that was normal for an elf, as they were typically not ready until they were five and 70. All that aside, the one thing she did know was that her physical needs and feelings for him were strong, and she would need to do something about it eventually. But for now, she was content to watch him and let him be a kid…for a bit longer anyway!

Agham-Ix left the tub and dried off quickly while Thaddeus sat in the hot, soapy water a bit longer and enjoyed the quiet, while he thought about Kama and how much he missed her while he was with Anacra and Li'Faran. He thought of her as his big sister, though they were about the same height, but she was far more experienced than he was, at least in magick. He did not realize that she was just as naïve as he was when it came to more physical pursuits, but he liked the way she looked and enjoyed the scent she wore regularly. Kama knew that Thaddeus liked her. They did not realize at this time that their love for each other would grow and be the reason why Thaddeus would stay in this world without reservation.

CHAPTER 26

❦

EVIL TRIES ANEW

After the last disastrous meeting with Thaddeus, where he lost half of one of the whip-like appendages coming out of his shoulder, Thanatos thought that he needed to try something new. He realized just how dangerous Thaddeus was to him and how easily he could be eliminated on the slightest miscalculation or errant spell that he cast. He thought that perhaps he was thinking too small and needed to look at the grand scheme of what he was tasked to do. He was focused on individual villages but realized that he was tasked with eliminating all life on the Continent and that while eliminating a village was a good thing, he needed to think much bigger to achieve his goal as it would take a very long time to hop from village to village and eliminate them one at a time due to the resistance that the humans, Barbarians, and Narsum would put up.

In a moment of clarity, he had an idea. And while somewhat unpredictable, it would have an effect on the remaining population on the Continent: a massive pandemic, spread by him, at night. Since he had the power to spread disease without using magick, it was perfect. He surmised that while some would be healed, others would die. If he combined that with poisoning the water supplies that some of the humans had, it would work even faster. He would fly around at night and spread a virulent disease among the people and their animals; he surmised he could cover a lot of ground in the air and not be seen because he would be doing this at night.

During the sun, he would hide, but at night, he would come out and spread disease against the humanoids that he so desperately wanted to eliminate to please the Dread Lord. As night approached, he prepared himself.

While he was a capable flier, owing to his demonic nature, he knew that he used energy rather quickly while in the air, and needed to land every so often to replenish his energy stores. He didn't think that was an issue at night because he was alone, and it would be easy for him to land, recharge, and take off again without anyone knowing that he was there.

Meanwhile, Kama made a discovery whilst exploring her new home in Samsrun. It was a circlet with a large red jewel in the center. It seemed to call to her, and so she put the circlet on and felt an aura about the home. It was a positive aura; she saw it as a slightly blue hue to everything she was looking at. As she concentrated, she was able to detect other auras in places that were further away, some positive and some negative. It was like she knew how people were feeling.

While she was concentrating, the elder Thaddeus appeared behind her, tapped her on the shoulder and said, "So, ye've found it. I was wonderin' when that would turn up…"

Kama jumped, quickly turned to face the elder Thaddeus and said, "Nifas soltra!" reverting to her native tongue.

Thaddeus laughed and said, "Sorry I startled ye, but since ye are a female and a Wizard, that item will work for ye. It's called the Heart of the Queen, and it detects auras of places…so that ye'll know how that area's people are doing. If they are doing well, ye'll see a bluish tint, but if not, ye'll see a reddish tint…at least that's how Sapphira described it to me. Like I said, that item only works fer women. Not sure why that is."

Kama said, "I see the auras—it's amazing. I'll know how people are doing all the time and can tell Thaddeus where there might be a problem…brilliant!"

The elder Thaddeus thought to himself, *Just like Sapphira and I used to…* As he thought of her and how special she was, not only to him, but to all the peoples on the Continent.

Thaddeus said, "Well, best be gettin' back now. Don't want the Moon Goddess to miss me, but I thought ye should know what ye've got there and how ta use it. Goodbye!"

As the elder Thaddeus dematerialized, his younger namesake came out of the bathroom, with a fresh robe on as he saw Kama and said, "Hey, what's that thing on your head? It looks really nice!"

Kama lit up when she saw him and, as she looked at him, saw a deep blue aura about him as he approached her. It wasn't just a tint, or a hue, it was as if his whole being was colored blue. She knew that he was very happy to see her, as lustful thoughts briefly entered her mind.

She said, "It's the Heart of the Queen. It only works for women. It detects auras of people and places; I know how groups of people feel, whole cities and villages even."

Thaddeus said, "Wow…really? That's so cool. How am I feeling right now?"

Kama said, "You're happy at the moment."

Thaddeus replied, "Yup…I'm clean and feel pretty good at the moment. But I think another magick lesson is in order, what say you?"

Kama said, "Aye. Let's get into the laboratory. Time to make some of those advanced poultices we were working on."

They walked to the lab and started the lesson, just as Thanatos took off into the night…

Since he was in the mountains, he decided that this would be an ideal place to begin spreading his disease. As he passed over a Narsum village, he opened his mouth, and a vile stench exuded from it as the disease poured out and mixed with the cool mountain air. As he passed over the village, he heard the sounds of merriment and that disgusted him. He wanted them to suffer.

As he flew over the mountains, he was covering lots of ground and spreading his disease far and wide. His mouth was almost constantly open, spewing the vile malady onto the unsuspecting creatures below. As he got low on energy, he would land, recharge for a moment, and continue on his nightly journey. So far, his plan was working perfectly; he wasn't using magick at all, no one could see him or know he was there. He realized that going forward that stealth and silence would be his friends in his nightly flyovers. He thought that a full season of spreading this sickness over the mountains should yield some acceptable results, even though he knew that his abilities in this arena were only at half-strength.

Soon enough, reports of a strange disease started to make themselves known across the villages and towns of the Dragonscape Mountains. The messengers of the time, pigeons and hawks, flew messages all around the entire mountain community, wondering what this disease was and how to combat it. Healers tried to use every method they could think of, but they noted that the disease was highly virulent, contagious and above all, extremely fast-acting, and all they seemed to be able to do is to provide a bit of comfort to the victims for it took less than two suns for the most vulnerable to die. Once contracted, one's life expectancy with the disease was five suns, for the hardiest and healthiest among the Narsum, perhaps seven was the upper limit which was not enough time for the medicines of the sun to have any hope of stopping the progress of the disease once it started.

As Samhein continued, many thousands of humans and Narsum would contract this horrific disease and die. The laughter and merriment that Thanatos once heard whilst flying over the mountains was replaced by the wails of the victims, the crying of those that were still alive over their dead relatives and this pleased him, knowing that he was the one responsible for their misery and suffering. Thanatos finally thought that he had a winning strategy, and for the first time in a long time, he smiled at his stroke of brilliance.

Across the mountains, the wailing of the victims, and the crying over the dead and was replaced by silence as a few more suns passed by. The sounds of people were becoming an increasing rarity as the disease continued to spread into the mountains, finding every last pocket of life and ensuring that it, too, would pass away.

During this time, Kama continued to experiment with the Heart of the Queen, but it was not attuned to her yet and her abilities with it were limited. She could see the city of Samsrun and a few hundred arms outside of it, but that was it. Thaddeus was ever vigilant with the Eyes of the King, but he detected nothing as no great magicks were being used anywhere on the Continent that he could see. They could not hear or see what was going on in the mountains far to the East, until Toril came to see him whilst he was reading a tome with Bjor'ma.

Toril said, "Champion, there is a matter which you need to attend to in the mountains; many are dying there..."

Agham-Ix said into his mind, "Thaddeus, something is happening in the mountains. My brethren need us."

Thaddeus leapt up and said, "Let's go. I'm ready!"

Thaddeus teleported himself, and Agham-Ix to the mountains in the Narsum village where Anacra and Li'Faran lived, and he was shocked at what he saw. Dead bodies everywhere; some recently buried, but some were just lying outside. He noted that even the carrion birds were staying away from them. He fell to his knees and cried. Though this village was blessed, it did nothing to prevent the spread of disease. He thought of Anacra and Li'Faran as he and Agham-Ix raced to Anacra's home on the edge of the village. He opened the door and stopped dead in his tracks. Anacra was dead, but he did not see Li-'Faran anywhere. As he checked around the house, it was deserted.

There was one thing he was thankful for, that as a Champion of the Light that he was largely immune to diseases of all sorts, as he bent down over Anacra, caressed her soft black hair and said, "Goodbye, mother. You will always be in my heart."

Just then, he heard a noise from another room, and before he could react, he saw a large Narsum coming at him with an axe. He wasn't quite fast enough as it struck him in the head, but at that moment, he realized just how hard his skin had become as the axe broke, and he was able to scramble to his feet and saw Li'Faran, still alive. She was seething, in some kind of hysterical state, but after seeing who it was, she calmed down a bit and screamed, "Puris den makar shirin!" and then broke down crying as she saw that Anacra was dead.

Thaddeus was scared of her now, knowing the only thing standing between him and an enraged Narsum was Agham-Ix, and while he was confident in his familiar's ability to protect him, he picked up Agham-Ix and said in his mind, "I think we should stick together. I don't know what she is going to do; she's kinda scary in this state…"

Agham-Ix nodded and said in his mind, "Yes, this is the fabled Narsum rage…it's not as strong in female Narsum, but can be just as deadly."

Thaddeus said in Manton, "Li'Faran…it's Thaddeus. I'm here. What happened here?"

She looked up at him, he could see that she was half-enraged, half-greiving. Her normally light green face was red in many areas and he could see that she was crying as she said, "Mom and village dead now…I alive. I think that when you clean room, it stopped me from being sick."

Thaddeus replied, "Okay…glad I cleaned your room then. But let me check you over just to be sure you're okay."

She said, "Okay…and sorry about axe…I thought you were thief."

Thaddeus checked her over, and she appeared free of disease. He took a water vial from his healer's bag, put a white powder in it and shook it up and said, "Li'Faran, drink this. It will help you."

Li'Faran took the vial and drank it down. Within a few moments, she felt better and said, "Thank you, brother. You said that I come with you if I want… nothing left for me here but sadness…can we bury Mom now?"

Thaddeus said, "Aye, we can. Let me prepare a site."

He went outside and dug a hole using earth magick. Thaddeus silently and reverently put a large blanket over her and levitated her out of the home and into the hole.

He said, "Li'Faran, would you like to say a few words?"

She said, "No...no one around but us."

Thaddeus said, "Very well. But I have something to say, by your leave, of course." Li'Faran nodded and Thaddeus said, "I consecrate the body of Anacra to the Ancients, may they watch over her and guide her. May they bless her as she enters their domain, and may she live among them happy for eternity."

He repeated this for no less than 25 others that were strewn about the village, unburied, as the stench of death lay heavy on this village. No songs were sung, no chants could be heard, no birds flying overhead, only the sounds of the wind, carrying the dead to their final resting place as Thaddeus hoped they would be accepted into the Crying Fields. Finally, as the first sun set, he finished his labors and said to Li'Faran and Agham-Ix, "I'm ready to leave this place, though I think we will have a lot more work to do, as I have a feeling that this same scene has been repeated across the mountains. Let's go home."

Thaddeus teleported Agham-Ix, Li'Faran and himself back to Samsrun, totally exhausted both physically and magickally.

As he arrived at his home in Samsrun, he said, "Li'Faran, I welcome you to my home. You'll be safe here."

Li'Faran said, "I help you when you go back to mountains tomorrow. I am strong."

Thaddeus said, "Yes, you are strong, but against this disease, I fear you may not be. But perhaps I can help there and bless you each sun, so that you do not become infected."

Kama came walking into the study and saw an extra person she was not expecting and said in a different sort of tone than usual, "Who have you brought back?"

Thaddeus said, "Kama, this is Li'Faran, my half-sister. We have the same father. She was the only one left alive in her entire village; the rest are dead of some disease. I checked her over, and I found no trace of it."

Kama said, "Li'Faran, that's an Elven name. It means, 'Unknown Life,' usually reserved for those whose lives will be different because of their birth. I can see that it would apply to you given the circumstances, but where are my manners? Let me show you around, get you set up in a room, make you comfortable."

Kama led Li'Faran away, and as they walked away from Thaddeus, he noted that they were quite a pair. Kama was short, slender with delicate features, and Li'Faran, much larger, stronger, not to mention prone to rage, but with potential as Anacra had said. He felt that he owed it to Anacra to try to teach Li'Faran some magick. After all, her father was a Wizard.

After about a toll, Kama came back and said, "I've never seen one of her kind before, and to have an Elven name…wow! She's smart, too. She said that you cleaned her room which prevented her from being sick."

Thaddeus said, "I cast a purification spell on her and her room. If you would have seen it, you would have understood why."

Kama replied, "I'm sure…and you said that you have the same father? How is that possible?"

Thaddeus said, "Let me show you this letter from my father…and hers."

He handed Kama the letter his father had written him along with the tome and the wand. After casting a spell enabling her to read it, she said, "It all makes sense now. Not only was your father a user of magick, but your mother was, too! While that is common in Elven families, not so much in human ones, which means that she has the potential to learn magick as well."

Thaddeus replied, "Aye, she does, but I will need her to help me bury more bodies tomorrow and try to find out what happened to these people. Though I think I know who is behind all this. None other than Thanatos. He must have a natural ability to cause this disease, but there must be a cure. I'd have to be there to effect it, and I don't even know where he is or where he will strike next. Kama, I need you to come with us tomorrow. You're much better at magick than I am, and you might see something that I don't. Fear not, we will stick close together, so no harm will come to you."

Kama said, "Finally a chance for adventure, and don't worry. I'm a big girl. And I've got a few tricks up my sleeve."

Thaddeus laughed and said, "I'm going to take a bath now…I need to rest and study tomorrow before we head out."

Kama said, "Okay…good night! See you tomorrow!"

CHAPTER 27

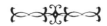

A CURE AND A DISEASE

The next sun, the four of them set off to other known villages in the mountains thanks to Li'Faran's knowledge of the area and her knowledge of Narsum ways. In the fifth village they visited that sun, there was one man who was alive, a human named Garal, he also served as the hawkmaster in this area. His collection of five hawks was certainly impressive, and he explained that this was a sort of crossroads for the hawks. They would stop here to rest, and he would send another hawk to deliver the message to the village. He explained that he can actually communicate with the hawks, and they seem to understand him. He had more knowledge about what was going on than most did owing to his position and he was still alive because he lived deep in a mountain cave, behind a waterfall. He was never outside at night, nor were the hawks.

He said, "Strangest thing, no one is sendin' hawks anymore. Got the last one in a couple of suns ago, but nothin' since. Heard about some disease out there...how bad is it?"

Thaddeus said, "It is bad, as we have been to several villages and have seen many dead. We honored them but moved on. We are headed for the dragon caves to see if the rest of the Narsum are there, would you mind if I give you a blessing of the Light? It will protect you from disease."

Garal said, "Sure, bless my hawks, too. They are my life!"

Thaddeus blessed all in the cave with the power of the Ancients and set Garal up with some food.

After that, the four of them moved on and approached the jagged peaks of the mountains. Flying above them was a dragon, though the two suns made it hard to distinguish what kind it was as it was far away, though it appeared to be getting closer as Agham-Ix said into Thaddeus' mind, "My father approaches! He's been looking for us."

Thaddeus said to the rest of the group, "The dragon up there is Agham-Ix' father. Not to worry, everyone, maybe he knows what's going on!"

Slowly, a large dragon approached their position as the four of them stood quietly on the high plateau they were on. He finally landed with a thud, shaking the stone they were standing on. He appeared as a large dragon looking exactly like Agham-Ix only much bigger, as he landed in front of them. They saw the stone cracking under his tremendous weight and were worried it would give way, but this was where stone dragons are most at home, as the rock slowly repaired itself. Agham-Ix' father was 18 arms long, small for an adult dragon, but weighed 650 stone and had the same coloration as his much smaller son.

Thaddeus bowed down to the large dragon in front of him and said in dragon tongue, "I am honored by your presence, and speak to you as a kindred spirit and as a Champion of the Light. I would ask a boon of you…if you know what is causing the disease that afflicts the humans and Narsum?"

Agham-Ix' father said in dragon tongue, "I am honored to meet my son's familiar and am grateful to know a Champion of the Light in my time. My name is Haron'Unve, and I welcome you and your group to my territory; if you are looking for the cause, it is not natural, spread by an evil being who flies at night. There is a way you can protect us. I hope you brought your strength with you, as you will need it. You have the knowledge in your mind and the means to cast this mighty magick, channel the Ancients through you…feel them as their power fills your mind, then do what you have come here to do."

Thaddeus looked back in his mind, into the vast storehouse of knowledge he had thanks to Alotraxas, and into his mind came a ritual that Toril had performed many cycles ago. A ritual with the wand of Light, one that could cleanse this mountain range, and oddly enough he knew that it was a stronger version of what he cast in Li'Faran's bedroom a few nights ago. As he pulled out the blackwood wand from his robe on that sunny Samhein morning, he felt the energy radiating from it, as if it knew what he had to do and was preparing itself. He held the wand high in front of everyone and said, "The Ancients have blessed you, and so do I."

As he said those words, he could feel the power of the Ancients through him, he could feel the thousands of Champions of the Light before him who have spoken those same words.

Kama, Li'Faran, and Agham-Ix stood transfixed as the whole of the wand turned white, and Thaddeus started to glow with a brilliant white light. He said in a booming voice, well beyond his normal speaking ability as if 50,000 voices were speaking through him at the same time, "I, Thaddeus, call upon the Ancients to protect this mountain range from the scourge that has infected it, I ask that all who still draw breath be cured of the affliction poisoning the noble creatures who inhabit this place. Behold, the glory of the Ancients!"

A bright white flash blinded all for a few moments as the spell Thaddeus cast went far and wide across the mountain range. As the light subsided, and their vision returned, they noted Thaddeus was still standing, though a little wobbly as he fell to his knees, having expended a huge amount of energy in one fell swoop.

Haron'Unve said in dragon tongue, "You have done well, Champion. Few have ever needed to cast such magicks, but those who have, are remembered."

Thaddeus tried to stand up but realized his legs would not support him as he said in a breathless voice, "Glad to...have been of service..." as Haron'Unve flew off, albeit slowly as all stone dragons do.

As luck would have it, Thanatos was regenerating deep in a mountain cave several leagues away, and as he stood up to prepare for his nightly disease-spreading flyovers, he noticed something, something that wasn't quite right, as if a piece of him was missing. He felt that his ability to cause disease was gone, like the sickness was cured, and that the "mother" of the disease that was placed in him was gone! He didn't understand, he was doing so well; people, animals, and Narsum were dying by the thousands—the Dread Lord was pleased with him...

Then he knew. It was Thaddeus...AGAIN! He raged at this revelation but was careful not to cast magick lest he have another run-in with Thaddeus. Thanatos knew that Thaddeus' abilities were becoming stronger by the sun, and he would have to be dealt with somehow. But how? Thaddeus had proven that he was the better every time they had met.

He didn't have time to think about how to eliminate Thaddeus at the moment, as he needed a new plan of attack. He surmised that the disease sapped the strength of the Narsum and humans, but not by enough, as there were still enough of them to mount a substantial defense against him (or so he thought). So, he thought about what to do next. Then he had an idea, why not have a different disease instilled in him? His original disease plan worked until Thaddeus came along and ruined it. He knew that it would be a few suns before Thaddeus would find out about this new disease, and hopefully, it would take longer for him to discover what was going on because there were less folks now to tell him.

Thanatos thought about what the Lord of Blight would say and if he acquiesced to Thanatos' request, he would be subjected to that pit of nasty goop again along with who knows what else, but so long as the Dread Lord's wishes were carried out, then he was willing to undergo whatever was needed to make it happen. He willed himself to the depths of the underworld and once again set foot in the realm of the Lord of Blight.

The Lord of Blight said in a gravelly whisper, "Welcome back, Thanatos. The Dread Lord has kept me apprised of your progress…it is going well, yes? What else can I, the Lord of Blight, do for you?"

Thanatos said, "The disease has been cured. There is a Champion of the Light up there thwarting all my plans, not to mention beating me in every engagement we have had. I need something else to carry out his wishes." The frustration in his voice was evident as he proceeded to expound to the Lord of Blight his trials up above.

Finally the Lord of Blight said, "I've been working on something that may help you…but there are some…side effects…to the carrier. What say you?"

Thanatos thought and said, "Why are your powers all so deadly to the wielder?"

The Lord of Blight said, "My powers are deadly to all, they do not discriminate between friend and foe; the only thing that keeps you upright is your demonic nature, but as I said before, even that will not completely protect you. Look around you, even the Gorpin here suffer from this place. All things rot and die…why should you be any different?"

Thanatos thought and said, "Aye, let's check out what you've come up with."

The two demons went deeper into the Lord of Blight's domain. The horridness of the odors here defied description causing Thanatos pause as he continued through what was quite possibly the worst smelling place anywhere. Thanatos thought that if he was human, he would have rotted away by now, and he was right, though even he could feel the rot and decay creeping up his legs as he continued to traverse the Lord of Blight's realm. Finally, they reached a door made completely of some slimy muck, opened it up, and in the room beyond, there was a table and a small glass vial on it, which was the only clean thing in the room. The vial was supported by what looked like a rotted human hand, along with the usual slime covered walls, the horrific smells and the general rot and decay that was so much a part of this place.

Thanatos couldn't believe that HE was feeling like he would rather be anywhere but here, probably from his former association with Bjor'ma, who must have imprinted some of his half-Elven predilections onto him during their brief time together.

The Lord of Blight picked the vial from the table and said, "Here it is… the culmination of many lifetimes' work. The very essence of death. We have spent lifetimes with all that rots, decays, and dies, concentrated that ultimate finality through the foulest means possible, and have distilled this single drop from it. This is perhaps my most ambitious work…to be able to extract the very essence of death into a liquid that can be consumed by you!"

The Lord of Blight continued, as he got closer to Thanatos with the vial in hand, "Consuming this single drop will make you what I like to call Death Incarnate! Death will follow in your wake, and all will wither and die in your presence. All you are and all you will be is Death. You will have only two powers should you decide to take this single drop. The first is causing death to all who are near you, but perhaps the greatest power of all, bringing death to not only yourself, but to every living thing in a vast area; say the size of the Continent and beyond. You see, in the end, there is no good or evil, there is only Death! What say you?"

Thanatos wondered for a moment. With the contents of that vial, he could affect the Dread Lord's wishes in one masterful stroke, but then he would cease to exist. He didn't want to die, as he was sure that the Dread Lord would have more tasks for him once the peoples of the Continent were eradicated, but he wasn't sure what they would be. He was sure there had to be something.

He said, "Mayhaps you would allow me to speak to my master before I take that? I would know what his thoughts are on the matter."

The Lord of Blight said, "Of course, speak with your master. Mayhaps he has a different plan, but know that this is here, should you want it."

Thanatos went to the Dread Lord and said, "My Lord, I would treat with you."

The Dread Lord said in an aggravated tone, "I know why you are here, though with your recent success in the field, I am puzzled as to why you aren't there, DOING MY WILL!"

Thanatos said, "My ability to cause disease has been taken from me; my other powers are not as effective in carrying out your will, and the Champion of the Light is becoming stronger by the sun. He has a new weapon at his disposal, a wand of some kind, he foils our plans at every turn. I humbly beseech you for guidance in carrying out your will."

The Dread Lord said, "So, the Champion has the wand of Light, does he? Hmmmm…that does pose a problem for you. With that, as I recall, he can thwart just about anything that you can do, but he has to know about it first…mayhaps another disease, then? Something that kills, something that saps the strength from them. Remember that we have the advantage of surprise and the fact that communications are slow…use that. There is no need to sacrifice yourself, just have the disease replaced. You will be far more useful to me alive than dead. Keep out of sight, work your magick, and above all, stay away from the Champion! Given his strength, he is a deadly adversary to you, and with a wand of Light in his hands, he is invincible to anything that you can do against him."

The Dread Lord continued, "Work quickly, but above all be patient in your work, take some pleasure in the deaths you have caused and look forward to those yet to come. As a demon, you should revel in your victories and take lessons from your failures, but no matter what you do, above all, be careful… the Champion has eyes everywhere. One slip, and he will dispose of you without remorse, pray that does not happen, or Bjor'ma's fate will be yours as well!"

Thanatos nodded, bowed low and said, "Yes, my Lord. Thank you for your sage advice!"

As he started moving away, he felt better. He didn't have to die, he just needed to have the disease in him replaced; that didn't sound so bad as he went back to the Lord of Blight to have another disease instilled in him. As he approached the stinking vileness that was the Lord of Blight's domain, he said, "Lord of Blight, the Dread Lord has made his wishes known, he wishes me to be alive and has requested that I have the disease replaced in me to effect his will."

The Lord of Blight said unto him, "Are you prepared…? It will take some time to remove the curative effects of the Champion from you, before another disease will take to you."

Thanatos said, "Aye."

The floor disappeared under his feet and once again, Thanatos experienced the Pit of Desecration, though this time it felt like he was in there for a very long time. He could feel the goopy muck permeate his person, joining itself with him, and removing any curing effects he might have carried with him. After an indeterminate amount of time, he arose slowly out of the semi-fluid muck as the Lord of Blight said to him, "The disease is one with you. It will take time for it to flourish within you. Two suns should do it, then go and create havoc in my brother's name!"

CHAPTER 28

THANATOS VS. DEITIES

Two suns passed by and Thanatos felt better than he had in quite some time. He could feel the disease in him, it was stronger than before and felt like it could kill faster. It just needed some time. This time, he decided to go to the Deep North, into the frozen wastelands, occupied by only the hardiest souls. He thought to bring disease and death here would be slow to travel to anyone, as he knew that those here were primarily outcasts and criminals, though there were some small hamlets in this very sparsely populated area.

He appeared in the middle of a raging storm, as Sarodan never completely loses its grip on this area. All around him, the wind whipped the snow around him as he was cold and soaking wet in a matter of seconds. He flew through the snow, and found the entrance to a small cave. He investigated the cave but found it to be uninhabited, a relatively safe place to wait for nightfall to come to start the Dread Lord's conquest of this area. He started to get his bearings and decided to attack several small hamlets in the area to spread his disease to first. He waited until the two suns set in the sky before he went out that first night. As the temperature dipped, he remembered his last venture to this area and how powerless he felt at the hands of the Champion. He thought that things were different, and this time he would be more successful. He flew over the first hamlet; he could see fires within homes and smoke rising from chimneys, sounds of animals and people preparing for yet another cold night here in the Deep North. He flew low over this village and released the disease within him onto the unsuspecting populace as the cold winds picked up, and it started to snow again. This same scene repeated itself over several hamlets that night. As he was spreading disease, he smiled, knowing that he was that much closer to the total annihilation of everyone here. Thanatos knew that he would have to wait to see if the disease was effective before he went to a different area, but felt good about his chances, given the extra-long "soak" that he had in the Pit of Desecration. The Dread Lord told him to be patient, and so he would be…hanging around the area, waiting to see the first signs that his disease had taken hold.

What Thanatos did not count on was that he was a shining beacon of evil in this place and this fact was not lost on one individual in particular…the Snow Queen. She was much more motivated to hold onto her worshippers as long as possible because she bore witness to what happens when a deity loses their worshippers, and she didn't want that to happen to her. Her appearances were more frequent than in the past, and as a result of this enhanced presence on the Continent, this area was much colder and experienced far more snow than it did in the past. Local residents were surprised but thankful for the Snow Queen's blessing because though it made life more difficult for them, they knew that it would be impossible for any army to make its way up here to attack them, so they took the tougher weather in exchange for safety…which was common in the Barbarian way of thinking. You received something, and so something had to be paid in return. Some of the local residents, in particular humans who had emigrated here from the West, though not totally inured to the cold were told that this was the Barbarian way and to be thankful for this measure of safety given to them by the Snow Queen.

In his travels across this section of the Deep North, Thanatos was having a tough time as the high winds and driving snow made it tough to see where he was going. He was also experiencing a heavy buildup of ice all over his body, weighing him down, requiring him to stop more frequently for an energy boost than he would like, but he still felt like he was accomplishing something as he continued to spread his disease across this area…that is until he met the Snow Queen herself.

Thanatos felt a presence around him as he was flying about, which he thought was odd as he knew that there was almost no magick in this area.

He said into the wind, "I can feel you. Reveal yourself and face me."

He heard a seductive female voice say, "I am here and all around you, can you not feel me caressing you? Can you not feel my cold embrace, and my icy wet lips? You are not welcome here. Leave at once…or face my wrath."

Thanatos wasn't sure what to say, but he knew that he was being challenged so he decided on his usual bravado as he said, "I do not fear you; there is nothing you can do about my presence here. I go where I please."

The Snow Queen said, "Ah...but there is something I can do!" The wind whipped up even harder as the Snow Queen said, "You see, I have friends in many places, places known and unknown where the Light is always bright."

A sliver of fear pierced Thanatos' normally tough rhetoric but still appeared unfazed as he said, "Your people will die soon, and then you will be no more, while my masters take over this place...stand aside or die now!"

The Snow Queen said, "Empty threats do not become you, Thanatos. You know what will happen if you try to cast any spells against me, but I can cast them with impunity against you!"

As she said that, an icy blast of wind blew into Thanatos' face.

Thanatos did know what would happen if he cast a spell against her: the Champion of the Light would come, and he would be defenseless against their combined onslaught; maybe he would be crushed by another rock or some similarly horrible fate, as he remembered what the Dread Lord said, "Be patient and stay away from the Champion; he has eyes everywhere..."

He decided to retreat; he would live to fight another sun. He would have to be quicker about his attacks in the future, get in and get out just as fast. He knew he was faster than most in the air but was unsure how he would fare against a deity on his heels, flinging cold and ice against him.

He said, "You've not seen the last of me. Your people will be dead soon enough, and there is nothing you can do to stop it...HAHAHAHAHA!" He flew straight up and away from the accursed Deep North and headed South. He flew high enough (or so he thought), to avoid detection by anyone.

As he maintained a height of several leagues above the Continent, he attracted the attention of another deity, this time the Moon Goddess, who was incensed at this totally evil creature flying high above her territory. Given that there were only a few deities left in this part of the multiverse, she had a much more expansive view of her territory than most as she viewed her territory as anywhere the Three Moons shone through with a few exceptions. In short, she viewed most of the Continent as her territory now and was determined to defend her territory against this blight flying above it.

Thaddeus was at her side as always as she said, "Thaddeus! See what is above my lands."

He said, "Aye, that I do…looks like a demon if I'm not mistaken. Wonder what he's doin' there…? Probably tryin' ta avoid the young man on the surface. I'll take Sairys and check it out fer ya."

Thaddeus rode Sairys to intercept the intruder as Thanatos continued to fly high over the Continent, spreading his disease as he went, figuring it wouldn't hurt and that it would eventually find its way down to the Continent. He was not moving quickly, conserving his energy and taking a "long view" of events. He knew that he would have some victories and some losses in this struggle, but was determined to be the victor in the end and then the Dread Lord would reward him for his continued faithfulness. Just then, he sensed something coming in fast behind him, as bright lights exploded all around him.

Coming out of his reverie, he was momentarily surprised to see a 60-arm long dragon and a wizard riding on top heading straight for him. He dove quickly and tried to outmaneuver the dragon and was having some luck in doing so as Sairys, though a capable flier, was not as maneuverable in the air as a smaller creature, as it took a lot of energy for him to quickly change direction.

He saw the dragon falling away but was surprised again as he heard a man behind him, "Ye can outmaneuver my friend, but not me. Let's slow ye down, shall we?"

Thanatos felt a spell wash over him and found that he was slowing, as if he was heading into a strong wind. The man behind him was casting another spell as Thanatos cast a spell of his own as he headed higher, only to be shot down by Sairys and his high-energy breath weapon.

Thanatos only lost a little height as Sairys' shot only grazed him, but once again realized that he was in trouble and could not hope to escape from this pair without leaving the Continent completely. Powerful magick was being cast at him, and while he tried to dodge those spells, one finally got through as he found himself answering a question posed by a flying wizard in a blue robe and hat, he said, "Dread Lord," though he did not remember the question that was asked of him. More magicks were cast and though he took some physical damages from the barrage of spells that were cast at him, Thanatos played his trump card, opening up a black portal in front of him and escaping to the Dread Lord's realm before the elder Thaddeus could finish him off with spells.

Thaddeus re-joined Sairys as they flew back to the Moon Goddess' domain. When he got back, Thaddeus said, "Well, that was refreshin'! Haven't done that in a long time, eh, Sairys? Just like old times, chasin' the bad guy.

He escaped o' course, but I think we clipped 'is wings a bit!" He stoked up his pipe and said, "Did find out somethin' interestin' though. He's workin fer the Dread Lord…I remember that name from one of the books I read. He's a greater demon as I recall…gonna be tough to thwart him, but he can't come here thanks ta my protégé on the surface. Looks like we found the intermediary…not much of a fighter, but 'e probably got other skills making 'im mighty dangerous. Should probably see what's goin' on with the boy. It's been a couple o' suns, but in the mornin', I think. Continent should be safe fer now."

Meanwhile, Thanatos flew through the infernal gate and landed in his quarters in the Dread Lord's domain. He opened his regeneration chamber and looked at his wounds, inflicted by that wizard and a dragon. He noted some burn marks, a couple of scratches and some ice chips in his black, rubbery skin. He thought that he could regenerate and go back to it tomorrow night. He thought that perhaps this would be best, to fly out, spread his disease as quickly as possible then return here to regenerate in safety. He would not stay on the Continent any longer than was necessary, as it was clearly not safe for him any longer, as he was too easily detected by the Champion or his many eyes on the ground. This way he could inflict damage on the populace, but not be accosted in any way…but he would lose the ability to actually see the disease doing its work. He knew that he would miss that because that was part of the pride he took in his work, to see how his disease would affect the humans and how much they suffered because of it. *All their healing magicks, all for naught*, he thought, as the disease would spread unchecked and unabated, soon to take over the Continent and eliminate everyone on it. Then he knew he would be ready for his showdown with the Champion of the Light; with the Dread Lord's power behind him, he would surely defeat that paragon of good as they would desecrate his body and declare complete victory over the Light for the first time in a thousand cycles. What glorious times those would be, he thought, as he closed the lid to his regeneration chamber, smiling.

CHAPTER 29

A CELEBRATION

Many suns passed, and life on the Continent continued, though somewhat diminished due to yet another disease spreading among the tribes and humans of the Deep North and Far North. This virulent outbreak was deadly to anyone who caught it, but the disease seemed to be very selective, targeting older folks and those who were already weakened, or injured. The shamans of the Far Northern tribes could do little to stop this disease from spreading, but continued trying as the populace was concerned that all the wisdom and knowledge of times past would not be carried on to the next generation.

Most of the Continent was still barren, though in many areas of the North, South, and West, farmlands were growing again, and wildlife returned to the now unoccupied cities and towns, looking for food. The natural world was once again taking over where humans and elves once were, and it was only in the periphery of the Continent could one find any humanoid life. The center of the Continent was seemingly firmly in the hands of Nature. Amidst all this, in the former capital city of Samsrun, an auspicious occasion was taking place, one that would be remembered for many cycles in the future; the younger Thaddeus had finally completed his magickal training, not to mention had significant battlefield experience, and had experience with minor demons, thanks to him opening up his home to Bjor'ma.

A celebration was planned in his honor, for he had completed a 10-cycle course of study in a little over a single cycle, which was amazingly fast. Granted, for most of that time, he had an ancient dragon spirit in his head, but the fact remained that he completed it in record time and to show his competence, completed the rigorous final exam with flying colors and was granted the title of Wizard, as that is what he believed he should be called owing to his magickal skill. Despite all the trials he endured, like seeing the very moment of death on a few occasions, watching others die because he was too late to save them, he attained the very pinnacle of human achievement on the Continent and was now prepared to fully carry out his duties as not only the only human wizard left on the Continent, but also as a Champion of the Light.

Of course, other things were brewing for our young Thaddeus, besides his upcoming graduation. He was also being trained for something else, life. As a part of that life, the thought was that he would naturally want a woman to accompany him through his journey along with his familiar. One contender for that role was Kama, his Elven tutor. Though technically a spirit, she had already made it known that she was attracted to Thaddeus, but understood that due to his youth, had not developed feelings of love for the much older Kama. Though approximately the same size now, Kama knew that he would grow, and she was unsure how he would treat her, as Elven men are famously gentle to their mates.

The other contender that Thaddeus had was Li'Faran. Though she and he had the same father, to her mind, that did not necessarily preclude her from potentially attracting him as a mate to her. Narsum society looked favorably upon young people who had the same father, but not the same mother, being together as one, especially if that father was a warrior. The thought was that his strength would find its way into the children, and any male children born of this union would undoubtedly be warriors of the tribe. Though she was physically superior to the young Thaddeus in every way possible, she had a kind and caring streak in her and wanted to care for him, just as Narsum women were trained to do from birth. Though she was his half-sister, she could often be found with him, teaching him the physical pursuits of fighting with weapons and fists. She also taught him how to maintain his body through exercise and good (albeit Narsum) nutrition. Thaddeus came to see her more as "one of the guys" owing to her physical prowess, though she was undeniably a woman, as her breasts were six times the size of Kama's.

Having two women, each very different and attractive in their own ways was a different experience for the young Thaddeus as he was never a super popular kid in school with the girls, and only liked one girl back home, though he was unsure about her. Here at least, he knew that Kama really liked him because she told him and he knew that Li'Faran liked him, too, as they were both trying to woo Thaddeus in their own unique ways.

Between them, stood Agham-Ix, who as his familiar served Thaddeus as his protector, and in some ways, his mentor in matters of love along with Toril, the last Champion of the Light, who appeared infrequently to teach Thaddeus about courtly manners, how to interact with the elite classes and most importantly, etiquette. It was his view that Thaddeus might well be a leader of people, even at his young age and Toril thought it best that he be prepared for such an eventuality.

Toril also helped Thaddeus with learning about love. As a human himself, Toril had lots of practice with the fair sex. He was a confirmed bachelor for much of his life, but later on, his wealth and station secure, he chose to take a wife at 55 cycles old, as he believed that he could provide for her properly. Toril instructed the young Thaddeus about ladies and what to say, and more importantly when to say it. He also instructed him in one rule that was drilled into his head, "Respect all ladies, regardless of wealth or station." Toril told him that one rule was oftentimes the difference between success and failure in his duties as a Champion of the Light. Ladies would often approach him and give him information that he might not have had otherwise simply because he treated them with the utmost respect, no matter what.

Toril went further than he normally would have, due to Thaddeus' age and instructed him in more personal items, like his personal upkeep and proper grooming that would be expected of him as a Champion. He even gave Thaddeus many lessons in the physical parts of a relationship, including the who, what, when, where, how, and why were given to him and were repeated on many occasions. He also tried to steer Thaddeus towards Kama, insofar as her suitability as a wife for him. He explained that he might not be looked upon as favorably if he had a Narsum for a wife, especially among more polite society and that elves, while not the norm, were deemed acceptable as wives for human wizards. Of course, his opinions were his own and he thought he was doing right but Thaddeus didn't understand why that mattered, and Toril said, "Perhaps in time, you will understand this, but now is not the time."

Eventually his graduation sun came, as Thaddeus took his place among a long line of wizards before him, and though his station was unique at this time, just as he was, he really enjoyed all the attention, not to mention the food and other victuals that were part of this celebration. The giving of gifts at this time was a long-standing tradition at the magickal academies, and the guest list included some big names on the Continent, like Thaddeus Brimstone, General Morshand, The Moon Goddess, The Snow Queen, even a fairly large contingent of elves in honor of Kama attended this grand celebration. Among the guests invited were also a fair number of dragons, as Agham-Ix was now the familiar of a full-fledged wizard, which was a rare thing among his kind.

Thaddeus received gifts this sun that he would treasure for a lifetime. The first of which was presented by his elder namesake who said, "My dear Thaddeus, it was one cycle ago that I took ye from yer room in that other place and brought ye here. Ye asked me if ye could talk to yer pa whenever ye wanted if ye stayed with us, and I said ye could. I stand before ye with such a device: it's a mirror which allows ye to look at an' talk to yer pa, Patrick the Younger. Yes, I know of him, and I'll tell ye the tale of how I met 'im later. Also, tradition dictates in the world I come from, whenever a new wizard graduates from school, his mentor provides him with a spellbook and journal of his own, so here is yers. As I said ta ye afore, a good wizard is a diligent wizard, and a diligent wizard is one who writes his discoveries down, so ye can look back and remember all the good ye had done. Congratulations, Thaddeus, yer a wizard now!"

General Morshand, all 6'9" of him, dressed in the furs of a Barbarian general said, "Ye've saved many of my troops in battle, and I hope ye never need them, but every warrior needs a weapon. And while yer weapon of choice might be magick, there are times when ye need somethin' else…a backup, if ye will. So I present ye with these twin short swords, made in the finest Barbarian tradition with iron and steel. Good luck, Thaddeus!"

Kama stepped forward and said, "Thaddeus, you and I have spent a lot of time together over the last cycle, and over that time, I have taught you about the elves, elfish magicks, and the traditions of my people. Tradition dictates that whenever an elf finishes a course of study, regardless of specialty, they are typically given a gift that represents who their instructor feels they are. In working with you in the past cycle, having seen you engage in battle yet still wonder what lies ahead for you and the Continent, I wanted to give you something that will help you divine what may lie ahead in your adventures. In the finest traditions of my people, I present to you a Diviner's Stone. My Elven friends brought it this sun in the hopes that it serves you well as a wizard!" She followed it up with a hug and a kiss on the cheek, as she wiped away a tear in her eye.

Not to be outdone, Li'Faran said, "My brother, from the first moment I saw you, I knew that we were connected in some way. When I saw you eating with the warriors of the tribe, I had feared that you would take a liking to being one with them, but when you came to me and we talked, I knew that you were unlike them and more like my brother, steeped in magick as our father was. When a Narsum becomes a warrior, he is awarded something that the whole village had a hand in making for him; the idea comes from the tradition that he will defend the whole village, so when he has this "village token" with him, he carries all of us with him no matter where he is, so that he is always defending us. In the finest traditions of the Narsum, on this occasion, I present to you, your village token. Taken from bits and pieces of my home village, which every Narsum had a hand in building, though there is nothing left of it now, I pray that you remember the good you did there and the honor that you bestowed on me and my tribe. Thank you!"

There were no dry eyes in the house after Li'Faran finished her soliloquy. Everyone knew what had happened to her village, and all assembled were amazed at two things...first that she was so articulate and second that she managed to assemble his token so beautifully. In truth, Kama helped her with both things, and as she finished her soliloquy, she winked at Kama in thanks to her.

That performance would be tough to top, but next up on the gift-giving stage was the Snow Queen as the temperature in the room dropped significantly. The Snow Queen said, "You have served my people well, and I have welcomed you as one of my people; additionally, I have blessed you with a token of my thanks for your acts of courage and bravery on behalf of my people. However, there is one more small token that I have only bestowed once before to a true hero of our people and now, with all of you as witnesses, I present you with this...a legendary artifact, Siras-Nar! Taken from the very heart of the Deep North, this tiny icicle of the purest water known, will bolster your ability with cold spells, will ensure that you are always warm, no matter where you are and will mark you as a true hero in the eyes of my people."

Finally, the Moon Goddess stepped up to speak, and said, "Of all of you, I've known this boy the longest, as he spent most of the last cycle in my domain, learning the art of spellcraft. During that time, we have not spoken much, but on the rare occasion when we did, I found him to be of good character, always doing what was right, instead of what was easy. On this occasion, given his unswerving loyalty to all of us gathered here, and to celebrate the completion of a long road of challenges, I present you with this…a Moon-shield. A small shield, too small to be of any use in combat, but renders the user's mind invisible to all who might search for it. Congratulations, young man. You've done very well!

She also said into his mind, "You know, I LOVE how you look at me. Haven't had that in a very long time!" She winked at him as the assembled crowd clapped and cheered as the festivities continued.

After that, a loud roar could be heard and all went outside to hear what the assembled dragons had to say, as Alotraxas piped up and said, "Deities, friends, and honored guests, we are gathered here to mark a very auspicious occasion, the achievement of something miraculous. One cycle ago, this was an ordinary boy, but this sun, we mark the beginning of his ascent to manhood as we welcome him into a unique group, that has only one member, that of full-fledged Wizards. We also acknowledge his inclusion in another group, one you all know about, those who have been charged with watching over the peoples of the Continent since time immemorial, I speak of that elite group known as Champions of the Light.

"Having watched a previous generations' experimentations with magick, I have a unique perspective on this matter and a unique gift for our young man. When magick first came to the Continent, we developed the Natural Law and instilled it into the minds of Wizards everywhere, but then as now, there were those who did not follow the Law and chaos resulted. Fortunately, at that time, Toril was still alive and was able to protect the people from their powers until we were able to exile them to another place. From that time to this, we have been without a Champion of the Light, as it seemed that mankind was no longer worthy to continue to receive those gifts given to them by the Ancients…That is until this brave young man came here and pledged to help us in our time of need. His desire to help us was unflinching even when faced with pure evil, his need to let the Continent know that the forces of good were still willing to fight for what was right and his courage in facing all this, without a personal stake in whether this world lives or dies. That, friends, is why I deemed him worthy of my knowledge and tutelage over the last cycle and why we are gathered here this sun.

"As you all know, I am the last Ancient still sworn to uphold my duty to mankind, something that I have never shied away from, and in honor of this young man's hard work and sacrifice on our behalf, I honor him with this… Toril's Eye! Toril, would you honor us with your presence?"

Toril appeared rather suddenly in the courtyard, seemingly dressed for the occasion and said, "Ah, Thaddeus. I see you have my eye…Allow me to explain. We all have two eyes in our head, but sometimes, you need eyes elsewhere, which is why I invented this—a mobile eye, one that can sprout from anywhere on the body. Simply think of where you need another eye, and it will appear there. Simply swallow this, and you will have a free-floating eyeball inside of you, ready to see anywhere your adventures might take you, along with a few magickal enhancements, of course. This eye can see in the dark, can see magickal energies and heat radiations. I found it very useful when I served as a Champion of the Light."

Thaddeus took the miniature eyeball and swallowed it (which was totally gross) and within a few moments, an eye appeared in his hand, then behind his head, then between his other eyes. It was like magick (because it was), and all the guests clapped and cheered after Alotraxas' delivery.

The party continued on, and Thaddeus played with his new magickal trinkets and the village token that Li'Faran had given him. Of all the cool things he got, it was the village token that he felt strongest about. It had little bits and pieces of her village, like a leather strip from a suit of armor, a strip of cloth from her mother's dress…a husk of grain and a shard of metal…also included was a chip of stone, presumably from one of the buildings and a charred bit of wood. She also gathered a "stick doll," a common toy for children and the last thing was a shard of pottery from an earthenware jug used for ale. He remembered that sun with perfect clarity, and as he was looking at it and remembering, Li'Faran happened to notice what he was doing and went over to him and said, "You like it?"

Thaddeus replied, "This means more to me than anything else I got…it helps me remember why I'm here. More importantly, it came from you, the only relative I have in this world. And I'm so glad that you're here and safe. When I realize how close you came to dying that sun, I'm so grateful that I didn't lose you and grateful that I have a very hard head!"

Li'Faran got a little choked up and said, "All your friends bring magick stuff. I don't have magick; I can only give you village token. I feel so out of place here…not like home…"

Thaddeus remembered what Toril told him in a case like this and said, "Li'Faran, you gave me a gift better than all the rest. You gave me a gift from your heart and from your people…I will never forget those people that we buried. This token is all that is left of them, and I will cherish it always."

He continued as he hugged her, "Besides, you and I are actually related. That is something that no one else in this room can say, and while they are all good friends, you are a great sister! Oh, and I forgot to tell you: you look amazing…so beautiful!"

Thaddeus kissed her and took her hand and brought her back out to the party. Truth be told, Li'Faran had never worn such finery before, but she did feel pretty, but horribly out of place, especially with real deities in the room.

The celebration continued long into the evening, but one by one, the assembled guests left, leaving only the young Thaddeus, Agham-Ix, Kama, Li-'Faran, and Bjor'ma in the home. Many who were in attendance that sun noticed Bjor'ma in his new state, but despite their powerful attempts at changing him back to what he was, he remained a pink blob with eyes. After the last guest left, the young Thaddeus and Agham-Ix plopped on his bed and went quickly to sleep. Kama and Li'Faran checked in on him some time later, and they noted that he held onto the village token while all the other gifts he had received that sun were in this room, but none was closer to him than the only non-magickal thing he had received that sun as Kama said, "You know, he's quite taken with that. Thank you for allowing me to help you make it."

Li'Faran said, "You're welcome. It was fun to make that together. He's a special kid and my brother."

They both smiled and quietly left his doorway and went to sleep.

Bjor'ma was still slithering around the house as he usually did late at night, and he left something by Thaddeus' door. He wanted Thaddeus to have something, but had no way of telling him that he had a gift for him. Thaddeus would have to wait until morning to reveal his last gift.

CHAPTER 30

BJOR'MA'S SECRET

Thaddeus awoke the next morning, opened his door and found a piece of parchment on the floor just outside of his door. He picked it up and saw a crudely written note. It said:

Thadeus,
*   It hard to write but wanted to tell you of gift. Find capital of west in castle south hallway third door on right...you find chest in floor...it was mine now yours...you good Wizard now...*
*   Bjorma*

Thaddeus couldn't believe it, Bjor'ma had learned to write, but how? He went to look for Bjor'ma and found him in the library, but he wasn't moving. Thaddeus went up to him and noted his eyes were closed. Thaddeus decided not to bother Bjor'ma until he awoke, as he was still unsure what would happen if he was startled. He decided to have some breakfast, but he was the only person awake in the house.

He reflected on the events of the last sun and the last cycle and asked himself, "Now what?"

He had completed his magickal training, he was a Champion of the Light, and a hero by most accounts...but what was he expected to do now? He needed some guidance, but first he wanted to ask the people who were closest to him, so he waited for them to get up while he toyed around with some of the gifts he got the sun afore. He didn't know how to work the Diviners' Stone, but he thought that Kama would. He took the tiny icicle that the Snow Queen gave him and held it in his hands, and he felt warm despite the coolness of a late Simcha morning. He decided to keep that on him at all times because he was frequently cold.

He opened the journal and spellbook that the elder Thaddeus had given him and inside he found a note which read:

Dear Thaddeus,

I present to ye, yer journal and spellbook, now I know what ye might be thinking...what am I going to do with a book, haven't I read enough? Trust me, I thought the same thing when my mentor gave me my journal and spellbook...but over the cycles, I found it to be a valuable tool...when ye write something in here, ye've preserved it and it becomes immune to the ravages of time...it is there for ye when ye might need to remember it, which is particularly useful when ye get older.

It has been an honor to teach ye what I know, just as I did in life...in effect, ye are my last pupil and perhaps the most miraculous one, as ye've learned 10 cycles of knowledge in but a single cycle. I've included all the spells that I taught ye in here, but left many pages for yer thoughts and adventures as ye progress through life. Also, ye'll never run out of pages as this book will automatically add more as needed.

In closing, know that ye'll never be alone as I'll always be with ye.
Your mentor and friend,
Thaddeus Brimstone

Thaddeus smiled as he read the note, remembering all the times he spent with Thaddeus, both in his mind when he was back home and since he arrived here, particularly in the early suns of his time here. It amazed him that he was now a wizard as well, and while not as experienced as the elder Thaddeus was, he figured that his elder namesake must have started out just like him at some point. He was sure that plenty of adventure would be coming his way...He could not have known just how right he was.

While he was reminiscing, Li'Faran awoke, and he heard some noise in the kitchen. He went to investigate and said, "Hey, sis! Great party last night!"

Li'Faran noted that he was carrying the pouch in which she put his village token, and she smiled at him as she said, "Yeah...and thank you fer helpin' me.

Not used to all that. We can practice with yer new swords, and I get to use my axe against ye…hehehe…gotta keep up with yer trainin'."

Li'Faran thought that she had to be a big sister and brother to him, she felt it was necessary to teach him about weapons and defense, as he had no one here to do that for him. She felt that his life might be saved one sun by what she was teaching him, and that it would help him attract a mate, at least to her mind. She knew that a male Narsum had to be strong to get the best possible mate, and though he was about as far away as one could get from a male Narsum at this stage in his life, she viewed it as a work in progress, and that this work would pay off when he was tall and strong, able to care for and defend his chosen mate. They ate a traditional Narsum first meal of meat and bread, though Thaddeus piled on a whole bunch of vegetables and fruits to his plate that didn't appeal to Li'Faran.

After breakfast, they went into the courtyard for weapons training, and Thaddeus was amazed how effective his new swords were; it was like they were made for him as he found them light and well-balanced. Despite the ferocity of Li'Faran's attacks on him, he held strong and was able to counter some of her blows. He knew that he was not training to learn to attack, but rather to defend against a physical threat. She taught him all manner of defensive movements designed to get him out of a tight spot so he could bring his magick to bear against any given foe. After a hard morning workout, Thaddeus inspected his new swords and noted no nicks or cuts on the blades, nor were they scratched at all. It was evident that Li'Faran put a lot of power behind her attacks, as her axe was nicked in several places as she said, "Good swords must be made of Barbarian steel…very hard and strong."

They went in to rest, and the pair saw that Kama was up, watching them practice as Thaddeus said, "Morning, Kama! Does the sun find you well?"

Kama said, "Aye! It does. Remember our experiment later on; discoveries don't make themselves!"

Thaddeus said, "Let me rest for a bit, and we can get to it…got a question for you though…"

Kama said, "Ask," as she was not expecting any really deep questions, or anything about her specifically as Thaddeus said, "Now that my training is done…now what?"

Kama smiled and said, "You know, I asked the same question after I graduated from the Academy, and my mentor told me, 'Now you practice what you've learned and one continues learning and discovering.' Speaking of discovery, I'll need to show you how to use your Diviner's Stone. It's a very useful item; perhaps even divine a few things for you, just so you can get a feel for how it works."

Thaddeus nodded as he saw Bjor'ma slithering towards him as he said, "I got your note. How did you learn to write?" Bjor'ma produced a quill pen from his body as Thaddeus said, "You never cease to amaze. I hope to be able to shake your hand one sun, and I intend to find that chest this sun. Thank you for honoring me this way."

The elder Thaddeus had attuned his extradimensional home for his young protégé during his last visit, and it was now ready to take Thaddeus anywhere he might need to go. So, he stepped aboard with Agham-Ix and said, "Capital of the West, in the castle, south hallway, third door on the right." He felt some magick flow around him, and the craft was off. The elder Thaddeus had also built in a few improvements; the first was to ensure that a part of it was always touching the ground to prevent the Entities of Evil from coming here, and he made it more "kid-friendly" by replacing his prized tobacco plants with a miniature library, featuring a small selection of tomes that he found most helpful while travelling. He did leave the golden chalice on his favorite chair though and attuned it to his young protégé's touch. When he touched it, it filled up with a clear liquid. Thaddeus took a sip and felt his mind really focus on what was ahead as a bell signaled the end of the trip.

He opened the door and arrived in a once opulent room, ravaged by swarms of undead creatures, not to mention the elements. He walked into the room and started looking around. He noted that most of the things in here were broken or destroyed, and he hoped that whatever did this, did not find the chest that he was here to find. He searched around the room carefully, amidst the broken remnants of what was once an opulent place. He figured that he would need some magickal help because he thought that whatever it was, he was looking for would be hidden magickally and he was right. He cast a Magick Detection spell, and within a few moments, he found a magickally marked floorboard under what was a fine four-post bed at one time. He carefully pried the board up and found a small chest underneath it. It was finely made of what looked like bronze and was small enough to fit in his hand.

On the miniature chest, he noted some magickal script which said, "Trace the magickal symbol on the board on the top of this chest to open."

Using his finger, he traced the symbol he saw on the floorboard. He heard a click from the chest and he opened the lid slowly and carefully. He was so excited to open this chest; his first treasure chest bequeathed to him by a former Wizard. As he opened it, he saw a large clear gem, he willed Toril's Eye onto his hand and found it was highly magickal. Also inside he found a note, written in Elven, which thanks to Kama he could read. It said:

Greetings to you,

If you are reading this, you are a Wizard. One of two things could have led you here, either sheer luck and happenstance, or I bequeathed this to you, and you were able to find my most prized possession. Either way, what is contained in this chest is yours now. In this chest is an Amplification Crystal, an extraordinarily rare magickal gem which I found in the Southern Great Forest where such crystals are sometimes formed and harvested by enterprising Wizards like myself. Using this, I was able to amplify my ability to control the minds of men, making me able to actually control the mind of King Noran I. This crystal serves as a means to take any natural abilities you may have and amplifies them. Note that it does not work for spells, only abilities that are already inherent in your mind.

To use it, keep it close to you for seven suns to allow it to attune itself to you...once that is complete, you'll find that any natural abilities that you have will be amplified to a great degree. On the bottom of the chest is a key which opens the lock to my personal safe behind the portrait of myself as I was in life...inside are many thousands of gold ducats, earned and saved over a lifetime, which I also bequeath to you.

Bjor'ma, Royal Advisor to King Noran I

Thaddeus pulled out the crystal and found a small key under it. He went up to the portrait of Bjor'ma as he appeared in life. Though it was faded and torn, Thaddeus saw enough of it and thought that he didn't look like a good man in the portrait, but perhaps he was, but controlling the mind of a king didn't sound like a good thing to do. He wondered who Bjor'ma really was as he took the portrait down and found a lone keyhole in the wall paneling. He inserted the key and opened a large safe, which was taller than he was, absolutely loaded to the gills with gold ducats. Thaddeus thought that this money could be used for reconstruction purposes, but he didn't have the strength or time to move all this gold, so he locked the safe back up again and put the key back into the miniature chest he found, thinking the gold would be safe here until the time for reconstruction came, some of which could be started here in the West.

He climbed back aboard his new "car" and said, "Home," and he felt the rush of magick as it took off again. He decided to keep the amplification crystal but thought that he should have it checked out first by the elder Thaddeus, just to be sure. On his trip home, Agham-Ix said into his mind, "This is a nice way to travel; all the comforts of home," as he stretched out on a mound of cushions. Thaddeus looked at him, smiled, and thought that Agham-Ix liked being his familiar, and he certainly liked having Agham-Ix around; no matter what happened in his life, he knew he would always have a friend to talk to.

Within a toll, the trip was complete, and Thaddeus arrived back in his Samsrun home. Kama was the first to greet him as she said, "Where did you go? I missed you!"

Thaddeus said, "I took my new car for a spin around the block to see what she could do, and I found this chest with a large magickal crystal inside, which Bjor'ma said I could have, and you should see the pile of gold that he amassed—it should help with reconstruction efforts across the Continent once the evil is gone from this land."

Kama looked in the chest and said, "I know what that is…it's an Amplification Crystal. They are very rare, I've only seen one once; my Elven mentor had one…He said it amplified his ability to teach. I wonder what it will amplify in you? It could be anything. Know this though, once done, it cannot be undone. Whatever the crystal amplifies in you, it stays that way. One question though: what's a car, and what did you mean by taking her around the block?"

Thaddeus laughed and said, "Sometimes I forget that I'm not back home and use terminology from my world. Sorry about that, but to explain what I meant…a car is a means of transportation in my world, they are often referred to as 'she' to remind us to treat them gently, and taking 'a spin around the block' means that I took a short trip to test everything out. I've told you about cars before and how my pa would drive me around 'cuz kids like me can't operate cars until we are a bit older."

Thaddeus was satisfied at Kama's explanation as to what the Amplification Crystal was and that it was safe for him to use, but he wondered what it would amplify in him. He didn't have any special talents that he knew of; that is before he learned magick, so he was unsure as to what it could possibly amplify in him. He went looking for Bjor'ma, fortunately for him, pink blobs are easy to find and said, "Bjor'ma, I found the crystal and the gold. What do you think it will amplify in me?"

Bjor'ma didn't seem to react to his question at first, but then heard a faint scratching sound from underneath Bjor'ma. A few moments later, Bjor'ma moved, and on a small piece of parchment was written, "Not sure."

Thaddeus heard another faint scratching sound and another slip of parchment appeared as Bjor'ma moved again. Scratched onto the parchment was, "Hope you enjoy crystal and gold, and always follow Law. No be like me or you end up like this."

Thaddeus said, "I will always follow the Law and be a good man. Speaking of that, were you a good man in life?"

Thaddeus heard a faint scratching sound as a third strip of parchment was revealed from underneath Bjor'ma which said, "No...and now I pay price for it."

Thaddeus said, "You've suffered much, but I will find a way to help you because everyone deserves a second chance." He smiled, touched Bjor'ma, and got up to leave the library where Bjor'ma could usually be found, still amazed that Bjor'ma had figured out how to write notes to him.

CHAPTER 31

EVIL FLYING HIGH AND FAST

Sarodan came to the Continent and though cold and brutal, especially in the North, it left the land, but in its wake came something that was not natural. Thaddeus had not heard about anything amiss on the Continent, but that was only because of the slow communications of the sun, as there were folks dying by the hundreds in the Deep North and Far North. A highly virulent and potent disease was slowly decimating the population, but it was thought that it was a "normal" thing, as only the hardiest souls could survive this far North. While the Barbarians who had been living here for hundreds of cycles were used to the cold, most of the humans who emigrated from the much warmer climes of the West were not. They fell victim to this disease seemingly much easier than the Barbarians did; part of the reason was due to the distance between Barbarian hamlets, and those of humans.

Barbarians prided themselves on self-sufficiency and would rarely trade with each other thus limiting the spread of any disease among them, but with humans that was not the case. Humans lived in hamlets that were much closer together, thereby facilitating trade and the exchange of ideas, but also it accelerated the spread of disease amongst the populations of humans spread over the vast area that comprised the North's two distinct regions. No one had any idea what this disease was, nor how to cure it, as it seemed to evolve over time…before it was only taking the old and infirm, but now seemed to be changing, gathering strength; so much so that it was enough to infect otherwise healthy individuals. No one detected the single high-flying creature that would only come out at night to spread this disease far and wide amidst the

North. Once done with his nightly flyovers, he would return to the Dread Lord's domain to regenerate. He had even asked the Dread Lord to mask his evil emanations and magickal abilities, so he would not be detected as he flew over the land by anyone who could sense evil or magickal powers. Things seemed to be going well for Thanatos, given his new outlook on the eventual conquest of the Continent, or so he thought. Even the Dread Lord was impressed but thought that he could be doing more as he summoned Thanatos to him as Simcha came to the Continent in earnest.

Thanatos said, "Reporting as you commanded, my Lord!"

The Dread Lord was sitting in his throne room, high above the polished black basalt floor where the lower demonic presences skittered and slithered about. His primary weapon, a charred, wicked looking, flaming trident was to his side, ready to pick up and throw at anyone who displeased him.

The Dread Lord said, "You are doing well, Thanatos. The disease is spreading, and the Lord of the Dead reports an uptick in the new recruits to his army. However, you can and should be doing more to spread this sickness. To aid you in your task, I will give you the ability to fly faster over the land. No one will be able to catch you, and you will be nothing but an anomaly to those who are watching the night skies. Instead of just flying over the North, fly over the periphery of the Continent, including the elves to the South…the purpose here is to sap their strength before the final glorious conquest of the Continent will begin. Once enough have died, we will begin to spread darkness across the land and all will wither and die."

Thanatos replied, "Yes, my Lord! How will my airborne velocity increase, my Lord?"

The Dread Lord said, "With these…" He threw a pair of blackened wings at Thanatos and said, "Fallen Angel Wings. A rare thing, but I give them to you so that you can continue to serve me and spread this disease as quickly as possible."

Thanatos quickly put the wings on his back and said while bowing low to the Dread Lord, "Thank you, my Lord. I live to serve you!"

The Dread Lord said, "Now go, regenerate, and prepare for tonight's flight!"

Thanatos went back to his regeneration chamber and thought how fast he would be now. He thought he could outfly anything, and he would be right on that count, as Angel Wings enable the user to fly faster than anything living. Fallen Angel Wings were the same as their goodlier counterpart, but instead were dedicated to evil and projected a strong aura of evil, which Thanatos didn't mind at all. He smiled as he thought about all the evil he would be able to do as he stepped inside his regeneration chamber and closed the lid.

Meanwhile, back in what used to be Samsrun, Thaddeus had spent seven suns with his new Amplification Crystal; he didn't feel anything different about himself or his magick. He could cast all the same spells he had before and had the same knowledge of healing and protection that he had before. He remembered that the Crystal didn't work on spells, but natural abilities. He thought long and hard as to what his natural abilities might be...what was he good at before he came here? His answer was that he was average at just about everything...except one thing: the acquisition of new knowledge. He knew that he excelled in school and had the grades to prove it, could that be his natural ability? Could he take in new knowledge better than most?

He decided to test his theory and found a tome that he had never read before in the library and sat down to read it as he normally would have. Agham-Ix crawled up on his lap as they read together and then the strangest thing happened, after reading for about a toll, he discovered something: he remembered everything that he just read with perfect clarity. It was like he could actually see every word that was written, he could actually recall the page it was written on it in his mind and read the page over again in his mind. Agham-Ix had fallen asleep, as reading was not his forte, but he wanted to be close to Thaddeus, and truth be told, Thaddeus liked the fact that Agham-Ix was there; unfortunately, because Agham-Ix weighed as much as he did though, Thaddeus didn't necessarily feel all his weight on his legs, he found that he was pinned to the chair, as he found it impossible to move the 40 stone that Agham-Ix weighed. Instead of waking up his weighty friend, he kept reading, and remembering; it was like he had a tome in his mind, and as he read, the tome would fill up, and he could "flip" pages back and forth in his mind with ease. He thought to himself, *Wow! This is great...I can read and remember everything now...that Amplification Crystal really works!*

Though he couldn't get up, he called out to Bjor'ma, who called the library his home, and a few moments later, he saw the pink blob slithering over to him.

He said, "Bjor'ma...the Amplification Crystal really works! I always enjoyed reading and picking up new knowledge, and now whenever I go to recall something that I've read, I can actually see the page in my mind and read from it...this is amazing! Thank you so much!"

Thaddeus heard a faint scratching sound on the floor as he saw Bjor'ma slowly reveal another scrap of parchment which read, "You're welcome…glad I could do some good."

Thaddeus smiled at Bjor'ma as Bjor'ma slithered away to find another book to read. That was when Li'Faran came barging into the library and said, "Brother. Time to practice. Come on."

Li'Faran did not notice Agham-Ix laying on Thaddeus due to the large tome on his lap, but as she came over, she noticed him. Thaddeus knew that Narsum were strong, but he didn't realize how strong they were, when Li'Faran slowly lifted Agham-Ix off him and put him on the floor without waking him.

Thaddeus said, "How did you?"

Li'Faran cut him off and said, "Narsum are strong! I make you strong like me!"

They went out to the courtyard and had a good workout, including weapons practice.

During weapons practice, Thaddeus saw her go into what he thought was the legendary Narsum rage, but she was faking it as she was unable to just get into rage mode as quickly as the men could. He didn't know that it took a lot more for Narsum women to enter rage than it did for men. He feared for his life, but he kept a cool head and used the defensive techniques he learned, emerging unscathed after a half-toll of battle with a larger and stronger foe.

As the second sun was setting on the thoroughly exhausted Thaddeus, Thanatos was preparing for his maiden flight with wings. He opened the black portal where he usually did, high in the Deep Northern mountains where he was unlikely to be seen by anyone. As he waited for nightfall, he tentatively tested his wings and found that they seemed to be doing quite well. That's when it started to snow.

As the temperature dropped, he had a feeling of deja vu as he felt a presence nearby. As good as his vision was, he couldn't see this presence, but rather heard it. He heard a female voice say, "Thanatos, you are not welcome here, and I banish you from my lands on pain of death. Go now and never return."

Thanatos turned in the direction where he thought he heard the voice and said, "Or what? You are nothing…and cannot command me."

The voice said to him, "Perhaps I cannot, but I know someone who can."

He heard a whisper go past him, but it was too fast for him to understand what was said.

Thaddeus was having a snack with Li'Faran when he heard, "Come now, Champion—you are needed!"

He teleported to the very spot that the whisper emanated from as he said, "YOU AGAIN!"

A bright light emanated from Thaddeus as the snow stopped, and Thanatos could see Thaddeus standing on the top of a mountain with a light robe and hat on, with twin swords on his belt and a large white staff in his hands.

Thaddeus said, "Now we finish this…"

Thaddeus willed himself to fly as Thanatos was spreading his new wings as he said, "Will you face me or run away like the coward you are?"

Thanatos said, "I am different now, and I choose to run…"

As he said that, he bolted away with a speed that Thaddeus had never seen before…and so Thaddeus gave chase as he took off into the night. Thanatos was surprised just how fast he was going, but much to his surprise noted that Thaddeus was gaining on him. What Thanatos didn't realize was that Thaddeus, as a Champion of the Light, had access to the powers of those who were dead and could use those powers only when he was faced with evil. Alotraxas himself granted Thaddeus the ability of "Light Flight," which is a bit faster than Angel Wings could carry someone. Thaddeus had never gone this fast before as he started to shoot bolts of pure white light from his staff and finally was able to see Thanatos trying to dodge the bolts of light and get away from him. Thanatos poured on the speed as he descended but just couldn't shake Thaddeus, as Thanatos noted bolts of lightning coming from behind him. Thaddeus knew that lightning was faster than Thanatos could ever be and just kept shooting; he grazed Thanatos on a few occasions as the disease he was spreading continued to fall from his demonic body.

Thaddeus had an idea as they were both heading straight down as Thanatos was going about as fast as he could; he called Agham-Ix, who teleported to him instantly and just as the young dragon appeared on his back, he pulled his blades out and teleported directly in front of Thanatos who couldn't stop in time and wound up striking Thaddeus' hardened body while being on the wrong end of Thaddeus' twin blades. He said with a snarl in his voice, "The Light takes you now!" as Thaddeus and his swords glowed brightly in the night sky as black goop started to pour from Thanatos. His very lifeblood was falling to the ground as he tried to back up and get off the swords which went all the way through him as the light from Thaddeus was literally eating him alive. He finally managed to slide off the blades and said, "You've won tonight, but I'll be back!"

A black portal opened up behind him, and he fell through it. Thaddeus kept the light in the sky bright, as if to announce yet another victory of the Light. Thaddeus flew home slowly with Agham-Ix taking in the wonderful Simcha night.

Thanatos landed hard on the floor and slid to a stop as he struck his regeneration chamber. A black goop covered the floor where he slid, and it pooled around him as he lay there. He managed to pick himself up and flop into his regeneration chamber knowing how close he came to death tonight. He could feel how strong Thaddeus' abilities were and knew that he didn't stand a chance against him; it was like he was fighting all the Champions of the Light at once, which gave him an idea. Perhaps there were others who could join with him when it was needed. He would dwell on that as he closed the lid on his regeneration chamber, and it started to mend his crippled form.

Thaddeus arrived home a few tolls later as he and Agham-Ix flew home together. Thaddeus noted that his white robe was now covered with a black goop, and as he looked at his blades, he noted that they were totally unaffected by being inside of a demon. He smelled horribly, like a dead corpse as the black goop dripped on the floor of his home. He desperately wanted to get out of these clothes and into a bath. He and Agham-Ix drew a bath for themselves and excitedly talked about their latest victory.

CHAPTER 32

SAMHEIN ARRIVES

Two full seasons passed by before Thanatos could get out of his regeneration chamber as his wounds were so grievous. He was grateful that he escaped and could continue in service to the Dread Lord. He knew that his sacrifices would be rewarded and once he was standing at the right hand of his master, his task complete, all the trials and suffering he went through would be forgotten. With that thought, he left his chamber to talk to the Lord of Blight. He knew that he would once again experience the Pit of Desecration to reinstate the disease that he was carrying after his run in with Thaddeus which is an experience he would rather not go through, but he knew it would be worth it in the end.

As he entered the foulest part of the Dread Lord's realm, where the Lord of Blight dwells, he knew that he would complete his mission this time.

The Lord of Blight said unto him, "Thanatos...back again? What can I do for you?"

Thanatos said, "That Champion is stronger than I thought. I am in need of your...unique services."

The Lord of Blight replied, "Aye, that you are. Are you prepared?"

Thanatos said, "Aye," as once again the floor dropped out from under him, and he found himself in the Pit of Desecration. He wondered if it would be a different disease this time, one that killed faster than before. As he was experiencing the feeling of the black sludge permeating his very soul, he felt hopeful in his ultimate success and as he remembered it was now the season of Samhein, which reminded him of an idea.

After floating around in the vileness for a few tolls, he rose out of the Pit and went to speak to the Lord of the Dead. The Lord of the Dead looked like a military man and carried himself that way as well. His regal home was at the top of 6,666 steps, which most of the undead that were in his endless legions could not climb.

Thanatos climbed the stairs and said, "Lord of the Dead, I am Thanatos, and I would treat with you!"

The Lord of the Dead stood 13 arms high, as he came through a portal, dressed in a black suit of plate armor, a large black blade and glowing red eyes that peered out from a full-face helmet. He said, in a deep, slow voice, "Thanatos, I have heard of your campaigns and your losses to the Light. I hope you are here with some good news."

Thanatos looked down and said, "No, Lord, I have once again lost to the Light, but I had an idea that might even the odds. I noted that the Champion of the Light has many friends and many eyes, and access to powers that no one has heard of or seen in thousands of cycles. Mayhaps we have friends and eyes as well, that I might have access to the next time I face him?"

The Lord of the Dead stood silently for the longest time, but finally said, "No. Those that join our ranks are turned into what you see here, mindless husks, milling about the endless plains of the dead. Mayhaps a soul or two from the Vault might be of assistance? They can provide knowledge, but little else, unless you can convince…No, I don't think you could…Could you?"

Thanatos said, "Convince who? I have to try something…"

The Lord of the Dead said, "Go to the Hollow Mist graveyard, in the city of Samsrun. There you will find a mausoleum, enter and speak to the resident therein. Know that he doesn't entertain fools, but if he would be willing to join your cause, mayhaps you'll have something. Know that you will have to offer him something in exchange for his services, and he will try to kill you if you displease him. Also know if you do this, you will have a target on your back, not only from the Champion, but from those that join you. Good luck, Thanatos!"

Thanatos was scared for the first time in his short existence because he knew that Samsrun was where the Champion lived, and he had never come this close to him willingly. He hoped that he could remain undetected because he did not think that he would survive another run-in with the Champion, and if he did, it might mean another season or two regenerating. The magick he had in him was masked, so he thought he would be safe, so long as he did as the Lord of the Dead instructed.

As night fell on the third of Samhein, Thanatos stood in front of the Hollow Mist graveyard, a vast place filled with wood and stone markers of all shapes and varieties. Some of these markers were elaborate, and some were simple, but he did note a heavy fog only over the graveyard, as if someone wanted to hide their presence here. He opened the heavy iron gate and set foot into the graveyard as the heavy fog took him in. He felt on edge because he wasn't sure what to expect, or what spirits roamed about through this vast cemetery. After about two tolls of wandering around this place, he felt a little more at ease as he came to a really big stone building; it was radiating energy, though Thanatos didn't know why. He could only surmise about who or what was in this building. He approached the sealed stone doors and noted a large, black wrought iron knocker on the right side of the massive doors. Above the doors was highly elaborate stonework and a name, Vruhans, which was beautifully engraved amidst the stonework.

He took the heavy knocker in his hand and struck the door with it. The ground shook a little as he did this, and he froze…What if the Champion felt that? Though after a few moments, the Champion did not appear, and he heard the sound of stone scraping against stone as the massive stone doors opened to him revealing the cavernous interior. Thanatos slipped inside as the heavy stone doors closed behind him. He felt like he belonged here, as he felt a presence in the room with him. A very powerful presence. He knew that his demonic nature would protect him from just about anything but he was still concerned based on the amount of energy he felt now approaching him.

He heard in a hauntingly low tone, "Who approaches?"

Thanatos said, "It is I, Thanatos, an emissary from the Dread Lord himself. I would treat with you this night."

Silence followed after Thanatos identified himself as the energy surrounding him got stronger. From the back of the mausoleum, he saw two small purple lights appear in the darkness. It got cold all of a sudden as he heard in the same low tones, "You are a demon…You have entered this place at the behest of the Dread Lord, I can sense his taint upon you. You need help against a Champion of the Light. I am willing to assist you in this glorious task, but first I would know something, what do you offer?"

During his long flight, in his thoughts about how he was going to approach this, Thanatos had forgotten that he would have to offer something. He was confused about this because to his mind, the glory of serving the Dread Lord was enough, but he decided to improvise and said, "I come with something that no one has offered you in your entire existence, an offering of glory. With your help, we will be able to eliminate a Champion of the Light, think about the honor the Dread Lord will rain upon us if we are successful in this inglorious task!"

The low haunting voice said, "You come with an offering…of nothing? Highly irregular…and UNACCEPTABLE!"

Thanatos felt that he had made a wrong move here as he felt the amount of energy in this dark room spike up as a force took him off his feet and he hit the stone door behind him…hard.

Thanatos scrambled back to his feet as the room brightened ever so slightly, taking on a blood red color as Thanatos finally saw what he was facing. It was a spirit to be sure, but this one was dressed as a Wizard with purple glowing eyes. He could sense the energy coming from this being and a twinge of fear entered his mind. The being in front of him said, "You come here seeking help, but offer nothing in return? Surely one is a fool to think that I, Vruhans, would deign to assist you without payment, and I do not entertain fools. When you have an appropriate offering, return…" He felt the same force take him off his feet, and propel him backwards, again; only this time he went through the door instead of hitting it. He felt the fog envelop him again as the stillness and silence of the cemetery once again took command of his senses.

Thanatos sat in the fog for a bit and thought about what he could offer as payment. Surely Vruhans had no need for gold, and obviously wasn't loyal or beholden to anyone. What could someone like that want to secure his services for a short time? What if he needed Vruhans' services for a longer period, what then? How could he command such a creature? He remembered what the Lord of the Dead told him, that he would have a target on his back the entire time should he choose to hire someone to help him. He decided to think on it, as he took to the air and did his nightly flyovers to spread his new disease on the unsuspecting population of the Continent.

As the disease fell from him over the towns and villages of the Elves, he was deep in thought, thinking about whether or not he wanted a mercenary to help him, and if he did, what could he offer as payment to that creature?

Did he want to risk betrayal at the hands of a helper? He was already betrayed once by Bjor'ma. Did he want to risk that again, only this time given the powers that Vruhans had, he might be totally destroyed instead of gravely injured. He knew that as the Champion got stronger, he would have to work that much harder to carry out the Dread Lord's wishes, and it would be nice if he had a little extra ability in his corner to counter anything that the Champion might do. As he was thinking, he decided on a new tactic: approach Vruhans from a position of power. That way, he would want to serve, but for how long? He knew that such a bargain can be very dangerous, especially given the power that Vruhans had and would have to be worded carefully.

As he was rounding the southeastern corner of the Continent, he came up with an idea. Why not use the Champion to help? If the Champion knew about the presence of evil close to where he lived, he would be duty-bound to try to eradicate it. Perhaps after fighting off the forces of good for a while, perhaps Vruhans would seek him out and strike a bargain...yes, that would do nicely, he thought. He decided to cast a spell in the graveyard the next night, which surely would attract the Champion. He would make a hasty exit, but the evil building would remain and the Champion would work to eradicate the evil within. He smiled at his new plan as he gained altitude as he started his run over the Dragonscape Mountains so as to not be detected by dragons or anything else.

The night's disease spreading went off without a hitch and Thanatos went back to the Dread Lord's domain while putting the finishing touches on his plan. He went into his regeneration chamber and was confident in his new plan to gain the powers of an undead Wizard in his corner.

He took to the air the following night and decided to visit the graveyard afterwards to put his plan into action. After a long flight around the Continent, he once again arrived at the Hollow Mist graveyard. The fog inside the gates was thick as it was the previous night, but Thanatos didn't care this time because he wasn't staying for long. He cast his spell and retreated into the fog to see what would happen, ready to make a quick exit should the need arise.

As he predicted, Thaddeus showed up with Agham Ix. He remembered just how hard the Champion's skin was having crashed into it two seasons ago and cursed Thaddeus for having such a powerful ally so close to him.

Thaddeus looked around and said, "There was magick cast here, Agham-Ix. I can see it. But I don't see the source...hmmmm...the Hollow Mist graveyard, never heard of it, and that fog can't be natural as it only affects the graveyard but not outside of it. Let's see if we can lift it, shall we?" He reviewed in his mind some of the things that he could do and decided on a Rest in Peace spell. This incantation would bless the dead and make them a lot less likely to rise up again. Additionally, it would consecrate the graveyard to good, driving out any evil spirits.

Thanatos listened intently and heard Thaddeus speaking what sounded like a spell. As he heard that, Thanatos went to hide behind the large mausoleum in the rear of the graveyard knowing that he couldn't be detected there. What he saw was miraculous. As the spell was completed, he saw an increasing field of energy coming towards him as the fog lifted. As the field of energy got to the mausoleum, it seemed to not be able to penetrate the energies that surrounded this stone edifice as it continued on its way to the very limits of this place. With the fog lifted, Thaddeus "turned on the lights" and allowed his Ring of Light to illuminate his way. He felt the good he had just done as he walked through the graveyard along a wide stone path. He saw innumerable stone markers, some new and some old, but felt no evil anywhere as he continued his journey into the graveyard, looking for the source of the magick that he detected.

Naturally, Vruhans felt this incursion of good in his graveyard and went out to investigate, not realizing that Thanatos was nearby watching all of this. Vruhans stopped in his tracks and saw a Champion of the Light coming towards him slowly. His fog had been lifted, and the ground here had been consecrated to good. He was not happy at seeing this and thought that it must have been Thanatos who brought him here in retribution for not helping him because nothing had disturbed him here for hundreds of cycles. He fumed quietly about what to do as Thaddeus approached closer, still not having seen him.

He decided to roll out the welcome mat as he could tell that this Champion was stronger than most, having dealt with them in the past. He also noted a stone dragon on the Champion's shoulder, and knew that the Champion was a Wizard and that physical attacks would have little effect. Thaddeus got closer and sensed an evil presence as he said to Agham-Ix in his mind, "There's an evil presence here. Be on your guard."

Thaddeus approached the large stone edifice and noted that the evil was strongest here as he heard in a low haunting tone, "Greetings, Champion…I am Vruhans, what brings you here to my humble home?"

Thaddeus went immediately into full defense mode as the spirit materialized 50 arms in front of him as he said, "Cross this sphere at your peril, spirit, for I am well-protected from the likes of you."

A white colored sphere encapsulated the pair and Vruhans said, "Aye that you are...very impressive. I know better than to cross swords with a Champion of the Light; I have had experiences with your kind before, but I think we have something in common, you and I..."

Thaddeus said angrily, "I don't have anything in common with you, foul spirit. I am duty-bound to destroy you!"

If Vruhans had eyes, he would have rolled them as he said, "Yes...Yes...I know all about your duty, but before you attempt to rid this world of me, mayhaps you should listen, as we have a common enemy you and I. Perhaps you know of him. His name is Thanatos."

Thaddeus did not drop his guard as he said, "Aye, I have heard that name afore, but I have defeated him several times already, and if he shows his cowardly hide here, I will defeat him again."

Thanatos listened in as the exchange continued, from a position of relative safety, behind the edifice of stone, not knowing how this terse exchange was going to play out, but he was hopeful it would erupt into a battle.

Vruhans said, "That would explain why he tried to recruit me to help him against you but had nothing to offer me in exchange for my...considerable talents."

Thaddeus remembered the spirits' name, Vruhans, in a tome he read. According to the book, Vruhans was an evil Wizard, one of the last of his kind in the First Age as it was called. He experimented with extending his life and was rumored to already be over 125 cycles old, which was unheard of at that time. He was killed by a group of Wizards who found his experiments to be against the will of the Gods and was buried here, deep within the Earth, never to rise again. Various spells were cast on his sarcophagus to prevent his return, but apparently, they didn't work as he was now talking to Thaddeus.

Thaddeus said, "What is your intention, spirit? Now that I know of you and your association with evil, you know what I have to do."

Vruhans said, "Yes, that is something that we both know, but perhaps you will stay your hand for a moment, I have a proposal for you."

Thaddeus retorted, "I don't make deals with your kind, prepare to defend yourself, the will of the Ancients will be done this night!"

Vruhans said in a more menacing tone, "You aren't going to make this easy, then…very well!" Vruhans decided not to waste time with smaller magicks and tried his most powerful spell first. He cast a spell, the likes of which had not been seen for many hundreds of cycles and had since been lost to time, but as one of the last of the First Age Wizards, he knew this spell well and had used it successfully on many occasions to neutralize his foes. He cast a Mindwipe spell. This spell wiped a mind clean, removing all magick, thought, and memories from it. It would have reduced Thaddeus to standing dazed before him, allowing the powerful Vruhans to dispose of him at his leisure. There was no mortal defense against this spell, but fortunately for Thaddeus, he had an item to thwart this powerful bit of magick. The Moon Goddess' gift to him, a Moonshield, which was hidden under his hat, provided the only known current defense against this effect as a bright light erupted from his wand of Light and 50,000 voices could be heard coming out of Thaddeus' mouth, "Vruhans, your evil ways stop this night."

Vruhans was surprised that his most powerful spell did not work as his opponent seemed to be casting a spell of his own. As the two engaged in magickal combat, spells flew back and forth between the two combatants while Thanatos looked on with delight. Bright lights and mystical words were heard as Thanatos wondered how long Vruhans would last against the Champion's onslaught and when he would ask Thanatos to help him.

CHAPTER 33

THANATOS' FINAL TOLL

While he was thinking about the perfect time to make his presence known, Thanatos had an idea. He remembered that there must be a source of power for Vruhans to do what he was doing; after all, he was dead. While Vruhans was distracted, he quietly snuck into the mausoleum and jumped down the hole at the back of it. He landed on top of his sarcophagus and tried to move the lid. It was so heavy that Thanatos could not budge it. He cast a spell that boosted his strength, and even with his newfound strength, it barely moved. He gave it one last push and opened it enough to get his arm in there. When he saw a purple glow from within the sarcophagus, he grabbed hold of it and pulled it off the skeleton inside. He looked at it, it was made of gold and very gaudy looking. It had a large purple stone that was glowing in the center of it. He realized that this was it, Vruhans' source of power, the whole reason he was able to survive this long and donned it as his own.

As he put the gaudy piece of jewelry over his head, he felt an incredible rush of power as knowledge of First Age Magick entered his mind, and the accompanying magickal boost was the most intense that he had ever felt. Thanatos thought that with these newfound abilities he could easily defeat the Champion, and with Vruhans next to him, he would be nigh unstoppable and the Continent would be his, while the Champion would be dead in some forgotten corner of the multiverse. While he deviated from his plan a bit, the results were really looking up, and this power boost was certainly unexpected.

He heard in his mind, "What do you wish of me, master?"

Upon hearing that, Thanatos knew that he had hit paydirt. He could not have imagined that he would be in total control of a powerful Wizard! He thought to himself that he was in a position of supreme power as he was now in total control of Vruhans, a powerful Wizard. He said, "Kill the Champion and bring his body to me," as he confidently strode out of the mausoleum to witness the end of the Champion.

While Thanatos was getting his power boost, Vruhans and Thaddeus were locked in magickal combat, with neither one able to overpower the other, until Vruhans sensed something: his phylactery was moving, and it shouldn't be, as it was on a skeleton buried deep underground in a sarcophagus that took a team of oxen to lower into place. Vruhans was in shock, and as his control of his abilities slipped away, he said, "Thanatos has my phylactery. He is my lord and master…I must…follow…his commands."

Thaddeus screamed out, "No! You don't!"

Thaddeus thought quickly about what to do and rushed Vruhans with his white sphere in place. As the floating Vruhans touched the sphere, Thaddeus saw a flash of purple smoke, and Vruhans was gone. Just as Vruhans disappeared, Thanatos ran out of the mausoleum wearing a large, gaudy piece of jewelry with a large purple stone in the center right in front of Thaddeus having sensed something was wrong.

Thaddeus sprang into action first, and a bright white flash emanated from his wand, blinding Thanatos for a few more moments as he reeled back inside the mausoleum. This was just enough time for Agham-Ix, realizing that he was in a stone building, to ask the stones on the ceiling to release a large iron chandelier that had been hanging there for many hundreds of cycles to fall. The stones obliged him, and Thanatos found himself under several stone of iron as the chandelier hit him. Blinded, half crushed, and held fast, Thaddeus took advantage of this, and said, "Thanatos, now you die!" as he approached Thanatos with his Wand of Light.

Thanatos could see the tip of the wand lighting up and knew that his end was coming fast; he said, "NO!" and tried to push Thaddeus back to delay his inevitable death. He could feel the power of the phylactery on him and was able to keep Thaddeus at bay for a few moments but could not keep his force shield up for very long, as his lifeblood was once again pouring out of him, and he started feeling weaker. Thanatos knew that he was in trouble, and while he could open a gate, he could not get through it because of this huge piece of iron on him. He was trying to move the large iron chandelier on him, but his strength spell had worn off, and he couldn't cast another because he had most of his magickal ability removed to avoid detection.

Thaddeus heard in his mind, "Now is the time to strike; hit the purple stone on my phylactery, then kill him. I wasn't always a bad man..."

Thaddeus was tired and had exhausted most of his spell arsenal fighting Vruhans, but realized that this was the moment of truth, this was the moment where true heroes are made as he pulled out his twin short swords, dropping his staff to the floor as he and Agham-Ix charged forward to meet evil head on.

Agham-Ix was the first to get there, and Thanatos quickly discovered that having a 40 stone dragon on top of you is debilitating at best and found that he was having trouble moving as Agham-Ix attacked with his razor sharp, stone-like claws. It was like having sharpened rocks digging into his legs. While Agham-Ix was doing his best to filet a demon, Thaddeus took advantage of the distraction and struck the purple stone of the phylactery that Thanatos was wearing, shattering it and rendering the phylactery useless, as his second blow penetrated Thanatos' head as he said, "Now, the Light takes you, demon!" His sword glowed white, and Thanatos, unable to move or defend himself further, succumbed to the glowing sword in his head and promptly exploded, never to return to the Continent again.

The force of the explosion pushed Thaddeus back against the stone doors of the mausoleum. He barely had time to turn away as large pieces of iron came flying at him due to the explosion. He was also very lucky as Agham-Ix happened to get pushed in the same direction and was actually in contact with him as the large iron pieces struck him so he was not harmed. He sat there for a few moments, not injured but a little dazed from the experience.

He noted another spirit materializing in front of him. He was too tired to deal with another evil spirit, but this one wasn't evil, in fact, it looked like a kindly old wizard with a purple glow around him as he said, "Champion, you've done well. I was not always a bad man, and as I told Thanatos, I do not entertain fools, which he was to try to secure my services without payment, and then desecrated my body and stole my phylactery...ah, well. What do you expect of evil? I go to the Crying Fields now to await judgement. I hope I will be deemed worthy of entrance. Goodbye and good luck!"

The spirit disappeared, and once again the graveyard was quiet as Thaddeus got up, picked up his swords and his staff. He took one last look inside the mausoleum and blessed it in the name of the Ancients. He left the mauso-leum, closing the door and blessing it, realizing that it still had an evil aura about it. He walked home, talking with Agham-Ix about Thanatos' defeat and perhaps now the Continent would be safe once again. Unfortunately, evil would not be so easily defeated.

Meanwhile, in the Dread Lord's domain, the Dread Lord, sitting on his throne, felt Thanatos' defeat as his own and promptly raged about it, kicking anything and everything he could find to kick, skewering lesser demons with his trident as he went. He had such high hopes for his favored servant, but he knew that there was no coming back from being impaled by a weapon wielded by a Champion of the Light. After he calmed down a bit, he proceeded to work on a new servant, one who was better than Thanatos, because Thanatos was designed after Boral with similar likes, dislikes, and abilities in deference to Bjor'ma. Since both were now gone, the Dread Lord was free to create the ul-timate evil being.

It took another season to replace Thanatos, but finally on the fifth sun of Sarodan, his creation was completed. The Dread Lord named her Heriotza. Her name has no translation to any language spoken on the Continent in mod-ern times, but the Dread Lord looked back in history and found a name that used to strike fear in the hearts of the ancient peoples of the Continent. He-riotza was a fierce female warrior who brought death to all who were unfaithful to the Ancients, those who betrayed them, or were cowardly, or who were in some way unfit to worship the Ancients. Her judgement was final and absolute; nothing would sway her or prevent her from killing you. The odd thing was that she was beautiful by most standards because the Ancients had a very dark sense of humor. They thought that the last living thing that a person should see on the Continent should be attractive, as they were facing an eternity of ugliness as if to say, "This is the last attractive thing you will ever see…enjoy it while it lasts!"

The Dread Lord made her taller than most females on the Continent, standing a full 6 arms high, though she was very shapely and muscular all at the same time. Her face was slender and oval shaped, with long black hair com-ing down to the middle of her back. He gave her light colored skin, warm green eyes, thin red lips, firm and round breasts, a narrow waist, and hips that sat atop long slender legs. She was every male's fantasy woman, the only dif-ference was that she was the last fantasy any of those men would ever have.

He dressed her very scantily to further extend her allure to men, she wore only a leather bra and tiny panties, and a pair of thigh-high leather boots. He gave her a high feminine voice, upped her pheromones, and gave her a permanent pleasant scent as the icing on the cake, so that men she faced would be distracted by that as well.

As her ancient counterpart was, she was a fierce warrior and blindingly fast, using weapons designed for speed instead of power. She used the long dagger as her favored weapon but was also skilled with various missile weapons, in particular the throwing dart which was one of her favorites, especially tipped with poison. Finally, she had some resistance to magick, but had no offensive magickal capability to decrease the chance of her being detected by the Champion or his friends. She did have one other power; she was able to enter the dreams of men. The Dread Lord knew about this power which was one of the reasons he picked this ancient ability for his ultimate evil being to have. He knew that most men were lustful, sexually unsatisfied, and would fall easily to her charms. She would attempt to seduce them as they slept, and if she was successful in seducing her target, and the man had sex with her in their dreams, the man was marked and would soon die.

The Dread Lord approved of his creation and said to her, "Heriotza, report to the Lord of Blight as you will be a carrier of disease as your predecessor was, and go to the Lord of the Dead for weapons and training. We have a season before we set you loose on the Continent…let's use that time wisely."

CHAPTER 34

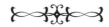

TWO NEW BEGINNINGS

While Thanatos' replacement was in the works, Thaddeus and Agham-Ix had some well-deserved rest for themselves and Thaddeus' thoughts moved towards reconstruction and healing the land from the scourge that had, for a time, infected it. Those who were infected by disease around the Continent got better for the most part and the regular hum of life resumed around the Continent. The season of Samhein was the perfect time to pursue other things, like magickal experiments and the like. It was also a great time to begin reconstruction efforts. He decided to start locally and would venture out into what was once a thriving city of a half million people. He consulted old maps of the city and tried to design a city for that many folks again, but he had zero experience with city planning and thought that he could use some help. He went far and wide, searching for someone who could assist him in rebuilding a city. He found someone in Taras'la, a half-elf named Cormar.

He told Cormar that he wanted the city of Samsrun to be returned to its former glory. Cormar, who planned many Elven cities in his former life, jumped at the chance to put his training to work, and for a Champion of the Light no less! Thaddeus noted that whenever he travelled to another hamlet, town or village, he found that he had an increased standing in the community, despite the fact that he was only 10 cycles old at this time. No one viewed him as a child, but as a hero, whose words were to be heeded as it was commonly known that those who have served as Champions of the Light were paragons of good, who only had their best interests at heart.

While in Taras'la, Thaddeus saw someone…someone that would change his life and the relationships that he had forged with the other women in his life; he saw Sarana for the first time. Sarana was a human girl, about his age. The sages who wrote about this time in history disagree whether he saw her after he had spoken with Cormar about the new city of Samsrun or before that historic meeting took place, but they all agree that it was an important moment in his life. The sages noted that this was the first time in this world that he met a girl his age that caught his eye.

She looked perfect to him with long, darker blonde hair, a white chemise and blue bodice on. The First sun shined on her hair just so, reflecting the ornament that she always had in her head. He was smitten with her, and though she didn't notice him at first, he felt compelled to speak to her as he said to Cormar, "We'll get started to Samsrun in a moment, I want to speak to that girl first…"

Cormar said with a certain knowing air, "Right. Take your time…"

He confidently approached her, but for all his experience with women and his recent deeds of skill and bravery, he was still very nervous…he said, "Good sun, my name is Thaddeus, might I know yours?" She turned to face him and was at first driven to smirk due to his wizardly clothing, but said, "Aye, mi name is Sarana…I've not seen ya afore…are ye a wizard?" He replied, "Aye, the last wizard on the Continent and this here is Agham-Ix…he's a Stone Dragon."

Sarana had never seen a wizard or a dragon before and was impressed. She had never been approached like this, as the boys in the village were afraid to approach any girl, but somehow this boy was different and seemed unafraid of her. (In reality, though, he was very nervous).

She said, "Walk me home…mayhaps we can talk, you and I."

As the three of them headed east to walk Sarana to her home, Thaddeus had three conversations going on at the same time, the one with Sarana in Manton, the one with Agham-Ix in dragon tongue, and the one with Toril in an ancient tongue called Liwet.

As they walked, Sarana said that she lived with her parents, and her four sisters on the far end of town. Thaddeus said, "I live in Samsrun, with my two sisters close to the center of town." For the first time, he referred to Kama as his sister, which he kind of thought of her as, at least at the moment. Thaddeus listened to her talk about her life and the voices in his head until they arrived at her home about a half toll later. In truth, he was paying far more attention

222

to the conversations in his mind, telling him how to act and what to say. As they arrived at an average looking abode for the area, Sarana said, "Thank you for walking me home; I hope you will call again!"

She kissed him on the cheek and waved to him as she opened the door to her home. Thaddeus walked away from the home, but felt like he was walking on air. He didn't know that Sarana had gone upstairs and was spying on Thaddeus through her open window as she watched him walk away…she wasn't sure what she was feeling, but she felt very safe with him beside her, even at his young age. She felt that he could protect her from just about anything, and though she didn't know it at the time, she was right in that estimation.

Thaddeus caught up with Cormar and said, "Are ye ready?"

Cormar said, "Aye. Have ye taken a shine ta her?"

Thaddeus said, "A sparkle perhaps, but not a shine…yet! She asked me ta call on her again…mayhaps I will."

Cormar said, "Ya won't find one nicer than her and she's easy on the eyes too! Haha! If'n ya like her, ye best make yerself known ta her pa, so ye can court her!"

Thaddeus opened the door to his extradimensional home and bade Cormar in by saying, "It's better than walking to Samsrun! Ye be fine…not ta worry!" Cormar said, "That's a fine bit o' magick ye got there."

Thaddeus said, "Aye, let's be off to Samsrun…there's a lot of work to be done."

The two entered the craft and within a quarter toll, they were back in Samsrun. Thaddeus said, "Welcome to my home; you are welcome to stay here whilst the work is done, or find other accommodations that might suit ye better."

Cormar looked around and said, "This'll do fine fer me. Now what did ye have in mind?"

The two spent many tolls going over city plans in the study as Li'Faran walked in and said, "Hi, Brother. Who've ya got there?"

Cormar looked over at the voice and was shocked to see a Narsum this close; he had only heard of their ferocity from stories told by his ancestors but had never actually seen one.

Cormar said, "Who is this? A Narsum? Here?"

Thaddeus said, "Not to worry, my friend. This is my sister, Li'Faran. She is really smart, mayhaps she has some ideas?"

Li'Faran said, "What ye doin' with these maps?"

Cormar said, "Good lady, we are planning on rebuilding this city to its former glory. I plan such things and lead teams of builders."

Li'Faran said, "I'm good at building, and I'm strong!"

Thaddeus said, "Mayhaps you'd like to stay and add your thoughts to this project? We'll begin on the first of Simcha, but there is so much planning to be done before then."

Li'Faran joined the Thaddeus and Cormar, and their dream for the city started to take shape. They focused on infrastructure and on finding a reliable water supply, then what should be where and where people should live, work, and trade.

Sometime later that same sun, Cormar asked, "We've made a good start on the plans, but I have a question: How are ye going to rebuild? People are gonna want gold to help ye, myself included. Do ye have the gold to build a city?"

Thaddeus said, "Aye, that I do. And as for you, what wage do ye believe ye would want to undertake this mighty task?"

Cormar figured he should shoot the moon here and said, "500 gold ducats fer the cycle, and 1,000 when the city is done."

Thaddeus listened to Toril in his mind and said, "250 gold ducats fer the cycle whilst construction is happening, free accommodations and food here for that time, then a position of nobility fer ye and yer family in the city paying 250 gold ducats per season; 10-cycle contract of service…what say ye? Also, I'll pay you a 10-ducat bonus for each family that moves in here from yer village as well."

Cormar's eyes lit up. He was to become a noble, in a city, with a Champion of the Light in it! His dreams for his family would all be possible now. He said, "Aye, I agree to yer terms!" as he took Thaddeus' hand and shook it.

Thaddeus said, "Meet my head of security, Li'Faran. She and her brethren will need places to stay, so that will be yer first task. Build barracks for her security force ta keep the builders safe while they work."

Li'Faran looked shocked and said, "Me? Head of security? Brother, I don't know anything about that…"

Thaddeus interrupted her and said, "Stop any bad people that try to harm the builders and teach your troops as you taught me. I would like an all-Narsum security force. Bad people will think twice when confronted by the ferocity of the Narsum, wouldn't you say?"

Li'Faran said with a lowered head, "Men won't take commands from me. I'm just a girl, remember?"

Thaddeus said while looking into her downturned eyes, "Yes, you most certainly are. Mayhaps we can change all that misogynistic nonsense. You are my sister, and I will command them to take orders from you, and I will pay them in gold. If they won't take commands from you, then they don't have to work for us; we will find others who will. Li'Faran, you are so much more than 'just a girl,' and I want you to have every opportunity to shine as you deserve nothing less!"

Li'Faran said, "Thank you, Brother! We find good troops and builders, too!"

Cormar said, "How...never mind, I don't think I want to know..."

Thaddeus said, "It's a long story, but in the meantime, I'd like you to meet my other 'sister.' Her name is Kama, and she is an elf."

Kama was in the library reading with Bjor'ma when she saw Thaddeus and Cormar come in.

Thaddeus said, "Kama, this is Cormar from the village of Taras'la, he is going to help us rebuild this city. Cormar, this is Kama, my magickal tutor and best friend. She will be making sure that the city aura is positive at all times and taking steps if she finds that it isn't. We want most folks that move here to be happy as I know ye can't please everyone, but we are going to try."

Cormar was definitely checking Kama out as he liked Kama's small frame and delicate features, when he noted the large pink blob at their feet looking at him as he said, "What is THAT?"

Thaddeus said, "Oh...his name is Bjor'ma. He's a guest from out of town; he's very quiet, you won't even know that he's here. We have quite the crew here, but we insist on one thing, harmony and cooperation. Nothing less than that will be tolerated."

Thaddeus said, "There now, we are all introduced. Kama, would you get Cormar set up in a room please? He's going to be staying here while we plan and build our new city. Cormar, if you'd like, you can bring your family to stay with you as well, but there are places that they will not be able to go, like here for example. It is up to you, though."

Kama said, "Right this way, Cormar. I know the perfect room for you..."

Thaddeus knew that Cormar liked Kama's body but also knew that she could easily defend herself from anything he might try. He touched Bjor'ma and heard a faint scratching sound from underneath him. A few moments

later, he moved and revealed a parchment which said, "I knew him as a boy...
good man."

Thaddeus smiled and said, "Yes, I checked him out magickally, and I
sensed nothing but good from him. And no magickal ability to speak of."

The planning phase continued through the season of Samhein and Sarodan, as more detailed maps were drawn up of what the city would look like
when it was done. Cormar also was a good engineer and planned on having
aqueducts and fountains in the city through an ingenious system of pumps,
which it didn't have before. He also wanted to incorporate what Thaddeus
called street lights, only these were oil lanterns mounted on high poles with
special cones on them directing the light down to the street below. The idea
of a castle was brought up and was ultimately dismissed, as it was decided that
the city would be run by committee, not a monarch. The government building
was to be a modest building of stone and not stand out in any way.

While all this planning was happening, several things were going on outside the city. Li'Faran was trying to drum up some soldiers amongst the Narsum and found about 200 warriors and their families all willing to move to
Samsrun and more importantly take orders from her, as she was the sister of
the Champion of the Light, which most Narsum had some knowledge of. She
was also able to convince seven teams of builders to come to the city to work
their craft under the direction of Cormar. They started building the barracks
to house the security force, where the Narsum would live whilst executing
their duties. It was decided that the Narsum would be split into four different
companies and occupy different areas of the city to ensure that they had eyes
and ears in all parts of the city at all times. Many of the Narsum were also expert horsemen and brought their steppe horses with them. They were paid at
the end of every season in gold, along with a 10-ducat bonus for just showing
up. Thaddeus had started withdrawing from the huge gold hoard he found in
the West and discovered that it seemingly went on without end; despite the
amount he had withdrawn, it still looked full. He also recorded a full account-
ing of what he had withdrawn and had the recipient sign a piece of parchment
stating that he/she had received a certain amount of gold, which matched what
he withdrew for them. He wanted to prove, in case he was ever asked, that the
money went towards its stated purpose, reconstruction, and that none of it was
being misused. With the new influx of Narsum, it didn't take long for more
Narsum to show up in addition to some humans. Tradesmen and craftsmen

started returning to Samsrun, in addition to farmers, to whom Thaddeus granted large tracts of land to grow food for his burgeoning community.

Towards the end of Samhein, Samsrun had a population of 739 beings, of which 309 were Narsum. Li'Faran was doing well at commanding the security forces, and all the Narsum believed that she was a fair commander though she donned a rather unique uniform for herself. She believed that she should dress simply as a Narsum woman and would almost always be found in her plain brown dress. She did not wear armor, though most Narsum didn't either, save a few bits of leather and metal, and perhaps a helmet, though she did carry her favored weapon, an axe, with her while she was on duty.

Kama detected the aura of the city was average as more folks started to emigrate to Samsrun and did not detect any dissent from anyone, save a few grumblings every now and again, but she was quick to answer those grumblings and followed through on what she said she was going to do, keeping the city "blue," as she put it.

Thaddeus, as the de facto leader of this community was not only directing everyone and everything in the city of Samsrun, but also pursuing Sarana in Taras'la, visiting her about once every five suns or so, as his duties would allow. He would always come early in the sun and had since met her sisters and her parents, who seemingly encouraged their middle daughter to pursue this relationship with Thaddeus, seeing who he was and the life that he could provide for her, and by extension for them.

CHAPTER 35

A BIG MOVE

Sarana's father, whose name was Edward, though supportive of Thaddeus and the life he could provide for his middle daughter, had some reservations about moving 600 leagues north to Samsrun, as he was a farmer and blacksmith, the only one left in the village. He felt bad for the people in this village, as they would have one less person to grow food for them, and no one to repair things for them. When he told Thaddeus of his thoughts on the matter, Thaddeus had an idea that could potentially resolve the issue and asked for a meeting with the Taras'la council of elders. That night, they agreed to see him given his station and at Edward's insistence. Entering the hut, Thaddeus was surprised to see this oddball collection of nine older men who formed the leadership committee since the elves left. Thaddeus did a little checking on them and found that they had no magickal ability to speak of but noted their minds were sharp as he said to them as the first order of business.

"Gentlemen, my name is Thaddeus, and some of you may know me as a Champion of the Light. I come to you this sun with a proposal. I propose that this entire village moves to the city of Samsrun, 600 leagues from here. I can provide you with protection, land, and clean water and a place to set down roots to raise your families. I realize that it is a long way from here, and the clime is different, but you will be safe there, as I will personally protect each and every one of you. I noted that many of the people here are farmers with herds of animals, you will be granted land at no charge, so long as you or your family continue working the land, and so long as you sell your produce and meats at reasonable prices. To those of you who are shopkeepers and craftsmen, you, too, will be granted space to ply your respective trades. And lastly, to the council of elders, the city of Samsrun is run by committee, of which you would be a part, so that you and all your people will have representation in government. I would ask that you prepare to move during Sarodan, and when Simcha arrives, that you move. There will be protection coming with you, as I will have two companies of Narsum warriors accompanying you on your journey. What say you?"

Thaddeus heard them debating for a while until one of the men stood up. He appeared older than the rest and was reliant on a cane to keep himself upright as he said, "Young man, I have been in this village for over 70 cycles. While we are happy here in Taras'la, many have stated a desire to leave, just as the elves did. Up until now, we had nowhere to go that would be suitable for our entire community. We will take your proposal under advisement, and when a decision is rendered, you will be informed. We will now hear the next order of business…"

Thaddeus left the simple hut, confident that they would come, and if they did, Sarana and her family would be coming as well, which would mean that he could see her much more often.

Thaddeus stayed in Taras'la at the local inn, a holdover from earlier times when Taras'la was a popular place for travelers to stop and kept up by a local family. In truth, he only appeared to be renting a room; he was actually staying in his extradimensional home, as it was very well-equipped for him and provided him a place to keep his spellbooks that was safe from anyone. He rented a room to support the local economy and to wait whilst a decision was made about his proposal. Of course, his primary reason for hanging around was to start courting Sarana in earnest. They were together every sun, even if only for a few tolls in the evening, she would always make time to spend with him, seemingly encouraged by her parents.

On his second night in Taras'la, Thaddeus and Sarana were outside of her home, and she could see a candle still burning in the window, meaning she still had time according to the "courting light." This ancient Elven tradition was mainstream here in Taras'la and was the norm, so Thaddeus accepted it. It worked simply enough in that when the couple went out, the courting candle would be lit, and when it burned out, courting time was over and the young lady had to be back home.

She said, "I had a wonderful time with you this night. You're a true gentleman."

Thaddeus said, "As did I, sweet Sarana..."

Then she did something unexpected, as they were standing outside under the three moons, she leaned towards him and kissed him on the lips, which Thaddeus returned with equal fervor. Thanks to Toril's coaching, he learned how to kiss and more importantly, when. He took her gently in his arms and held her close, as she put her arms around him. They stood outside for a while like that, holding each other and kissing under the moonlight. He was in heaven; he was living a dream he had often, kissing a pretty girl. She could feel the passion from him and was impressed at his ability to kiss her properly while being respectful at the same time. After a long while, Sarana eyed the courting light, and it was almost out, so she reluctantly said, "I have to go, the courting light is almost out...Will I see ye again tomorrow?"

Thaddeus said, "Aye, I hope ta have a decision from the council tomorrow. Good night!"

The courting light went out, and Sarana's father opened the front door to see his daughter turning towards the door and Thaddeus walking away.

He said, "Welcome home, I trust you two had a good time. Mayhaps the young man would like to have dinner with us tomorrow? Your mother and I have some questions for him."

She said, "Aye, I'm sure he would like that!"

Early the next sun, Thaddeus was sitting outside the inn with Agham-Ix. He noted a young boy, about his age approach him and said, "Thaddeus?"

Thaddeus said, "Aye, what can I do for you?"

The boy said, "Message from the council fer ye..."

Thaddeus took the message and gave the lad a silver coin.

The boy's eyes lit up and said, "Thanks!"

The message was written in Elven, and he thought it strange that the message should be in Elven, but then again, the council members were all older folks, and he assumed that they never bothered to switch to Manton. It read:

Your presence is requested by the Taras'la Council of Elders this night at Mrilto's rise...a decision about your proposal has been reached.
Very truly yours,
Gideon, Keeper of Taras'la History

Thaddeus said to himself, "Finally...and it's about time too!"

Thaddeus knew that Mrilto was the last of the three moons to rise and generally occurred later in the evening, so he would have some time with Sarana before his meeting with the council. Thaddeus spent the sun writing in his journal and writing down ideas that he wanted to share with Cormar when he returned. He also spent time with Agham-Ix, talking with him and learning more about dragonkind. Thaddeus enjoyed these talks with Agham-Ix sitting on his lap, just watching the ebb and flow of town life unfold before him. He knew that if he was successful in getting these folks to move, that he would have 2,000 or more under his protection, which he thought was important. He hoped that this would attract more people, which as he was taught would increase his tax base, and he could see more gold coming into the treasury instead of leaving it.

As midsun approached, he noted Sarana coming towards him and said to Agham-Ix, "Let's see what this sun brings, shall we?"

She said to him, "Thaddeus, my pa asked if you'd like ta share dinner with us before yer meetin' with the council!"

Thaddeus asked himself, *I wonder how she knows about that…I haven't told anyone.* Thaddeus said, "I'd be delighted."

Sarana said, "Mum sent me ta the market ta git some stuff. Would ye like ta come?"

Thaddeus said, "Aye, let's head out." He said to Agham-Ix, "Here we go…"

Their trip to the market was pleasant enough, and Thaddeus paid two silver ducats for what they bought, as Sarana talked about everything and anything. Thaddeus noted that she wasn't very focused and tended to switch from subject to subject very quickly, but chalked it up to the fact that she, like himself, was 10, and had not gone through his level of schooling. In fact, Sarana had never been to school, as it did not exist for anyone here in Taras'la. Education was not seen as important enough to supplant helping the family get work done on the farm. She was home-schooled for the most part, and like many of her contemporaries, could not read or write, but she really had no use for such skills at this point in her life. She spent a lot of time helping her father on the farm, mostly taking care of their herd of livestock and the endless cleaning up after them.

When they arrived at her home, Thaddeus hesitated as Sarana said, "Will ye come inside? Ye can help if'n ye like, and of course, Agham-Ix is invited as well!"

Thaddeus said, "Aye!" and ventured into her home.

It was an average home; it smelled a little but was otherwise reasonably appointed as Thaddeus was the only male in the house, as Sarana's father was still out on the farm. Thaddeus noted that Sarana's older sisters (they were 15 and 13) were checking him out, and he was doing likewise as he noted the same color hair that Sarana had and their female parts were "already installed" while Sarana's had not quite come in yet.

They were particularly enthralled with Agham-Ix and her two younger sisters took to petting him, and Thaddeus was thankful that Agham-Ix was practically indestructible and able to withstand the two younger girls (they were seven and five) poking and petting him. He showed them he particularly liked having his belly rubbed. Their mother was fairly young as well, Thaddeus estimated that she was between 28 and 32; moreover, he could see where her daughters got their good looks from. She introduced herself as Lirta and said that he was an honored guest in their home as she went into the kitchen and all five of her daughters followed suit to start preparing the evening meal.

Thaddeus noted that they had a fairly efficient system set up and seemed to be in their element as they were preparing dinner. Thaddeus decided to bless the home in the name of the Ancients and did so quietly without anyone noticing as he sat on a stone stool and spoke with Agham-Ix in his mind. The two conversed for another toll, before Sarana's father came in from the fields.

He sat down close to Thaddeus said, "Good ta see ya again, my name is Edward, and I understand ye be standing afore the Council again tonight."

He extended his hand, and Thaddeus took it and gave him a handshake, but his hand was much smaller that Edward's was. He yelled out, "And how are my girls!"

They yelled out seemingly in unison, "We're good, Daddy!" He went over and kissed his wife and took to supervising the goings on in the kitchen.

The girls were busy for about a toll, and as things started to be put into the large oven to cook, the girls started to clean up. While the girls were cleaning up, Sarana's mother and father approached him, sat down as Sarana's father said, "So…ye been courting Sarana fer a couple of nights now, what say ye?"

Thaddeus was confused at first but let Toril advise him in his mind as he said, "She is a fine girl, and I'd like ta keep courtin' her if'n that's alright with you, o' course." He took a trick from his elder namesake's playbook and started speaking as they would to make them feel that he was one of them and not some high-minded intellectual, even though he was.

Sarana's father smiled and said, "Aye, it be alright with us, and though we haven't told the girls yet, no matter what the council decides tonight, we all decided ta move to Samsrun come Simcha. Better ta live in a place with a Champion of the Light than anywhere else, I'd say."

Thaddeus said, "Aye, I'd like that and I think Sarana would as well."

Truth be told, Lirta and Edward knew Thaddeus' station and knew that they would benefit from it if he decided to marry his middle daughter and probably before.

Thaddeus said, "I'll give ye some land as well in Samsrun; there's a nice plot that's close ta the city, but big enough where ya can keep yer livestock and grow crops. We can talk about the terms later, and everyone will benefit... Plus, as a blacksmith, I can give ye space fer a shop, in fact, one of the old blacksmith shops still stands, and ye can have that one, one of the finest in the city. If'n ye can get that up and runnin', more people will come, which will be a boon fer everyone."

Edward said, "Aye, it'll be good fer everyone."

Thaddeus said, "Once ye come ta the city, seek me out. I'll give ye some funds ta buy things ye will need and ta get the shop running." Thaddeus moved his hands about surreptitiously and cast a detection spell, specifically detecting evil. He looked around at them and their daughters and detected no evil, though he could see that Edward had a greedy streak to him. He also looked about for magick and found none anywhere in the home.

As Trirance rose, the smell of dinner was ever-present, and Lirta said, "Let's eat. I think everything is ready." She yelled out, "Girls...dinner!"

Soon enough there were eight people and a dragon sitting at the table. Thaddeus ate what he could, but it certainly wasn't what he was used to. This sort of peasant food was heavy and satisfying, but Thaddeus had become used to Elven foods and wasn't a big eater in the first place. Also, everyone in the home drank beer, including the younger girls. The thought was that beer was safer to drink than water, which Thaddeus didn't really understand. They made the beer themselves, and though Thaddeus didn't care for it, Agham-Ix did. All in all, Thaddeus had a good time and spent a large part of the meal checking out Sarana. He wished her mind was more open, so they could speak silently, but he thought that in time it would be.

After the meal, Sarana's father said, "We had best be off fer the council meeting. See ya all later."

It was a short walk to the council meeting from Edward's home. The three walked quietly along the well-worn paths that served as streets in Taras'la, as they approached the council building, which was a simple wattle-and-daub structure with some stones particularly at the base of the building. They opened the door and went inside where a bonfire was burning in the center to ward off the night chill. There were 15 other men in the building, nine of which were the council members themselves and six other folks presumably with requests and/or grievances.

Luck was on their side as the lead council member stood and said, "First order of business: Is the petitioner Thaddeus here?"

Thaddeus piped up and said, "Aye!"

The lead council member remained standing, and while leaning on his cane said, "We've reached a decision about yer petition. Know that it was not unanimous, but we have decided none the less. On a 6-to-3 vote, the council has decided to move the township now known as Taras'la to be incorporated with the city of Samsrun, effective on the first of Simcha. At that time, the township of Taras'la will cease to exist and be incorporated within the city of Samsrun."

He continued, "Ye mentioned security will be provided, yes?"

Thaddeus said, "Aye, I will send 200 Narsum warriors to escort you safely from here to Samsrun. Upon arrival, each family will receive 25 gold ducats to resupply and to begin constructing their homes. Those who ply a trade will be given space to continue to do so, provided they are in compliance with the original city charter, first laid out by King Joseph IV in 507. There will be plenty of work for those who wish to do it, and the rewards of that work will be felt by all citizens of our fair city!"

The lead council member sat down and said, "Next order of business…"

Thaddeus, Agham-Ix, and Edward left the council building shortly after the decision was rendered and went back to Edward's home and said, "Thank you for doing this for us. I just want a better life and more opportunity for my girls."

Thaddeus said, "Edward, I didn't do it for you. I did it for the entire Continent, and this is just a start; once the city is up and running, other cities and towns will be built, and they will need things, especially from a blacksmith."

Edward smiled and said, "See you later, Thaddeus."

Thaddeus waved to him as he entered the inn and then into his extradimensional home.

CHAPTER 36

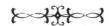

EVIL RISES ONCE AGAIN

During the season of Samhein, Thaddeus was pleased to see a continuous trickle of immigrants to the newest city on the Continent. To monitor his progress in building his new city, he had all new arrivals to the city directed to him, so he could provide them with directions, and most importantly, seed money. He knew that most arrived with very little in the way of money and supplies, and he thought that providing everyone with a means of supporting themselves until they could get established was a good practice and would serve to attract more immigrants.

As Sarodan came, Thaddeus took a risk and sent most of his Narsum security force under the direction of Li'Faran to Taras'la. Since they were headed south, he knew that Sarodan would not be as tough as it was in the North, but that also meant that he would have to stay here in town, as he would have to serve as the city's only defense with a handful of trained soldiers and militia. Truth be told, he was not concerned, as there had been no reports of anything amiss during the entire season of Samhein, and no one that he spoke with reported anything amiss where they had come from. It was as if evil was "taking a break" after the defeat of Thanatos, though he knew that they would never completely give up, at least he had given them pause, which allowed him to get his plans off the ground.

Meanwhile, in the Dread Lord's domain, Heriotza's training and outfitting was complete as Sarodan was finishing up. She got an upgrade in skill, armor, and weaponry. She took to wearing black scale mail armor, though it was obviously designed with her "assets" in mind and was very light, and she was now highly accurate along with being super-fast with the throwing dart. While her range was short, about 30 arms at most, her accuracy was close to 100 percent. The Lord of Blight made her a carrier of a virulent disease as Thanatos was, and tipped one very special dart with the Essence of Death he had created. He designed the dart to remove the Champion's protection from evil in one tiny area, and once removed, the Essence of Death would then be able to do its grisly work.

He told her, "Should ye run into the Champion of the Light, throw this dart at him. If it hits him, he should fall quickly and within a few tolls be dead, thus making your job a lot easier. Death comes for all of us, why should he be any different?"

She smiled at that remark, knowing that she had a defense against the Champion, one that would kill him. Knowing that she could kill him, she wanted to meet him, wanted to get close enough to stick this dart in his flesh and watch him slowly die. As she watched the last of his life force ebb away, she would take his body to the Dread Lord and present it to him as a gift, before wreaking havoc on the Continent.

As Evil was making its plans, Thaddeus decided to set up an infirmary and put Kama in charge of running it, knowing that there would need to be a place where sick and injured people could go to be well again. Most suns and many nights, he could be found there, healing the sick and caring for the wounded, just as she did, and it allowed the two of them to be close together, which they both enjoyed immensely. Some suns the work was exhausting, and some suns the infirmary's 75 beds were filled to capacity, but they knew that their skill and devotion to the healing arts would see everyone through.

On the seventy-third sun of Sarodan, the caravan from Taras'la arrived in Samsrun. It was a grand sun, and it seemed that Sarodan was letting up just in time to allow them to settle into their new surroundings. Thaddeus was busier than he had ever been before and served as traffic cop, banker, and information booth all at once. Li'Faran and her troops had performed admirably and were assisting the families to get where they needed to go. Thaddeus had mapped out where each family would stay based on the trade that they practiced. He saw Sarana's family and directed them to the farm that he had designated for them, but they saw that he was very busy and decided to settle into their new surroundings before worrying about the progress of the courtship of their middle daughter.

Three suns passed before everyone was settled in, and the population of Samsrun now stood at 2,784. Land was being worked, the sounds of construction were ever-present, and the sounds of the blacksmith's hammer along with the sounds of merriment could be heard as children played in the streets. As Thaddeus walked through the city, he was happy that he was able to make this happen for them after all they had been through. He knew that the families that chose to move here did so because of who he was and the promises that he had made to them. He wasn't about to let them down under any circumstances, though his perseverance was about to be tested in the harshest possible way.

As the night of the first of Simcha came to the Continent, evil started anew. Heriotza appeared for the first time and started to fly over the Continent to spread her disease anew. She flew fast and high, starting with the Elves to the South, then the Narsum to the East, and the Barbarians to the North. She also noticed Samsrun in the center of the Continent and felt the presence of good there.

After her nightly flyover, she set down to recharge just outside of Samsrun, spreading her disease in this place before she headed back to the Dread Lord's domain. She did not feel that she was seen by anyone and wanted to start to be seen as her ancient ancestor was. She wanted to focus on men because they would react to her as she wanted and be very easy to pick off. She thought that the women and children would die of disease, but she had a special affinity to killing men in her preferred way: in their dreams. She also hoped that she would be seen by the Champion but did not realize that he was just a boy. She would find out soon enough.

After several more nights, and more flyovers, elves and humans started to get sick again, though the disease was slowed in Samsrun owing to the Champion's presence there and his daily blessing of the city. Only those who went outside the city and came back in were at real risk of disease. Also reaching the Champion's ears were reports were of men dying in their sleep. Perfectly healthy men would go to sleep at night and not wake up again. Rumors started to fly about as to how this could happen, as this was a terrifying thing to many people; people started to think they were cursed, or that some magick was at play.

Even Samsrun was not immune to this phenomenon, as five men had died this way, all within the last seven suns. No magickal residues could be found on them, ruling out magickal effects, and no disease of any sort had infected these healthy men. They just fell asleep and did not wake up again. As the male death toll started to climb and disease started to take its toll, Thaddeus was faced with a real problem, how to assuage the thoughts of the populace in his city, not only against disease, but against this new sickness seemingly only affecting men.

Thaddeus could fight the disease, and for the most part keep it out of his city, but this new sickness was a real problem because for many families; the sudden loss of the man of the house was a difficult setback to overcome. In trying to find an answer, Thaddeus would visit with about 50 men each sun to see how they were and how they felt and if anything happened to them that they remembered, no matter how insignificant they thought it was. It took a few dozen suns for Thaddeus to make a connection, and he found it quite by accident.

He was visiting a man in his home, when his infant third child started to fuss in another room. As was the custom, his wife got up and took care of the child. While she was gone, he said, "Didn't want to mention it in front o' the wife. Had a strange dream last night...dreamt of this gorgeous woman. We had sex in my dream! It was awesome!" He went on to describe the woman he dreamt of; six arms tall, gorgeous body, long legs, long hair, soft skin...the works!

Thaddeus asked, "Has this ever happened afore?"

He said, "Naw, the wife always took care o' that, but since this kid came out...hasn't been happening fer a while."

Thaddeus knew that giving birth meant that the woman would be unable to have sex for a while given his medical studies under Kama, but it varied from woman to woman insofar as how long she would be unavailable for.

He said, "Okay...that's good information. Let me see if anyone else is having the same issue." He had always made the mistake of asking the man in front of his wife or his family, not realizing how sensitive a subject this was, owing to his inexperience, so he subtly switched up his tactic and started asking men these questions when they were alone. And that's when he came upon this similarity. Ten of the men that he had spoken with alone, all reported seeing the same woman in their dreams, which Thaddeus thought was highly unusual. Within another 15 suns, all 10 were gone; all had died in their sleep. He had solved the mystery, but now, he needed to figure out what to do about it, as it seemed to be picking up not only in and around Samsrun, but all across the Continent along with this disease.

He consulted Toril and asked if this had ever happened before in times past, and it had. Toril told him that about 47,000 cycles ago, there was an enforcer of sorts, one who punished men who had thoughts out of line with their professed deity. This deity whose name had since been lost supposed that men could not be trusted with their thoughts and needed to be told how to think, what to think, and when to think it. He decided to utilize an enforcer to ensure that his faithful were thinking properly and utilized the shape of a beautiful woman to accomplish his ends. Her name was Heriotza, and her name was rightfully feared, as she served as judge, jury, and if need be, executioner to those who had thoughts or dreams that were out of line. The thought was that if those thoughts or dreams could be put towards something that was more in line with what the deity in question espoused, then that person would be rewarded in real life so that all could see the benefits of only having the thoughts that the deity in question thought were appropriate. Unfortunately, that faith was short lived, and while the enforcer lived on, she had not made an appearance from that time to this. Toril wondered why she has been brought back after all this time.

Thaddeus said to Toril, "It must be the Dread Lord, as he focuses more on the mind. They are just using her power to kill; she only goes after men because the men who succumb to her charms in their dreams…die. I killed Thanatos, so this must be his replacement. I gotta give 'em points for originality—that's brilliant. The question is, how to stop it? We can't control everyone's dreams, but we can warn them."

Thaddeus called for Li'Faran who had just returned home after her shift and said, "Sister, first, welcome home. Second, I need you to get a message out to the populace; there will be a city-wide meeting at the city's main fountain tomorrow at high sun."

Li'Faran responded, "Aye, I will pass that along to the troops and to the people. Everyone will be there!"

The next sun, high sun came, and a large gathering of people could be seen at the city's new fountain, which Cormar had just finished as Thaddeus stepped up on a makeshift stage and said, "Good people of Samsrun, you all know me as Thaddeus, Champion of the Light, but this sun I bring dark news to you…but it is dark news that you need to know, especially the men amongst you. For the last several nights, men have been passing on in their sleep, and I know why. It is the Dread Lord, who is trying to sap the strength of our great city. He is using an ancient enforcer from times past that preys on men who have sex with her in their dreams."

Thaddeus noted that several of the men's faces changed at that statement and a lot of hurried conversations were being had as he continued, "I thought the best way to combat this latest attack on us was through education. Now that you know about it, if you see this woman in your dreams, do not engage with her, rebuke her with all your might. Doing so seems to be the only effective defense against her. Men, you are not weak for having these thoughts, they are normal and common for all men, but it is how we act on them that counts. Be loyal and faithful to your wives; your very life may depend on it. Thank you!"

Several families approached Thaddeus after his speech and all asked the same question: "What if you've already 'done the deed'? What then?"

Thaddeus said, "If you are marked for death, pray to the Moon Goddess for redemption, she may be able to help you. There is a simple shrine set up to the south; pray and hope that tonight is not your last. No magick can help you. Perhaps faith can assist." As he said that a throng of folks crowded the shrine to the Moon Goddess as Thaddeus thought to himself, *There must be a way to stop her.*

He went back to his home and thought; he made a few guesses trying to narrow down where she might be. He assumed that she was spreading disease as Thanatos had done, and she needed to be on (or above) the Continent for that to happen. If he could track her somehow and force a showdown with her, that might be to his advantage.

He surmised that Heriotza, like Thanatos, was flying above population centers to spread the disease, so he decided to travel to the Dragonscape Mountains with Agham-Ix. He cast a series of detect evil spells, making the range longer and the width of detection larger, whilst significantly decreasing the sensitivity of the spell, realizing that Heriotza would have to be very evil and would certainly trip his spell. He recast the spell several times that night and caught a blip on his "screen," flying north. He took off after the blip and saw a black figure flying slowly ahead of him. He cast a lightning bolt at it, heard a scream, and saw it head down, but it disappeared in the gloom of the night before he could capture and kill it.

He recognized that tactic as Thanatos did the same thing, escaping after being shot down or injured; he hoped he had done enough damage to kill her, but his offensive magickal capability, while formidable, was not where his elder namesake's was, at least not at this early point in his wizardly career. He smiled as he went back to Samsrun, knowing that he did something to the enemy and that they knew that he was onto them.

Back in the Dread Lord's domain, Heriotza tumbled rather unceremoniously into her chamber, landed on the floor, and noted that most of her scale mail was damaged. She looked as if she had been electrocuted; her skin was burnt, her hair was sticking out, and her pleasant scent now smelled like burning flesh with a hint of rose. She was furious and wondered how she had been caught. She was burnt over 90 percent of her body and thanked her demonic nature for her continued survival, but being a demon had nothing to do with the fact that she was still breathing…She was fortunate that the young Thaddeus did not yet have his namesake's ability with elemental forces, or she would have been charred to a crisp.

She knew that this would take a while to heal as she stepped into her regeneration chamber and closed the lid. She was looking forward to finding out who had fired the lightning bolt and marking them for death. How little she knew about her adversary…

A mistake that would cost her dearly.

CHAPTER 37

EVIL WINS A VICTORY

After a few suns, Heriotza healed up and left her regeneration chamber. She decided to lose the clothing that she was wearing, thinking that she would be even more alluring with nothing on. She wore a bandolier and belt to hold her long daggers and her darts but other than that, was totally naked, knowing that her allure would increase exponentially with nothing to hide her assets. She waited until nightfall to make her appearance as usual, starting in the South with the Elves, turning north towards the mountains, and finally in the North, then turning southeast and flying over Samsrun, now a large town with over 2,500 residents.

The mystery "man only" affliction had not affected anyone for a couple of suns, which Thaddeus attributed to the fact that he had stopped its host at least temporarily. Heriotza did not realize that Thaddeus had proverbially "put two and two together" and pegged her for the Continents' most recent troubles. He was also duty-bound to try to stop her.

The flyovers continued, and the mysterious ailment afflicting men only had resumed, despite Thaddeus' instructions on how to stop it, which was another situation where people were having difficulties with the fact that the Continent's only human Wizard and Champion of the Light was a 10-year-old kid. Men did what they thought they needed to, and unfortunately for them, many younger men were sexually unsatisfied. She was the first person in a very long time to prey on those men using their dreams and secret desires against them, and that is why Heriotza's plan was so brilliant, and why her ancient namesake was so very dangerous.

To try to combat this, Thaddeus continued with the instructions on how to stop those dreams, but even he seemed to realize that despite his best efforts, "boys will be boys," and there was little he could do about this most basic need of all men.

Thaddeus wanted to protect those in Samsrun and in doing so, consulted librams on artificing, or constructing magickal artifacts. He wanted to create a network of interconnected artifacts that would warn him if one of them was tripped by an evil being flying through its invisible beam. He was inspired by the Internet back home, but nothing like this had ever been tried here before to his knowledge…even the elder Thaddeus had no advice for him, but there were tomes which Toril wrote on the subject of artificing along with many of Toril's notes and theories, which Thaddeus delved into.

As time wore on, the disease spread by Heriotza and her method of killing men were starting to be felt, and for the first time in recent seasons, the population in Samsrun went down. Thaddeus worked diligently for several suns and finally came up with a prototype for a device that continuously cast a detection of evil spell in a huge area and would cast a Whisper spell when it was tripped, with him as the destination for the Whisper. He placed it atop his home in Samsrun and powered it up. It was a black cube shaped device, about a hand across. It did not glow, or make any noise as he wanted to ensure that they were invisible to anyone flying around. Then he and Agham-Ix sat next to the device and waited.

He didn't have to wait long; Heriotza unknowingly tripped the device as Prefgel rose that night. It worked flawlessly, and Thaddeus sprung into action. He immediately cast a Light of The Suns spell, which lit up all of Samsrun as much as the two suns would have which exposed the naked Heriotza as she was making her flyover.

He yelled out, "Foul demon, face my wrath!" as he launched himself skyward to meet his shapely opponent. Heriotza was initially surprised by the sudden change in light and was blinded for a moment, but quickly recovered seeing a small boy flying up to meet her with a staff in hand, encapsulated in white and with a dragon on his shoulder. She thought that this must be the Champion of the Light, though she was surprised by his youth and thought him a little less dangerous because of it.

She hovered for a moment as Thaddeus got a little closer to her; she didn't realize that she was now close enough for him to start casting air magick against her. She found herself at the mercy of a Sphere of Winds spell, which encloses the target in a sphere of air, so powerful that the target cannot escape from it without risking serious injury by the hurricane force winds that the spell generates. He placed a shield around the sphere, and Agham-Ix introduced pebbles, by the hundreds, into the small sphere. While the space inside the sphere was calm, the outer edge was a torrent of hurricane driven pebbles, which would have bludgeoned her to death very quickly.

Heriotza took this all in stride and made no movements, realizing that she would cease to exist if she touched the outer edge of the sphere. So, she didn't. She was confident in her abilities to charm any man and thought that he wanted to feel safe in approaching her, so she allowed herself to become trapped. She noted that he was flying closer whilst readying a wand.

He approached to within 100 arms and was taken aback by what he saw: a very shapely, very attractive and very naked woman wearing only a belt and bandolier. She could feel his gaze upon her but sensed no desire in his mind for her, which she found very odd and very annoying. Thaddeus was fortunate in that he had gotten to see a real deity upon his arrival here and though Heriotza was incredibly attractive, capable of inspiring lust in all but the most pious men, the Moon Goddess continued to be his "gold standard" insofar as the appearance of women was concerned.

She said, "You have me trapped good and well, Champion. What is your intention?"

He replied, "I intend to send you back to the hells that spawned you, preferably in pieces. I've already defeated one of your kind. You are no different!"

She said, "Oh, but I am different…my predecessor wasn't this…beautiful." She ran her delicate hands over her perfectly shaped breasts, causing her nipples to harden. She licked her lips and bit her lower lip as seductively as she could as she stared at him with her smoldering eyes. She said, "Come closer… I want to show you what a real woman can do…"

Thaddeus stayed focused on his mission despite her sexually oriented actions. It was like she was trying desperately to distract him, but he had 50,000 cycles of experience in his mind, and every Champion of the Light helping him stay focused. He caused his Wand of Light to glow brightly as he said, "Now, foul temptress…the Light shall reveal what you truly are!" As the wand got closer to her, she started to feel different…her soft, supple skin melted away, her perfect body revealing a patchwork of body parts seemingly slapped

247

together, her long, soft hair fell out completely, as did her eyes…when things stopped falling off of her, he said, "Ah…not so pretty now, are ye? The Light has revealed the demon within, an ugly thing wrapped in a pretty package. Now I do what I must…"

As he said that, the Wand got brighter, Heriotza shielded herself from it as he said in a commanding voice that was definitely not his own, "Now, Demon: I cast thee out from here, be gone and trouble us no more. So sayeth the Ancients!" The winds and shield surrounding the now horrific looking Heriotza dropped away as a bright flash emanated from the wand and Heriotza disappeared.

But before she left, he heard, "You've won this battle, take this as your prize!"

She was gone, but Thaddeus noted something…something black, penetrating his robe as he started to feel drained. Within a few moments, he latched on to Agham-Ix and said, "Take me home, my friend…something is wrong…get Kama…"

Those were the last words he spoke as Agham-Ix flew slowly back to his home. Kama immediately sensed something was wrong as she rushed back to Thaddeus' home to find him unconscious and totally unresponsive, but alive. Agham-Ix was very worried as he didn't want to die, but there was little he could do, he could only hope that Kama would be able to fix this. Kama noted the black dart that had penetrated his robe and removed it. It looked plain enough, and she noted no evil from it, but when she opened Thaddeus' robe to check him for injuries, she gasped.

The dart hit Thaddeus in his chest, and she noted a small hole in Thaddeus with black spidery tendrils radiating out from that spot on him, and growing. She panicked as she realized the gravity of the situation, and that she had no idea what to do to save what was the Continent's only hope for survival, but then her medical and magickal training kicked in, as she realized that he was a patient, and she was a trained professional, and she would find a way to save him. Knowing she needed time, she cast a powerful spell on him; it was risky, but it was the best she could do right now until she figured out a solution. She put him in a Stasis Cocoon. This very rare spell from deep in Elven spellcasting lore, requiring a target dedicated to good and a deity's intervention to cast, caused a magickal cocoon to be created around a being and most importantly, kept the being within it alive, stopping all bodily functions and all diseases and ailments in their tracks.

Essentially, time stopped for the young Thaddeus as Kama worked feverishly to save him. The Moon Goddess, knowing that Kama would not cast such a spell without good cause, saw what was happening and allowed the spell to be cast, giving some of her limited energy to Kama to effect this mighty magick, proving once again that Kama was indeed blessed by the Moon Goddess.

News travelled fast in and around Samsrun, as many witnessed the battle in the sky above them as night turned to sun, then back to night again as Thaddeus' spell wore off. Some saw him latch onto Agham-Ix as he slumped over his friend. The population wondered what had happened to Thaddeus, and many were concerned about his health. Upon hearing the news, Li'Faran stationed 25 Narsum warriors in and around Thaddeus' home to protect him while Kama searched for a cure. She worried about her little brother and visited him often. Outpourings of support came from the population, especially from Sarana's family. Sarana was allowed into his room, where Kama had erected the Stasis Cocoon so that she could see him.

Kama felt pressure as she never had before. Back in her home village, she had saved many people and had lost many people while she was a healer, but Thaddeus was not an ordinary person, and this was the one patient that she could not lose. She had to find a way to save him. She knew that with each passing sun, evil would grow stronger, and without Thaddeus to protect them, the city and the whole of the Continent might be destroyed if she failed.

The news of Thaddeus' fall travelled slowly to the farthest corners of the Continent. People worried because they knew that he was their protector against evil; eventually, the whole of the Continent was brought together in prayer, knowing that their future might well be in jeopardy if Thaddeus died. Dragons also made their presence known and worked to protect Thaddeus from any and all who might seek to harm him while Kama looked for a cure. For one brief shining moment, the Continent came together in a common cause, but no one, not even Kama, knew if he would survive.

Through these dark times, vigils were held, prayers were said, and Kama worked tirelessly to cure her student, her friend, and unbeknownst to her at this time, her future. The Continent held its collective breath...and waited.

CHAPTER 38

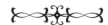

THE CHAMPION RISING

The Dread Lord was also saddened, as his finest creation was heavily damaged, returning to him as a mere shadow of what Heriotza once was, but there was enough of her left to regenerate fully, though it would take time—which he had, owing to the Lord of Blight's special dart striking the Champion of the Light. The Dread Lord knew that if Thaddeus died, he and his brothers could bring their full powers to bear on the hapless people of the Continent, and within a few short suns, annihilate the population entirely, returning it to the barren wasteland that the evil Ancients had envisioned in the distant past.

So, he put her in a regeneration chamber and waited, and brooded over what to do next. His plans, like the plans of so many others all centered on a young man, fighting for his life, and whether he lived or died. During this time, Thaddeus' home was host to all sorts of visitors, from the deities that he had met and treated with, to commoners wishing him well and everyone in between. The disease that was spread by Heriotza was eventually cured again, and men miraculously stopped dying in their sleep and reported not dreaming of anyone (except perhaps their wives!). Of all the people who wanted to save Thaddeus, Kama was first; she imagined what her (after)life would have been like without him; she thought of how much he meant to her and all the fun times that they had shared. While she worked to save him, she finally admitted to herself that she loved him. That revelation led her to double down on her efforts to save him and inspired her to search even deeper into Elven history to find something that would help.

She even went to the Elven city of Hin'taril, located on the Southern Coast, where the great Elven library still stood, and within it the most complete library on the Continent with over 8,000 cycles of knowledge and consulted the tomes there. She asked many other healers, some of which were her former instructors, to see if they had any ideas or clues about what had afflicted Thaddeus. No one she asked knew anything about it but said that she did the right thing in putting him in a Stasis Cocoon until she could find an answer. She spent many suns amongst her people in search of an answer, and it wasn't until many suns had passed that she finally found a clue.

What she found was an obscure reference to another tome that might have the answer she was looking for amidst the Narsum. She had no idea where to look, or if the tome still existed, but she had to find out. She went to the Dragonscape Mountains and searched for suns on end, asking village leaders and what few shamans were left after the last few devastating cycles about where the tome was and if it still existed. After a half season of adventure, in the form of searching high and low for an answer and speaking in the Narsum tongue (which she didn't like at all), she found herself in front of a large cave; it was her last chance to find an answer to cure Thaddeus.

Inside the cave was the legendary Narsum shaman, Burzel. Born of uncertain parentage over 200 cycles ago, Burzel was an anomaly amidst the Narsum. No one knew why he had lived for so long, but he was considered an oracle and possessed knowledge dating back over 40,000 cycles ago, as was commonly noted, the Narsum were the Continent's first inhabitants and had a long and storied history here.

She entered the cave cautiously, as it didn't look like anyone had come in or out of this place in a very long time. She was frightened, but steeled herself because she wanted so desperately to find a cure for Thaddeus. As she went further back into the cave, she was swallowed up by the gloomy darkness within. She cast a simple spell to make her staff glow and pressed on into the black abyss ahead. Through the winding passageways and the dank fetid smell that was ever-present, she finally came upon a dimly lit chamber, she noted it was warm and dry, in contrast to the moistness of the tunnels she took to get here.

Stacked ceiling to floor, upon rows and rows of makeshift shelves were tomes, stone tablets, and other curiosities from Narsum history and in the center of it all, moving about slowly, was a very ancient looking Narsum. He was a skeletal gaunt figure, dressed in a ragged robe, about seven arms high;

he had greenish-blue skin instead of the normal green and said in a low hushed tone, in the tongue of the Narsum, "Welcome, Kama of the Elves. The winds told me of your arrival."

Kama replied, "I seek a tome of knowledge..."

Burzel cut her off and said, "Yes, I know what you seek...a Champion of the Light has been afflicted by a strange sickness and you wish to cure him."

Kama wondered out loud, "How did you know?"

Burzel said, "I know much. In fact, that knowledge has kept me going all these many cycles...but what is this? A connection...? You love him! Aha!"

Kama was taken aback by this, even though she was told that Burzel was an oracle, she just admitted that she loved Thaddeus to herself not too long ago as he said, "That love you have for him is his only hope, because there is a way to treat him but it is difficult. He has been infected by the Essence of Death. This vile substance was once only known to the evilest Ancient; it was jealously guarded, and when Chagdrom died, the secret of the Essence of Death was thought to be lost with him. The fact that it has resurfaced is not entirely unexpected given its creator, the Lord of Blight, but then as now, there were those Champions in the ancient past who were infected by this most vile concoction, and they can be rid of this affliction. Know that only Champions of the Light can be sickened with the Essence of Death. It kills anyone else instantly."

Kama said, "What must I do? I'll do anything! Please tell me!" as tears started rolling down her cheeks. A great weight was lifted from her knowing that he could be cured. Burzel said, "The Essence of Death can only be countered by one thing: the Essence of Life. Unfortunately, while you can administer the cure, you cannot provide it."

Kama asked, "What do you mean? What do I have to do?"

Burzel said, "The Essence of Life is a drop of unadulterated good, distilled to be in its very purest form, it is undiluted by evil and has only one source. A Champion of the Light. You must find blood from another Champion, distill it down to a single drop, then have it purified and blessed by an Ancient. Once that is complete, you must take that drop and seal the entry wound where the Essence of Death entered. If done properly, the effect is immediate, and the Champion will awaken. If it is not done properly, the Champion will die. There you have it."

Kama, getting more upset by the moment, said, "But he is the last Champion of the Light, there are no others! He is going to die!" as she sat on the ground and started crying in earnest. She said, "All I learned and all I was taught can't help him…"

Burzel said, "You are wrong, mi'lady. There is another Champion still alive…"

Kama looked up with tears running down her cheeks and said, "Who? No one else knows of another Champion…"

Burzel said, "Ah, well what the Continent does not know is that 80 and 100 cycles ago, I was named as a Champion of the Light by the Narsum diety, Grom the Mighty. He was not an Ancient, but as a God, he possessed some power to name Champions of the Light, so he named me, as I was once a mighty warrior, but forsook all that for becoming a collector of knowledge and history among my people. Grom said to me, 'I make you Champion of keeping knowledge alive of Narsum…you find place and keep Narsum legend alive.'"

He continued, "I found this cave, and I've been here ever since collecting these bits and pieces of Narsum knowledge and lore. And I may have just saved the Continent…again!"

Kama looked hopeful and said, "Would you be willing to part with some of your blood? I can pay you…"

Burzel said, "You know, it's funny. About 100 cycles ago, I sensed a change in the Continent and made some preparations just in case. Among them was this…" In his skeletal-looking hands was a small clear vial; inside the vial was a single drop of white liquid. He said, "I did most of the work for you, the only thing you have to do is have this purified and blessed by an Ancient, preferably the one who made him a Champion of the Light."

Kama said, "What do you want in exchange for this?"

Burzel thought for a moment and said, "I want to be there when this is administered, and I would like the knowledge I have collected to be preserved in a proper library, where my people can go and learn of their proud heritage."

Kama smiled at him and said, "I have just the person to take on such a request. We will have a library built for all this in the city of Samsrun, and it so happens that the Champion of the Light has a Narsum sister. I know she would be honored to head up this task."

Kama said, "Are you ready to travel? The Ancient who made him a Champion is watching over him now, and his brethren are guarding our fair city along with the Narsum."

Burzel said, "Aye. Somehow I knew this would be an interesting time... let's go!"

Kama extended her hand to him, he took it, and they teleported to Samsrun. As Kama and Burzel returned to Thaddeus' home, the place was abuzz with visitors of all sorts, mostly just concerned Samsrun citizens. Kama appreciated them but thought that they got in the way a lot, particularly when she was checking up on Thaddeus, and then she thought about the endless questions that they would ask, which she always took the time to answer, as the pair headed out to the courtyard.

There, Burzel saw the largest collection of dragonkind he had ever seen. There were 14 in all, some walking the grounds and others flying about, all making sure that Thaddeus would be okay.

Kama yelled out, "Alotraxas, your presence is requested by the Champion of the Light. I am Kama, his proxy, as he is unable to call you himself."

She didn't have to wait long as Alotraxas appeared before her in all his glory. Standing at 75 arms tall, he was truly a sight to behold as Burzel bowed low and said, "I never thought I'd see a real Ancient...what an honor!"

Kama bowed to him and said, "Mighty Alotraxas, I stand before you with dire news, the Champion has been infected with the Essence of Death. If it were not for Burzel, I would never have known how to cure him, but the answer is in this small vial, a drop of Burzel's distilled blood. He is a Champion as well, so named by Grom the Mighty. Will you purify and bless this blood, so that he might be cured and return to his duties?"

Alotraxas said, "Ah, Burzel. I did know about you and your quest to assemble lore and the history of the Narsum...but I, Alotraxas, have a question for you before I bless and purify this blood. Do you give it willingly and without reservation of any kind? If so, what compensation have you or will you receive?

Burzel said, "Great Alotraxas, I know of your name, as you appear many times in Narsum lore. To answer your questions, I do give this willingly and without reservation, and I did receive a promise of having a library built in this city for my tomes and artifacts, so that all Narsum can come here and bear witness to their proud history and heritage."

Alotraxas nodded and said, "Burzel, you are wise as I would not bless this if you received something as crass as gold or valuables, but building a library for the Narsum is a noble deed, and I will honor this deed by blessing and purifying this drop of blood."

Kama put it in his huge claw and Alotraxas said, "As the last remaining Ancient, I bless and purify this blood and give it the power to cure a true Champion of the Light…" A white flash followed the incantation as the vial was handed back to Kama as Alotraxas said, "Go, cure him. He has much work to do still."

Kama was hardly able to contain her joy. She had the cure in her hand. She walked calmly and steadily towards Thaddeus' room; the Narsum guards cleared a path for her and Burzel as they entered his bedchamber. The Stasis Cocoon was still intact and working, as she said, "Moon Goddess, guide my hands."

She was very nervous and her hands were shaking as she felt a presence in the room and heard in her mind, *We will do it together, my child.*

The crowd in the room numbered about 50, and all were deathly quiet as Kama released the Stasis Cocoon and applied the drop to the very spot where the Essence of Death had gotten in, and she could see it working to remove the spider like tendrils that had grown into his chest, finally sealing up the wound he received as Thaddeus opened up his eyes and said just above a whisper, "Kama. Thank you for bringing me back…I knew you would find a way."

She screamed with joy and held him close as the crowd inside the room cheered, as they actually witnessed a miracle.

Kama said with teary eyes, "I thought I'd never see you alive again. I was so worried…"

Fortunately for Thaddeus, she was not Li'Faran, who would have crushed him, but he could feel her joy as he sat up and said, "Quite a crowd…well, I'm back. Thank you all for your support and your prayers!"

Agham-Ix smiled at him and said, "Welcome back, my friend! Glad to see you!"

CHAPTER 39

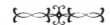

PRELUDE TO WAR

Thaddeus needed no recovery time even though he was laid up for just under a season as he ventured outside to cheers, roars, and other sounds of adulation as the populace was overjoyed that their Champion was back on his feet and able to protect them once again. Over the next few suns, life returned to normal in Samsrun, and while building structures in the city had never stopped, a new order came from Thaddeus, to build a library for the Narsum artifacts, tomes and librams so that all may partake in their knowledge and wisdom. He remembered that his father knew of their skill and knowledge and now he was especially thankful for that knowledge.

Burzel decided to stay in Samsrun to oversee the construction of the library and museum, and to curate the collection of artifacts he had collected over the last 180 cycles. The city had a population of just over 3,000 now, and Thaddeus enjoyed the fact that he was presiding over a growing city that was ruled by a committee of humans and Narsum.

Meanwhile, in the Dread Lord's domain, Heriotza had finished her regeneration cycle and emerged as she did before. As she reported to the Dread Lord, he said in a jovial voice, "Ah, Heriotza…completed our regeneration, have we? Well, I hope you've learned a valuable lesson about Champions of the Light. They are very dangerous and can kill you—just ask Thanatos. Though you struck a blow in my name, the Champion has recovered as you have, so we are back to the beginning. Clearly, we need something that will work faster, as the Champion has developed a device to detect you as you fly about spreading disease. We need to take the next step in severity as this

Champion is stronger and smarter than I thought. I will call for you after I have spoken to my brothers…"

The Dread Lord called silently for his brothers, and soon the Entities of Evil were together again sitting at a large black table of wrought iron. The Dread Lord stood and said in a grave, serious tone, "Brothers…as you all know, our efforts to conquer the Continent have been thwarted on many occasions, all because of the Champion of the Light being smarter and stronger than I could have foreseen. We need to take a step that presents more risk to us, but carries a greater chance of a successful outcome. You all know what must be done. We must risk ourselves. Each of us will put a part of themselves into Heriotza; she will venture to the Continent at the spot where we made our initial appearance, as it has not yet been found and blessed by the Champion. There, she will begin our assault on the Continent."

He continued, "Each of us must decide what powers we wish to give to her, as you know that once she takes possession of it, it cannot be returned until she returns victorious."

The brothers all assented and the Dread Lord called for Heriotza. She sauntered into the room, showing off her newly regenerated body as the Dread Lord said, "Heriotza, it is time for our final assault on the Continent. Our previous attempts have been thwarted, and we have decided upon a risky plan to assure your success in carrying out our will. Each of us will put a part of themselves into you and you will be able to utilize those given abilities with impunity. We are trusting you with parts of ourselves so that you might be successful in the conquest of the Continent. We will decide on what is needed for your success, then it will be up to you to execute our will. Return here in two suns hence to receive our gifts."

Two suns passed, and once again the Brothers and Heriotza gathered in the room with the large wrought iron table. Each was prepared as the Dread Lord said, "Brothers…are we ready for the glory that is to come? We follow in the footsteps of our Ancient Father, who gave us these gifts, and now we bequeath them to you, Heriotza, so that you may carry out our will."

Each Brother knew the risks to themselves and assented.

The first to step forward was the Lord of Blight as he said in a gravely tone, "Heriotza, I grant you the power to cause decay and rot, while being a source of death and disease…use my powers well." He then touched her soft, supple skin causing an ugly blotch of decay to take root there, but soon her demonic abilities worked to cover the blotch, and though she didn't look any different on the outside, on the inside, she could feel the death welling up inside of her. She felt weak at first as the Lord of Blight's power coursed through her demonic body but soon was able to stand tall again. The Lord of Blight felt very empty without the powers he had given to Heriotza but felt that it was worth the sacrifice to ensure success because the Dread Lord was never wrong.

The Lord of the Dead stepped up next and said, "Heriotza, I grant you my strength and martial skills, honed over thousands of cycles, and give you the ability to wield any weapon you may encounter. I also grant you the capability to call for aid, in the form of the undead to assist you in your conquest. Use my powers well and return quickly." He touched her arm, and she could feel the Lord of the Dead's strength along with a flood of knowledge on martial techniques along with knowledge of how to fight with any weapon ever created throughout history. She also called a spectre to her, as a ghostly form appeared next to her.

Last to step forward was the Dread Lord as he said, "I grant you the ability to be able to cast magickal spells. My knowledge of magick is yours." He touched her arm with a blackened claw and in an instant, a rush of knowledge entered her mind.

She stood frozen for a few moments as her mind took in thousands of cycles of spell knowledge. After the transfers were complete, Heriotza stood before all of the Brothers and said, "Thank you, my Fathers. Your faith in me is appreciated, and when I return victorious, all will hail and fear you!"

The Dread Lord said, "Now, go to the place on the Continent called the Dread Hallows. We have desecrated this place so that you might have a place to begin your conquest. Now go, my daughter...and return soon victorious!"

Heriotza left the Dread Lord's domain that same sun and landed in a place of absolute evil, the Dread Hallows. She saw and felt their mark upon this unholy place. The dead trees and soil, along with the fetid stench of decay filled this place as she thought about what to do with her newfound abilities. She saw the good on the Continent beyond the Dread Hallows, and using her newfound powers, caused a blight to come to the land. She could see it starting just below her feet and started spreading rapidly outward, beyond the borders of the Dread Hallows and onto the Continent. She thought, "Soon the peoples of the Continent will have no food, as their lands will wither and die by my hand…" She smiled as the blight continued outward, so noted by the death of the plants that had lived just a moment ago.

While Heriotza was giving her powers their first real test, Thaddeus sensed something using the Eyes of the King. He and Agham-Ix teleported immediately to it and saw Heriotza in a blighted patch of land.

He called out to her, "Ready for Round 2, demon?" He threw a large green ball of fire towards her as he saw her blight approaching his position. The fireball hit her and set her on fire, but he saw it did not appear to be harming her at all as she reciprocated in kind. Heriotza's fireball was smaller and the normal assortment of colors, but it went straight into his void stone. Thaddeus also observed her blight radiating out from where she was standing as he put the void stone's energy into the ground as he said, "You will not harm my people any longer!"

She said, "The harm of your people has only just begun!" She dematerialized after that, leaving the blighted Dread Hallows.

Thaddeus, seeing this blight upon the Continent decided to take action to rectify it. He cast the Ancient's Rite of Purification over the area and combined that with a Ritual of Cleansing and a Blessing of the Ancients upon this blighted land. After all that, it seemed to get better, as he cast a Detect Evil spell and spotted no evil emanations from the land, he was satisfied that this area was cleansed and free of the evil that was once there. He teleported back to Samsrun after that and thought about what to do next.

Heriotza kept Thaddeus busy for the next season, popping up here and there, causing some chaos, then disappearing, but as always Thaddeus was more than a match for her and managed to chase her away, leaving him to clean up her mess. Unbeknownst to Thaddeus, Heriotza was leaving behind a ghost at each spot she visited, the thought being that the ghosts she left behind could do her will, and she wouldn't risk being spotted whilst causing more chaos. Unfortunately, ghosts are notoriously fickle and will do whatever they feel like doing without regard for the requests of some servant of the Entities of Evil, but Heriotza didn't know that as she thought she had their total and complete fealty.

By the end of Somar, Heriotza had visited 20 different places on the Continent, with one exception—she had never been to Samsrun, because of what had happened before, and she didn't know what kind of defenses Thaddeus may have erected there to stop her.

Heriotza knew that all this skirmishing would lead to something bigger, as her ghosts on occasion reported increased security activities in and around the places she visited. She relished the thought of a final glorious battle when she would see the mangled body of Thaddeus, dead by her hand. Oh, the adulations they would place on her and the honor they would bestow upon her as she marched triumphant into the Dread Lord's domain…

But as always, her thoughts centered on how she would do it. He was obviously a Wizard and a good one, so she thought that she couldn't best him magickally. She saw his familiar, a stone dragon and knew that weapons were useless against him, and to top it all off, her looks didn't seem to sway him either. She thought that it was because he was just a boy, but didn't realize that she was being compared to a goddess by him.

She decided to use the Lord of Blight's talents against him and started to land in multiple places around the Continent and start blighting the land as she went. She reasoned that some would be stopped but others might grow large enough to deprive the people of food and water. She would land for an instant, start a blight, and take off again…she hoped that he would not be able to detect the miniscule amount of energy that it took to start a blight. She also decided to stay away from him, realizing that he could kill her and because of this fact; she also decided to not risk any more encounters with him until she had a plan.

She also started her dream killings again and stepped them up to a great degree, as it was still a big part of who she was, her original power, so to speak. She would concentrate her dream killing power on a single area and was killing up to 40 males a night. She wanted to sap the strength of the men and reduce the ability for the people to survive her other powers.

Her scorched-earth style of fighting was a gift from the Dread Lord, but she was always careful to pick faraway places; those who were far away from anything that could help them in their time of need. She didn't focus on a single area of the Continent, but switched it up and moved around a lot. Her methods were simple, methodical, and effective in executing the Dread Lord's will. She would do some surveillance on the ground and from the air. She would pick a location to attack and begin dream killing. After a few nights of that, she would descend on the village with decay and pestilence, unleashing insects and locusts on the people and their crops, then using the Lord of the Dead's martial abilities with her enhanced strength, she would kill what defenders were left; and finally, amidst all the misery and sadness she caused, she would set a disease upon the women and children, followed by razing the area with successive waves of fire, a victory dance of sorts. All this devastation took less than a sun to accomplish, and then she would disappear to repeat the cycle anew.

News was slow to travel to Thaddeus' ears, and truth be told, when he wasn't off fighting evil, he was always very busy because he discovered that running a town wasn't easy, especially for a 10-cycle-old boy. Though everything was going according to plan, it was the million little details, and the concerns of the citizenry, that took up the majority of his time as the city of Samsrun began to rise from the ashes, a shining jewel among the desolation of the rest of the Continent. He took great pains to protect the city as well, placing his newly designed "detection boxes" in strategic locations designed to encompass the city and alert him if there was any evil that tripped a box's invisible detection area.

Finally, on the sixteenth sun of Somar, a ragged looking woman entered the city and was spotted by a Narsum guard as she said, "Need Champion…" as she flopped over, seemingly dead. The guard carried her to Thaddeus, who looked over the ragged looking woman and cast the same spell he cast on Boral that night a while back, instilling life in her, at least temporarily.

She said, "My village…attacked by woman…killed everyone and everything, crops and livestock…left fire in her wake…all dead except me…Village of Mascolain in foothills…three suns from here…"

The last of Thaddeus' life energy left her as she promptly died there in his arms and he said to Kama, "Well, I'm off again. That woman is really pushing my buttons. Getting a little angry."

Kama said, "Thaddeus, that's what she wants. She wants to make you angry, so you'll make a mistake and give her an advantage. Don't let her get you angry. Keep calm and remember your purpose."

He said, "Thanks, Kama. You always know just what to say! Come on, Agham-Ix…let's go!"

CHAPTER 40

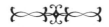

WAR!

Thaddeus arrived at Mascolain. What was a village a few tolls ago, was now reduced to nothing; all that was left were a few charred stones and burnt wood, though he managed to find a few skeletal remains. He buried what he could find and said a blessing over the fallen, but the perpetrator was nowhere to be found. He caught a trace of evil as he cast his Detection of Evil spell, but nothing more. Thaddeus took to the air and noted that it was a very isolated village in the foothills of the Dragonscape Mountains, and that it was small, he estimated a population of 100 to 200 lived there. He decided to pay the Hawkmaster, Garal, a visit while he was here.

He appeared in the cave where he first met Garal and saw that Garal was dead, having succumbed to disease along with four of the five hawks that he saw here on his first visit. One hawk was still on his perch but didn't look so good. Thaddeus cast a flurry of spells on the hawk, and within a few moments, the hawk looked as good as new, but Thaddeus was not trained in falconry, and he didn't know anyone around here who was, but he knew where to find those who were experienced falconers…none other than General Morshand's First Expeditionary Force. He took the hawk on his bare arm, as he didn't need the glove that falconers typically wear thanks to Agham-Ix and teleported to the Fortress, which was General Morshand's command post and home to over 100,000 Barbarian warriors.

When he arrived, he gasped, as there was no one here; the Fortress looked to be abandoned. It was stripped bare of everything, but a few telltale signs of what happened presented themselves. He noted some dead Barbarians who had died of disease, and he thought that the rest of them fled to their homes to defend their villages, but what about General Morshand? As he explored the massive stone structure, he came upon the building that once housed General Morshand and his inner circle of officers. He found the General there with his back to him and said, "General! What happened here? Where are all your warriors?"

The General turned slowly, revealing a gaunt shell of a man that took the place of one of the greatest warriors that the Continent had ever known. As he lurched forward towards Thaddeus and promptly fell on the floor, he said, "Thaddeus…men fled…disease and blight on fields…left to tend to families…all gone…we won many battles, we cannot lose the war! Help my people…please!"

Those words would be his last as life left him, and the fire he carried inside of him was extinguished. He took the General's sword and took to the air, looking for other fortresses in the mountains, but what he saw sickened him. Black circles everywhere on the land, blighted crops, dead or dying people, poisoned water—people suffering, and it was all because of her…the demon woman. He flew around for a few tolls, and it was all the same no matter where he looked. A proud people, all but wiped out because they couldn't get word to him to save them. Fortunately, some of the folks in Samsrun were from the North, but what about those in the Deep North? And the Narsum to the East? And the elves to the South? For the first time, he realized that while he was tending to the people in the city, the rest of the Continent was suffering. He recriminated himself because he should have been patrolling the Continent, not just building one city. He vowed to spend his suns patrolling the Continent for trouble, but he was only one person; he could easily miss something.

He had an idea. Could Kama help him? She could detect auras of an area; maybe she could help him if an area was being attacked using the Heart of the Queen, which she didn't wear all the time because she was constantly tending to the sick and injured. Thaddeus teleported back to Samsrun and put his new hawk on a perch while he went looking for Kama. She was at the hospital as always, which had a nice new roof and an expanded capacity of over 200 beds, most of which were occupied. He found her and said, "Kama, I need your help!"

Kama hugged him tightly and said, "I've been worried about you. Are you alright?"

Thaddeus said, "Yes, I'm fine, but the rest of the Continent is not. Are there others who could tend to these people?"

Kama said, "Aye, but what is wrong?"

Thaddeus said, "Put that circlet on, follow me, and I will show you."

Kama went back to Thaddeus' home, put the Heart of the Queen on, and took to the air with Thaddeus and Agham-Ix. She was able to see the entire Continent now as the Heart had finally attuned itself to her; she saw lots of red in the North and East and a very light blue in the South, with one spot of red seemingly in the middle of the South, close to the coast.

Thaddeus asked, "What do you see?"

She replied, "Lots of sad people. The elves are doing okay, except for one spot."

Thaddeus asked, "Where is it? Can you take us there?" Kama said, "Aye, I know that village; it's Hin'Taril, where the library is."

They teleported there to witness a scene that no one expected. A small army of elves, facing off against one woman. She was not in any hurry to get there, as the elves formed ranks and prepared for a battle. Thaddeus landed in front of the elves, along with Kama and said, "You will not harm these people, I forbid it, leave here or face death at my hands!"

The elves bore witness to the scene that followed which was described in stunning detail by the Elven chronicler, *Fean'Turas*...

...the Champion of Light, his Dragon, and Kama stood before her, a demonic presence set upon our ancient village, with the intent of laying waste to us and extinguishing our way of life. The Champion caused his staff to glow white as she continued her slow approach towards him. She did not waver as he laid protections on us and our brave aerie troops, before he focused on the approaching demon as she began to run at him. He erected a stone wall in front of her which she leaped over, but was caught in a magickal snare, and he fired five lightning bolts at the demon, seemingly without effect as she struggled to free herself from the snare that trapped her on top of the 12-arm high wall in front of the Champion.

She spoke in her vile tongue and lashed out at him, striking him with a flame whip, but it had no effect on him as he conjured a sphere of cold around her as the stones from the wall were flung at her, one by one. The stones did not harm her, but the cold seemed to slow her down. She was able to dispel the cold sphere and the wall as they stood there, barely 10 arms from each other…as she said with a demonic snarl, "Are you ready to see your pathetic life come to an end? Killing your people is too easy, I want to kill you and return home to my Fathers, victorious from the field of battle, having defeated the Champion of the Light in combat."

Thaddeus said defiantly, "You will never defeat me…"

The demon lunged at him, as a sword appeared from her arm, but Thaddeus was too fast for her, and took his twin short swords from his belt as he said, "I killed your predecessor with these…now they will take you as well."

She furiously attacked him with everything she had, but not one of her attacks were able to get through his superb defense. It was clear that her ability to continue attacking him was not waning despite the energy she was putting behind her attacks, but he was still in good form, as he seemed to be re-energized and renewed with each block that he performed. The fighting went on as the aerie elves went from being potential combatants to onlookers, as they started praying to the Moon Goddess to bolster and strengthen the Champion to withstand the furious attacks that were coming at him. He held strong for the longest time, steel and sinew, against iron and evil.

The two combatants, engaged in a classic fight of good versus evil, seemed to know what was at stake here as they gave their all to prove that their side was the better. On the one hand, a demonic woman, who had already taken thousands of lives, bent on the total annihilation and destruction of the Continent, favored demon of the Entities of Evil, and on the other the Champion of the Light, who had saved thousands of lives, and worked to protect the people of the Continent and our way of life. Onward they fought, the hearts and minds of those who witnessed this battle were praying that the Champion would win out, but he was fighting a defensive battle and did not seem able to strike a decisive blow to end this contest.

She landed a few hits on him, but they were quickly healed by Kama, the great and noble healer. Every so often, the demon would be momentarily distracted by an airborne stone, but Thaddeus was unable to take advantage of these opportunities, as the demon recovered quickly, and he used that time to reset his defenses. As the battle wore on, her demonic stamina started to give way, and it appeared that Thaddeus was biding his time for the perfect opportunity to strike, and he found it about a half-toll into this battle. She *appeared to want to end the battle because she was tiring and attempted a diagonal cut against him and raised her sword up high, he lunged up and forward and his sword found its mark. His blade glowed white as it cut deeply into her belly. As she screamed in pain, he followed it up with a sweeping low kick to her right leg, bringing her to her knees, as his second blade removed her head from her body.*

As her head flopped onto the ground, and her body collapsed, a cheer went up from the elves, the likes of which have never been heard before. The Champion seemed relieved to have won, but that happiness was short lived, as a spirit coalesced in front of the Champion, a black, evil spirit as we all heard, "You won the battle, but now I win the war!"

The spirit flew right into the Champion, and he appeared to stiffen for a moment...

In that moment, time stopped for him, and no one except Thaddeus knew what was happening as his body was temporarily home to two souls, one good and one evil. In his mind, Heriotza laid out a scene for him that was straight out of his fantasies, as he saw in his mind the form of Kama seductively approaching him. Unbeknownst to Thaddeus, Heriotza had the ability to appear as herself, or anyone who happened to be taking up residence in the thoughts of her victim. She chose to take on the form of Kama as she sensed a connection between the two of them and decided to exploit it, as that tactic usually resulted in her being successful in marking that man for death. He saw that he was standing in a dimly lit room, and there was a bed nearby as Kama came to him dressed in white, as she caressed him and laid down on the bed, silently beckoning him to her as she smiled and ran her delicate hands over her soft body. She opened her legs a bit; he could feel her desire and lust yearning to be satisfied as she bit her lower lip and said in a breathy, seductive tone, "I want to feel you inside of me. Come here and take me...I'm yours!"

Thaddeus really like the way she looked and wanted to be next to her as he cautiously moved towards her as he was still a little confused, but her beckoning to him was starting to weaken his resolve to question what he was seeing. As he continued to move slowly towards her, listening to her voice calling to him, trying to awaken desires in him that he had yet to experience, he was wondering why she was acting the way she was, he heard a familiar voice in his mind...

"NO! DON'T! STOP!"

He took his eyes off of Kama for the merest of moments as he looked around for the source of the sounds, and saw nothing. He looked towards the bed again and instead of seeing the beautiful Kama seductively laying there, he saw the form of Heriotza, long dagger in hand, lunging at him with a maniacal grin on her face. He recoiled back and started fighting with her in his mind.

He was scared that he could be the next to be marked for death, and there would be little that anyone could do to prevent it. Her demonic strength was evident as she was able to cut him a few times as they wrestled on the floor, but just as panic started to set in, he remembered his defensive training with Li'Faran. She taught him wrestling moves that could help him, and he was able to affect them against someone as large and strong as Li'Faran, so why not someone like Heriotza, who was apparently just as strong, but far lighter?

As the fighting continued in his mind, he finally managed to get her off of him, and he scrambled to his feet just in time to fend off yet another dagger thrust aimed at his heart. He had no weapon and no magick that he could bring to bear in this arena; he was unsure what to do but decided to bide his time and play a defensive game, which worked well for him in the real world having defeated her in physical combat. After what seemed like a long time, they were both tiring, and she finally made the mistake he was waiting for.

She overshot him with a dagger thrust, and he proceeded to break her arm with a move that Li'Faran taught him. She screamed and recoiled back, but Thaddeus had his foot in the way, and she tripped over it and lost her footing. As quick as Heriotza was, Thaddeus had the advantage of youth and Narsum training as he saw the long dagger on the floor and knew what he had to do. He quickly scooped it up and pressed the attack on his prone opponent, stabbing her deep in the chest. As she felt the cold steel plunge between her breasts, she said something that hearkened back to who she was, something that she had only said a handful of times over her long life, and only to the most pious and dedicated men that she had tested this way, "You've bested me twice, and truly a Champion's heart beats in your chest…I deem you worthy to worship the Ancients."

He got up and saw Heriotza laying there on the floor, bleeding out her lifeblood, all the while staring right at him through now lifeless eyes. He was exhausted, and as the vision that Heriotza had put into his mind faded, he saw the familiar form of Toril in his mind. Toril said, "Others are watching. You need to say something for the history books…something heroic I think…yes?"

Thaddeus nodded but was too tired to think of something to say as he saw Toril say something out loud as time resumed its slow march forward once again.

…as his face showed the strain of the battle within and he screamed out with the power of many voices, "You cannot corrupt me…I am a Champion of the Light… evil…will never take me! Be gone from me…you have…no power here!"

Thaddeus heard himself speaking, but it wasn't him, realizing that it must be Toril helping him once again. Toril turned to face him once again, he was smiling as he said, "You'll be alright now, but repeat after me…"

Once again, he heard himself saying words as he yelled out and saw the soul of Heriotza flying away from him in defeat…though what he said was recorded by Fean'Turas as the last entry of this epic battle. *Fean'Turas* wrote:

The spirit was expelled by the Champion's sheer force of will as he said with the power of many voices, "Come back at your peril, spirit, for I, Thaddeus, Champion of the Light, guard this place against the likes of you!"

The elves who bore witness to the event rushed Thaddeus and congratulated him, including the chronicler who described the battle, and as always Thaddeus thanked Kama for healing him and Agham-Ix, who all the while was throwing rocks at the demon to distract her, to give his familiar a fighting chance while allowing him to garner glory by defeating a larger and stronger foe. As he looked upon Kama again in the real world, he came to a realization…that he could love this woman. He figured that what he saw was a fantasy, but it felt so real. The one thing that Heriotza could not get him to feel was sexual lust for her because he had never had those thoughts and perhaps that was ultimately her downfall and his saving grace, that he was just a boy and had never known feelings like that for a woman.

He thanked Toril in his mind, as he was very close to succumbing to Heriotza and her trickery. He realized that he would have been marked for death if he lost that internal struggle against Heriotza.

Toril said in his mind, "As I have told you, you are connected to all past Champions, and you would not be the first man to fall victim to the charms of a beautiful woman, but you held strong, and I am proud to call you my brother…Fare thee well, Champion!"

He thanked Li'Faran in his mind for teaching him to fight the way she did; without her tutelage, he never would have been able to hold on as long as he did, and he would not have known the movements that led to both of his victories in combat. Not to mention, the ferocity of her attacks and her incredible stamina mimicked those of the demon, and he was thankful for having been trained so well by a Narsum.

Meanwhile, in the Dread Lord's domain, the Brothers fumed and raged. It looked like she was going to win thanks to the Lord of the Dead and his martial training. When that failed and she inhabited him, she had a chance to corrupt him, to turn him into their servant, to make him do their will, but it was not to be as she found his heart and his mind firmly on the side of good, and totally incorruptible because of his innocence. He had never experienced greed or hatred, and though he had been tempted by her disguise, he never experienced lust. When she was forced out of his body, Heriotza realized that she underestimated the Champion, as she had never faced a boy in martial or mental combat. She thought to herself, *I've never fought someone who was so innocent afore…I thought all men were corruptible…apparently some boys are not. I'll remember that next time…*

Heriotza returned to the Dread Lord as a mere spirit, devoid of all powers and abilities. The powers they entrusted to her were gone when Thaddeus removed her head, and without them, they could not cause anything more than mere annoyances to the people of the Continent for a very long time. The Dread Lord said to Heriotza and his Brothers, "We lost the battle this sun, but we will return stronger than ever…let us plan for our glorious victory, shall we?

CHAPTER 41

WHAT DOES THE FUTURE HOLD?

After the battle, Thaddeus stayed with the elves for a few suns to celebrate his victory but afterwards went home to Samsrun, along with Kama and Agham-Ix. He recounted the battle to the Narsum and thanked Li'Faran for teaching him how to fight with his swords and fists, which ultimately saved his life.

Li'Faran said, "You welcome, my brother. I make you strong warrior!"

Thaddeus replied, "You certainly did, you certainly did."

As a remembrance to the Continent's most famous fighting man, General Morshand, he placed the General's sword in his private study so that he would always remember the man that he was. Thaddeus thought that it was strange that though he had learned a lot of magick here, it was his skill with blades that won all those battles against demons, not magick. It was as if the General knew that would be the case and gave Thaddeus the weapons he needed to not only survive those battles, but to win them so decisively.

Everytime he saw the General's sword, he smiled and said, "Thank you, General. Your legacy lives on!"

The season of Somar came and went, then turned to Samhein as more seasons turned into cycles, and many things changed on the Continent, not the least of which was Samsrun. The rebuilding of the city of Samsrun was completed after five cycles, and now had a population of over 75,000 souls of all races; Barbarian, Narsum, human, half-Elven, and Elven. As the most populous and diverse city on the Continent at this time, the city attracted more immigrants, and it continued to grow.

271

Thanks to the city council, which had 50 members who were selected from all the races that were in Samsrun, the city was being managed well; the city's treasury was full of gold, and all the people who lived there were generally happy. Of course, that was closely monitored by Kama, who was quick to find dissent and corrected problems before they became really big problems. The city had a standing army of 2,500 melee troops, mostly Narsum and Barbarians, along with 100 female reconnaissance troops and an archer corps of women and elves numbering around 1,000. With solid city defenses, the city was one of the safest places on the Continent during this time.

As good as the city was, Thaddeus continued to take a worldlier view of things, as he continued to monitor the Continent for magick and did a "lap" around the Continent each sun. In his travels, he would stop in various places for a few suns at a time to see how others were doing, and ensuring that all was well. He spent a mere 15 suns per season in Samsrun to look after the council and the people in his home city. Due to this self-imposed but very demanding schedule, there were some consequences to others that he didn't intend on. The one thing he regretted the most was that he didn't have the time to pursue Sarana as he would have liked. She was saddened by this turn of events (as were her parents), but she understood that it was not meant to be, though the two would remain friends throughout their lives.

Six cycles passed by, and life of the Continent buzzed along as it always did. There were no great evils to fight for the Continent's resident Champion of the Light, though he always kept busy by visiting his friends all over the Continent and ensuring that they were doing well.

Thaddeus, now six and 10 cycles old, discovered something about having a stone dragon familiar, which wasn't necessarily a bad thing, he realized that he didn't look like a 16-year-old human, he looked 10. He realized that he wasn't growing as he should be, and that having such a long-lived familiar must be affecting him by extending his life and slowing down his aging and growing process. Agham-Ix was growing very slowly and was perhaps a half-hand longer than he was six cycles ago, but now weighed in at an impressive 55 stone, but that was considered normal for his kind.

Though he was busy, and he looked 10, in reality, he was 16, and started having thoughts that all 16-year-old boys have. His thoughts turned to romantic pursuits and who he should pursue to be his wife. On that front, Li-'Faran had found another Narsum warrior named Bortul. He was a huge

Narsum, standing eight arms tall, and weighing in at 22 stone, wielding a double-headed axe as his favored weapon. They were in a very serious relationship and could often be found together, just walking the streets of Samsrun and talking. She still considered Thaddeus her brother, and she made sure that Thaddeus kept up with his martial training, but took her romantic eyes from him in exchange for a much larger and stronger Narsum. Thaddeus thought that was okay, and enjoyed having Li'Faran as his sister and not as a romantic partner. He also enjoyed training with Bortul as he was stronger and faster than Li'Faran was and provided him with a greater challenge to progress in his defensive martial training.

Despite Thaddeus taking a worldlier view of things, and having many choices insofar as who he could pursue from all over the Continent; he chose the one person who had been there since the beginning, the one person who knew him as no other, the one person who told him that she loved him and would wait for him; he chose Kama. Truth be told, Toril was preaching that for six cycles, and Thaddeus finally took his advice.

The two were still about the same size, the same weight, and Kama knew his heart and how he felt about her, so they started courting each other on top of continuing their magickal studies together, but now as they sat close to each other in study, sometimes those study sessions would turn into romantic rendezvous and over time, they fell in love. Though they were apart from each other during many suns at a time, as she was Samsrun's lead healer and he was a Champion of the Light, duty-bound to protect the whole of the Continent, they still found time to be together and enjoy each other's company. Thaddeus learned that Elven courtships can last 10-20 cycles, as elves are rarely in a hurry to do anything, which was fine with him. Though he wasn't an elf, he identified with the Elven way of doing things and took a long view of events and knew that eventually they would be joined.

During this time, Thaddeus tried several times to transfigure Bjor'ma back to his normal self and failed each time, until one sun when he came upon a spell designed to strip a being's magickal defenses from them, then rendering them more susceptible to magicks, presumably to cause more damage to them. Thaddeus thought that he could use that to strip Bjor'ma's resistance away and transfigure him, so he decided to try it in his laboratory. He cast the first spell, and it seemed to work, then he cast the transfiguration spell, and lo and behold—it didn't work.

Bjor'ma was still a pink blob with eyes as he said, "Well, my friend. It didn't work, but I will keep trying."

He heard a familiar scratching sound under Bjor'ma and saw "It's alright… I know you are trying" on a scrap of parchment.

Thaddeus always made sure to treat Bjor'ma as a person, not as a thing and would ask him wizardly questions and take his opinions into account when making decisions. Bjor'ma was happy that he wasn't being tortured every sun and had the freedom to go wherever he wanted, but mostly stayed in Thaddeus' home, reading books and relaxing, waiting for the time when he could be with his mother again.

During these six cycles, the Barbarians in the North rebuilt their homes, and their fortresses, and under the direction of the Snow Queen, life continued as it always had; it was a hard life, but the Barbarians of the North are a hardy bunch, and the humans that decided to stick it out in the Far North, were rewarded by having a good (albeit cold) life high in the mountains. Peace reigned in the Far North and Deep North, thanks to the Snow Queen and Thaddeus, who would visit them often and ensure that the disparate tribes of Barbarians got along. Whenever he visited one of the 16 tribes, the Barbarians would literally roll out the "red carpet" for him and treated him as an honored guest. Reluctantly, he used a longpipe for the first time in his life to seal a trade bargain between Samsrun and the Bear Claw tribe. He found it to his liking, but it wasn't something he enjoyed as they did. He made friends wherever he went in the North, and while he was often the smallest person in the room, the Barbarians knew who he was and gave him great respect because of what he had done for them.

The Narsum to the East recovered as well from the diseases spread by evil and retained their homes in the most rugged terrain on the Continent. They rebuilt villages and towns amidst the unspoiled beauty of the Dragonscape Mountains. Thaddeus made it a point to visit the Narsum often; he learned their tongue, thanks to Li'Faran, and would often engage in trade bargains with them, as the Narsum were experts in crafts of all sorts, especially armor and weapons. In fact, all the armor and weapons for the standing army came from Narsum forges, for which they were paid in gold and other trade goods, which they needed to survive. He also visited the dragons in the mountains to avail himself to their knowledge and wisdom, and to visit Agham-Ix's father and siblings. Agham-Ix's father noted that Thaddeus had not grown very much and said, "You are growing and aging as we do...slowly. You will live a long life, Champion."

The Elves on the Southern Coast continued to flourish in their ancestral homeland and generally stayed out of the affairs of humans as they always had, but they welcomed Thaddeus whenever he would visit them, given his station as Champion, his knowledge of their language and ways, and the fact that he chose an elf to court as his potential mate. They saw him as an honorary elf and unbeknownst to them, and him, he would live as long as they would. As witnesses to his abilities and power not to mention his devotion to good, they held him in very high regard and always treated him with the utmost respect, which meant leaving him alone for the most part whenever he would visit. Despite their aloofness towards him, which he understood, he always enjoyed his time with the elves, often engaging them in esoteric conversations and would often join them in philosophical discussions that would last for tolls on end.

The one sad story on the Continent were the humans in the South and West, who were utterly wiped out in the War of the Wizards and the subsequent dark times that followed. Those populations never recovered, and even now, the South and West are slowly being reclaimed by natural forces. All told, over four million humans, fully three-quarters of the total human population perished during those times, and Thaddeus knew that it was all because of magick and those who did not follow the Law. Those who had died served to remind him that he would be the last true Wizard here on the Continent, and that he would never teach anyone else the magicks he knew, especially those of the elder Thaddeus. When he died, the elder Thaddeus' magick would die with him, leaving only elvish and shamanic magicks on the Continent, which it had before.

Of all the buildings in the West and South now falling to ruin, he did see fit to preserve one building in the West, the castle in what was once the capital city because of what he discovered here...Bjor'ma's secret stash of gold. He and Agham-Ix later cast a preservation spell on the castle to prevent it from falling into ruin and unbeknownst to everyone on the Continent except for him, the bulk of Samsrun's treasury was here, over 500 leagues from Samsrun. He reasoned that if the city was besieged in some way, there was enough gold there to rebuild the city again and because it wasn't in Samsrun, no one would be tempted to try to steal it.

CHAPTER 42

A FAMILY UNITED

More cycles passed by, people were born, lived, and died never having experienced for themselves the horrors that the Continent once knew, never knowing of the suffering of their ancestors at the hands of Wizards…which is exactly how Thaddeus wanted it. He added a wing to the Narsum Museum and Library, still curated by Burzel, to preserve relics from that time so that people would never forget about what had happened and to pay homage to the beings of all races that had died during that tumultuous time. As the Continent's last true Wizard, he cast magick very sparingly and never in public. In that regard, he was very different than his elder namesake, as he wanted to keep his magick as quiet as possible to allow people to live their lives. Of course, he would help people and make sure they were taken care of using magick, but never engaged in the egregious displays of magick of his elder namesake.

After 17 cycles of courting, Kama and Thaddeus were joined in a beautiful Elven joining ceremony in the Elven capital of Simas Garath, meaning "Safe Harbor" in the tongue of the elves. Thaddeus and Li'Faran had a unique distinction during this time in that they were the only non-elves in the city during the five suns of the ceremony. Of course, Thaddeus still looked like a kid at this stage in his life, but was nearing his full height of five and a half arms and weighing 11 stone, which suited Kama just fine. He was about as tall as the tallest elves in the city, but everyone knew where he was at all times because Li'Faran followed him everywhere he went as she wanted to make sure he was safe. Li'Faran also served as Kama's matron of honor, which had never been done before in the history of the elves.

After the ceremony, in deference to Li'Faran and what she meant to them, they decided to spend their honeymoon together as guests of the Narsum, though living in Thaddeus' extradimensional home. Their first night together was simply divine by their own recollections. They made love for tolls on end, and Thaddeus knew that they would be together for a long time, as he found a love so strong here, just as his elder namesake did all those cycles ago.

After Thaddeus and Kama were joined and had their honeymoon together, they came back to Samsrun. They resumed their duties and life resumed its frenetic pace for the Continent's most famous couple. Through all this, despite being totally fulfilled with his life here, Thaddeus sometimes thought about the life he left behind in our world. He thought about his father and what he would think of his only son being here. He had the device that his elder namesake made for him, but it only showed an empty house, as it seemed his father had gone somewhere and had not yet returned. Thaddeus knew that time in this world was different and did not panic, but he missed his dad and wondered what his life would have been like if he had decided not to help all those cycles ago. He wondered what would have become of him and the life he might have had. He didn't think his life would have been better if he had stayed in our world, and he knew for certain he would not have had an elf for a wife. He thought he made a good choice back then and thoroughly enjoyed his life and who he was. He wondered if his father would come and visit him here to see the wizard that he had become and the life he lived. These thoughts came infrequently for the young Thaddeus, but what he didn't know was that he wouldn't have to wait long to have his questions answered.

A couple of seasons passed, and Thaddeus was home studying a tome of rare plants on the Continent when he heard Li'Faran call to him, saying, "Brother...you have visitor!"

This was a common occurrence for Thaddeus whenever he was here in Samsrun as he said, "Okay, I'll be right there!"

He thought it was perhaps a concerned citizen or one of the council asking for his advice on a matter of importance, but he never thought he would come face to face with someone from his past. He entered the front parlor, where he normally received guests and noted a man standing with his back to him, warming himself by the roaring fireplace, as it was early Simcha. The man was wearing a robe and hooded travelling cloak, all in blue, along with what appeared to leather boots. The man was a human, though small, about Thaddeus' height and weight as Thaddeus said, "Good sun, sir…how many I help you?"

The man said in Manton without turning around, "Seems you've done quite well for yourself…a wizard, and a Champion of the Light. Very impressive. The city is abuzz with the fact that you've just taken a wife, an elf no less. An interesting choice, but not unexpected given your family history."

Thaddeus was suspicious and pulled out his Wand of Light as he said, "Who are you? What do you know of my family?" The man turned around, removed his hood and before he could say anything, Thaddeus said, "Dad? Is it really you?"

Patrick switched to English and said, "Aye, my son. It is I. I greeted your sister earlier, and she told me about my wife, Anacra, and what happened to her and her people, but I'm glad that Li'Faran is doing well…and apparently, so are you! I got your note this morning, after having been on a business trip for the last few suns, but I knew you'd be fine. Never thought you'd be here though, fighting evil and being a hero and all! Li'Faran caught me up on what happened here, and I'm glad your elder namesake brought you here. He is an amazing man and you…wow, I still can't believe it!"

Kama came walking in at this point, hearing voices speaking in a strange tongue and asked in Elven, "Who is that, and what tongue do ye speak?"

Thaddeus said to her in Elven, "My love, this is my father, Patrick. We speak in a tongue from my original world called English."

Kama said in Narsum, "I know of you. I read about you in Narsum tomes, many of which are here in Samsrun. I am honored to meet you. I am Kama, Thaddeus' wife."

Patrick was taken aback as here was a very diminutive and very beautiful elf speaking in Narsum, and he replied in Narsum, "You speak the tongue of my people…you honor me and them!"

Agham-Ix walked in and flew up on Thaddeus' shoulder and said in his mind, *That is your father? My father told me of him. He is a good man.*

Patrick asked, "Is that what I think it is? You have a familiar? And a dragon, no less?"

Thaddeus replied, "Aye, this is Agham-Ix, a stone dragon. Alotraxas the Ancient picked him for me about a cycle after I arrived here, and we have been inseparable ever since."

Patrick was stunned as he said, "You have spoken to an Ancient?"

Thaddeus said quite matter-of-factly, "Yeah, his spirit was in my mind for a while when I was learning magick, and I've seen and spoken with two deities, killed a couple of demons, seen lots of spirits, and we've got a pink blob living here named Bjor'ma...long story there!"

Patrick had to sit down, for never in his wildest dreams would he have ever thought that his only son would be that accomplished in the ways of magick.

Patrick said, "So...you'll be staying here, then..."

Thaddeus said, "Aye, that I will and from what I've been able to gather, I'll be here for a long time. You might not know this, but I've been here for 20 cycles already, and I'm looking forward to many more."

Patrick said, "This world is a wonderful place. I'm kinda sorry I left as well. Now that I know you're here and safe, I'll visit from time to time. Thaddeus, I'm very proud of you, you've carried on the family tradition, though you and I are alike in one way, we both married Wizards! I'd love to stay here for the sun and catch up, what say you?"

Thaddeus replied, "Aye...that will do nicely, Dad!"

Thaddeus and his father spent the sun together, with Kama, Li'Faran, and Agham-Ix. Patrick met Bjor'ma, and Thaddeus told him the tale of his first victory against Thanatos and how he met the pink blob that was before them. Thaddeus showed his father around what was now his home, but once belonged to his elder namesake, and even took him for a "spin" in his extradimensional home of which Patrick had seen before a very long time ago.

As the Second Sun was setting, another spirit came into the home, and Thaddeus, Kama, Li'Faran, and Patrick all smelled the same thing at the same time...a fruity smoke with a hint of anise as they turned and saw Thaddeus Brimstone and Sairys looking back at them.

The elder Thaddeus said, "Patrick the Younger, welcome back. Yer boy has done quite well fer himself. He's made this world a lot better than what it was. Couldn't let ye leave without saying hello to ye. I assume ye got my note..."

Patrick said, "Aye, that I did. Thank you for leaving it, but I wasn't worried when I read that he was with you. You're a good man."

The elder Thaddeus said, "Aye...always try ta be. Come ye back soon. Mayhaps we can chat like civilized gentlemen and reminisce about old times, aye?"

Patrick said, "It would be an honor...aye!"

Thaddeus disappeared, leaving behind his signature scent as Patrick said, "Well, my boy. I should be getting back. Though I'll only be gone a few moments in our world...I'll be back soon!"

Patrick hugged his son, Kama, and Li'Faran, and waved goodbye as he left Thaddeus' home and came back to our world. He smiled as he returned, knowing how special his son really was, a far cry from the boy he left only a few suns ago.

EPILOGUE

Hundreds of cycles passed by, seemingly in the blink of an eye and over that time, Samsrun became a huge sprawling city of over half a million residents, and through it all, they always had Thaddeus and Kama to help them through any difficulties, though thankfully there were few. Other towns and cities had been established during this time, and the Continent was thriving, having experienced the longest stretch of peace in Continent history, well over 500 cycles. Most folks recognized that it was Thaddeus who was responsible for this as he still continued in his sworn duties to protect the Continent, never letting down his guard, ready to respond to the slightest hint of evil anywhere on the Continent.

Thaddeus was now a man, aged 532, though he appeared as a human man of 50 at this stage in his life. Kama, a matronly looking elf of 596 still stood by his side, doing as she had always done, healing others and helping them as she was able. They were living a good life, but of all the things that Kama had always wanted, she wanted children the most, having dreamed of becoming a mother so often in her life, but her premature death took that ability from her. She often lamented about it when they were alone together knowing it was the one thing that they couldn't have. Thaddeus realized that they could never have children of their own, but he remembered that there were children in his fair city who were orphaned that they could raise as their own.

After discussing it at length, which was the Elven way, Thaddeus and Kama decided to adopt orphaned children as they were able. Over their long lives, they adopted many children so their home would always be filled with love and laughter. As it was over 700 cycles ago, their home was full to bursting during holy suns and other celebrations when their now grown adopted children would bring over their families, and so on—in fact, over 400 children owe their lives to Thaddeus and Kama, who opened up their home and their hearts to so many over the cycles.

Agham-Ix was now fully grown, and though he was small for his age during his youth, he wasn't anymore. He was now 19 arms long and weighed in at 725 stone, he was an impressive sight to be sure. He continued his long-standing tradition of accompanying Thaddeus on his duties as a Champion of the Light and sometimes wore his Crown of the Light while they were out and about. He was happy that Thaddeus was a good man and that both their names would be remembered for a very long time. He had even taken a mate about 250 cycles ago and now had offspring of his own, but he knew that his life was always dedicated to Thaddeus and vice versa, and over the cycles had figured out how to split his time between his duty to Thaddeus and his growing family.

Li'Faran and Bortul had long since passed away after a long life (by Narsum standards), and Thaddeus always welcomed her progeny into his home for any reason at all. Thaddeus counted 17 generations of her progeny had lived and died in and around Samsrun over his life, and the latest three generations were frequent visitors to his home, which he enjoyed immensely. Thaddeus never forgot the lessons she and Bortul taught him and practiced martial arts with the Narsum whenever his duties allowed to keep his skills sharp.

Throughout his long life, Thaddeus noted something curious about children, both his adopted children and those of his late sister. All of them seemed to be fascinated by Bjor'ma, who stayed as a pink blob all this time. The children seemed to love playing with him because he was impervious to anything they could possibly think to do to him. Particularly during holy suns and celebrations, some of the childrens' parents remembered that they played with him too when they were kids and laughed to themselves watching their children following in their footsteps. Bjor'ma realized that he finally managed to do something that he was unable to do in life, to bring a smile to a child. He thought that perhaps this was one of the many lessons that he was here to learn and perhaps why fate chose to let him live his life here. Having long since been forgotten by most, including the Dread Lord, he felt like he belonged to a family, and he was very thankful that he could serve a purpose in his current form. He reveled in the glee that he elicited in children, and while sometimes they would hurt him, he still loved entertaining children.

Patrick was true to his word and visited Thaddeus and Kama often, as he watched his boy turn into a man. He was genuinely proud of Thaddeus, being a Wizard and a Champion of the Light, taking care of millions of people, defending them against evil and ensuring that they would always know peace while having a family of his own. Patrick would often speak of his son in our world and how wonderfully he was doing, but he always said that his son found happiness and really made a difference in another land… how true of a statement it was, though no one in our world had any idea what he really meant.

While Thaddeus had the ability to come back to our world and enjoy all the conveniences that our modern life offered, he found all he could have ever wanted here in another land, with a woman that he could never find in our world. He found love and adventure here on the Continent, just as his elder namesake did and had no desire to be away from this place for any length of time. He resolved to live out his life here on the Continent, surrounded by people who loved and cared for him, for as long as he would live.

As the lens of our story pans out, we can see the whole of the Continent now, with many cities and towns, all sparkling like jewels against a cerulean sky. The millions of people now living on the Continent, all of whom have grown up during these peaceful times have all but forgotten the trials of the past. Those trying times, now remembered by only a few select people, stand in stark contrast to the quiet, peaceful times that the Continent now knows.

Panning out further, we see the whole of Terra against the endless starry skies beyond. While gazing at the sights of the multiverse, we pause to look in on some old friends, the Moon Goddess and her stalwart companions, Thaddeus Brimstone and Sairys. They spend their suns watching the Continent from above as the Moon Goddess turned to Thaddeus and said, "See my friend, everything turned out right."

Thaddeus took a drag from his pipe, exhaling a fruity smelling plume of orange smoke and said, "Aye, my lady…it did. The magick I brought here has come full circle. It started with a man named Thaddeus, and it will end with a man named Thaddeus. All is as it should be."

As our lens pans out and begins to fade, we look into the boundless blackness of the multiverse…we hear the familiar voice of the elder Thaddeus:

"Look there, a spark in the sky…hmmm…I wonder…"

The End

CPSIA information can be obtained
at www.ICGtesting.com
Printed in the USA
LVHW080043011021
699177LV00001B/2